MORGAN'S BOY

Lee raised his head slowly and looked at Morgan.

'It's just a room, Morgan,' he pleaded, 'only a room.'

The blow took Lee high on his cheek and swung him off balance, felling him instantly. He felt no pain. Shocked and dazed, he lay before the fire, the comb still tight in his fist. With dignity Morgan stepped up and took it from him. Lee's senses settled. He heard the sideboard open, and the muted clink of a key. He heard Morgan's heavy steps on the stairs. Pain poured into his cheek as he propped himself up on shaking arms. A door opened and closed upstairs. Then there was silence.

Time stretched further. Lee climbed slowly to his feet and walked delicately through the porch door and into the yard. Suddenly dizzy, he leaned against cool bricks until the fuzziness cleared. He rubbed his face and made his way uphill, anywhere away from the farm and the man he had wounded so deeply.

Morgan's Boy

ALICK ROWE

SPHERE BOOKS LIMITED
London and Sydney

First published in Great Britain by
Sphere Books Ltd 1984
30–32 Gray's Inn Road, London WC1X 8JL
Copyright © 1984 by Alick Rowe
Reprinted 1984

Publisher's Note

Set in 9 point English Times

Printed and bound in Great Britain by
Cox & Wyman Ltd, Reading

Chapter One

The five ridges of the Black Mountains lie like a huge hand, fingers outstretched, clutching together the English and Welsh borders. There is a popular saying that the Welsh are two nations: the Highland North and the Industrial South. In fact there are three. Along the border lives an uncertain people with generations of suspicion in its blood: a fear of the stranger, and for good historical reason. Holiday brochures describe the Black Mountains as wild, beautiful and secretive. They're also very lonely.

The farm, Blainau, was lonely, clinging apologetically to the skirts of the high ridge rearing up behind it towards the highest point of the Black Mountains a mile or so away. Morgan Thomas, who farmed Blainau, was lonely too.

January rain from the north-west slashed the small farm. Usually the old man, Pugh, who helped him, would have shared his loneliness, but today was Sunday and Morgan was alone. He sat by his fire but and, possibly for the first time in his life, reviewed his situation. Once there had been four to work the farm, many years ago: his father, mother and younger sister. Now they had all gone. Val had gone when she was seventeen, unable to endure the loneliness — a great reader of magazines which had presented to her the image of a life elsewhere where there were shops, dancing, others of her age. It had been a bitter blow to the whole family but Morgan and his parents, with a stoicism typical of the hills, had carried on. In 1970 his father had died, and he and his mother had reduced the scope of the farm and tried to continue their way of life. Three months ago his mother, Gwen, had also died (the Old Lady as he had always thought of her) and Morgan had found himself, for the first time, alone. Farm routine and the occasional friend like Pugh had sustained him through those difficult days, but friends

1

could not provide sympathy and support for ever, and, in these last few weeks, Morgan had found the sharpness of his situation almost intolerable.

In the dark living-room of Blainau he reviewed his position, the first of the early lambs, weak, not well able to contend with the weather, warming at his feet. Morgan leaned forward to check its heartbeat, glad of a living presence in this house, which had become for him such a poignant reminder of his solitariness. He got to his feet and moved towards the kitchen to make himself tea and his eyes fell, not for the first time, upon the telephone. The wildness of the weather outside and the disturbance within him suddenly combined to force an unusually positive decision from him. He opened a drawer and sought the telephone number of his sister, Val, in Manchester. He had not seen her since his father's funeral.

Val, in her neat, bright house in the outer Manchester suburbs, was on her own, too, and enjoying the novelty. Her son, Lee, was out with friends, and Alan, who lived with them, had performed his Sunday ritual of cleaning his car before a drink in the pub. When she answered the phone she was surprised to hear Morgan; at first she didn't recognise his voice and it took a while for her to gather her thoughts and interpret what Morgan was asking. His distress was well hidden, but memories of her brother enabled her to see through his reticence and it was with something like panic that she realised he was asking her for help. She guessed well enough the reason.

'Are you lonely on your own without Mam?' she asked, and, when Morgan seemed to suggest that she come to Wales and stay, her panic increased. 'I might be able to come down at the weekend,' she said anxiously, 'but, no, not to stay.' Then, gathering her distress into a lie: 'Morgan, look, the boy's just come in for his dinner. I'll ring you back. Okay? Look after yourself; we'll think of something.'

She put down the telephone, surprised that she should feel such concern and unease for the brother she had seen, after all, only twice since she left Blainau and its loneliness twenty years before. Lee had not come in for his lunch. Val sat and lit a cigarette.

Morgan stood a while before he put his receiver down; he had not known what to expect and was not disappointed. He returned to the fire and the weak lamb. He laid another log on

2

the flames and once more with great gentleness checked the lamb's heartbeats. They were strong. Morgan was satisfied: if he could nurse it through the first forty-eight hours, it would survive. It was a mutual dependence. Blainau had little more, these days, than sheep.

In the busy supermarket, where Lee worked, music rolled from speakers, remorselessly cheerful, and tills chirped with pleasure as a constant diet of cash was fed into them. Lee was stocking shelves when Carol, his girlfriend, tapped him on the shoulder and told him that Mr Ellis, the Manager, wished to see him in his office behind the stockroom.

Mr Ellis had a certain stoic quality too, not forced upon him, as Morgan's was, by his physical situation, but due to a never-ending stream of employees on Y.O.P. schemes, Y.T.S. schemes, other schemes, of which he was more than faintly suspicious. He looked at the tall, gangly figure of Lee and questioned long-sufferingly whether the boy had overslept until half-past one yet again today. Lee looked down at his boss, behind the desk, his face open and innocent, making no reply.

'If you don't want this job, there's plenty who do,' the man warned.

Lee nodded encouragingly. 'Great,' he said.

Mr Ellis shuffled through his papers, searching for the boy's Christian name. 'What's wrong with the job, Lee?'

'Boring, Mr Ellis,' Lee replied. 'It took me two minutes to suss out you stick the Kelloggs on the Kelloggs shelf, and two seconds more to guess you move the old stock up. Two minutes, two seconds, Mr Ellis,' he emphasised. 'I've been doing this job two bloody months.'

Ellis shifted uncomfortably under the boy's frank gaze. 'Come on, lad,' he said, 'you've done other things than stocking up, I know that.'

'Right,' the boy replied without heat. 'I make tea; I sweep floors. You're supposed to be teaching me a trade, Mr Ellis. I knew tea and brooms already.'

The music dimly entered the dingy office from the stockroom next door; there were crashes as goods clanked into the wire trolleys which would roll them to the shelves. Mr Ellis looked up once more at Lee, met, once more, that frank, open gaze and gave up.

'Call in tomorrow, Mr Turner. I'll have your money and papers ready.' Lee began to move to the door. Ellis leaned back.

'You know what I used to call the Y.O.P. scheme?' he asked 'Yobs Occasionally Punctual.'

Lee was appreciative. 'That's good, is that,' he said, turning at the door. 'You've got a great little team here, Mr Ellis. I bet the Sub-Area Manager's Assistant's Assistant is real pleased,' and he left. Ellis permitted himself a small smile.

At the end of the day Val let herself into the empty house and dumped a bag of shopping on the table as she slowly removed her coat. She yawned a little as she filled a kettle and set it over a flame. Upstairs in his tiny room, Lee heard her as he fed a small tank of tropical fish. Then, shaking off his apprehension, he walked jauntily downstairs for an encounter he knew neither of them would enjoy.

Val was scanning a couple of letters as Lee came in. She was surprised to see him. 'Finished early?' she asked. 'Work okay?'

Lee sat at the table and played with the cup Val had laid for herself. 'I packed it in,' he said casually. Casualness was important to mother and son: they used it as a smoke-screen behind which they could organise their true feelings. Val forced herself to finish the letters before turning to unpack the shopping.

Lee recognised the ominous sign. 'It was boring,' he said. 'So I jacked it in.'

She continued to unpack. Soon the kettle whistled. 'Let's have a cup of tea,' she suggested.

'I don't drink tea,' Lee said automatically.

Val emerged from her show of indifference. 'I do. I drink tea,' she said with a flash of real feeling. 'Think of somebody else for a change.' She moved to the stove to fill a teapot from the boiling kettle. 'You didn't get the push?' she asked. 'Not for stealing or anything like that?'

Lee was affronted. 'It was boring. I was late; just a few times I was a bit late, okay?'

Val put the teapot aside and moved to the refrigerator to find some milk. 'I've never been late for work in my life,' she said quietly.

'Fantastic,' her son replied, moving the teacup round and round the table. 'It was really boring; you just don't know.' Lee pulled a packet of cigarettes from his pocket.

'Don't smoke in here,' Val snapped at him.

Lee was amazed: he could see her cigarette still burning in the ashtray. 'You never minded before,' he said.

'From now on I do.' She banged the teapot on the table.

Lee rose and swiftly moved towards the door. He knew there was more to be said by both, but couldn't judge the right time.

Val spoke. 'I don't know what Alan's going to say about this.'

'I don't give a toss what Alan says,' Lee shouted back, as he walked out.

Val's energy suddenly evaporated; it had been a long day . . . she could do without this. She poured herself a cup of tea, feeling tired and dispirited, and reached for her smouldering cigarette.

When he heard the deafening roar of Alan's lorry, manoeuvring into its overnight parking place outside, Lee cared very much what Alan would say. He looked through his window at the bulk of the reversing vehicle, stepping back when Alan shut off the engine and climbed from the cab, not daring to have his anxiety noticed.

Alan had been living at the house for several months. He was a tall, powerful man, a Londoner, who had met Val by chance when delivering a load to the factory where she worked. Before long he had persuaded his employers to transfer him to their Manchester branch, where the friendship had developed, and soon afterwards he had moved in. Alan and Lee had disliked each other from the start. They were entirely different: Alan was industrious and energetic, whereas Lee was apathetic and easily tired. Alan had a job and liked his work; Lee saw no reason to work at all if the Department of Health and Social Security were willing to pay him for not doing so. Lee remembered his father, Ken, who had suddenly not returned home one evening, four years ago. At the time he had not felt this particularly sharply: Ken had been quiet, easily dominated by Val, hardly, at times, a presence in the house at all. This had maybe been one reason for the marriage's failure – and possibly a reason for Alan's attraction to Val. (Thank God, she had thought when Alan and she had become lovers. It's not too late. I have met a real man.)

Alan came into the back kitchen where a meal was set out on the table. He found himself a can of beer in the fridge and took it into the living-room where he picked up the evening paper. Val was watching television and showed no reaction when Alan leant over to kiss her. The man saw there was a problem and guessed what the problem was.

5

'Lee?' he asked. Val nodded. Alan sat beside her and laid an arm around her, drawing her closer. For a while they stared at the screen. 'Where is he now?' Alan asked quietly.

'Don't start anything, Alan' she said softly.

He kissed her again. 'Come on, love,' he said. 'Don't let it get to you.' She put her arms round him, grateful for his concern.

From the open door Lee watched his mother and her lover, aware he must tread carefully.

'What time's tea then?' he asked jauntily.

Val got up and moved towards the kitchen. 'When it's ready,' she said. Alan's eyes stayed on the screen. Lee hovered uneasily near the door.

'Your mother says – ' Alan began.

'I don't take notice of you,' Lee replied quickly, following Val into the kitchen, determined not to provoke Alan to the violence that had surfaced once or twice before.

Val was drying the teacups as Lee came in. He hovered at the door.

'It really matters to you? The job?' he asked. She made no reply, putting the cups away. Lee was uneasy; he wanted to be out of the house. 'What time's tea then? Only, I'm meeting Colin and – '

'I don't want you going out tonight,' said Val firmly.

Lee was surprised and apprehensive. 'Why?' he asked.

'Because you just go drinking to get pissed out of your mind, and because you're only seventeen, and because you got the elbow from work today and you should – you just should feel it, you know?' Her resentment and anxiety flared. Alan appeared at the door, drawn by Val's outburst.

Lee nodded towards him. 'Is this his idea?' he asked.

Val set about getting the meal together. 'Don't start,' she insisted.

Lee said, 'Look, I was a bloody skivvy there.'

From the door behind him, Alan said, 'It was a job.'

Val knew the signs. She said anxiously, 'Don't start, please. Either of you.'

Alan came further in. 'What did you do?' he asked.

Lee turned to his mother. 'The money was terrible. I wasn't much worse off before I took the bloody job.'

Val brought knives to the table. 'It's not just the job,' she said wearily.

Lee thought this over. 'Then what are you on about?' he asked.

6

Val wearily took the pepper and salt to the table. 'Let's just keep this easy, Lee.'

In the silence, Alan came further into the room. 'You got the push, did you?'

Lee sat at the table and, annoyed, said, 'Bloody wild-fire, yes.'

His mother turned to him. 'So what are you going to do?'

'I don't know, do I? Not this minute.' The mood was turning dangerously. Val and Alan exchanged a quick look.

Alan came to stand over Lee at the table. 'Money,' he said flatly. Val turned to him, shaking her head imperceptibly – a swift signal not to pursue the matter.

Lee saw it, too. He said, 'Money, right. I've got money; I've been working for two months.'

'Money for drinking every night?' demanded Alan. 'For going to see City every weekend? For your tapes? For your magazines? You must think we're stupid.' He leaned upon the table, bringing his face close to Lee's. 'You steal money from Val.' There was a pause.

'Balls, I do,' shouted Lee, scared now: he had not thought either had noticed the odd pound missing.

'You don't risk it with me,' jeered Alan.

Lee looked up at him. 'I don't risk it with anyone,' he snapped, then, with a sudden burst of spirit, 'just because you pay for a room here and screw my mother.'

Alan hit him. In the moment of shock that followed, Val tried to come between them, as Lee rose from the table, scared and hurt.

'Piss off,' he shouted.

Alan would not move. 'Don't insult your mother like that again. Ever.'

At last the tight group broke. Lee moved to the far side of the kitchen where he stood, shaking a little. Val stood between them, her eyes moving, frightened, from one to the other. Then Alan retreated a pace, shrugged and seemed to be willing to let the issue drop.

'You lie in that stinking bed of yours all day,' he murmured.

Lee, with a further flash of temper, shouted at him. 'While you're riding your big, macho lorry. Up yours with a Yorkie bar.'

Alan came for him again, fast, nudging the table in his anger. A cup fell and smashed on the floor. He lunged for Lee and caught him by the shoulder, as Val fought again to come between them.

'My house,' she said. 'My son.' Her forceful distress bled the situation of further violence. 'Go up to your room' she said quietly to Lee, who, almost in tears, protested. 'He started it.' Then, seeing the hopelessness of the situation, he turned and walked to the door, not looking back. There was a long silence before Alan bent to collect the fragments of the cup.

'He begs for it, Val, he really does.'

'That's enough, Alan,' she said, sitting, shaken, at the table. He took the fragments of crockery to the waste bin and sat opposite her, regarding her steadily as both tried to wind down.

'Val, we agreed when I moved in that if it didn't work out . . .' He left the unspoken threat hanging in the air.

Val saw it and was further distressed. She forced a smile. 'Come on, love,' she said anxiously. 'Ginger up. You were that age once.' He made no reply and Val felt the smile begin to slip. 'I've not had it easy,' she muttered. 'What are you saying?'

'I'm saying it's happening once too often. Sooner or later, one of us is going to get hurt.' His threat was still between them. Val gave it voice.

'Are you saying you want to go?' she asked quietly. No reply came from the man. She got up and moved quietly to him, kneeling at his side, her arms round his waist. She pulled him to her, trying to show how much she needed him, and embarrassed at having to give so much of herself. Finding little response, she moved coldly away and continued to reset the table. 'We've been over this before,' she said. 'I can't ask the boy to leave his own home.'

'He's getting between us,' said Alan, 'and that's what he wants. I don't like heavy scenes like this.'

There was a silence, and Val, remembering Morgan's surprising phone call, about which she had not spoken either to Lee or Alan, said quietly, 'My brother phoned last night. He says he's lonely. I could ask Lee to stay with him for a while. If he wanted to go.' Alan looked up with interest. She evaded further impossible thoughts in the routine familiarity of making their meal.

Much later that night, when the boy had not been down for his supper, Val took him a cup of coffee and a sandwich.

He was stretched out on the bed and made no movement as she came and sat near him, laying the cup and plate on his bedside table. She stroked his head which he moved away.

'Why do you let him do that?' he asked. 'It's your house.'

8

She promised he would not do it again, as she always did. 'It hurts Alan to see me upset,' she added. There was silence, except for the occasional vehicle speeding along the road.

Lee said, 'I hear him come into your room. How do you think I feel about that?'

She was brisk in her reply. 'Old enough to know it's nothing to do with you, I hope.' A motorbike passed noisily.

Lee glanced at her. 'My father never hit me,' he said quietly.

'He didn't care about us that much,' Val replied. She felt this exchange was moving nowhere. 'Since you brought it up,' she added, 'the sex bit's not important.'

Lee let the subject drop. He felt the tension in her. 'What do you want?' he asked suspiciously.

Val organised her resolve. 'Your uncle phoned last night . . .' There was no response. 'He's having a bad time.'

Lee's face was turned from her; he was listening intently, guessing something important was about to be said.

'He's very lonely; having a bad time.'

Lee began to see the direction of the conversation and was puzzled. He said, tentatively, 'I'm not a bloody farmer.'

Val rose from the bed. 'Fine,' she said. 'Tell me what you are and I might understand better. What are you? How do you see yourself?'

'I don't want to go to Wales,' said Lee, uneasy at her reaction. 'Why should I?'

Val shook her head, irritated and frustrated that he should care so little. 'To help me,' she pleaded.

'Boring,' said Lee.

Val moved to the wardrobe to put away his clothes. 'Like school was boring?' she said, wanting to hurt. 'Like this house is boring? Like the supermarket was boring? I've got a job, Lee.'

He knew what was coming. 'I know,' he said.

'You know, yes, and I check that twenty girls pack components into the right sections of the right containers.' She turned to face him.

'I know,' said Lee, wishing she would let the subject go. 'I know'.

Val would not. 'And I do the same thing, five days a week, from a quarter to nine until five-thirty and you talk about boredom.' She closed the wardrobe doors. 'Yes,' she said, 'work's boring: that's why they pay you to do it.'

Lee said nothing. His mother moved close to him again,

forcing a quiet and reasonable tone. She said, 'Morgan's been alone on that farm since your gran died, three months ago. He needs somebody there, just for a while; just to see him through a bad time. I need time to see if Alan and I maybe can . . .' The words fell away; she had said about as much as she could, and quickly kissed his head. 'We'll talk about it in the morning. Goodnight,' she said, as she moved to the door. Lee said nothing, as she left, then slowly sat up and sipped his coffee.

Alan was watching television when Val came into the room and sat down at his side. Both kept their eyes on the set, knowing the situation was still dangerous. 'Better if you don't come in tonight, Alan,' she said.

Lee was woken next morning by a strange, wet noise. Something swished; something plopped. It barely registered, but was sufficient to wake him a little. There was more swishing and another plop. Something crunched and Lee woke abruptly. His best friend, Colin, was standing at the fish tank, taking no notice of Lee, and apparently dipping into the tank searching for particular fish. He seemed to take one and slipped a wriggling gold shape into his mouth. He crunched.

Lee was speechless. He struggled to his elbows, appalled.

Colin turned to him. 'I like the Eaters best,' he said. He calmly looked at Lee's horrified face and said, concerned, 'Wasn't that an Eater?' But then a grin began to form on his lips and Lee began to smile too.

He dropped back on his bed, relieved. 'Oh, you sod,' he grinned.

Colin came to the bed, waving before Lee's eyes the sliver of carrot he was eating. He moved to draw the curtains and let in the daylight.

'What's the time?' asked Lee.

'Quarter to twelve. Where did you get to last night?'

Lee recalled the events of the previous evening. 'They wouldn't let me out, the bastards,' he said vehemently.

'Job thing?' asked Colin.

Lee nodded as Colin sat at the end of his bed.

'They're at the awkward age, your two,' he mused. 'Too old to have a good laugh but too young to let it all slide by.' He reached to pick up Lee's jeans and threw them at the boy. Lee got out of bed and climbed into them. 'Going to pick up your money from Ellis today?' asked Colin.

Lee zipped up his flies. 'She wants to get rid of me,' he said.

'I've got this uncle, somewhere in Wales, where my mother was born.'

Colin grinned. 'You don't have to do something you don't want,' he said. 'You're a big boy. Say no.'

Lee pulled a sweater round his shoulders. 'I could live round your place for a bit, couldn't I?' he asked carefully, but Colin, not keen, stretched out on the bed and said:

'You know what it's like — space and that.'

Lee nooded gloomily. 'It's not her,' he said.

'Roger the lodger?' grinned Colin.

Lee was suddenly indignant. He pushed his face close to Colin's. 'Have I got a mark? He went for me last night. Look.'

Colin was amused. 'Where?' he laughed. 'There's nothing there. You're cracking up.'

Lee grabbed a pillow and smacked it across Colin's head, giggling. 'I thought you were eating my poor bloody fish,' he said.

'You're cracking up,' Colin repeated, ducking away, laughing.

'You like the idea of signing on again?' Mr Ellis enquired. 'You don't find the prospect depressing?'

Once again Lee stood the other side of Mr Ellis' desk in the supermarket office. 'It keeps me off the streets,' he said cockily.

'An answer for everything,' his former boss sighed.

Lee agreed. 'That's education for you.'

'Clever,' said Ellis.

'Ta,' said Lee.

Tiring of banter, Ellis slid an envelope to the centre of the desk. 'Your money,' he said. 'Your cards. What now?'

'I'll likely go straight to the pub. Might mug a few grannies on the way. That's what you want to hear, isn't it?'

Mr Ellis smiled long-sufferingly. 'Sit down, Lee,' he said. 'I've got a boy your age.'

Lee opened his eyes wide. 'Is he a brain surgeon?' he asked.

Ellis smiled again. 'He wears earrings and goes about in chains,' he chuckled. 'Chains and leather; you can hear him a mile off, squeaking and clinking. I'm not saying I like the way he looks, but it's his life.'

'You must be disappointed, Mr Ellis,' said Lee with exaggerated sympathy.

The man smiled. 'No,' he said. 'He works a night shift at a motorway service station. It's not much but he's not on the dole; he's got status. You've not got status the minute you pick that envelope up.' Lee picked the envelope up and Ellis sighed heavily. 'We've done our best for you,' he said. 'You won't easily get another job on the Y.T.S. scheme.'

Lee opened the envelope to check the contents. 'Every cloud has a silver lining,' he said cheerfully.

Ellis got to his feet and moved to open the door. 'What do you want from life then?' he asked.

Lee finished checking the envelope's contents. 'A few laughs,' he said. 'A few mates.'

You're easily satisfied then,' Ellis said.

'I reckon that's the secret, Mr Ellis,' said Lee.

Ellis stuck out his hand. 'Would you believe I trained as a teacher?' he smiled.

Lee could easily believe it. 'Oh, yes,' he said, 'no bother.' He left.

Ellis, marooned with his hand in mid-air and the door shut on him, sighed heavily yet again and returned to his desk to check the daily intake of fish fingers.

Val was surprised to find Lee sitting at the kitchen table, waiting, when she came home. She was further surprised to find the kettle whistling on the stove and two crisp five-pound notes, side by side, near a cup and saucer.

'Hello,' smiled Lee.

Val looked at him suspiciously as she got out of her coat. 'What's this?' she asked, pointing at the money.

'Ten quid,' he said. 'For housekeeping.'

Suspicious of his consideration, but grateful nonetheless, Val sat as Lee poured boiling water into the teapot.

'What have you been doing with yourself today?' she asked.

'I went to the Job Centre,' said Lee, 'but there was nothing; I'll go again after the weekend.' He brought the teapot to the table. 'Oh, and Colin said I could stay at his place,' he lied casually, sitting down.

There was a long silence; Val reached into her bag for her cigarettes. She offered one to Lee and they both lit up. Quietly, Val said, 'Colin lives just two streets away.'

Her son shrugged. 'Look, we get on all right, you and me,' he said, desperately. 'It was okay before Alan came.'

Val drew on her cigarette. 'Not for me,' she said. Lee tried not to meet her steady glance. 'Alan tries, but you never notice; you don't take in anything you don't like. You can't give, can you? Your father couldn't give.'

Lee was puzzled. 'Give what?' he said, unconsciously proving her point.

'But you take, all right,' said Val heavily, sipping her tea. His eyes moved to the money. 'Oh, not that,' she said. 'That's the least. You take energy, patience, good will; that's why I wanted you to go to Morgan – he's got more than I'll ever have. You'd have fitted well together.' He smoked his cigarette in silence. 'All right,' said Val, 'if not Morgan, where do we go from here?' She looked directly at him and he saw her weariness; he saw her sagging shoulders, saw he was a complication she preferred to do without.

He got to his feet. 'Great,' he said, 'right.' He looked down at her. 'I'll go to Wales, if that's what you want.'

Val recognised the bravado for what it was and shook her head.

'When?' demanded Lee. 'Sunday? I mean I could go today except it's too late. That's okay with you, is it? You and him? You can keep your heads out of the gas oven one more night, can you?'

Val felt her patience going. 'Don't be ridiculous,' she snapped.

'No,' insisted Lee, as he headed for the door. 'It'll be a nice change, if someone wants me – actually and definitely wants me.'

Val was weary of it all. 'Don't go on, Lee,' she said.

'No,' said Lee, 'that's great,' slamming the door behind him as he left.

The pub was busy with its weekend clientele. It was about ten-thirty and a sudden influx of late arrivals added to the hubbub of the juke box, the ringing of the till and the general noisy chatter. At a table in the corner sat Lee, Colin and Carol, Lee's girlfriend. Lee and Colin, at least, had enjoyed the pub crawl; this was their fourth call and seemed likely to be their last. Lee was sleepy, anaesthetised by drink. Colin grinned, happily vacant, all around. Carol, an attractive girl, looked from one to the other.

'Wake up,' she said sharply, nudging Lee – who fought his way back through the clouds of drink.

'No, it's great,' he said. 'It's a great goodbye, is this.' A glass smashed somewhere and everybody cheered.

Carol gave up and drained her glass. 'You won't be gone forever,' she said. 'They can't force you to stay if you don't like it. A big farm is it? Horses and ploughs, and haystacks and things?'

Lee thought hard. 'Yeah, as far as I remember. I've only been there once — went with the old woman when I was about twelve.' He gazed absently into his glass.

Carol turned to Colin, who was grinning vacuously around him. 'We'll go down one weekend, yeah?'

Colin switched his attention to her. 'What?' he asked.

'Bloody hell,' she said, fed-up. 'It's like talking to a three-year-old.'

'He's pissed,' said Lee, grinning.

'We're all pissed,' Colin declared.

She tried again. 'Why are you going so soon?'

'Shake them up a bit,' said Lee, putting on his bravest show. 'It was good. You should have seen the old woman's face.' He laughed, but was in truth not much amused. There was a long silence.

'My shout,' called Colin, suddenly climbing to his feet.

'Pint,' said Lee, sliding his glass across the table.

'Blue Moon,' said Carol.

Colin picked up her glass and gazed at the vivid blue remnants of her drink with distaste. 'How can you drink anything that colour?' he asked, shaking his head.

'No problem at all,' she pouted, as Colin staggered towards the counter.

'I'll miss you, Carol,' said Lee, sentimental with drink.

'Yeah,' said Carol casually, 'I'll miss you.'

Lee threw his arms round her in a sudden excess of emotion and she fended him off as gently as she could.

At the counter Colin ordered the drinks and tipsily surveyed his companions. At his side an old woman drank alone, and he smiled at her.

'Who are you?' she asked suspiciously.

'Dracula,' he said.

The woman stared at him without surprise. 'My husband's over there,' she said. 'If I screamed he'd come running. He's a professional wrestler is my husband.'

Seeing there was no one remotely near who could possibly be her husband, Colin turned away, but the woman grabbed his sleeve.

'So watch it,' she threatened.

Colin looked at her, baring his teeth, and gently snarled. As the landlord fetched the drinks, Colin leaned back on the counter and watched Lee and Carol grappling. It had been a good night out — a good farewell to his mate. He wondered how Lee would make out in Wales and where the hell in his tidy, crowded home he would find room for Lee's fish.

The National coach wound its way to the Castle Inn at Pengenffordd, where it pulled to the side of the road and stopped. Its doors hissed open and three passengers alighted. As the third passenger crossed the road to enter the Inn, Lee shivered in the sudden cold and followed the direction of his mother's wave, to where Morgan stood by his Land Rover. Lee was uncertain what response was called for; it was a problem common to all three. Val took Lee's arm and they moved towards her brother, as the coach doors swung to and the vehicle moved off. All round him the hills were covered in snow; it was bitterly cold and very muddy. Lee adjusted the weight of his rucksack to give himself time before he must meet the uncle he had not seen for five years.

Val and Morgan clumsily embraced.

'How are you, Morgan?' she asked warmly. He made no answer and she turned to Lee, who was only now arriving. 'And here's the boy,' she said.

To Lee's intense embarrassment, Morgan scrutinised him from top to toe as if he were one of the farm animals. 'Grown since,' he said softly.

'He's seventeen now,' said Val proudly.

Lee felt that sense of not being there, of being invisible, while adults talked about him. He could not meet Morgan's steady glance. They hung about.

'Still the same old banger then,' said Val, tapping the battered Land Rover. 'Put your rucksack in the back, Lee.'

Lee was grateful for being told what to do, and moved to the back of the Land Rover. There was no back door and the vehicle smelt of animals. Val smiled at Morgan as he held open the door for her to climb in. Lee clambered over the tail-gate. As Morgan walked round the vehicle to climb into the driving seat, Val suddenly dropped her defence and looked anxiously round at her son.

'There's room in the front,' she said, wanting him near, but Lee took no notice. Then Morgan was switching on the engine and Val was smiling again. She knew she was smiling too much.

Morgan turned to her and said very quietly, 'See the Old Lady and Gentleman, Val?'

15

Val knew what he was talking about and that she had no choice. 'Yes,' she said, 'I'd like that.' The Land Rover pulled from the car park at the Castle Inn and began the descent towards Blainau.

It was a short drive by country standards, but Lee found it long enough. The Land Rover turned from the main road and crisscrossed a grid of minor roads before climbing sharply. The sudden jolting rattle of a cattle grid beneath the wheels alarmed him and his mother turned and smiled. He, too, knew she was smiling too much. The old Land Rover pulled noisily across the brow of Llanelieu Common and the whole western block of the Black Mountains was suddenly before them — an impenetrable, high wall, impressive and daunting, clouds softening the sharp, top ridges and a layer of snow extending down to where fields had once been laboriously reclaimed from the bare mountainside. They came to a T junction and the Land Rover descended steeply. Another cattle grid rattled beneath them and then Morgan was pulling up at the side of a small, bleak church.

Val and Morgan stood at the side of the two-month-old grave. The inscription on the headstone said simply, 'Ivor Thomas. 1905 – 1970. With the Lord,' and, below it, a newer inscription, 'Gwen Thomas. Loving Wife. 1916 – 1983.' Lee hovered uneasily at the gate of the churchyard, watching his mother and uncle. The wind was bitter and the silent emotion that seemed to be manifest at the graveside embarrassed him. He pulled the collar of his anorak higher and looked down at his training shoes, already dirty and letting in cold mud. He could see Morgan's eyes wet with emotion and looked away. He knew he was in an impossible situation and was angry with himself for provoking his brother's arm. At last Val took her brother's arm.

'Let's get to the farm now,' she said firmly. 'I told Alan to fetch me at seven.' Seeing the adults coming towards the gate, Lee climbed back into the Land Rover. Val felt she should explain his indifference. 'Lee's a different generation,' she said. 'Don't worry about him.'

Arm in arm, Val and Morgan walked through the gate and down stone steps to the road and the Land Rover, where Lee was already huddled, cold, in the back.

'That's one of the oldest churches in Wales, Lee,' said Val, for conversation, as she shut the door behind her.

'Fantastic,' murmured Lee, feeling more and more that he had nothing to offer this place and that in turn it had even less to offer him.

When Lee jumped from the Land Rover at his mother's sharp command to open the gate, his sense of uneasiness sharpened into something near sudden panic. Blainau was not as he remembered it. In the dying light of the January afternoon it looked oppressive and alien. The Land Rover drove past him into the yard and Lee swung the gate shut and squelched across the muddy yard to where his mother was already stepping down. A dog was barking furiously from a barn and Morgan moved to release it. Lee did not like dogs, but his mother saw his uneasiness, and, as Cap, Morgan's sheepdog, bounded into the yard, she made an effort to allay his fears.

'Come here, boy. Come here. Good dog, that's a good dog,' she said easily. Turning to her son, she said, 'No need to be afraid of him.'

'I'm not afraid,' said Lee, stepping back anxiously to avoid the dog's excited greeting.

Morgan moved towards the door of the house and saw the boy's uneasiness. 'Get down,' he called and the dog obediently moved away to a neutral part of the yard, where it watched the arrivals with interest.

Val pointed down to a scraper near the door. 'Wipe your feet on that.'

Lee did as he was told and followed his mother and the stranger that was his uncle into the house.

If the outside of Blainau and its situation, huddled at the foot of the high ridge, in the gathering dusk, had alarmed Lee, the inside almost frightened him more. The house was small and, to his eyes, dirty. It smelled slightly of animals and was dark even when Morgan switched on the lights. He stood bemused inside the door. Val saw his hesitation.

'Come on,' she said briskly. 'Let's get you settled first. Bring your rucksack.' She moved towards a door in the living-room which opened onto a set of stairs. Lee followed her, not knowing what else he could do, regretting bitterly now the bravado which had led him to this strange house and this strange man and this strange country, where he simply felt he could have no possible life.

Val climbed the stairs to a small landing and turned towards a door, knowing where she was going. The dark landing and the creaking stairs further convinced Lee that it was all a mistake. Suddenly he sat down at the top of the stairs, not meeting his mother's questioning and anxious eyes as they turned upon him.

Val, disappointed but not surprised, half-expecting some such reaction, simply asked, 'All right, Lee. What do you want?' She had known his misgivings the moment they had left the coach, and she shared his feelings. She had hoped against hope he would accept the situation and knew, now, that he could not.

There was silence in the house. Outside, Cap barked twice and Lee suddenly heard Morgan moving to another room beneath him. He still would not meet his mother's eyes.

'Do you want to come back home?' she asked.

'I don't know,' he said. 'I mean it: I don't know.' He shrugged miserably, unable to find the right words.

Val said quietly, 'It's not home, is it? And it's not how you remember the farm?' Lee nodded. She took a step or two nearer her son and said tentatively, 'It's not Morgan? He doesn't frighten you?'

There was a pause before Lee suddenly took the initiative and stood up, grabbing his rucksack and moving past her onto the landing. He turned to her. 'Which room?' he said. Bewildered and exasperated with the changes of mood, Val passed him without a word and opened a corner door.

The room was small and overlooked the farmyard. The furniture was old, though someone had made an effort to dust it. The room smelled unlived in. There was a low chest of drawers, a wardrobe, a high, narrow bed and a wooden chair and table. The wallpaper was faded. There was a cheap print of flowers on one wall and, above the bed, a scriptural text.

Val knew the room well, and when her son, feeling he must make some remark to help them both, asked, 'How do you know this is the room?' she said quietly, 'I know; it used to be mine.' She moved to the bed and slipped her hand inside to check it was aired. Satisfied, she turned back the coverlet and moved to adjust the curtains. 'You've got a marvellous view,' she said.

Lee sat on the bed, his rucksack at his side, not knowing what to do. 'What will Alan say if I come back home?' He hated asking the question.

'I thought what Alan said never bothered you,' she said briskly, but, seeing his complete helplessness, she softened. 'He won't say anything,' she added.

Lee's voice was dull and defeated. 'Not tonight maybe, but

18

anytime there's any hassle, he'll start right in on it. You know he will. He'll say I couldn't handle this.'

'You'll have to decide who you're more scared of then,' said Val wearily, 'Alan or Morgan.'

Lee was suddenly annoyed with her. 'You bloody keep on about being scared,' he said.

His mother looked levelly at him. 'Seventeen is not a child. You're forever telling me you can look after yourself.'

Lee suddenly seemed to have made a decision. He quietly unfastened his rucksack and began unpacking.

Val said quietly, 'You're not being punished.'

Lee knew better. 'Is that right?' he said coldly, continuing his unpacking.

Val moved to open drawers for him to put away some of his clothes, and gingerly she switched on an ancient electric fire. 'Lee,' she said urgently, 'try to like it.'

He moved towards the chest of drawers, with a hand full of singlets, socks and pants. 'You can't try to like anything,' he murmured. 'You either do or you don't.'

Val watched him return to the rucksack. His face was cold and remote. She turned to leave and Lee heard her feet clatter downstairs; heard the door at the foot of the stairs close; heard distantly the quiet conversation between his mother and her brother. He allowed himself to look closely at the room for the first time and was not impressed. He moved to the window and looked out. It was, as his mother had said, a wonderful view, but Lee was in no mood for it. He pulled the curtains closed and sat on the bed. He thought — what am I doing here?

In the kitchen Val was also unpacking. 'I brought us a meal,' she said, 'and I'll clean round for you a bit if there's time.' She placed on the table the components of the meal she had brought.

Morgan stood, watching her. He said, 'The boy looks like his father.'

Val smiled. 'I know,' she said. 'Everybody says that.' She put on the apron she had brought.

'Happy enough is he?' asked Morgan.

Val smiled again. 'Don't ask me,' she said, 'I'm only his mother.' She moved to her handbag. 'What about money now, Morgan?' she asked.

Morgan seemed puzzled. 'I'll pay him if he works, fair play.'

'You can sort that out between you,' said Val, taking a folded set of notes from her handbag and firmly handing them to Morgan. He shook his head but Val was insistent. 'Take it. Kids are expensive. Then I can tell him you've got it if he needs it.' Morgan seriously considered this a second or two, nodded, took the notes and carefully placed them in a tin on the sideboard.

Val continued preparing the meal as Morgan hovered around her. She sensed he needed to talk, but the situation was so uncertain that she realised, to her shame, that she would prefer not to hear what he might say.

'Bad is it, big brother?' She could not look at him and Morgan, troubled, moved his head, as if in pain. She laid a hand on his arm. Val moved to him. 'I knew it must be, to make you phone.'

Morgan said quietly, 'I didn't expect it, Val. When dad died, there was still the Old Lady and I was younger then. But it knocked the stuffing right out of me when she passed on.' Tears welled in his eyes. 'I didn't expect it.'

Val squeezed his arm gently. 'You're like my boy up there,' she said. 'It takes a lot to admit you're human. And I'm glad you phoned.' The man's head was down. She removed her hand and said briskly, 'Come on, Mor. "Ginger up". That's what Mam would say.'

Morgan, trying hard not to distress her, made himself smile. 'Yes,' he said, 'she would.'

Val turned back to the table, taking frozen vegetables to the draining board, under which she knew she would find saucepans. 'What about the paperwork, Morgan?' she asked. 'Are you up to it?'

Morgan gave a short laugh. 'Closed books to me. She could do it, but damn if I can. I've got an accountant chappie in Aber now,' he said.

Val remembered Pugh. 'How's Pugh?' she grinned. 'He must be getting on.'

Morgan laughed again, making more of an effort. 'Fit as a flea,' he said. 'I don't know what I'd do without him and that's a fact.'

'Supper won't be long,' Val called across the room, finding, to her surprise and pleasure, that her flat Manchester voice, for so long her normal accent, was now rounding out to match his Welshness. The mood had lightened.

Morgan said, 'Aren't you going to wait for your man?'

Val shook her head, 'He'll have something before he leaves.'

Morgan smiled again. 'Got him well-trained, say?'

20

Val turned to grin at him. 'Not that one,' she said. 'You can't train that one.'

Lee was glad to see headlights questing through the frosted darkness towards the farm. The yard light was on, but served only to intensify the darkness all round him. He had been waiting outside for Alan for almost twenty minutes.

Alan was surprised to find Lee waiting for him.

'You found it then,' the boy said.

'Just about,' Alan replied, slamming the car door and stepping carefully upon the frozen mud. 'I didn't know if this was it or not, until I saw you.'

Lee smiled. 'That's why I came out to wait,' he said.

Alan was faintly wary of the unusual solicitude for his well-being. He carried a large cardboard box and a plastic shopping bag. 'It's bloody cold,' he said, shivering, as Lee opened the gate for him. They gingerly moved across the slippery yard towards the house whose door was opened by Morgan. The two men summed each other up. Morgan, formally suited; Alan, tall and casually dressed. Alan nodded at Morgan. 'Evening,' he said.

'Go in, please,' said Morgan, standing back for Alan and Lee to pass.

'What's that box?' asked Lee.

Alan smiled. 'I'll show you inside,' he said, as he passed through the door, Lee following him quickly in.

Alan was surprised, as Lee had been, at the spare dinginess of the farmhouse. It was, in fact, the first farmhouse he had ever been inside; his notions of farmhouses were bright, cheerful, like the ones he'd seen on the television ads. Blainau was nothing like that.

He stepped into the living-room where Val came up to him, smiling, and they kissed self-consciously. Alan looked round the room, Val catching his sense of slight bewilderment.

'And you've met Morgan,' she said quickly.

Alan nodded. 'We said hello,' he confirmed.

Val turned to Morgan, wanting them to like each other. 'This is Alan.'

Alan put out his hand. 'How are you,' he said. Morgan replied shyly that he was very well. Nobody seemed to know what to do next.

Morgan suddenly said, 'Sit down, why not,' and Val left to find another cup in the kitchen. Lee followed her, leaving the two men together. Alan gratefully warmed his hands at the fire, while the sense of complete difference hung in the air between them.

'You're out in the wilds here,' said Alan, willing to be friendly. Morgan considered this and nodded. 'Nice to see an open fire,' he tried again.

Morgan had never considered this. He looked at the fire he had known the whole of his life and then back to Alan. 'It sucks the dust from a room,' he agreed. Alan gave up and they sat in awkward silence.

In the kitchen Val quickly packed the last of the containers which had brought their evening meal, and talked earnestly and quietly.

'We've got to get off soon,' she said. 'I don't want to leave you here if you hate it.' Lee shrugged. 'I've given Morgan money if you need anything,' she continued. There was no reply from Lee; Val's anxiety increased. 'Look,' she said, 'phone me tomorrow, all right? See how you make out. If it's hopeless we'll collect you the next day, after work, all right?' Lee nodded. She looked at her miserable son, suddenly feeling guilty for having forced him into this position.

The door opened and Alan came in with the cardboard box and the carrier bag. He nodded briskly to Lee. 'You all right?'

Lee was irritable. 'Everybody keeps asking me if I'm all right. Yes. Great. Fantastic. I'm not a kid,' he muttered.

Alan looked at Val, seeing her anxiety. He handed over the box. 'I knew you'd miss your music,' he said.

Lee saw his mother pass an uneasy smile at Alan as he took it. The box revealed a brand new stereo radio with a cassette deck. In other circumstances the boy would have been delighted, but, feeling cornered and dismissed from his familiar life, he shrugged.

He grumbled, 'I didn't bring any tapes.'

Alan held out the plastic bag towards him. 'Tapes,' he said.

And suddenly Lee was genuinely grateful to him for this connection with home. 'Thanks, Alan,' he said, turning his attention to the radio to hide his feelings.

Val said to Alan, 'I said we'd pick him up on Thursday after work if he doesn't like it.'

'Why shouldn't he like it?' asked Alan sharply. Lee sensed the antagonism between his mother and Alan and bent to examine his generous gift, unwilling to meet anyone's eyes.

Alan nodded imperceptibly towards the door.

'I'll get my things together,' Val said and moved from the room.

Alan came to stand opposite Lee at the table. 'Give it a go, a real go,' he said. 'Try.'

There was a brief silence as Lee stolidly looked through the tapes in the bag. He said quietly, 'I'm sorry, Alan, about the other night.'

But Alan was not to be charmed. 'Give us a chance,' he insisted. 'Your mother and me, we need time together. Do you know what I mean?'

Lee looked up, objecting mildly. 'She's my mother.'

Alan was sharp with him. 'Don't you even think of it,' he said. 'Let her be her own woman for a change.' The man steadily looked at the boy who could not hold his gaze.

Lee nodded down towards the radio. 'Thanks for this,' he said and moved towards the door.

Alan moved with him, laying a friendly arm on his shoulders, as he moved out. 'You'll be okay,' he said confidently. 'It's a great place. I'd have loved it at your age.' Lee opened the door and stood back so that Alan would have to move through and drop the hand from his shoulder.

In the living-room Val was putting on her coat when Lee and Alan came in. Morgan had left to open the gate. Alan picked up Val's bag and both turned to Lee.

'I'll see you then,' he said, not moving.

Val frowned anxiously. 'You're not coming to see us off?' she asked.

Lee looked at her steadily. 'See you,' he repeated.

Val sensed that his petty refusal to see them to the car was a rebuke, a standing on dignity. Alan saw it too, and putting his arm round Val, he moved her towards the door, calling over his shoulder, 'Take care, Lee.'

Val turned one last time as she left. 'Phone us tomorrow night,' she said, not wanting to leave him like this. Lee nodded, as Alan moved Val outside and closed the door behind them. Alan had recognised Val's mood all too well – she was too soft with the boy; it would be good not to have his surly presence in the house.

As they moved through the yard, Val said unhappily, 'I don't like leaving him in that mood.' Alan made no reply as he opened the car door for her.

Morgan came towards them. 'I'll take care of him,' he said to his sister.

Alan settled in the driver's seat. He grinned up at Morgan. 'Get him working,' he said, as he switched on the ignition.

Val called, 'Look after yourself. I'll see you again soon.'

Morgan nodded and stepped back as Alan slammed the driver's door shut. The car's wheels spun a little on the mud at the verge of the road.

Alan looked over at Val and grinned. 'Are you Welsh always like this when you trip over your roots?' he asked. 'Where does that accent come from? It's a riot.'

Val said nothing as Alan put the car into gear again, was more careful with the accelerator and spun the car slightly as it moved into the centre of the road.

Morgan waved as they passed; Alan pressed the horn in reply. Morgan swung the yard gate shut and watched the lights of the car as it threaded its way along the lonely road. His dog came to his side as he turned back towards the house. Morgan whistled it to its home in the small barn.

Lee was not in the living-room when Morgan returned. The man bent to put more wood on the fire and heard from the kitchen a burst of music, then static, then the measured tones of a foreign news broadcast as Lee aimlessly sought stations on his new radio. Morgan was aware that this was an important time: their first moments alone. He sat in the chair to think. It was strange to hear someone else in the house again; comforting but unsettling. At last he rose and moved towards the kitchen.

The boy also knew the importance of the moment, but felt merely rejected and irrelevant. He spun the dial until he found Radio One, grateful for the link, however tenuous, with what he considered his real life. Morgan came through the door and Lee switched the radio off.

'They're away then,' said Morgan, 'and there's ice on the roads. A long drive home.' The boy would not answer him. Morgan moved towards the small upright stove and warmed his hands. 'I have a drink of beer about this time,' he said.

The boy shrugged, unwilling to make it easy. 'Did you ask for me to come here?' he inquired, 'or was it their idea?'

Morgan, behind him, noted the set, tense shoulders. 'What difference, say?' he asked quietly.

'Why did you phone us?'

Morgan thought this over seriously. 'Your mother's family, boy,' he said. 'My sister.'

Lee turned to look up at his uncle. 'She left here when she was seventeen,' he said. 'She's only ever been back twice. I don't call that particularly close.'

'She's still all the family I've got left,' said Morgan, intimidated. 'Bar you,' he added.

The boy aimlessly turned on the radio; music filled the kitchen; he switched it off again. 'What did she tell you about me?' he asked.

Morgan was thoughtful. 'She said you can't settle.'

Lee laughed without humour. 'I fight with Alan,' he said.

'Then you're lucky to have someone to fight with, boy,' his uncle replied.

Lee twisted in his chair again, to look Morgan directly in the eye. He had decided to be cruel. 'You don't have to live here,' he jeered.

Morgan laughed quietly. 'I'm forty-seven, boy,' he said. 'I was born in the Old Lady's room upstairs. For school it was down to the village and leave at fourteen. I don't know much, but I know this farm, and that's all I know. You're right. I don't have to live here' — he was suddenly angry — 'but where else should I go?'

Morgan's sudden sharpness cut through Lee's sullen mood. He turned his attention back to the radio. He turned it on and music filled the room.

'And will you work?' said Morgan, above the noise.

'I'm not here to work,' said Lee. 'I'm here to get me out of the way.'

Morgan nodded. He moved slowly so that he and Lee were face to face. He reached over and switched off the radio. 'I'm lonely, boy,' he said, 'and my name's Morgan.' Lee would not meet his eyes, partly aware of the effort it had taken to force this strange, embarrassing confession from his uncle. 'Have you ever been lonely?' asked Morgan.

Lee got to his feet. He picked up the radio and moved to the door. 'Yes,' he said, matter-of-factly, as if to say 'who hasn't?'

At the door, he turned, troubled by a sudden thought which struck him acutely and obliquely, turning into an anxiety that he knew he would have to voice, though he hated breaking into the image of indifferent hardness he had been fashioning. Morgan looked up at him.

'Where did my grandmother and grandfather die?' Lee asked. 'In this house?'

Morgan felt a sudden rush of sympathy. He, who had known all his life the familiarity of this farmhouse, suddenly understood something of what the boy must be feeling. He said gently, 'Not in your room.'

Lee was grateful for not having been made fun of. He nodded. 'Night then,' he said, and moved into the living-room.

Morgan said quietly, 'Goodnight.'

The man stood entirely still, hearing someone else in the house, opening the stair-door; hearing someone else's feet tread the stairs to the landing. Morgan wondered at the relief he felt at hearing the familiar boards squeak under someone else's feet. He heard Lee's door close. Then he found a can of beer in the cupboard, picked up the local newspaper from the shelf and sat at the table, not wanting so much to read as to have an excuse to be silent and let the impressions of the day settle. Someone was in Blainau again — someone who was family.

In his bleak bedroom Lee turned off the electric fire and stretched out on the bed, hearing the silence and the sudden susurration of wind in the trees. Very distantly a dog barked and Cap, in the outhouse, barked back a routine reply. Something metallic rattled across the yard, blown by the wind; then there was this terrifying silence once again.

This cannot work, Lee thought. Why did I let it happen?

Relieved by the idea that his mother had promised to fetch him home on Thursday, he leaned down to fill his room with Radio One. The inane chatter of a familiar disc-jockey soothed his scattered thoughts. He forced himself not to panic and to wait until tomorrow, when he would ring home and ask to be collected.

Chapter Two

Lee did not sleep well. The wind that had vaguely disturbed him blew more strongly after midnight, and he lay in the unaccustomed bed imagining voices calling through the gusts. At some time he must have dozed for an hour or so, because he woke to hear rain drumming on the corrugated roof of the barns opposite. For a while the rain and wind combined – the doors to the cowshed groaned and grated under the onslaught. At four o'clock he got up and gingerly trod the noisy landing to find the bathroom, not wanting Morgan to hear him in case the man got up too, forcing enquiries, conversation. On return to his room, he switched on the electric fire and knelt before it to regain some of his lost warmth. He heard the humming of the wire elements as they glowed, and realised the rain and wind had stopped. When he drew the curtains he saw thin flakes of snow licking the glass. He left the fire on and climbed back into bed. Tomorrow he would phone Val and the next day they would come for him. He fell asleep wrapped in that comfort and woke late.

Lee did not know it was late. What was late here? He heard, through his early-morning dozing, Morgan get up; he heard the man trying to be quiet as he clanked cups in the kitchen. Some time later he heard a car draw up – he was aware that the darkness had passed – and there was an exchange of greetings: Morgan and some other, older voice. Then there was more muffled clanking of crockery down below. He must have slept again, for when he finally woke with any determination, it was to hear the older voice calling wordlessly to the rattling of barn doors and the answering lowing of cows. Lee stretched, rubbed tired eyes and reached down for the comfort of Simon Bates, who was suggesting that, on such a dreadful day as this, there was little to be done except phone the boss and claim to be sick, reach for the coffee and listen to Duran Duran's latest.

Unaware of Simon Bates' advice, Morgan and Pugh were mucking out the cowshed, with the thin layer of snow already melting from the roof. Pugh asked where the boy was but got no answer. In fact Lee was asleep again. His disturbed night was catching up on him; he did not mind. As he dozed off into dreamlessness, he felt he was as safe in his bed as anywhere else.

Pugh Davies had helped Morgan on the farm for two years. Well past retirement, he had found that sedentary life in his daughter's house in Talgarth left him irritable and dissatisfied; he had been glad when one of Morgan's neighbours had dropped the hint that work at Blainau was very hard for Morgan and his mother. One day he had asked his daughter to drop him at the farm on her way to work and had suggested to the Old Lady that she take him on part-time. Pugh had been a farmer in his own right, until his wife had died and life had become a struggle, affecting his health; he understood the hard ways of hill-farming. He had slowly become indispensable to the Thomases, and when the Old Lady died he became essential, not only for his work but for his company. Pugh, with his dry wit, was often the only other human Morgan saw from day to day. His daughter dropped him at the farm every morning, on her way to Abergavenny, and collected him on her way home. Everyone benefited.

Pugh was washing his hands and Morgan setting out mugs for their mid-morning break when Lee came hesitantly into the kitchen.

'Get up late in the town, is it?' grinned Pugh, drying his hands on a grubby roller towel.

Lee looked at him coldly, recognising the voice he had heard earlier and seeing a small gnome of a man with a drooping moustache.

Morgan introduced him. 'Pugh, this is.'

'The power behind the throne,' added Pugh, trying for friendliness. None came. When Morgan asked if he'd join them in a cup of tea, Lee sullenly stated he did not like tea, and, when the men chatted to him about the early morning snow, Lee pulled out a chair, slumped down on it and complained about the hard bed and the sleepless night he'd endured.

Neither of the men seemed impressed. Morgan brought the teapot to the table and Pugh found a biscuit tin in the cupboard and each took two. Morgan asked if Lee was hungry; he shook his head. But when Pugh held the tin before him, he eventually took a biscuit and when the old man, grinning remorselessly, imperiously shook the tin, Lee gracelessly took another. The three munched; the men sipped hot, sweet tea. There was silence. Lee felt Pugh's eyes on him, sorting him out, unimpressed so far. Instinctively he reached for his packet of cigarettes, crushed in the pocket of his jeans: there was one left — he had meant to stock up somewhere. He lit his last smoke.

'There a shop near here?' he asked.

Morgan nodded, glad to be helpful. 'Down in the town,' he said.

Lee was glad for that excuse to break from the farm for a while. 'How far's that?' he asked, and was less glad to learn that Talgarth was five miles away. 'Is there a bus?'

That seemed to amuse the men, adding to the boy's discomfiture. There were obviously no buses.

'Where's the nearest pub?' he tried again. Again amusement.

Pugh chuckled, 'Five miles. By God, you must be craving,' and then they were sipping tea again, in silence.

'You lending a hand today?' Morgan's voice was casual but Lee saw the eyes flick away to Pugh and guessed they must have been discussing him.

'Useful — another pair of hands,' added Pugh, encouragingly. Lee said nothing, making much of his smoking, avoiding their glances. Pugh chuckled. 'Workshy, is it?' he asked, with a trace of mockery.

Lee was stung to reply: 'I can work when I want to.' The old man found this amusing and Lee began to tire of being the butt of unknown jokes.

'Nobody ever gave *me* the chance, boy,' Pugh said.

Lee was stung again. 'I've got a name,' he said.

'I'm likely nameshy,' replied the old man complacently, dipping a biscuit into his tea. '*You* ever had the option of working, Morgan?' he asked innocently, looking to the other man for complicity.

But Morgan had had enough of the game, seeing Lee's discomfort. He shook his head at Pugh, warning him off, but Lee was already on his feet and out of the room. His steps clattered upstairs. There was the creaking of boards and then the shutting of his bedroom door.

'Let him settle,' Morgan said, but Pugh smiled as he licked damp crumbs from his lips.

'He's no use to you; he's like all the young 'uns round here. He'll be away, soon as he can'.

'He will if you keep at him,' Morgan said sharply, rising from his chair to follow the boy. Pugh contemplated the rebuke, nodding. He reached for the teapot.

Lee was struggling into his thin town anorak as Morgan came into the room.

'You don't want to mind Pugh,' he said, moving to draw back the half-pulled curtains.

Lee asked the way into town, refusing Morgan's offer to drive him there if he would wait until dinnertime. 'I'll go now,' the boy said firmly, knotting a scarf loosely round his neck.

Morgan stayed at the window, gazing out. 'No good is this,' he said, 'no damn good at all.'

Lee turned to him. 'I didn't ask to come here.'

Morgan swung to face Lee, suddenly angry. 'Nobody asks to be born, but we got to make the best.' He instantly regretted his tone, seeing the boy's anxiety. (Morgan thought: I'm not used to dealing with people. I talk to them like cattle.) Softly, he asked Lee if maybe he was homesick, and, seeing the boy's face twist in scorn, said gently, encouragingly, 'Give it a go then?'

This way of attack was familiar to Lee. The boy looked directly at him; the man's eyes slid away. 'It's dead simple to you,' Lee said. 'You want help or company or something, so you just phone up. They want me out of the way, so I get sent here.' His tone unsettled the man.

'But you're family, son,' he said, almost plaintively, as if that explained all.

Lee smiled briefly; he recognised that blackmail too. 'Don't lumber me with that,' he said, moving to the door.

Morgan followed him doggedly. 'That's family, is it,' he persisted, 'being lumbered?'

Lee sought the most hurtful reply he could find. 'It's lumbered you.'

Morgan was hurt. He said softly, 'Your grandfather — he'd have taken a strap to you for that.'

Lee smiled, pleased with the result of his thrust. 'Great,' he said, 'that's family.' He moved again to the door and was suddenly aware of Morgan at his shoulder, again suddenly angry.

'What's to do then, say? Phone your mother, is it? Collect you tomorrow?'

And suddenly Lee was angry too; what right had this man to keep on at him like this? 'Leave me alone,' he shouted.

Morgan pursued him to the top of the stairs. 'Last night you said you knew about being alone.' It was a plaintive cry; Lee recognised its true ring.

He turned to Morgan. 'Where did you say this town was?' he asked.

Morgan paused, knowing he was out of his depth. 'You don't want to be wandering off on your own,' he said, lamely. Then, seeing the boy turn and move from the bottom of the stairs into the living-room, he called after him, 'There's a gate across from the yard. Go straight across the field. You'll see Talgarth. Save you a mile.'

Lee didn't stop; he walked through the porch and into the yard, towards the gate Morgan had mentioned.

Pugh was pulling on his work-coat at the door when Morgan came slowly down the stairs. 'No change in the work force then?' he chuckled.

Morgan snapped at the old man. 'You were awkward enough when you was a boy by all accounts. Give him a chance.'

Pugh found the length of binder twine in his coat pocket and tied it round his waist. Morgan pulled on his stained duffel coat which the Old Lady had bought for him, as best, eight years ago. He regretted his sharpness with Pugh; he regretted his inability to communicate with Lee.

Some of this must have shown in his face, for the old man saw it and responded, though misreading the causes. 'You never heard from the Estate?' he asked, tentatively. 'Time you heard about the tenancy, boy. Three months now since the Old Lady passed on.'

Morgan drew on his boots. He, too, was worried about the tenancy and Pugh was right: he should have heard about the succession by now. 'They won't want me out,' he replied.

Pugh nodded as he opened the door and the cold air of the porch hit him; he caught his breath briefly and strained to see Lee, far in the distance, walking across the ten-acre field towards Talgarth. 'The boy'd take some weight from us, Morgan,' he said. 'Carry up a bit of feed; get at some ditching.'

Morgan joined him in the porch, closing the living-room door behind him. 'It's not just the work,' he said softly.

Pugh understood. 'Bit of company,' he affirmed.

Morgan nodded. For a second or two, they watched Lee cross through a distant gate into a further field before Pugh broke the mood.

'Fix the fence by the brook?' he asked.

'I expect so,' said Morgan, moving to the workshop where the tools were kept, looking round for Cap to come trotting to his side.

Meanwhile, Lee was learning about sheep. The field he was crossing contained about eighty, most of whom had noted with interest his entry to their pasture, whose meagre grass was thin and very short, nibbled to the mud. It was late morning and their daily feeding time was mid-afternoon, but they were prepared to stretch a point; they were hungry and two legs walking meant food. They began to move hopefully towards him. And they began to bleat, loudly.

The noise penetrated Lee's thoughts first. He looked round to find himself a magnet for a fieldful of sheep. He was not afraid of sheep, but he had never been a focal point for a flock's attentions before. The sheep nearest him pressed closer still and those furthest away began to run. All began to bleat strongly as he passed, unknowingly, the point where they were used to being fed. The running became more urgent; the noise became strident. Feeling foolish, and grateful that he was not being observed by anyone, Lee quickened his pace. The sheep quickened theirs. Sheep surrounded Lee, impeding his controlled flight forwards, and urging him on behind. The bolder and closer finally began nudging him. He looked quickly round: a group of about a dozen were rushing towards him, joining the rest who were now deafeningly insistent in their complaints. He waved his arms; he even said 'Shoo'.

The sheep closed round him, noisier, bolder, until at last his nerve broke and he ran, training shoes slipping on the muddy ground, pursued by eighty frantic, demanding sheep, until he was able to clamber inelegantly over a gate and leave the indignant bleating behind. He walked on towards Talgarth, whistling to rebuild his confidence and flicking the field from the corners of his eyes, in case others should come rushing on him in the new field. But the field was empty. He came to one final fence before he found himself on the common, near the cattle grid, and got his bearings. He decided he would try to find an alternative route back. The wind was strong and bitter on the common; he walked quickly on, grinning at the idea of flight before ravaging sheep.

Lee walked upon concrete, between houses once again, with

some feeling of relief. Talgarth was not Manchester, but it was recognisably a place of shops and people, where an anonymous stranger had some place in the scheme of things. There were streets, with street lighting. It was civilisation of sorts. Lee began to relax.

In a street near the town square he came upon an electrical appliances shop where a man stood gazing into the display window, a pork pie in one hand and a cider bottle in the other. Eccentricity reassured him: Manchester had its full share. Inside the shop window several television sets were showing an identical picture: a woman was talking, demonstrating something. Lee paused to find out what the man found of such interest, straining to hear the transmission through the thick window glass. He sneaked a look at his companion. He was of indeterminate age; his hair was grey, long and greasy, tied at the back; a grubby, too-small trilby sat on his head; he wore a tattered mac and heavy, worn boots; his face was lined with ingrained dirt. He intrigued Lee.

The man, in his turn, showed no interest at all in the boy at his side.

'If you went inside, you could hear too,' Lee said, helpfully.

The man shot him a suspicious glance before turning his attention back to the silent screens within. 'Aye,' he agreed mildly, 'I could.' He drank from his bottle.

Lee divided his time between the man and the screens; the man was more interesting. 'Are you a gipsy or something?' he asked. It was, for some reason, the wrong question.

The man turned a cold, blank face to him. 'Get from here, boy,' he said softly.

Lee was affronted: 'All right. Keep your hair on,' he replied, wondering, as he spoke, if that, too, was a wrong thing to say. It was.

To Lee's surprise the man swung towards him and shouted, furiously angry, 'Get from here!' The sound attracted glances from passers-by. Embarrassed and bewildered, Lee hurried round the corner.

He came to a fish and chip shop and felt hungry. He reached into a pocket and gathered up his cash: it would have to be either cigarettes or food. Lee reasoned that whatever Blainau's shortcomings, it could at least provide food. He pocketed his money and crossed a bridge into the small, grey square as a clock somewhere above him clunked noon.

In the square there was a newsagent. Lee liked newsagents —

wherever you went, a newsagent's shop was almost always the same: a wall of magazines, a small counter, chocolate and sweets, cigarettes, stationery. Lee wandered over to the magazine display, enjoying the warmth. He reached for a girlie magazine — the choice was limited — and was aware of the newsagent moving to the counter, watching. He nodded and was pleased when the man nodded back, smiling, not shouting.

Lee was vaguely aware of a motorcycle drawing up outside. The centrefold girl was grotesque: pneumatic and leering. He reached out to replace the magazine as the door pinged open and a boy of about his own age came in. The newsagent reached below the counter to find a small pile of papers and magazines. He dropped them on the counter: the local weekly, *Horse and Hound*, *Tropical Fish*.

'Mr Gregory, Mrs Gregory, and your own,' the man behind the counter said.

The boy slipped the *Brecon and Radnor Gazette* and *Horse and Hound* into his jacket and briefly perused the magazine that was obviously his own.

'How are things at Plas Newydd?' the newsagent asked.

'Fine,' replied the boy, disinterested, not looking up from his magazine.

Lee moved forward as the other boy slipped *Tropical Fish* into his coat and moved to the door.

'Remind Captain Gregory that's four weeks on the bill, Matthew, will you?' the man asked.

'Fine,' murmured the boy as he left.

Lee quickly ordered his packet of cigarettes. He was greatly in need of any sort of ally, and this boy — Matthew? — with his leather jacket and motorbike and an accent that seemed, from what Lee had heard, un-Welsh, might have to do. They had *Tropical Fish* in common; it was his own regular magazine at home. He paid for the cigarettes and hurried out.

Matthew was strapping on his crash helmet as Lee came out. Uncertain of how to approach him, Lee hovered outside the shop, drawing a cursory glance. Lee smiled tentatively, not risking another put-down. The boy pulled on gauntlets and moved astride his machine.

'I saw your magazine,' called Lee. Matthew stared at him for a second or two before switching on the engine. 'You're into fish then,' Lee added, a shade desperately. Matthew turned to look fully at Lee; he had a handsome, open face. Feeling suddenly foolish, Lee shrugged.

Matthew said, 'Why?'

Lee shrugged again. 'No reason. So am I.' Matthew adjusted the magazines inside his jacket. 'Live round here, do you?' Lee persisted.

Matthew looked steadily at Lee, seeing a stranger who wanted to be friendly; Matthew, too, needed friends. He nodded to the pillion. 'Get on,' he said.

Matthew was a good driver and knew his machine well. Lee was less of a good passenger − the occasional lift on a low-powered townbike was the limit of his experience. But both enjoyed the few miles between Talgarth and Plas Newydd. Matthew drove fast, showing off, but safely, and Lee soon mastered the speed and sway of the bike and found the trip exhilarating on the empty winter roads which would be unsafe, later in the year, with the influx of tourists, but, on a cold, dry, January day, provided no problems.

Neither of the boys thought much about the other − problems of balance entirely filled their minds. If either had any such thought, Lee would have wondered why Matthew had so easily accepted him and needed to impress, while Matthew, in turn, would have questioned the value of subjecting Lee to the people he lived with.

They turned from one side road to another, until, at last, Matthew swung the bike from the road, across fields, and they entered what had once been a cultured parkland, making for what seemed a ruin of a house, between gateposts that held no gates and whose walls had long fallen and the stone used elsewhere. Each, in his own way, was sorry that the drive had come to an end.

As Matthew braked and switched off the engine, Lee became fully aware of the house before which they had stopped. He blew on his cold hands and briefly boggled at the scale of the place; one wing was a total ruin and seemed about to collapse, the central section was shored up by buttresses, windows smashed, and the other wing looked little better. Nevertheless, it was towards this last section of the building that Matthew led him. Matthew was turning out to be mysterious.

'Is this your home?' Lee asked, as Matthew pushed open a large, ornate door, crumbling round the lintels.

'No,' the other replied. The mystery deepened.

Inside, the scale was vast, too, though Lee could see that everything was in need of decoration; somebody had indeed made a poor attempt at plastering a section of the hall. Lee thought that maybe the whole of his mother's house in Manchester could be fitted into this one room. It was cold.

Matthew led Lee towards a grand staircase where they met a small, dapper man, coming down, muffled in wool, to whom Matthew handed over the local paper and *Horse and Hound*. Lee hung around in the background, wondering, for the first time, if his visit were an entirely good idea. The man noticed his slight discomfort and asked Matthew who his friend was.

'Lee Turner,' the boy replied: 'he's interested in fish.'

The man showed no interest. 'Dreary damn things if you ask me,' he said, as he continued his way across the hall and through an archway. Lee watched him.

'Matthew Gibbs,' said Matthew, holding out a hand.

Lee took it, unused to formality. 'Oh, right,' he said, following on as Matthew led the way up the vast, dingy staircase to an equally depressing landing.

Matthew's room was a revelation. It was, as he explained, one of the best, even with its decayed plasterwork, worm-eaten floorboards and rotten woodwork. It had two enormous fish tanks, bigger and better than Lee's. Where Lee had Guppies, Matthew had Silver Shark and Plecostamus and he was trying to breed Discus. Lee was impressed and a little envious. Matthew refused a cigarette. Lee lit up and looked at the rest of the room: the cheap furniture, battered school trunks – and the wall.

The wall screamed to be considered. Over an area of ten square feet a montage-mosaic had painstakingly been created from newspapers, magazines and posters. The effect was intricate and claustrophobic. (Four walls of this would drive anybody crazy, Lee thought.) He drew on his cigarette and moved closer.

'You're really into all this,' he said, after a long and careful examination.

Matthew was pleased; he nodded. 'I'm going to join the Paras,' he said. The wall was a close patchwork of army life and weaponry – ten square feet of arms and the men; on a small table, beneath, lay a Red Beret. The Paras predominated. Near the beret stood a row of books, all about fighting men. 'I've got an interview next month.' Matthew watched Lee carefully, pleased at the impression his work seemed to be having.

Live and let live, thought Lee. He turned from the display. 'Was that your old man in the hall?' he asked. Matthew was half-amused, half-affronted. They left the strange room to find food downstairs.

Harry Gregory – the Captain, as he preferred to be called, though Eileen, his wife, questioned, in her more wicked moments, of which there were many, the need for anybody to retain such status titles, particularly so lowly – had come from Zimbabwe shortly after Independence, disenchanted and virtually dispossessed of the fruits of a lifetime's work on their tobacco farm. Through a strange combination of bad luck, judgement and playing the game, they had brought out with them only the most basic allowances. Through her family connections and the cashing-in of a few insurance policies the Gregorys managed to buy the habitable section of Plas Newydd, preferring the status of country landowners to the more anonymous and comfortable life of many of their fellow ex-patriates who were now, like them, complaining bitterly about U.K. prices, U.K. practices and their lot in general, from the warmer south coast. Cocooned in woollens and tweeds against the British weather, and wrapped in the haze of alcohol-assisted nostalgia, the Gregorys, like many others, lived a life of confused regrets, envy and hostility, and often turned, for want of a sharper target, against Matthew, whose parents they had known in Rhodesia, as they still insisted on calling it, and who paid them twenty pounds a week for their son's keep. Far from seeing to their responsibilities in statu parentis, Harry and Eileen looked upon the boy, grumblingly, as a paying guest and a none-too-profitable one at that.

Matthew, on his part, was used to a life of boarding schools, holiday homes and the annual brief visit to Zimbabwe, where his parents, doctors who had once enjoyed a private practice, seemed vaguely astonished at the presence of a son and, although solicitous for his entertainment, were not sorry to see him leave. Matthew had a sister, who was more to the Gibbs and Gregory taste than this quiet, remote boy, who wanted, for some reason none knew, to share the aggressive, communal life of the Parachute Brigade; none of them had considered that Matthew might be as ignorant of motivation as they. Matthew, in short, for all his quietness and solitary ways, was considered a burden wherever he went, with his fish tanks – always costing a fortune to move – and his Honda Superdream, constantly needing space and attention. He had left school with three inadequate O-levels six months earlier, and, apart from a fortnight's summer camp with the school C.C.F., had spent the entire time at Plas Newydd, waiting for the succession of interviews, aptitude tests and selection courses which would, he hoped, end at the Training Barracks in Aldershot.

Lee was hungry. On their way through the bleak baronial hall to the kitchen, Lee offered history of his own, trying to impress. He told Matthew of his problems at home ('They kicked me out'), exaggerating the bravado and imagining future plans. One of Colin's friends had worked a month on an oil rig and Lee had been impressed. Now he lied blandly to Matthew that it was his intention, too. They walked into a large, decaying kitchen, where Harry Gregory was trying ineffectually to keep ill-mixed plaster from falling in dismal lumps to the floor. He slapped and banged it on the wall, cursing beneath his breath, swaying on the ladder placed six inches too far away for efficiency.

He was pleased to see the boys. Fluent in the language of command, in spite of Matthew's mild protestations, the Captain had Lee on the ladder bemusedly spreading plaster and Matthew accompanying himself on a wood-cutting expedition within minutes. Plas Newydd was heavy on labour and he had never had reason to think that potential helpers might prefer otherwise. As he led Matthew from the room, Eileen sauntered in, drawn by the voices.

'Such excitement,' she said as they left, the Captain briefly introducing Lee, of whom Eileen took no notice whatever for some time, as she flicked idly through her *Horse and Hound*.

Lee pressed the plaster wherever he assumed it was needed, occasionally flicking a glance at the slight woman pulling a large woollen shawl close round her shoulders, and turning pages, bored. Lee himself began to feel bored and wondered the best way to get himself from this cold, cheerless house. Blainau was warmer than this.

Eileen Gregory had been a great beauty and was still a woman of striking composure. A small smile which might be mere politeness, subtle mockery, mild amusement or genuine encouragement was always on her lips. She was, in general, enigmatic. Courted and made much of in her youth, she had an incisive mind; friends and family had been puzzled, even dismayed, when she had decided upon Harry, forty years previously. He, too, had been handsome, and was, like her, still striking, but he had never been a great intelligence, not one for organisation, forward planning or instant decisions. In fact, his lack of determination had been what had attracted her. (This man will always be a child, she had thought, and I shall always have the advantage over him.) The frustrations of such a bond had been many and had worn away the sharp edges of a creative relationship. She had loved Rhodesia, where almost all her life had been spent. Wales was alien to her spirit.

She pulled the shawl tighter and dropped her magazine on the table. 'Have you noticed you can't get a decent cup of tea in this dreadful place?' she said vaguely, bringing a large box of teabags to the Aga.

Lee climbed down from the ladder. He had never met anyone like Eileen or the Captain. He collected more plaster.

'Cups on the tray,' she commanded.

To his annoyance, Lee found himself automatically obeying. She asked him his Christian name only to mock it. ('What odd names parents give their children these days.') She elegantly scrounged a cigarette from him, and, finally, when he was confused enough, she fixed her thin smile full on him and demanded to know what he couldn't do. He didn't understand. The smile grew warmer, or bleaker.

'*We* couldn't farm where we'd spent our lives farming. Matthew can't scrape enough O-Levels together to make a future, so he's going to the Paratroops. The girl who flicks a casual duster tells me she likes working here because she couldn't leave home. What are you doing here? You're not a native, with an accent like that.'

Lee had had enough. 'You keep on asking questions,' he grumbled.

Eileen liked that: few people spoke directly back to her. 'This is Never-Never Land,' she declaimed grandly, and when the Captain came in to take tea to the wood shed and demanded anti-freeze, she told him, without surprise, that he'd find half a bottle in the living-room cupboard. Lee had no idea what they were talking about and returned to the security of the plastering. 'Didn't we once have a servant called Lee?' she shouted to Harry, seeking his whisky in the living-room across the hall.

Although only four o'clock, it was growing dark as Matthew drove Lee to the cattle grid on the common. Lee looked round, getting his bearings. He had refused a lift all the way to Blainau; Plas Newydd and the grandiose Gregorys had intimidated him.

With some embarrassment, he realised he felt protective towards Morgan and the tiny, grubby farm.

The two boys hung about together in the cold dusk, aware of their mutual need for friendship. Matthew suggested they might take a drink together at a local pub, if he were still around in a day or so; he'd borrow a crash helmet for Lee so he could ride the pillion legally. Lee confessed the oil rig was only the vaguest of ideas and walked gingerly across the grid, towards the distant hills. He turned and watched Matthew circle the Super Dream. He grinned. 'Those Gregorys of yours are bloody mad,' he called.

Matthew grinned back, raised a gauntlet in farewell and roared away, dipping below the crest of the road. Alone again, Lee listened until the bike's roar became a distant buzz, and then nothing. He checked the scrap of paper in his pocket bearing the Plas Newydd telephone number, wrapped his scarf more firmly round his neck and walked swiftly towards Blainau, cold hands thrust deep into his anorak.

Lee was about half a mile from Blainau and beginning to wonder if he were lost when he heard Morgan in the field where he had undergone his earlier ordeal with the sheep. Relieved, he moved to a gate on which he leaned, watching his uncle working Cap to round up the flock. It was impressive. A nonstop string of commands, curses, encouragements and endearments flowed as the dog crouched, crawled, streaked suddenly to gather in a loose group. Lee was deeply impressed, guessing a little at the years of patient perseverance necessary to enable a man and dog to work so effortlessly as one. It was a new view of Morgan, as well as of Cap, whom he had imagined simply as some sort of guard-dog. He realised also that Morgan was enjoying himself.

Innocent of his unseen watcher, Morgan was relaxed and firmly in control of a part of life of which he understood every aspect. Lee suddenly felt an eavesdropper, knowing that Morgan would be embarrassed at his presence. He moved quietly past. As Blainau appeared, further along the road, he could still hear the cursing and encouragement. Feeling cold, he quickened his pace, suddenly anxious to reach a place of partial familiarity.

Pugh was in the living-room, buttoning up his overcoat. As Lee made directly for the fire, he hung up his tattered working-mac, then sat, waiting for his lift home. 'You found your way then?' he asked.

Lee didn't turn, keeping his hands near the flickering flames. 'Why not?' He was casual in his cool reply.

Pugh grinned. 'I told Morgan you'd be safe back before dark. He was worried for you.' Lee picked up a log and laid it on the fire. Warmer, he turned to face Pugh, who was steadily watching him, aware of his silence. Quietly the old man asked, 'Don't think much to it all, say?'

Lee did not know how to answer. He shrugged. 'It's just different,' he said.

'That don't make it bad.'

Lee nodded agreement.

Pugh got to his feet and moved to set more wood among the growing flames, while Lee sat heavily back into the old sofa, aware that he was tired and hungry. Pugh leaned towards him confidentially.

'He's been the best of friends to me, has Morgan,' he said gently. Lee looked up; the old man's face was solemn. 'He don't say much, but when my missus died, he come up champion.' Warm in the fire-glow, Lee pondered this glimpse of yet another Morgan: friend and comforter. 'It's been a poor time for him since your gran passed away.'

Lee said sharply, 'I know,' unwilling to allow any kind of obligation to be laid upon him.

Pugh nodded gravely; he warmed his backside. The grin carved his face again. He laughed. 'By God and he give me a telling-off for what I said to you this morning; no mistake.' Pugh laughed once more, as if it were the joke of the day. He wiped his eyes, and, seeing Lee was unamused, said, through his laughter, 'You don't want to mind me, boy.' He subsided to the occasional chuckle and at last to silence.

The wood crackled and spat a spark. Pugh dropped his foot on it. Very distantly a car could be heard approaching. Pugh moved towards the door and picked up a canvas bag into which he peered, checking. The car grew closer.

'I saw Morgan in a field with Cap.' Pugh looked up from his bag; Lee's eyes were on the fire. 'They were . . .' he didn't know the precise term; he shrugged — 'getting sheep together.' Something of what Lee had felt, seeing the work, must have communicated itself.

Pugh said softly, 'I've seen him work three, four dogs, no trouble, when there was the work here.' The car horn sounded jauntily as Pugh opened the door into the porch. 'There she is,' he said. He seemed about to leave but turned, finally, towards

Lee. 'Morgan says you can't settle, boy. We all gets times like that. There's time here, and room.'

Lee sensed the old man had prepared this specially for him, and, had he been less warm, less tired, might have snapped back, mockingly. Instead he found himself accepting the man's involvement; Pugh actually cared about it. Before he could gauge a response sufficiently guarded, the man added, 'Let him talk, son. Morgan don't say much to me,' and then he was gone. Lee heard his steps in the yard and a brief exchange with Morgan before a car door opened, slammed shut and the vehicle moved off. Cap barked and Morgan told the dog to shut up.

Morgan came in warily, recalling the mood of the morning. Lee sat still and silent in the deep sofa. 'Tired?' Lee nodded. 'Hungry?' Lee nodded again. Morgan pulled off his boots and hung his filthy duffel coat besides Pugh's mac. 'Ham and eggs?' he asked.

Lee was still off his guard. 'Great,' he said, pleased and surprised. Too late he composed his face to its usual neutrality.

Morgan smiled freely at Lee's confusion; his spontaneity and warmth drew a rueful response from Lee, who almost smiled back.

Morgan moved to the kitchen. 'What did you think of the town, say?' Lee got to his feet and followed. Morgan found a bowl of eggs, from his bantams in the yard, picked up a pan and flicked a cube of fat into it. He lit the stove. Lee sat at the table, shrugging, but encouraged by the sizzle and smell he began to tell Morgan about his day — about the man who had shouted at him. (Morgan laughed: everybody knew old Bryn — no harm in him.) He talked about Matthew and the Gregorys, aware that, apart from Matthew, the day's chance meetings had been less than successful. He suddenly stopped.

Morgan fried their food. He said, quietly, 'Poor sort of place, this, you think, then?' It was important not to ruin this communication.

'I saw you and Cap with the sheep,' Lee said.

Morgan nodded as he flicked the gammon steaks over. Lee watched him carefully but his uncle showed neither annoyance nor embarrassment. It was almost as if the man was pleased he had been seen and was accepting humbly the unoffered compliments.

'And I had a chat with Pugh,' Lee added. 'How old is he?'

Morgan laughed as he broke the eggs into the pan and the appetising sizzling intensified. 'Anybody who calls *me* "boy" ' —

Morgan grinned, over his shoulder — 'have got to be damn near derelict.' He laughed as he dodged the egg around and reached for another. Lee smiled. Morgan looked back over his shoulder again and their eyes met and held for a moment. Each felt strangely embarrassed. 'Cut some bread, why not?' said Morgan, and Lee moved to do so. He was very hungry.

Dinner at Plas Newyyd was more formal and less appetising. The smell of wet plaster — as Eileen noted — did nothing for one's appetite. Neither, as Harry secretly thought, did Eileen's steak pudding. Turning, as ever, upon Matthew for a little vicious amusement, they asked him about Lee — 'Your homely friend' — and when the boy repeated, without rancour that Lee had thought them mad, they laughed a great deal, genuinely delighted.

'Poor Matthew is improving,' Eileen remarked, mistaking the boy's truthfulness for another move in the game.

With the table cleared and the washing-up done, Lee rang home, uncomfortably aware of Morgan's presence in the room. His spirits sank when Alan answered. His mother, said the man, was in the bath.

He asked Lee how he was making out. With a glance towards Morgan, sitting wearily near the fire, Lee felt forced to reply non-committally. Alan asked him how the weather was. Lee knew he had to speak to his mother — admitting that he found Blainau too alien, too much for him, was hard enough with Morgan able to hear, but to admit it to Alan was more than he could do. 'Can Mum phone me back?' he asked. It seemed she could not: she and Alan were about to go out for the evening. The man asked how the new radio was, how Morgan was treating him. Lee had, again, to be non-committal.

Alan paused, as Val came into the room, knowing her concern for the boy, and lightened his voice for her benefit. 'We don't have to turn out to rescue you then?' he asked winking at her as she stood at his side, waiting to talk to Lee. 'I'll tell her you're all right then,' he said firmly.

Lee glanced towards Morgan whom now, for some reason, he could not bring himself to hurt. 'Did Colin come for my fish?' he asked. Colin had. 'You got back safely last night?' They did. They were both okay? They were.

Four people listened to the silence and Lee knew he was losing his opportunity. He spoke urgently, closer to the mouthpiece.

'Look, Alan, this is a right stupid arrangement. I'm not a farmer.' He saw Morgan's head rise slightly and felt bad.

Alan smiled at Val. 'That's right,' he said, 'you'll learn.'

'It's not simple like that. Can you come and get me, like Mum promised?' Now Lee had begun, he had to go on, but Alan said: 'This must be costing your uncle a fortune. Take care, Lee. Keep up the good work.' ('Alan,' shouted Lee, desperate and powerless two hundred miles away.) 'We're grateful — Val and me. You're giving us time. Take care,' he repeated, putting down the receiver. 'He's fine,' he said to Val, smiling.

Lee slowly replaced the receiver in Blainau, knowing he had lost and knowing he had, in some way, betrayed Morgan. He moved to sit on the sofa, not meeting Morgan's eyes. 'He wouldn't let me speak to her,' he said softly. The wind briefly hit the house and sheep bleated close at hand. Lee stared into the fire.

Morgan got up. He moved to his coat. Lee looked anxiously at him, fearing rejection here also. 'Get your jacket on, boy,' said Morgan.

There was a silence too in the Manchester house where Alan and Val were not going out — just as Val had not been in the bath.

'You could have let me speak,' she said, quietly bitter. Her tone surprised and annoyed Alan.

'Look,' he protested, 'the boy was fine. You heard.'

'I heard *you*,' she replied.

Alan, worried by her clear thinking, moved on the attack. 'You're soft with him, Val. One hint he's got wet feet or a runny nose and you'd be begging him back. He's got to learn we've got a life to lead too.' Val was silent; she nodded slowly. Alan patted the space at his side. 'Come on, love,' he said softly. 'Relax.'

Val sat, stiffly obedient, ignoring his arm around her, holding back from its gentle, insistent pressure.

'And no letters,' he added sternly. 'No phoning behind my back.' The pressure continued; she yielded against him very slightly. 'It's not fair on any of us. Let him settle.'

For a while Val sat in silence, then, 'You'd better be right,' she said softly.

His hand moved to turn her face to his and he kissed her. 'Trust me,' he murmured, stopping further words with a firmer kiss. She swung round to him, suddenly needing him, suddenly lonely.

44

Morgan drove his Land Rover into the car park in a sudden flurry of snow. The lights of the Castle Inn shone across the road. There were two other vehicles parked near the telephone kiosk whose dim light lit their way, as they left the vehicle. Lee recognised the place: this was where he and his mother had arrived in the coach only yesterday – it seemed longer ago. He followed Morgan towards the pub, grateful for the gesture. Pubs were more familiar ground than farms, small, Welsh towns and decaying mansions.

The bar was warm and welcoming. A table of four were involved in a card game and a man was standing at the counter, talking with the landlord. A burst of laughter rose from the cribbage players as Morgan and Lee walked in; someone had played a cunning hand. The oldest of the players greeted their arrival.

'It must be Christmas or the telly's on the blink,' he said. 'How are you, Morgan?' Morgan nodded.

The Landlord, Les, came over, smiling gravely. 'Morgan,' he pronounced as if confirming a fact.

Another card player called over, 'How be, Mr Thomas?'

A third giggled. 'What are you drinking?' Morgan ordered a pint of beer. Lee said he'd have the same.

'You can't have the same.' Les gravely stated another fact. 'You can only have similar.' He turned away.

'Pint?' Morgan asked the boy.

Les was already pulling the beer. 'It's all pints here,' he said, mildly offended. Lee was puzzled. 'Unless you got a doctor's certificate.' Lee looked to Morgan: doctor's certificate? He looked at Les who winked, slowly. A joke. The Welsh sense of humour, Lee supposed: God Almighty.

The players snapped cards onto the table and Lee looked incuriously over to them. The man who had initially heralded their arrival was about Morgan's age, bearded, smaller. On either side sat two younger men, still in work-clothes. The fourth player played on, silently impassive, his back to Lee as another hand finished noisily. The giggler angled back on his chair, catching Lee's glance, then dismissing it.

'Buy us a drink, Morgan,' he called over; this seemed to amuse him hugely.

The other young man looked over as he shuffled the pack. 'When you getting married, Morgan?' he asked. His companion giggled as Morgan looked over blankly.

'That your wife, Mr Thomas?' the joker called. Lee's glance moved to the table, affronted for Morgan, but all attention was now on the cards.

Les brought over a pint and Morgan moved it to Lee, nodding to the table furthest from the crib players. Lee sat and sipped the beer, looking over again to the card table. He felt less than comfortable; it was a situation he recognised and had often thoughtlessly taken part in — baiting the weak one, the one you knew would not respond, or who, if he did, would provoke further taunting. He had never been on the other end of the joke and did not like it.

The older man must also have disliked the situation for he called over, asking Morgan, sensibly, if he had any early lambs. Morgan said there was one.

One of the younger men, concentrating on his cards, asked, 'Who's that with you, Mr Thomas?' and Lee felt a sudden strangeness at hearing himself referred to as, 'My sister's son.' Cards snapped down. The giggler giggled into his drink, his attention on the game. Lee relaxed a little: the mocking seemed to be over.

'What do you think of your uncle's place, boy?'

Lee looked back to the table. The older man's eyes were on him, curious but friendly. Lee shrugged, casting for the right answer.

Then one of the youngsters laughed. 'It's a bloody palace,' and his companion choked on his beer.

The bearded man frowned. He tapped his cards on the table, authoritatively. 'Is anybody playing this game?'

The laughter subsided. A hand was laid down: 'Fifteen — two, fifteen — four and a pair.' A score was pegged. Les brought the second pint to the counter. (Wildfire, thought Lee. He'd not last long behind a bar at home: you'd die of thirst waiting.)

Morgan moved to the counter. 'I'll see to that, Les,' the man with the beard called, but Morgan firmly put his money on the polished top and Les took it.

Other jokes followed against Morgan. Not good jokes, not even really bad jokes: just an unthinking, unmalicious patter designed to confirm status. Morgan and Blainau were joke status, inferior. Lee began to heat — as much against Morgan's passivity as against the two young card players.

Morgan saw the boy's discomfort. 'Don't give any mind to

them,' he said. 'The one with the beard – that's Tom Griffiths. Neighbour of mine. Good farmer. Good friend. We was at school together.' (Neighbour? Lee boggled. How near? How far?) 'The two with the mouth work for him. Good health.' They drank their beer in silence.

'Oh, you jammy sod,' shouted Price, the more intelligent of Griffiths' workmen. Graham, the other, giggled as the silent fourth lay down a winning hand.

Morgan leaned closer to Lee. 'Hard to tell Alan the truth. He'd think you were soft, wanting to go home.' Lee nodded. Morgan surveyed him, steadily. 'Will you go home?'

'Do you want me to go?' asked Lee.

Morgan looked down to his solid hands round his pint on the table. 'Nothing to do with me,' he said quietly.

Les drew the man at the counter another pint. A vehicle passed slowly outside.

'Gone quiet in the corner,' giggled Graham. 'What's all this drinking then? The Old Lady wouldn't have approved.' This was daring and everybody knew it.

Morgan stood, draining his glass. 'Drink up, son,' he said.

Price said, loudly enough, 'You done it now,' and Graham giggled.

Griffiths rapped his cards on the table. 'That's enough,' he said and, as Morgan and Lee made for the door, he rose to meet them. 'Come on, Morgan,' he smiled. 'They're too stupid over there to mean anything. You have one with me now – you and the boy.'

But Morgan was already opening the door and bidding goodnight. Lee looked over at the grinning pair at their table.

'Goodnight, Uncle Morgan,' they chorused.

But Morgan was already outside with Lee close behind him, upset on Morgan's behalf.

In the bar, Griffiths heard the outside door shut and sighed. (Poor bloody Morgan, he thought.) He looked to his farm workers, but they were chatting quietly now, Morgan forgotten. Griffiths choked back the reprimands. 'Deal them out,' he said as he moved back to his seat.

Morgan built up the fire. He had said nothing during the long drive among the hills and Lee had respected his silence. The boy hung up his anorak.

'Can of beer?' Morgan asked, no hint of embarrassment or displeasure in his voice. Lee found this sudden switch hard to

47

understand. 'Long old day,' Morgan added. Lee guessed that maybe it was Blainau alone that gave this man his security, appreciating all the more Morgan taking him elsewhere, for his sake.

'Why did you let them do that?' Lee had to ask. Morgan stared blankly at him; it was as if the whole half-hour had been wiped from his mind, had never happened. 'All that would have started something back home.'

Morgan seemed at last to realise what Lee was talking about. He smiled. 'Too much to drink and not enough to think about,' he said, looking at Lee, puzzled that the boy should take the incident seriously.

'Did you know they'd be there?'

The smile eased away. Morgan replied softly, 'They're always there.'

For a few brief seconds Lee saw a depth in Morgan's eyes; he saw a childhood where They Were Always There – at school, on the way home, at discos (did they have discos here? Did they have them then?) at market, at the pub. They Were Always There. Lee felt a sudden, bleak sadness. Then Lee could see nothing beyond Morgan's now smiling eyes. The man moved towards the kitchen. Lee followed.

'Why didn't you say anything back? Are you scared of them?'

Morgan laughed, reaching into the cupboard. 'Them? No. They're all talk.' He brought two cans of beer to the table. Lee noticed two grubby glasses on the sideboard and fetched them.

Morgan paused before pulling off the ring of the first can, seeing a worry, a disconnection, in the boy's face. 'If you're different, you get picked on,' the man said. It was an accepted fact. Lee nodded; he saw the truth too well in that.

Morgan held out a hand for a glass. Lee watched his big hands carefully pour the beer. Different. He remembered the man with the bottle and pie; he remembered Matthew with his fighting wall; the Gregorys and their foreign language; the man in the pub.

'How are you different?' he said, affronted. Morgan was the most recognisably human of all the people he had met that long day. Morgan recognised Lee's concern for him and was moved. He poured the other can. 'I can change my room round, can I?' Lee asked dully.

Pleased, but unable to show it, Morgan lowered his lips to the glass. 'I expect so,' he said.

Chapter Three

The weeks passed. Lee changed his room round — not that he could do much with it, but it was a gesture which he and Morgan understood. He began to think less about Manchester, where he knew the emotional politics were complicated, and when his mother phoned, with Alan out on a job, he was non-committal, refusing her the peace of mind he knew she needed but giving her no definite cause for unrest. She phoned twice more and then stopped; Lee guessed that she and Alan were enjoying a honeymoon period which both reassured and irritated him. He spoke no more of it to Morgan.

Lee was beginning to enjoy the change and began to show a guarded interest in the working of the farm; he even took Cap secretly to a field of sheep and tried, with little success, to work the dog, mimicking Morgan's commands and endearments, which simply confused the animal. Morgan bought him gumboots and an overall. The simple rhythm of routine began to supply an underpinning security. For the first time in his life, he began to feel he was important.

He began to make acquaintances: Mrs Lewis, the driver of the school bus which passed Blainau twice daily, nodded and smiled, while her passengers grinned or gaped. Matthew remained an enigma but the two boys accepted each other, and Lee occasionally called to see him at Plas Newydd where the Gregorys became less strange, though never familiar. Matthew, in his turn, spent more and more time at Blainau, liking Lee's companionship, liking Morgan and Pugh for their unquestioning acceptance, helping out when he wished and generally grateful for being away from the continual chill of Plas Newydd and the Gregorys' bitter sniping. Three weeks passed.

Lee lost contact with Colin — never one for letters or phone calls — but Carol, surprisingly, wrote regularly: a catalogue of catalogue of humdrum happenings at home and work; what Mr Ellis had said to so-and-so; how the shoplifting rate had suddenly increased. Knowing his concern, she wrote of his fish, which Colin was tending, and how she occasionally saw Val and Alan together at this pub or that — they seemed to be making out really well, which was nice. Lee never bothered to write back. The kind letters came from another world.

In any case, Lee was interested in Sarah Griffiths, whose father he had met in the Castle Inn and who nodded and peeped his car horn if he happened to pass the boy. Sarah was, he guessed, about sixteen. He saw her twice a day as she passed to and from school. He tried to be about at least once as the bus drove by, to smile nonchalantly or wave. Sarah so far had not responded.

Aware of his immobility, Lee had persuaded a reluctant Matthew to teach him the rudiments of riding the Honda, but what he enjoyed most, which sometimes surprised even him, was working Morgan's ancient tractor. He found himself singing boisterously as he bounced it through the February mornings, hauling loads through the fields. It had become his sole prerogative to take bales of hay to feed the sheep.

Sometimes, with no definite work to do, Lee would drive the tractor nowhere in particular for the sheer joy of it, which became a source of amusement to both Pugh and Morgan, and an occasional hazard to gates and other road-users.

The weeks succeeded one another. Morgan grew to like the boy and did his best to show it, while Lee came to admire his uncle's stamina and strength. If time weighed heavily in the evenings, the long silences worried neither. Lee became resigned to Welsh television of which the reception was, in any case, poor; Morgan learned to shut his ears to Lee's music tapes and even to recognise a number or two.

There was no feeling of permanence for Lee, however — he always knew he would go back to Manchester sometime — but neither was there any urgency then. It was time-out for him — as Alan had asked for Val and himself. He also began to feel unusually healthy. In short, Lee was finding out about himself by being in contact with a novel and outside stimulus.

'Who's that?' people would ask, as he shopped in Talgarth. 'You know Blainau, under the hill?' would come the reply. 'Morgan Thomas? That's Morgan's boy.'

Lee was indignant when he told Morgan of the first time he overheard it, ('It's like I'm some kind of bloody pet.') but

Morgan had smiled, secretly proud.

One irritation he could not overcome was Morgan's sense of tending Blainau on behalf of his dead parents: a mere caretaker. Their deaths hung over the man and farm like a winter cloud. Their bedroom, where Morgan and Val had been born, was kept strictly locked. Morgan would not say why.

One day there was a gathering. Though most sheep were weather-wise and came down to the valley at the early signs of snow, a number — usually in isolated groups — stayed on the hills, straying far from their farms. Two or three farmers would come together to ride the tops and bring down any sheep that could be found, which were sorted, according to their markings, and placed with their respective flocks.

Morgan had left at first light, with Griffiths and Price, together with Jesse Watkins and his son, Glyn, near neighbours. They would return before dark, and meet with other farmers, to distribute the strays. It was a long, hard day for all concerned — men, ponies and dogs alike. The valleys were cold enough, on the edge of the snowline, but the wind was always bitter high up, and the snow seldom less than three or four inches deep at this time of year, often more.

When Lee got up, it was to find Morgan and his pony already gone. Cap's noisy farewell — prone to fight with other dogs he had been left behind — had woken Lee some hours earlier.

Lee carried fencing posts to the tractor at the side of the road. In the box behind the machine more posts waited, with a roll of wire and the necessary tools: a sledge-hammer ('pudding-bumper,' Morgan called it), a wire-tensioning lever, staples, wire-cutters and a hammer. Lee enjoyed the fencing, liked the satisfaction of a taut, flawless stretch between vertical stakes. Pugh was to help him when the old man had finished mucking out the cows. Lee dropped the stakes in the box and looked at his watch. Eight-forty. The school bus would pass within five minutes.

He climbed into the bucket-seat and pressed down the starter, but the engine groaned, strained and did not fire. He tried again; the engine failed again. Lee sneaked another look at his watch; he wanted to be on his way so he could pull suavely from the road to wave the school bus past, not marooned half-blocking its progress. He pressed down again. The engine churned less enthusiastically. (Battery, thought Lee.) At that moment Mrs Lewis turned the corner, two hundred yards away, and it was too late to abandon the tractor and shout to Pugh for help.

Lee pressed twice again, with no result. 'Bloody thing,' he shouted above the straining engine. The bus drew up behind him and he turned towards the grinning faces and smiled feebly. Mrs Lewis patiently waited as Lee tried one last time, before giving up: he would be impressing nobody today. He waved the bus past.

Mrs Lewis inched the minibus round the stranded tractor to high-spirited insults from her passengers, while Lee smiled bravely at Sarah, in her usual place. It was the closest they'd been. She stared stonily back, fed-up with the banter these twice daily non-meetings were drawing from the Gwillim boys in front and the girls behind. The bus edged into the clear and tooted. As it gathered speed the girls in the back seat threw obscene gestures in good-hearted derision, and then the bus was turning out of sight and a highspot of the day had gone, leaving Lee inept and foolish.

He jammed the starter down in frustration and held it down. The noise drew Pugh. 'She's cold,' he cried, aware of the diminishing power of the battery. Pugh hurried to the side of the tractor, casting quick expert eyes at the controls. 'You've got the stop out,' he said aggrieved, pressing home the offending part. Lee tried again. The tractor strained, then turned over, sweetly.

'Magic,' grinned Lee, as well as he could. He turned in the seat to operate the hydraulic lift and the box behind rose clear of the road. He slammed the tractor into gear and made for the distant gate. Pugh watched him go, considering the lengths a boy would go to be noticed by a girl, then turned back to his cows, muttering.

Two miles distant and five hundred feet above Blainau, Morgan held the scraggy sheep in a sitting position in the snow, forcing its lips apart to examine the teeth. It was old and independent, as it struggled in his grasp, and the marking on its rump had long grown out. 'Look at the wool on her,' shouted Morgan to Griffiths, holding the ponies on the ridge above. 'Must have missed her last year.' Morgan let the animal free. It ran a few metres, then began to nuzzle in the snow for grass, its panic instantly forgotten.

'Old 'un,' called back Griffiths above the sly, bitter wind.

Morgan climbed to the ridge, took the reins of his pony and swung into the saddle. 'She won't go far,' he said. 'We'll pick her up on our way down.'

Griffiths banged his hands together against the cold and they rode steeply uphill, the ponies careful about footing among the sharp, snow-covered stones.

'Damn and she's strong enough,' grinned Morgan. 'See the old girl struggle?'

Griffiths grinned back as his pony picked a way up a narrow track, no more than a straggling indentation. He liked to see Morgan with sheep; it was the man's natural expertise — the only one he seemed ever to have had. He came to a clearing and kicked his pony into a gallop.

Morgan turned, to see Price riding close by and made to follow Griffiths, but Price matched his pace. 'Don't see you much up Castle Inn, Mr Thomas,' he called.

Morgan had no time for the younger man: he was rude and disrespectful, not even native to these hills, but a refugee from Cardiff who had turned up camping the previous summer, and stayed on, finding work with Griffiths. He was supposed to be sharp with his tongue, a joker towards slower minds and a good worker. 'Things to do, boy,' muttered Morgan, his words half lost in the wind.

'Don't like the company?' the youngster jeered.

Morgan turned in his saddle and watched the cool, mocking eyes of the boy. He swung back and urged the pony on. 'We've got strays to gather,' he called, following Griffiths, who was now joining Jesse and Glyn, well ahead, nearing the flat plateau where the snow would be deeper and the wind stinging.

Price called his pony into a canter. Morgan was a joke; could never have a laugh or relax. Price shook his head and rode on, alone.

In the warmth of Blainau's kitchen Lee read a letter, as Pugh washed his hands and they waited for the kettle to boil.

'Get the dirt off,' Lee said, without looking up. 'I washed that towel, last night.'

Pugh gave his hands an extra rinse before moving to the roller towel (Good job, the old man thought. Morgan never noticed dirt on a towel.) Pugh fetched the biscuit tin from its shelf; the boy must have given it a wipe-over, too, and the shelf itself had lost its sticky dust. Good job. Blainau was distinctly less grubby. Pugh put the tin on the table and sat opposite the boy. The postman had brought a letter, for Morgan; it stood angled against a sauce bottle. Pugh munched a biscuit, watching Lee's face.

'Lady friend?' he ventured. 'She's loyal. I'll say that. Do she know about Sarah Griffiths?'

'Get lost, Pugh,' returned Lee, without heat.

Pugh leaned back, laughing. 'I am lost with your love life, boy: lady friend back home and Sarah Griffiths down here.'

Lee glanced up. 'I've never even spoken to Sarah Griffiths,' he protested.

Pugh got up to attend to the boiling kettle. 'Damn,' he said, 'and you done near everything else, bar lying in the road when the school bus come by.'

Lee read on: bad news. 'One of my fish died,' he murmured.

Pugh nodded sympathetically as he filled the teapot. 'It's a hard old world,' he agreed.

Lee glanced up sharply and had to smile. Pugh's face, too, creased into a grin. He brought the pot to the table as Lee folded Carol's record of Mancunian events and slid it back into the envelope.

'What do you think of it all now, say?' asked Pugh. 'Now you got muck on your boots?'

It was a serious question and Lee thought it over seriously as he reached for a biscuit. 'It's all right,' he said.

The old man knew it was as much of a gesture towards satisfaction as Lee could make and nodded happily as he poured his mid-morning tea. Lee got up to make himself coffee, which Pugh always seemed to forget.

A long column of sheep stretched along an unseen track as the dogs brought them down. It had been a useful gathering: they'd found about a hundred − not bad for February, with more snow threatening. The men rode, dotted along the line, tired and cold but glad to be moving down.

'You should have brought the boy,' Griffiths called over to Morgan, as they paused at the top of a gulley to let the dogs work better. 'Should have shown him some gathering.'

'He's all for the tractor.' Morgan called back. Griffiths nodded, smiling. The youngsters always liked tractors. He remembered Sarah's excitement when he had taught her.

Together, he and Morgan watched Price working one of Griffiths' dogs, laughing at his curses as a few canny sheep dodged from the column and he shouted it round to gather them up.

'Not much work for your dog now at Blainau,' Griffiths said, as they moved across to deter the line scattering further.

Morgan shouted at three sheep deciding to run his way, waving his arms to turn them. He looked towards Griffiths' blank face as they moved on down again, the panic in the sheep subdued. Morgan grinned: it was an old joke between them. 'Plenty,' he called over his shoulder. It was a a joke, yet not wholly a joke. Griffiths was locally acknowledged as a prodigy of a farmer; careful of his affairs but always willing to adapt and expand. He paid highly for expert advice and was never afraid of the new. Morgan tried never to compare his own farm with his neighbour's, but they had been at the local school together, and, although Griffiths had won a scholarship to Brecon High School and gone on to do well at Agricultural College, they had age, background and much else in common, and others besides Morgan would set the one man's achievements alongside the other's. ('Morgan's parents held him back,' they would say, though not in Morgan's hearing.) Griffiths would have liked some of Morgan's land, and Morgan knew which way the joke-but-not-quite-a-joke would go now.

'When you going to sell me that ten-acre field, Morgan?'

'Not mine to sell.'

'The Estate'd let me have it, if you said.'

'It's a Blainau field: my Dad brung it back from scrub.'

'You're a hard man to deal with, Morgan.'

'Have to be with a sharp bugger like you.'

Both men laughed as the column came down to the tree-line and they saw the old hillfort of Castel Dinas at last. From there it was ten minutes to the road; five more to Blainau where Gwyn and Arty waited to help with the sorting at the sheep-pen.

'We're too old for farming, Morgan.'

'Oh aye?'

'Get the concrete down and the caravans in, man. Let them get on with it.'

'You're the big man. I'll follow you.'

And more laughter. Each despised the farmers who ruined hard-won fields for the cheap return from tourists. A caravan seeking a site overnight would get short shrift from either.

In the darkening end of the day, the farmers set out with their strays: Jesse and his son drove the larger part peaceably down the Blainau road to Rhydycaer. Arty loaded half a dozen in a Land Rover with help from Gwyn. Griffiths left his twenty in the Blainau sheep-pen for Price to collect the next day, as he always did, and Morgan's own sheep now nuzzled at the sparse grass in his field at the side of the yard, happy not to freeze muzzles in the constant search for food high in the hills.

Pugh had left half an hour ago and Lee and Matthew were watching cartoons on television when they heard Cap barking at the clatter of hooves on the road, and, next, the deep hum of the hinges as the gate swung open to let the men in. Lee got up to switch off the set; Matthew dropped a half-log on the fire.

Cramped with cold, Griffiths, Price and Morgan stamped in and made for the fire, where they chatted over their day. Lee and Matthew stood aside, excluded, until Morgan asked Lee to bring the bottle of whisky that he kept on top of the kitchen cupboard. Lee already had a kettle boiling for their tea and left to attend to their needs; Matthew followed.

The men relaxed in the warmth.

'The boy from Plas Newydd up here much, Morgan?' asked Griffiths quietly. 'Slow on their bills, I hear. Keep themselves to themselves,' he added.

Morgan felt moved to defend Matthew. 'He gives us a hand. It's hard enough for newcomers round here, any age. The boy's all right.' Griffiths nodded and turned to toast his backside.

Price moved away and sat on the sofa. 'Send your boy up Castle Inn, Morgan,' he teased. 'We'll show him the ropes.'

Griffiths laughed. 'What *you* got to teach anybody?' he said.

Morgan looked solemnly down at the young man. 'He've got more sense than waste his money.'

Price laughed, shaking his head. 'Take it easy, Morgan,' he said, amused. Griffiths winked at him, behind Morgan's back, and Price laughed on while Griffiths turned to Morgan and talked sheep.

Lee and Matthew served the tea and left the men to it. In his room Lee slipped a Status Quo tape into his cassette and stretched out on his bed at ease, smoking. Matthew sat on the floor, close to the electric fire. Murmurs rose from below, muted. Lee reached for his letter from Carol.

'Does this girl at home know you're trying to knock Sarah Griffiths off?' asked Matthew.

Lee read on. He said, 'Don't *you* fancy Sarah Griffiths?'

Matthew smiled. 'No,' he said emphatically.

Lee felt an edge of irritation. Matthew could be very righteous. 'No smoking; no sex. Keeping your body for the Paras,' he mocked. Matthew was not amused. Lee tossed the letter aside and blew a smoke ring. 'Everybody smoked in Vietnam,' he ventured. 'I saw it in a film. They all smoked dope.'

Matthew shook his head and snorted. 'God, you're thick, sometimes,' he said mildly, returning to his comfortable position. He raised a hand to catch the warmth from the fire.

Lee continued to look down on Matthew, slightly affronted. 'Okay,' he said. 'Let's see this fantastic body in action.' Matthew dropped his hand. 'No, come on,' Lee persisted. 'Prove yourself, boy.'

Matthew, for all his quietness, was always capable of surprise. For a while he said nothing, as Lee blew another smoke ring and coughed briefly, content at having won that particular round, but, suddenly, Matthew twisted over and performed ten fast press-ups, the floor creaking rhythmically beneath his balanced weight. He lightly jumped to his feet, breathing easily while Lee clapped. He said, 'Your turn.'

Lee smiled complacently. He lay back, grinning. 'Wouldn't want to,' he said, denying the challenge he knew he couldn't equal, and secretly a little impressed. 'Not unless Sarah Griffiths was underneath,' he added, taking, as ever, the last word.

Morgan called from the stairs that Griffiths and Price were leaving and Lee swung from the bed, stubbing out his cigarette in the brimming ash-tray. He smiled at Matthew and moved from the room, marooning Matthew and his challenge. Matthew sat on the bed, able now, secretly, to gasp a little and recover.

Lee collected the empty cups and took them through to the kitchen where Morgan stood, reading the letter that had come for him that morning. The boy moved to the sink to pour hot water.

'When'd this come?' his uncle asked quietly.

Lee told him, squirting washing-up liquid into the bowl and dropping the cups in the water. He turned to Morgan. 'Matthew can stay for a meal, can't he?' But something was wrong; each knew it, though Morgan passed off the moment instantly.

'I expect so.' The man never moved. Seeing Lee's concern sharpening, Morgan turned the subject. 'Get the bottle back on the cupboard,' he said brusquely. Lee wondered if he had received bad news and was about to ask, but decided otherwise. He took the bottle from the table and pulled a chair to the cupboard, stepping up easily to reach to the top. He stepped down, his attention full on Morgan. Morgan dug in his pocket and held out several pound notes, crumpled. 'You been working,' Morgan explained.

Lee tried to make connections but failed. He smiled. 'No, ta.' Morgan's hand stayed out and Lee sensed the gesture meant a great deal to him, but accepting wages from Morgan put him under an obligation which he had decided to deny. He shook his head. Morgan finally stuffed the notes back into his pocket and moved towards the living-room. 'You all right?' Lee called after him. There was no reply. Lee turned to the washing-up.

Watching an unintelligible programme in Welsh, Matthew also sensed something was wrong, seeing Morgan enter slowly, a letter in his hand. The man paused between him and the television set.

'Want your chair?' Matthew asked, half-rising.

Morgan hadn't noticed him. His eyes turned towards the boy, troubled.

'Say?' he asked quietly.

'Your chair.'

Morgan thought it over, shook his head, then, dropping the letter on the low embers, he swiftly turned and moved back through the door to the stairs.

Matthew sank back into the armchair, watching the letter crinkle at the edges, noticing a printed heading and a formal, typed arrangement, before it burst suddenly into flame, curled and blackening. Morgan's steps creaked overhead.

When he came down an hour later for supper, he seemed less distant, though still subdued, and the evening passed well enough.

Morgan sat in an office in Hereford, waiting. He scratched a spray of mud from his suit with a grubby fingernail, which he hastily cleaned in his teeth. All round him unfamiliar sounds intruded: the clatter of a typewriter, female laughter, heavy traffic in a main road from a suddenly-opened door. He pulled at his tie, coughed behind his hand, and looked round at the efficient security of the room. It reminded him of a room he had seen as a boy when his father had taken him to the Big House. It spoke of confident, traditional authority. Morgan shone up the toecap of a boot on his trouser leg and waited for Tom Duncan to find time to see him. Duncan was one of the new breed of Estate Managers — young, open, trained to the work at college. Morgan looked at the heavy bookcase, immaculately stacked with leather-bound ledgers and reference books. He wished Colonel Edwards still managed the Estate: the old boy had been keener on a clean farmyard than financial return, but you'd known where you stood. The letter — unexpected, precisely dictated in a solicitor's office — had shaken and outraged

Morgan. He had decided to put matters straight: to come to the man with the power.

Tom Duncan walked into the room, a smile on his face and his hand outstretched. 'How are you, Morgan? Pull your chair up.' Morgan stood, shook his hand and drew his chair to the desk where Duncan was already seated, leafing through a file. The younger man looked up briefly. 'Glad you came in.' Morgan nodded. He had left Pugh and the boy to a busy morning: hedging to be done as well as the routine chores, and Griffiths' sheep to be collected and seen off.

'Another bad spring, do you think?' Duncan was still leafing through the file, eyes down. 'Can't be as bad as last year.' Morgan agreed, hearing his own voice timid and muffled. He coughed again behind his hand. He had not told Pugh or Lee where he was going as he'd passed them at the roadside, noting with approval that Pugh seemed to be passing on his expertise in hedging. Duncan looked up with a smile and Morgan harnessed his thoughts to the needs of this meeting. Duncan tested him: 'You got our solicitor's letter then?' Morgan nodded, almost deciding to say that he'd burned it. Duncan leaned across his desk. 'The first thing, Morgan, is that there's nothing personal in this,' he said sincerely.

The idea took Morgan by surprise: nothing personal. He fought down a rising anger. 'Personal enough to me,' he muttered.

Duncan appreciated the response. 'It's simple economics. Look at it that way – '

'I know economics,' Morgan interrupted, fidgeting.

Duncan groaned inwardly; it was going to be difficult – as he had expected. 'Good,' he said smoothly. 'Then we'll see eye-to-eye.'

He looked down at his file. 'Almost fifty years since your father took the tenancy of Blainau.' He nudged the meeting into another direction; hill-farmers spoke of liking a direct, no-nonsense approach, but seldom took it themselves. It worked and Morgan relaxed; the past was always safer than the present.

Morgan looked Duncan proudly in the eye. 'September the eighteenth, 1935,' he recited.

Duncan appeared impressed. 'Exactly right,' he smiled, and, catching the current, added, 'times change, Morgan. The farm's been running down over the years; long before your mother died.' He waited for the reply, prepared for the oblique.

'Colonel Edwards never had no complaints,' Morgan

murmured. 'He spoke well of us.'

The Colonel would speak well of anyone producing a bottle during his visits or poultry at Christmas, thought Duncan. He nodded encouragingly: 'I know that.' Catching the favourable current again, he said, 'Pigs and cows were making good money then. Now you're shepherding a couple of hundred sheep on pasture that's been run down,' and, moving off at another angle, 'it can't be easy for you, on your own,' with just Pugh Davies to help.'

It was the wrong angle. Morgan leaned forward, animated. He told Duncan that listening to advice had been Pugh's biggest mistake. 'A farmer in his own right before he sold to the Estate. And look at him now.' He leaned back, a good point made. Duncan spread his hands on the desk, looking mildly at Morgan's face, watchful with suspicion. He smiled. Pugh had got a good price and was happy in retirement, living with his daughter and his family, working for Morgan. What was wrong with that? Morgan shook his head, knowing everything was wrong with selling your birthright.

'He got his health again,' countered Duncan. He reminded Morgan, pointedly, of the desperate state Pugh had worked himself into, trying to run the farm alone, after his wife's death.

Morgan saw the point and countered 'There's nothing wrong with me, sir,' but, sensing the farmer's defensiveness, Duncan pressed on.

'And in a few years' time? Or if you have an accident or fall sick? What happens when Pugh prefers his warm bed to turning out early for you?'

Morgan cast round for a good, sharp reply, but found none; it was a fear he had turned over in his mind many times. 'We'll face that when it comes,' he mumbled.

Duncan was gratified at winning the first set. He consulted his list. 'A hundred and twenty acres; three hundred sheep.' He wound himself up for his next volley as Morgan nodded – more or less three hundred. 'When both your parents were alive – three of you working – the farm could just about manage.'

Morgan was stung. 'We managed well,' he protested. It was less than the truth and both men knew it.

'With just you and your mother, the scale had to be reduced, yes?' Morgan held his silence: the man was right. Duncan drove on. 'Pigs went. Half the cattle.' He flicked a glance at his notes. 'Good grazing deteriorated to rough pasture.' He leaned back, seeing the cold truth strike, and slightly regretting it. 'Now there's just you. And Davies.'

'I got my sister's boy with me.'

What does that mean, thought Duncan. What does he actually mean? He said blandly, 'Good. That must help.'

Morgan pursued what he saw as an advantage: 'He's a good lad and a willing lad and he learns well. We can see Blainau to rights.' Morgan was impassioned, but Duncan was largely unimpressed. A secretary tapped on the door and laid a sheaf of letters on the desk. She smiled politely at Morgan as she left.

Morgan asked quietly, 'How long have I got?' He had come to the question at last and Duncan, feeling sorry for the man, moved ground a little. 'Neither of us want the trouble and expense of the Land Tribunal, do we? Solicitors, accountants' fees? Under the terms of the Act I'm obliged to see if we can't make a settlement on common ground.'

Morgan was not to be diverted. 'How long?' he repeated softly.

Duncan gazed at the country man. (This can be a bastard job, he thought. All this man's life, all he knows and cares for, and I have to persuade him to give it up.) He said quietly, 'The Tribunal would want the matter settled within a reasonable time. I'd guess about a year. Maybe longer,' he added, seeing the worry furrow Morgan's brow.

Then the brow smoothed as if a decision had been made. 'That's long enough for me,' Morgan said, satisfied.

It was Duncan's turn to be worried. 'I doubt it,' he countered, 'unless you've got the capital to reclaim a great deal of land and buy in a lot more sheep.'

Morgan sat back, still content with what he'd heard: more than a year; a lot to be done, but three to do it now — four if the boy from Plas Newydd could be useful. Time ahead. For Morgan the meeting was over. Duncan saw he had gone as far as possible; he had another meeting at noon. He pushed back from the desk. 'Anyway,' he said, 'the solicitor's letter was just to inform you officially that the Estate would contest your succession to the tenancy on grounds of suitability.'

Duncan prepared to stand and shake hands — details could wait until another meeting — but Morgan had taken objection to something. He glared. Duncan sat back wondering what had triggered this.

'Damn' — Morgan was sharp and tense — 'I can make Blainau pay. I *am* suitable.' There was a brief silence.

61

'Don't take it personally,' Duncan reiterated, 'I'm at the sharp end, face to face with you, trying to give you an easier life and not involve the Estate's solicitors, accountants and advisers.' He was aware he had said the wrong thing again.

Morgan was on his feet, angry. 'What's this "Estate" with accountants and advisers? It was a man — flesh and blood — give my father the tenancy; a good man, too, who'd carry his gun up behind Blainau for a bit of sport.' Morgan was shouting now. 'What's this "Estate", with you at the sharp end? *I'm* the Estate, and tenants like me. I know who's at the sharp end, sir.' He jabbed a finger at Duncan, 'and it damn well ain't you.'

Duncan was used to being shouted at. It cut no ice. He set his face, holding Morgan's angry eyes in the coldest of stares. Morgan dropped his hand, hearing typewriters, traffic, voices. The anger fell away under Duncan's aggressive neutrality. He sat like a dumped sack and coughed nervously behind his hand. Duncan chose his time. He let embarrassment seep through Morgan like a stain.

'In the interests of us all,' he said, quietly cold, 'the Estate would be prepared to make a deal with you.'

Morgan stared at the floor and listened like a chastened child.

In mid-afternoon Lee and Pugh came cheerfully down from the fields, where Lee had enjoyed his first attempts at hedging under the tetchy tutelage of the old man. They came into the yard and Pugh returned the chainsaw to the workshop, while Lee moved into the house, past the Land Rover, to tell Morgan the work they'd done.

He looked into the living-room, but the fire was dead and the room empty, so he swung round into the kitchen where Morgan was seated at the table, still in his suit, silent and subdued. Lee was too content to notice his mood. He washed his hands at the sink.

'Where've you been skiving off to?' he asked, jauntily accusing, his back to Morgan. Lee was selfish in his well-being: he didn't gauge the pause before Morgan replied, or even note the deadness of his voice.

'Business,' he said shortly.

Lee dried his hands. 'Business?' he laughed, mocking, 'you don't know anything about business,' and he turned, smiling, to talk about the day's events.

But Morgan was looking at him, serious and spiteful. Lee's smile began to slip. 'Get out from here.' The words came out slowly, and were calculated to hurt. Lee hesitated, wondering wildly if this was Morgan's notion of a joke. Dimly aware it was not, a nervous smile crept uneasily to his lips. Then resentment of the long drive home and the brooding on his official lack of suitability to run the farm that his father had carved from nothing, all gathered into one uncontrolled moment. 'Get out,' Morgan shouted. 'Do some damn work for a change.'

Lee stared and began to bristle. 'What the hell's wrong with you?'

Morgan swung in his chair and shouted again. 'Get out!'

Lee was deeply affronted. 'I'm not your bloody dog,' he said coldly, as he walked swiftly from the room, meeting Pugh and almost knocking him aside. Lee slammed the door behind him, striding into the yard. At the door Pugh stared, bewildered, before turning into the kitchen, concerned for what he might find.

He found Morgan sitting sullenly at the table. Pugh guessed where he had been — had already worked out Morgan's length of absence in terms of distance, the appearance of the letter, the wearing of the suit, and, finally, this. 'Been to the Estate.' It was not a question, though Morgan nodded, averting his unhappy eyes.

Pugh took a chair to the cupboard and climbed with clumsy care to reach the bottle of Scotch, as Morgan watched him.

'How long before you're better in your bed at home, mornings?' he asked softly, comparing the heavy movements with Lee's thoughtless step-and-reach of the day before. Pugh set the bottle before him and found two glasses. He pulled up a chair and sat opposite his friend, waiting to be shown how to help.

'They want me out,' Morgan said. Softly, without heat, he told Pugh the deal he had been offered. If Morgan would simply give up his claim to Blainau's tenancy and let the land revert to the Estate, he would be given cheap, adequate housing, in an Estate house, for the rest of his life. He would sell off stock, feed and machinery for a lump sum to live on. The Estate's accountants would advise him how to invest the nest-egg if he wished.

Pugh listened carefully, knowing how the possibility of such a deal must affect Morgan. He tried to be positive. 'Money in your pocket and a roof over your head.'

But Morgan wanted to talk, not listen. 'I done it right,' he insisted. 'I put in for the tenancy when the Old Lady passed on.'

He felt all the injustice of one who had seen the sun set and had just been told it would never rise again. He could not understand. 'Don't tell the boy,' Morgan concluded.

Pugh sat quietly. He knew about tenancies and the Land Tribunal. He did not know if Morgan could improve Blainau sufficiently within the timespan the Tribunal would impose. Like Duncan, he doubted it. 'You better tell the boy something,' he said. 'He damn near scorched me on his way out.'

Morgan nodded. He had regretted his temper the moment he had unleashed it. He got to his feet and walked heavily to the door. Pugh poured himself a whisky. 'I won't let you down,' he called.

The yard was empty but Cap lay outside the workshop door, sniffing the gap beneath. As Morgan came from the house, he sat up expectantly. Morgan moved to the door and opened it. He and Cap went in.

An old ewe was penned by bales in a corner, with a very young lamb, draped in the skin of another. Lee was leaning upon the hurdle, watching her, as Morgan called Cap to stay at the door, so as not to frighten the animals. The man moved to stand at the boy's side. They watched the sheep in silence.

'That old sheep's a wanderer: found her on the hills on her own. Same last year. Tough old girl – on her own against foxes, poor weather. Wonderful mother, mind. She'll take to any lamb who loses the ewe.'

He moved his head very slightly so he could see Lee's face in the gathering dark. Lee's eyes stayed firmly on the sheep. 'What's the point?' he said. 'They both end up meat.' Morgan looked at the ewe as the lamb suckled. He said nothing.

'Why did you shout at me?' Lee turned to face his uncle. 'It's what happens at home is that. Something happens – nothing to do with me but I'm the one who gets it. Then someone – him, or her, or you – they wind down and they don't explain and they don't say sorry; not exactly sorry. They just change the subject and come creeping round you to show they're not going to shout anymore for a bit.'

Morgan would not face Lee, but was moved at this dignified and justified account of adult behaviour. He laid a hand on Lee's arm, but the boy shook it off and moved to the door. 'I'm not a kid, Morgan.' He moved into the yard. Morgan heard his steps on the stone. 'Or a bloody lamb,' Lee murmured angrily to himself at the porch-door, noticing the wind was getting up.

The wind that Lee had barely noticed in mid-afternoon, swung into the north-east by evening and intensified. Hill-storms had alarmed him at first: their violence was a new experience for a boy used to the compact shelter of a city. The noise had overwhelmed him − the fist-like buffeting against the house; the banshee screaming; the machine-gun rattle of loose corrugated roofing; unseen, unknown objects bowling and scraping across the concrete yard. He had stayed close to Morgan who sensed his fear and, by calm, smiling example, had diminished it. Lee came to appreciate the squat sturdiness of Blainau and its position underneath the sheltering ridge.

There was little shelter from a north-east storm; the wind hit the deflecting hills five miles away and rolled, gathering strength, along the line of the ridge to swirl down upon Blainau. The farm took the full force.

Even so, Lee was not alarmed. After an early supper, he sprawled before the fire with half his attention on the television set, whose picture glazed and shuttled as the aerial on the roof was buffeted this way and that. The picture was poor at the best of times. He switched it off and, bored, wandered into the kitchen where Morgan was trying to make sense of a pile of paperwork: invoices, bills, receipts.

Lee stood watching. He asked Morgan if he were going to sort his papers all night, hoping for a game of draughts or cards, but his uncle murmured that he had to get them straight. Lee walked to the window and peered into the blackness. A spatter of rain dashed against the glass. 'I'm bored. I'm going out.'

Morgan was aware of the boy's mood: a slight distancing. They were not yet back on easy terms with each other. He added a column of figures, getting a different total from a previous effort. 'Where will you go?'

Lee shrugged. 'Suppose I'll phone Matthew.'

Morgan turned again to the column. 'It's blowing up nasty,' he warned. 'The boy won't turn out on a night like this.'

Lee peered again into the night. It wasn't too bad; he'd known worse. 'I'll ring anyway,' he said, moving to the door.

Morgan managed a total that matched. He grunted and put the relevant papers aside, reaching for more.

Matthew came to collect him at seven-thirty, with the spare helmet fastened to the pillion. As Lee ran across the yard, the rain lashed briefly against him and the corrugated doors of the cowshed groaned and rattled. The animals inside bellowed uneasily and Cap barked from his bed in the workshop. 'Stuff this,' Lee shouted, as he fastened the helmet and straddled the bike behind Matthew. Matthew grinned and they roared down the road. It was good to have a dependable friend, Lee thought, yelling in mock alarm as the wind slyly ambushed them at the corner. Matthew screamed joyfully. The bike moved up to the common. Matthew screamed again. It was exhilarating. Why not? thought Lee, screaming with him.

Lee sat on Matthew's bed, flicking through a magazine. 'Stuff this,' he said again, as the rain slashed the windows, rattling the ill-fitting frames, bubbling through onto the towel, already soaked, that Matthew had jammed against the gaps. Matthew grinned at him, angling back on a chair before his montage of weaponry in action. Lee tossed the magazine aside and looked round.

'Your mum and dad must have a bob or two,' he said, half-enviously. 'Your bike; your fish; paying for you to stay here.'

Matthew held out a hand for the magazine which Lee threw to him. 'The Gregs were the only ones who could have me at short notice. They're all right: they leave me alone.' He turned the pages idly.

Lee had never thought of other sorts of Gregorys, taking in other sorts of Matthew when school holidays came. 'Must be funny,' he said, 'being shifted round all the time.'

'Doesn't bother me any more. I don't notice where I am.'

Lee considered this. 'That's weird.' Matthew looked up. 'No, it is, Matthew. It's weird.' Matthew couldn't see why; it was his way of life — nothing strange about it. Lee lay back. 'You're weird yourself.' Matthew threw the magazine aside. He leaned forward, setting his chair on all four legs, suddenly interested. Nobody had ever thought him weird before. 'How am I weird?' he asked.

Flat on his back, Lee waved towards the fish tanks, then to the bloodthirsty montage. 'Looking after fish here; blowing people to bits over there.'

Matthew blinked. 'It's not like that,' he protested.

'It bloody is,' insisted Lee. They listened to the storm.

'Do you miss your mother?' Matthew asked.

Even a fortnight ago, Lee would have deflected or ignored the question. He glanced sideways at Matthew, who was looking steadily back. It was a genuine interest. 'Yeah, a bit,' he replied, sitting up. 'It's better now I'm doing things on the farm.' He dropped his eyes, slightly embarrassed at the admission.

'What about your father?' Matthew persisted.

'Do you miss your two?' Lee asked, countering, unused to such personal questions.

Matthew smiled slightly. 'I don't get on with my father. It's better with my mother.' He stopped. Then, feeling a bewildering compulsion to talk about his remote parents and the sister he had been so close to, he began, 'What happened was – ' but swift steps approached and the door swung open.

'What are you skulking up here for?' demanded Eileen, sweeping in, the inevitable glass in her hand. 'I've been waiting downstairs to be entertained.' She smiled brightly at them. 'Orphans of the storm must stick together.' She waited for entertainment. None happened. She noticed the silence. 'Have I interrupted your boy talk?' she asked, as the moment of intimacy fell to pieces in her grand presence. She looked round for somewhere to sit. Lee got awkwardly to his feet and nodded to the bed. Eileen sat and looked brightly at him. 'You must need your head read, roaming about on a night like this.'

She sighed and sipped, staring at the fish. 'You still have a white shirt from school, I imagine?' she asked.

Matthew assumed the question was directed at him, used to Eileen's oblique ways. 'I don't think so,' he replied, not even puzzled.

She looked enquiringly at Lee. 'No,' he said, hoping he was reading the right conversation.

'What about trousers?'

'I've just got two pairs of jeans,' he said, looking over Eileen's head to Matthew who was no help, grinning.

Eileen studied Lee's jeans, shapeless, wet and muddied from the drive. 'Wear the other pair,' she said firmly.

Lee saw a possible line of thought. 'Is this about your party?'

Eileen winced. 'Party may not be exactly the right word,' she murmured. 'Presumably you're both capable of handing round drinks?' She caught a smile passed above her and felt a little gratified. 'You could look quite presentable,' she tested. The smiles turned to grins. She looked questioningly at each, enjoying the boys' attempts to stifle their amusement. She rode on the moment. 'And we must have a girl, too, for the kitchen.'

Matthew turned innocent eyes to Lee. 'What about Sarah Griffiths?'

Eileen caught Lee's accusing glance of betrayal. 'What,' she cried grandly, enjoying herself, 'is Sarah Griffiths?' (Good, she thought: entertainment.)

'She's a friend of Lee's.' Matthew was all helpful sincerity. 'He could go and ask her.' Lee raised his eyes to the ceiling. 'You could do that, Lee, couldn't you?' Matthew said.

Eileen caught secret signals and was further gratified. She rose and strode to the fish tanks, where a particularly ugly fish had caught her attention. 'Is she clean?' she asked. 'Is she honest and a cut above the village harpies?'

Lee was excused further embarrassment by Harry's plaintive voice at the foot of the stairs, demanding where everybody had fled to. 'We're in the military aquarium,' his wife called back. Unsteady footsteps weaved upstairs, along the landing, preceding the unsteady entrance of the Captain.

'Something large outside just took a purler,' he exclaimed. 'It was probably the waterbutt.'

Matthew saw an escape route. 'We'll go and take a look.' He jerked his head towards the door, unseen by the adults, and Lee took his cue.

'Right,' he said, and then they were out of the room and giggling fast down the stairs.

Harry sat heavily on the bed. Eileen turned her attention from the unpleasant fish to her tipsy husband, with similar distaste. He smiled foolishly. 'The Lee child has to get back somewhere in the hills.' She made it sound as if the boy somehow bore complete responsibility for the storm raging outside.

'Matthew mustn't take him.' The Captain was adamant. He pondered the problem. 'They'd blow off the road,' he added mildly. 'I'll get the car out.'

Eileen looked at him in amazement. 'How much of that have you drunk?' she asked.

Harry felt mildly insulted. 'No more than you, I suspect.'

She moved across the room towards the military wall. 'Let his uncle collect him: he has a Land Rover, I assume.'

The Captain, however, had made up his mind. He hauled himself to his feet. 'Is he helping us out for the shindig?' he asked, and, receiving an imperious nod, he continued, 'then I'll do him a favour now.'

An exceptional blast of wind hit the house. (February in Britain, thought Harry; the bedpan of the year. What, for God's sake, are we doing here?) Eileen pulled him from his thoughts. 'Did you write to little local Franklyn?'

Harry assured her he had. Since the sole purpose of the coming shindig was to wheedle money from Mr Franklyn's bank, his invitation had been the first. He drained his glass. 'It'll cost a fortune,' he said miserably. 'But you'll sort it all out. You're the clever one.' He beamed at his wife.

'I always have to,' she said. 'You can have precious few brain cells clinging on, the way you put the Scotch away.'

Harry nodded in agreement. Then, feeling boredom creep in, together with a need for justification, he intoned, 'As we grow older and pleasures fewer, we must work very hard at those which remain.' Proud of his aphorism and enjoying a rare thin smile of appreciation from his wife, he held out his arm grandly. 'Shall we descend?'

Eileen took a final glance round her. 'Isn't this room of the boy's excessively strange?' she mused.

Gregory followed her eyes from the montage on the wall to the fishtanks. 'Killing and caring,' he stated.

She took his arm. 'Ah, the British Empire,' she sighed, as they crossed through the door.

'Ah,' echoed Harry tragically, closing it behind them.

When the Captain's car drew up at the Blainau gate, the storm was at its highest and the yard in confusion. Gregory and Lee were aware of the yard light, dim behind rods of rain, and a milling of shifting cows, before Lee opened the door which the wind flung hard back against him. The noise was horrendous. The frightened lowing of the cows and Cap's frantic barking were suddenly apparent beneath the howl and gust of the wind. Another sound drew attention: fast hammering against metal. Lee stared at Gregory and moved to the gate, instantly drenched.

Morgan was in the yard, shouting inaudibly to them against the wind. Lee climbed the gate. Gregory, aware of crisis, apprehensively forced his way from his seat and stared uncomprehendingly at the chaos before him.

Lee forced his way through the heavy, moving bodies of the cows. A fierce rattling at his side drew his attention to a loose sheet of corrugated iron caught in the eddying wind, jagged and dangerous as it lifted and slanted fast against a bellowing heifer. Gregory began to fumble at the clasp of the gate, prepared to help. He wished he had drunk less.

Some time earlier, the wind had raised a loose edge of the

69

barn's corrugated doors. Working looser, it had been prised from the insecure nails until, held only at one corner, it had torn itself free. The gale had surged through the gap and burst the next sheet easily from its moorings. The simple fastening of the door itself had snapped under the buffeting, weakened by pressure from inside as scared beasts pushed out in panic. Once the wind had blown the whole door flat back, and flapping against the stone wall (the clanging had drawn Morgan out), the rest of the sheets had begun to break away from the framework, each more easily than its neighbour. Morgan was frantically driving home the remaining nails and had managed to refasten one of the free sheets by the corner. He had been struggling to manoeuvre the unwielding metal into place and secure it with new nails as the car had driven up.

Lee appreciated his problem as soon as he was close enough for Morgan to shout in his ear. He shouted back for instructions. Gregory gingerly eased himself along the side of the barn towards them. As Morgan found nails, Lee struggled to hold the flapping metal in place. It writhed and flapped in his grasp, almost breaking free again. Then Morgan threw his weight against it and hammered home one nail, then another, then a third. The sheet held in place now, though not yet secure. Morgan shouted for Lee to bring one of the free sheets rattling between the cattle. As the boy reached, lost and finally held it, he heard more fast hammering, then Morgan was with him and they slanted the sheet into the wind and to its place. An edge jagged the palm of Lee's right hand, and, pulling it back, Lee reached for a less dangerous hold. Morgan hammered.

Seeing the plan, Gregory bent for a wide sheet of metal, docile in the lee of the yard wall and lifted it. Unsheltered now from the face of the wind, it took him like a sail and he staggered back, helpless among the cows. He dropped his shoulder to angle his load and staggered to where Lee and Morgan had all but secured their second sheet. They took it from him. Seeing Lee's cut hand, Harry peeled off his sodden gloves and thrust them at the boy, retiring, aware of his thumping heart and rasping breath. It was a job for younger men, but he leaned his weight to help keep the new sheet in position while Morgan hammered it home. He looked miserably towards his headlights, beaming into the slanting rain, and wondered how much juice there was in the battery. The bedpan of the year, he thought, as Morgan hammered near his ear. Dear God, Dear God.

*   *   *

An hour after they had arrived, Gregory spoke to an anxious Eileen on the phone while Lee, in the kitchen, held his hand out for Morgan to bandage. They listened to the one-sided conversation as Morgan gently wound the dressing, smiling at the drama Harry was unfolding and particularly at the heightened account of his own part in it. ('No, we coped,' they heard him say. 'Terrible business but we managed.') The phone went down.

'You all right?' Lee asked his uncle.

'Black and blue,' the man replied, solemnly smiling. The Captain came in, tired but proud. Outside, the wind dropped and the rain dwindled to spasmodic bursts.

Morgan was proud, too. Even Lee thought something big had been achieved. As the Captain drove slowly away down the Blainau road, they sat either side of the table and Morgan closed the lid of his First Aid box as Lee sipped coffee. 'You did well,' the man said, jerking the last few drops of Scotch into his own cup. (The Captain had emptied most of the bottle; he felt he deserved it, if only in compensation for his devastated gloves. Best kid, too, he had sadly thought, as they lay on the table like two small, drowned animals.)

'You did most of it,' replied Lee, shy at giving and getting compliments.

'Should have seen to that job a while since. That's the trouble,' Morgan said fiercely. 'Two on the farm never gets round the lot.'

Lee yawned and climbed to his feet. 'Bed,' he said.

Morgan looked into his coffee, stirring. 'Pugh, could'n'a did what you did.' He suddenly looked up. 'A good young 'un on this place and we'd soon show 'em, boy.' Lee smiled and nodded, hearing not listening. Morgan searched his face. 'What d'you say to it, son?'

Lee was too tired to follow complicated thoughts. He smiled again. 'Yeah,' he said, moving to the door.

But Morgan was so proud. The only man he had ever worked with in dangerous conditions was his father: a fire on the hill in tinder-dry fern; a blizzard miles from home, finding sheep. (Family, Morgan thought: family.) He heard Lee begin running water into the old bath upstairs and wondered if he'd manage, with his bandaged hand. But Lee would manage. Family.

Tired as he was, the adrenalin still ran. For the first time he was aware of a mass of dull aches in his arms, on a thigh. He rubbed the worst, his left shoulder, proud of his boy and pleased with himself. Even pleased with the Captain. Recalling the half-seen vision of Harry Gregory in full sail among the cows, he laughed almost until tears filled his eyes.

Hearing the laughter, Lee grinned as he stepped into his bath. As the laughter hooted on, he began laughing, too. 'Shut up, will you!' he called out. Blainau rang with laughter.

The next day – Sunday – was dull but dry. There was no wind. Lee slept late. By the time he woke, Morgan was already in church at Llanelieu. Lee reached for the music on his radio and waited to feel like getting up. He had slept deeply, without dreams.

Morgan sang with the congregation. Hymn 373. 'God Moves In a Mysterious Way.' He was in a strange and febrile mood; his sleep had been fitful and full of ideas and hopes. As he affirmed that God rode above the storm, his mind slipped back to the storm of the previous night: the boy had done well; he himself had done better with the boy there – setting the example. Griffiths winked to him as they sang about God's mysterious ways, riding above the storm – there had been some damage at his farm, too.

Morgan sang about taking fresh courage:
The clouds ye so much dread
Are big with mercy, and shall break
In blessings on your head.
The hymn spoke to Morgan of trust and faith:
Behind a frowning providence
He hides a smiling face.
As the dozen or so launched into the final, triumphant verse, led by the harmonium under full pedal-power, Morgan found himself struck by the meaning of the hymn. Certainly, there were clouds on Blainau's horizon: one in particular – the Estate's threat about the tenancy. But what if that, too, should break into blessings? A smiling face behind a frowning providence. And all this because a God, whose intentions are mysterious, can ride upon a storm. And a storm had bound him and the boy closer together, closer to Blainau.

Morgan's faith was not complex: his attendance here each Sunday was as much the habit of a lifetime as an awareness of God in his life. It was a link with the Old Lady and Gentleman who, even now, lay quietly near at hand. But, like them,

Morgan believed in a life after death, a time when he would stand again with his father and mother — as they had done with theirs — and would be praised or blamed for what they had seen him do on earth. If Morgan's Christian beliefs came closer to ancestor-worship than a study of Christ's ways, he would have been confused to learn it.

The congregation sat, but Morgan, in his heightened awareness kept open his hymn book. The words he had sung so many times had never before possessed meaning. It was a sort of revelation. He read them again. And again.

Lee examined his hand. It was not as badly cut as it had looked, and he had had a course of tetanus jabs last year at school. He wound the bandage awkwardly into place. A plaster would have served better: he'd get some from Talgarth tomorrow. Meanwhile, he put on the new anorak he had bought from Abergavenny market for a fiver (it had fallen from the rack into the mud and was marked; he'd waited till the end of the day and haggled.) He checked his face for spots, wanting to look his best: he was going to see Sarah Griffiths about the Gregorys' party. The bandage gave him a sort of heroism, he thought, as he left.

The sermon was a further revelation to Morgan. The vicar, comparatively new to the parish and desperate for approval, took the storm as a theme. He spun a swift connection through a handful of biblical storms and their significance, before taking up the words of Hymn 373 which had so impressed Morgan.

'We talk of Acts of God. Even our insurance forms call them that.' He smiled upon his congregation. 'Yet we have seen that Acts of God always have a meaning, always point a way for his followers.' He was trying to pull his talk towards the idea of tradition, which was the true subject of the sermon, and wanted to link it with the final hymn, 'Christ Is Our Cornerstone,' Hymn 379. He had seen a way and was rather pleased. 'And yet,' he continued, 'in spite of our recent "tempest" ' — he smiled again — 'I hear of no houses flattened or roofs blown far and wide. Our forefathers knew what they were doing. They built on firm foundations, for which we honour them. "Honour Thy Father and Thy Mother",' he flung out at random, ' "that thy days may be long in the land thy Lord God giveth thee". You see, my friends,' he said, 'it sometimes takes an Act of God to bring home the force of tradition.'

He continued, inexorably nudging the sermon towards the idea of a cornerstone, not noticing Morgan's rapt face and shining eyes.

It was Lee's first visit to any farm other than Blainau. He had passed many on the road to Talgarth and, by and large, they much resembled Morgan's farm — mostly bigger, but much the same. The Griffiths' farm was different. It was the biggest and cleanest farm he had seen; it had a modern silo tower, rearing among a complex of barns and other buildings whose use he could not guess. He walked past a small reservoir and understood better how Morgan's precarious shambles of a farm could draw jokes and snide comments. The farmhouse itself was painted white, and sat among flowerbeds. As he walked to the ornamental gate, he noticed two huge modern tractors, a van and an organisation of machinery. He was impressed.

He heard voices as he pushed open the gate, and looked round for their source. In an older barn, close to the house, Sarah and Price stood close together, unseen. The clang startled them and they came out quickly, noticing Lee. They were awkward and nonchalant. Lee smiled and nodded.

Sarah looked as though she, too, might be out for a walk. She wore a black duffel coat over her sweater and jeans. Price was in his working overalls. Just as the silence began to be noticeable, Price said loudly to her, 'I'll check the van over then.' She nodded and moved, not unfriendly, towards Lee.

'Brought a message up for you,' Lee said. 'From Mrs Gregory at Plas Newydd.'

Her eyes opened in enquiry. She smiled. 'Better come into the house then.' She glanced briefly towards Price, still standing watchful at the barn, then the man moved towards the vehicles. He and Lee had not spoken at all. She nodded towards his bandaged hand. 'What have you done?'

Lee grinned modestly. 'Corrugated. From our barn, last night. The wind got in.' Sarah passed through the gate, leading the way to the house. She smiled back at him.

'You're not getting any better on that tractor.'

Lee smiled back, beginning to feel slightly enchanted. 'I see you in the bus.' he said. 'Sixth Form?'

She pouted prettily. 'No such luck. O-level Year.'

'How many are you taking?'

'Ten,' she said. Lee gulped. She saw his surprise.

'Why? How many did you get?' Lee shrugged, entirely modest.

'Didn't get any. Woodwork, English and Scripture: CSE's.'

'Have to be an undertaker then.' They laughed. She opened the door as her father's car drove into the yard. She laughed again, this time at his annoyance. 'Stay for dinner,' she said. 'They'll ask you anyway. I'll show you round the farm, after.'

Then Tom Griffiths and his wife were walking towards the house. Griffiths smiled and said hello, remembering Lee's name and Mrs Griffiths asked him to stay for a meal. Lee was polite and grateful, not only for Sarah's presence, but for meeting new people. He realised that life at Blainau could be restrictive, even claustrophobic.

'Mr Griffiths?'

They all turned at the door. Price was calling from the gate.

'I checked the van and seen to the cattle.' Near her father and in Price's eyeline, Sarah gave the slightest shake of her head. Price understood. 'So I'll be away then.'

'That's right,' said Griffiths. 'See you tomorrow.'

Lee followed Sarah and her mother into the house. Griffiths pulled the door shut behind them all. Price walked towards his pick-up truck, annoyed.

Morgan walked the upper limit of his farm below the ridge, a lamb in his arms. Cap trotted at his side. He had stayed a long time at his parents' headstone, letting his thoughts settle, asking for advice.

As he walked into his farmhouse, the phone rang: Lee, from Tom Griffiths' farm, asking if he could stay for a meal. Morgan felt a great calm. The meaning of the storm and the sermon was extended. It was the advice he had asked for. He ate a meal alone, but not lonely, before checking for early lambs in the high fields. The ewe he had noticed yesterday had lambed, but not well. She would take no notice of the scrawny, spindly-legged creature she had given birth to. Morgan bore it towards the farm, directly below.

As he came down from the fields, he saw Lee jogging along the road and into the yard. He had not realised it was that late. Walking had clarified his thoughts even further. He now knew what he would say.

He set the lamb in the workshop pen and moved into the house, where Lee was in the living-room, scraping mud and muck from his shoes onto a sheet of newspaper, humming tunelessly to a tape playing at his side. He looked up and greeted Morgan happily as the man pulled off his boots and hung up his coat.

'Good meal?' Lee nodded. He prised a stone from the patterned sole of a shoe. 'Pretty girl.' Lee nodded again. 'That's right.' Morgan's emphasis drew the boy's attention. 'That's right,' the man repeated emphatically. 'And Tom Griffiths, he's not a bad sort. Good farmer.'

Lee looked up at Morgan, seeing the solemnity. He was too happy to be much concerned. He went back to scraping the shoe. Morgan turned to a drawer and took out keys. 'Something I want to show you.'

Lee searched Morgan's solemn, set face and laid down the shoe. Sensing a moment of importance, he turned off the tape and stood uncertainly. Morgan moved to the foot of the stairs and waited for Lee to follow. When Morgan nodded the way ahead, he asked, 'What is it?' and began climbing the stairs.

On the landing the boy waited while Morgan moved past him to the door of what had been his parents' room. He unlocked the door. Lee became interested. This was the one room of Blainau he had never seen. Earlier questions ('What's in the spare room?' 'Why do you keep it locked?') had produced no concrete answers and Lee had let the matter drop, thinking it strange but not worrying: most things at Blainau had been strange in the first few weeks. Now Morgan unlocked the door, pushed it open and stood back for Lee to enter.

The boy hated it. He knew that the moment held significance for Morgan, but as he stepped into the darkened, musty bedroom, he hated it. His nose wrinkled at the mixture of smells: the slight dampness, yes, but an overriding, unidentifiable musk which he recognised, with an unexpected alarm, as human – an old smell, sour. Morgan drew back the curtains and light flooded in, revealing the dark shapes. Lee looked round, hating it, not knowing exactly why.

'Take a good look.' Morgan's voice was holy, very quiet. 'A real look.'

Lee looked round slowly. It was at once obvious that it had been his grandmother's room and that nothing had been moved since the time of her death. It was a shrine to the memory of the Old Lady, and – to Lee – infinitely creepy. Heavy, old furniture stood, polished – by Morgan, Lee supposed, though he had never seen the door open. On a dressing-table stood brushes, (there were white hairs in the bristles) and an ornate comb. The bed predominated: plain, brass bed-ends (polished, too). A pallid Christ hung from a surprisingly ornate cross directly above it, one arm crumbled to reveal thin wire beneath.

Lee swung round, alarmed, as Morgan opened the wardrobe door. A number of dresses could be seen inside. And Lee hated it, wondering what his response should be, not wanting to offend his uncle, who was now staring intently at him. Lee shifted his eyes to a chest of drawers on whose top stood a host of framed photographs. He moved towards them.

The largest frame held a picture of a burly, bearded man in a black suit with a small, bright-eyed woman at his side; each stared, unsmiling, towards the camera. Lee supposed that they must be his grandparents soon after their marriage. He looked towards Morgan who nodded, reading his thoughts. He was surprised to see two pictures of his mother, when young; one was taken outside Blainau – Val, at twelve, posturing awkwardly, an embarrassed grin on her face. There was a wedding picture: his mother and father (a similar print had been in Val's room at home before Alan arrived). Strangest of all, there was a large picture of a baby; slotted under the edges of the frame were snapshots of himself – a toddler but recognisable; a school picture at ten; on holiday in a deck-chair at thirteen; another school snapshot of only two years ago. With a shock he realised his mother must have sent them here.

Morgan stayed by the wardrobe, watchful and intent. 'Your Grandad was a hard man: black and white, right and wrong. Hardest worker I ever seen. A strong man. When he took Blainau over, you would'n'a know'd it, everybody said. But she had the brains behind him; she had the softness. Strict in her ways, mind, but she had a way of softness. She thought of you, boy. Look. You can see the pictures. Only met you once but she had you in mind.'

Lee searched his uncle's face for clues to the meaning. Why show him this room? Why now?

'They'd both have been gladdened to see what we did last night, you and me together.'

So this opening of the shrine, this sharing, was his reward, the boy thought. Morgan's fists clenched and relaxed; clenched, relaxed. 'They did see it.' His voice rose. 'I don't doubt that they did.' He took a pace forward, eager now to have the boy's approval and understanding.

'We could see this place back to rights. I watched you with Pugh; fast learner. I seen it when you been with me. Seen you take Cap to try to work the sheep. That's right, boy. That's good.' He came closer to Lee. His voice lost pace. 'I was sharp with you yesterday, when I come home. Wrong of me. Only I'd been to the Estate. You saw me burn a letter.' Lee tried to follow the twists, and at last, with sadness and alarm, he saw the probable direction his uncle was driving.

'They wants it out from the family: Blainau. Blainau have been

77

run down too long, they says. Fifty years in the family and nothing when we come here. It's a long shot, son, but we got time. Damn near two years. Look to the future.'

Again, Morgan paused, wanting reaction. Lee, knowing whatever he said could only disappoint, looked away in silence. Morgan smiled shyly. 'Hard life for me at your age,' he said. 'No time for courting. I never knew nothing else but this farm; I was made shy. But you're educated. You can get on with people — that's your mother in you.' Morgan moved closer again. His heavy fists clenched, opened, reclenched as he came at last to his point.

'And maybe it was intended. Can you see?' Lee, mesmerised by this amazing passion, shook his head, licked his lips nervously. 'You in the town, can't settle, coming to be with me, here, can't settle. Maybe it was meant. Last night was meant: to show us what we can do if we want.'

Morgan faltered, his gaze strangely and suddenly modest.

'And in two years you could get a wife.' He glanced up to see Lee's expression sharpen to incredulity. 'Damn, your Grandad was married by eighteen,' he affirmed vigorously. 'A good woman behind us and we'd be well away. I shan't last for ever. Look to the future, son.' His eyes came up to Lee's face, shining with vision. 'They wouldn't try it on then; wouldn't take the tenancy from the family.' Their eyes stayed locked. Morgan yearned for a good response. 'What say, son?' he whispered finally.

What could Lee say to this simple, passionate neatness? Lee married (to Sarah, he presumed), and taking the farm over at Morgan's death. It was so crazy that, at another time, in another place, he would have laughed. He did not laugh now. He did nothing. Morgan's eyes, heavy with disappointment, dropped from Lee's impassive face. The man supposed he had spoken too much too soon. He guessed his vision had overwhelmed the boy. 'Talk later?' he begged quietly. Lee nodded and Morgan moved towards the door. He shut the open wardrobe and smiled a little, wanting to reassure. 'I can leave the room unlocked now. You come when you want.'

Lee heard his slow steps move downstairs and the porch doors open and close. He heard Morgan call for Cap. He heard the yard gate clang. Soon there was silence. Lee walked from the room without a glance. Halfway to his room he realised he had left the Old Lady's room open and hurriedly turned back to pull the door shut, almost as if a presence inside might escape.

Matthew was out when Lee arrived. Rather than return to Blainau and Morgan, he killed time cutting wood for Gregory until the distant buzz of the motorbike drifted across the fields. They ate some toast in Matthew's room and he stayed for a meal, guilty that Morgan would worry about his absence, before they drove to the Castle Inn to try to lighten the mood. Matthew was sympathetic but no help. They sat in a corner, munching crisps and drinking beer. It was a cold night and one other customer talked to Les at the counter in a quiet monotone.

Lee returned to the long quarter of an hour in his grandmother's room. He could not help himself. Morgan had given him so much since he had arrived, raw and arrogant, from the city. Now the man had opened his heart and let out his deepest hopes and Lee could not fulfil any one of them.

'The worst thing is him just sitting there, waiting for an answer.' Lee folded the crisp packet into a square.

'You'll just have to tell him the truth,' said Matthew. Lee folded the square smaller. He knew Matthew was right. Matthew rose and took the glasses to be refilled.

In the car park, opposite, Price's pick-up truck pulled in, its headlamps catching the Honda full in their beam which glanced off the two helmets strapped on seat and pillion. The beam snapped off and Price came to look at the bike. Graham, his workmate, was with him. They briefly conferred and Price stepped quickly towards the phone box in the corner of the car park.

When Les put down the phone and hurried back into the bar to call Lee and tell him that Morgan had had an accident and was at Blainau, Lee never wondered how anyone could know where he was: Matthew had not even told the Gregorys their destination. He assumed, in the back of his mind, that somebody must have guessed, or seen them pass in the direction of the pub. His whole concern was for Morgan and what could have happened to him. The aspect of Morgan he had lately seen was so strange, so unlike the man, that a number of unidentified fears sped him, with Matthew, over the road to the Honda. Even when Price and Graham stepped from the pick-up, he assumed they had come from Blainau and anxiously enquired what had happened.

Price laughed softly and Graham giggled. Lee still could not understand.

'There's been an accident to Morgan,' he said urgently.

Price reassured him there had not. Silence fell around them. Lee looked round to Matthew. The boy stood near his bike, his helmet in his hands, halfway to his head, staring at the two young men. Lee looked back at them.

'What's all this about?' he asked, puzzled.

Price stepped forward. 'Take your coat off,' he said quietly. Lee looked again to Matthew, as Graham sauntered a few paces towards the boy and stopped, facing him. Matthew fumbled awkwardly with the helmet. He lowered his eyes.

'Take your coat off, pretty boy,' Price repeated.

Lee realised he was about to be in trouble. The relief that Morgan was all right briefly gave way to a sharp sense of apprehension which he controlled; he had been in fights before. Two against two. He and Colin had always coped. He wished he knew why this was happening: country against town, he supposed. Locals against newcomers. He was uneasy: his fights at home had been for more definite causes than this — and less coldly set up.

'This is bloody ridiculous. I'm not getting in a fight with you.'

'Then you're going to end up a fair mess.'

Lee was still unconvinced, still confused, 'Why?' he asked. Price was insistent.

'Get your fancy coat off.'

Lee looked again to Matthew, for guidance, support, anything. His friend had not moved. Cradling his helmet, he stood passively before Graham, eyes on the gravel of the car park. Lee began to realise, uneasily, that he could expect no help from him. He put a hand to the zip of his anorak, then looked up at Price. 'I don't even know you.'

He saw nothing in Price's face but determination. Hoping Graham would stay out of it or that, at least, Matthew would prevent his participation when it came to it, Lee finally faced up to the fact that he was about to fight and unzipped his anorak. He began thinking about tactics. Price was squarely-built and fit. The anorak was halfway off, pinioning his arms for a second, when Price punched him, hard and expertly in the solar plexus. Lee jackknifed as he hit the ground, too shocked to cry out, gasping desperately for breath. Price came down fast on him, holding his head hard into the gravel. He choked and fought for breath.

'You spoiled my afternoon today.' Price spat out the words close to his ear. 'Know what I'm talking about? You think I *like* working Sundays? You spoiled *her* afternoon too. Know what I'm saying?' He ground Lee's face into the gravel. Lee tried to nod through his pain. His breathing was loud and violent. 'Don't step in where you're not wanted.' He gave Lee's head a final twist, grazing his face, and climbed to his feet. Graham looked over at him, then back to Matthew who had not moved throughout.

'Big, brave mate you got here,' he grinned.

Price jabbed a finger towards Matthew. 'You keep quiet about this.' The eyes never left the floor. Graham giggled.

'And you keep quiet too.' Price turned his attention back to Lee, still gulping for air at his feet. 'Morgan's dog now,' he mused. 'Where'd Morgan be without him? Lot of poison put out for rats round here.' The threat was real enough. Lee found a little spare breath.

'Piss off,' he gasped.

Price debated whether to kick him and decided there was no need. He said, in a casual, conversational tone, 'You'd be better away from Morgan. Share the bed, is it? Never thought why he ain't married? A pretty boy like you'd do as well as a wife.'

Then, jerking his head towards the lights of the Castle Inn, he moved away, easily dismissive. Graham shook his head in happy disbelief at Matthew and joined him. Their steps clacked jauntily across the road. Their voices and then their laughter drifted to Lee as he struggled to his knees. The pub door opened and slammed; then there was silence.

Lee laid his head back and breathed long, uneven draughts of air into his lungs; the pain in the pit of his stomach was like cramp. He climbed delicately to his feet. Matthew's voice came to him. He had almost forgotten the boy was there.

'It's my physical soon. If I'd broken an arm . . . smashed my hand . . .'

Lee swayed in the frosty night. His stomach twisted in spasms and he bent over for relief. He straightened slowly and breathed in more air.

'You'll be great in the Paras.' Lee prepared to walk. His breathing was regular now, though the ache where he had been punched was hardening to pain. Matthew stepped towards him. Lee turned carefully.

'Keep off,' he shouted, hurt and angry. Lee began to walk, slowly at first, towards the road. Matthew turned and ran to his bike, switching it on, revving hurriedly. The beam of his headlamp picked out Lee, moving along the road towards Blainau. Matthew throttled into a burst of speed. He braked at Lee's side.

'Get on, Lee, please,' he begged.

Lee walked painfully on. Matthew drove the bike to his side again.

'Lee? Get on.'

Lee's temper flashed again. 'Leave me alone,' he shouted, finding a rhythm for his feet, never even looking at Matthew, wobbling miserably at his side.

In the bar of the Castle, Graham threw practice darts while Price paid Les for their beer.

'You didn't phone earlier, did you?' he asked, the slightest grin on his otherwise solemn face.

'Me, Les? No,' replied Price, all innocence. 'Why? No trouble was there?'

'No trouble,' said Les, taking the money to the till. 'It must have been some other trouble-maker.'

Graham handed the darts to Price and lifted his pint. 'Plenty of them about,' he giggled.

'Hooligans,' affirmed Price, throwing a double nineteen.

Morgan was asleep in his chair when Lee came in. It was a journey of three miles between the Castle and Blainau. Lee saw him from the porch door and was glad. He closed it quietly and moved upstairs. He was too tired for Morgan's visions.

It was the creaking of floorboards and the soft closing of the door directly above the living-room that woke Morgan. He looked at the clock on the dresser and lifted his head to catch other quiet creakings and the weight of Lee dropping into his bed. He shook away his sleep and moved to the stairs, worried.

The light was off in Lee's room. The boy heard Morgan's anxious approach with something like despair. He could not face him. Quiet, urgent tapping at the door closed Lee's eyes in wretchedness. The light snapped on, showing Lee flat on his bed. Morgan gently closed the door behind him and approached, seeing the graze on his pale face and the tiredness in the dark smudges beneath his closed eyes. It was Morgan's turn to feel inadequate in a situation not of his choosing.

'Lee?' he said softly.

No answer came for a long time. In his exhaustion, Lee simply hoped the man would go away, knowing he would not. Morgan hovered anxiously at the side of the bed. He saw mud stains on the boy's jeans; he guessed he must have fallen. Lee's voice was low and level.

'These boots are killing me.'

Morgan hastened to undo the laces, glad to be practical. He eased the boots off with difficulty over Lee's heels. The socks beneath were rucked around his instep. Lee's eyes stayed shut.

'Drunk, is it?' ventured Morgan. Lee lay immobile. 'Best sit up.' Morgan, needing to be practical, leaned over Lee and put his hands behind his shoulders to help the boy into a sitting position.

The eyes snapped open as Lee felt Morgan's hands on him. Involuntarily he shouted, 'No,' Price's sneers clicking unwanted into his tired mind. Morgan stepped back, alarmed. Levelly, Lee said, 'I can do it,' and painfully moved across the bed, grateful for the cool wall at his back. He unzipped his anorak.

'Coffee?' Lee shook his head. Morgan's anxiety suddenly burst out. 'Where you been, boy? It's after one.'

'Walking.' Lee's eyes closed slowly. Morgan was astonished. 'Walking where?'

Lee's tired, low voice tried hard to find the right words. 'It's just a house on a farm, Morgan; just stone and wood. It's people that matter, not places.'

Morgan looked at the boy, still puzzled, still half-suspecting he was drunk. 'Things get done differently here,' he added.

Morgan asked if Lee had had some accident. The eyes stayed shut, but, for one moment, the beginnings of a smile twisted his lips.

'No,' he said. 'This was intended all right.' The smile smoothed itself into nothing. There was no sound in the room for a long time. Then Lee opened his eyes and looked steadily at his uncle's bewilderment. He hauled himself from the bed and began to take off his anorak, gently. Morgan stepped forward to help him.

Lee stopped dead. His eyes closed again. He felt low and dispirited, tired with it all.

'Just leave me alone.'

Morgan dropped his large hands and stood for a moment, helpless. Then he nodded, turned and left the room. His steps creaked downstairs. Lee shut the door behind him and wearily undressed.

On the road, a little way from the yard gate, Matthew sat astride his bike, feeling wretched and guilty. He saw at last the light in Lee's window disappear. He waited a while longer, then switched on his engine and drove past Blainau towards Plas Newydd. Cap barked until the roar of the motor had dulled to a murmur, but did not wake Lee who was already asleep.

83

Chapter Four

Rain in the Black Mountains tends seldom merely to fall; it cascades, it envelops and, during winter months, it drives hard in sideways. The rain seeks out ill-fitting roof tiles, window frames not perfectly secure, a gap beneath a door and any guttering not entirely clear of the mouldering remains of autumn leaves. Plas Newydd had its share of all these and on 20th February the rain had been driving at the ruin of a mansion for almost three days.

Harry Gregory, with an unerring sense of disaster, had chosen the night of the twentieth for his party to impress the bank manager. The kitchen table groaned beneath a mountain of expensive food; more than enough for twenty guests, although only a dozen had been invited. On a side table a reserve stock of wines and spirits stood ready to supplement the already ample supply in the living-room. The invitations had specified half-past seven and it was now five to eight. A car approached the building, its tyres noisy on the wet roads. Harry, midway through pouring a Scotch for himself, dapper in his regimental blazer, looked at Eileen, chic in a kaftan which had been much admired in Rhodesia, as she sat near the fire and looked towards the door.

Lee also cast his eyes towards the door, hoping that something would happen soon. He felt ridiculous in his new, white shirt and small bow tie on which Eileen had insisted. At his side, Sarah Griffiths, already gathering the signals of impending doom, looked at all three quickly and secretly prayed that somebody would arrive. The car did not stop. Changing gear almost outside the house, it continued on its way.

Eileen sighed deeply and looked at her husband, who, avoiding her gaze continued the pouring of his drink. She imperiously thrust out her empty glass towards him, and Sarah rushed to collect and deliver it to the Captain for refilling. It was their second drink since they had gathered at seven-thirty. Lee sneaked a look at the clock. All four of them had a sense of difficult times ahead, none more so than Harry Gregory himself.

Gregory sloshed gin and tonic into Eileen's glass and silently handed it to Sarah, who returned it to Eileen, sitting still and dangerous at the fireside. 'What a wonderful time of year to throw a party,' said Eileen, her voice designed for maximum criticism of all arrangements.

Gregory felt it strike home. 'How did I know it was going to pee down like this?' he murmured. 'We should have put people off.'

Eileen smiled thinly. 'And what should we do with the food?' she said. 'Throw it away? This has cost a fortune.' All four relapsed into an uneasy silence.

Matthew came down from his room. He had not seen Lee since the fiasco in the car park and the situation was doubly difficult for him because the cause of it stood the other side of the door. He, too, felt more than slightly absurd in a stiff, white shirt and bow tie, and had indeed mildly protested when Eileen had presented it to him, but she had insisted: there was a proper way of doing things. He guessed that their servants in Rhodesia had looked something like himself. Outside the door he paused and then made himself enter.

Matthew came into the frozen atmosphere. At a small table near the door stood Lee and Sarah. Lee looked pointedly away and Sarah, innocent of any tension between the boys and of her part in it, smiled.

Eileen snapped at him, 'Come in if you're going to.'

Matthew came in and shut the door behind him, partaking of the uneasy silence. Rain hit the window; wind rattled unidentified objects outside.

'People are bound to be late,' said Harry. 'The roads must be swamped.'

'It's very wet on the roads,' Sarah agreed, anxious to continue the conversation now it had begun, and Harry was grateful to her.

'Yes,' he said. 'Everybody will turn up at the same time. It's always the way.'

Eileen was not to be mollified. 'Considering the Morrises live just up the hill . . .' she began – the Morrises were their nearest neighbours and had a small farm.

'If they've got flooding,' interrupted Gregory, 'they've got flooding.'

'How can they have flooding?' said Eileen sharply.

'*We've* got some flooding at the farm, Mrs Gregory,' said Sarah helpfully. Eileen ignored her well-meant interruption.

Silence fell again as Matthew, once more, tried to catch Lee's eye and failed. Another car approached; a bigger car. All listened intently. They heard its tyres on the wet road, heard its gear change near the corner – and then a horn tooted. The relief was enormous and suddenly there was a great deal of movement.

'There you are,' cried Harry, moving towards the door.

Eileen rose to hustle the children from the room. 'I'll let you know when we want things in,' she said, rolling high the incongruous sleeves of a woolly cardigan beneath her kaftan.

'On with the motley!' cried Gregory, and putting an arm around her shoulders, he gave a friendly squeeze.

'I just hope this isn't your friendly, local bank manager and his little, bleating wife arriving first,' she said.

Gregory would not allow his goodwill to be dissipated. 'I just hope he makes it,' he said. 'He's the one we need to impress.'

The doorbell rang and Gregory left to answer it. Eileen prepared her smile and moved to the open living-room door to await the arrival of her first guests.

In the kitchen the two boys found themselves briefly alone, and Matthew smiled tentatively.

'Haven't seen you about for a while,' he said.

Lee still would not meet his eyes. He murmured, 'Been busy.'

Matthew persisted. 'I rang up a couple of times. Your uncle said you were working.'

Lee folded a table-napkin in the manner Mrs Gregory had taught him. 'I know,' he said. 'Morgan told me.'

Sarah entered, smiling, unaware of the tensions, wanting merely to ally herself against the strange atmosphere of the living-room. She waved towards the laden table and said to Matthew, 'You'll be having this lot for breakfast, dinner and tea!' Matthew made no reply and Sarah turned to Lee. 'How's the tractor driving coming along?' she asked. Lee shrugged and continued folding table-napkins. Sarah gave up, not knowing that anything should be wrong between them.

The first arrival was Tom Duncan. Harry ushered him into the hall and closed the door against the terrible weather. They made polite conversation and Tom handed over a bottle of Scotch as a contribution towards the evening festivities.

In the living-room Eileen felt that there was no great need to impress Tom Duncan and relaxed a little. 'Tom,' she said, moving to take his outstretched hands.

He kissed her cheek. 'Good evening, Eileen,' he said jovially, noting, with some despair, that he was the only guest.

'We were beginning to think that February festivity was a dreadful mistake,' said Eileen.

'No,' lied Duncan. 'Exactly the right time: cheer us all up.' Gregory poured Tom a drink and all three moved towards the fire. 'Did the load of wood arrive?' Duncan asked.

'Most grateful,' replied Gregory. 'You must let us know how much we owe you.'

'Oh, absolutely not,' said Duncan and they drank gratefully.

'Do you know Richard Franklyn and his wife?' asked Eileen. Tom did. 'They're coming over from Brecon,' she went on.

Duncan picked up the anxiety behind her words and quickly reassured her. 'The main roads are fine,' he said. For some reason all three laughed. 'Cheers!' said Tom.

The doorbell rang. Gregory moved towards the door. 'Did you hear a car?' he asked. Tom and Eileen settled down for some routine, inconsequential chat.

James and Mary Austin were soaked.

'You're soaked,' cried Gregory. 'Come in, come in!'

'We're drenched,' agreed Mary.

'We're two drowned rats,' confirmed James. 'We walked.'

'Good heavens,' murmured Gregory, noting the fact that they were alone — they were supposed to have brought their three children. Having helped the Austins from gumboots, waterproofs, hats and umbrellas, Harry herded them towards the living-room door, mentally totting-up how many guests had actually arrived and how many had been invited: the Morrises and their son, the three Austin children. He groaned secretly at the cost and hoped like hell that Franklyn and his wife would show up soon.

Duncan and Eileen were talking about June, Tom's wife, when the Austins burst into the room with a fit sense of bonhomie and Harry bustled to get them a drink.

'We were just saying we didn't hear a car,' said Eileen.

'They walked over,' called Harry.

Mary squealed. 'Don't mention cars!'

.'Our car,' said James, 'is dead. It's been standing out during all this awful rain and rigor mortis has set in!'

'Where are your youngsters?' demanded Eileen, catching Harry's eyes briefly.

Mary was more than a little apologetic. 'We thought we'd better leave them at the house,' she said. 'They weren't very keen on the idea of walking over.'

Don't blame them, thought Duncan. 'A long walk?' he asked.

James grinned and took his Scotch. 'Long enough,' he said, making for the fire. 'We've got a holiday home, the other side of the common.'

Mary smiled. 'Pant-bach,' she said.

Harry picked up Eileen's slight nod towards Tom Duncan and rushed forward. 'I'm very sorry. Do you know Tom Duncan? He manages the Cae-Nest Estate.' A welter of introductions ensued.

'James Austin,' said James, thrusting out a hand.

'His better half,' said Mary, thrusting out another.

'Have a little nibble,' said Gregory, holding out a dish of nuts into the already complicated arrangement of arms.

'That's a very racy suggestion, sir.' cried Mary, and all laughed and laughed and laughed. They knew they were in for a grim evening.

The extended burst of hearty laughter penetrated to the kitchen where the three youngsters stood waiting for their call. Sarah came to Lee and asked him how he had come to Plas Newydd. Hearing the terse reply that he had cycled, she offered a drier lift back to Blainau when her father brought the car to collect her. Lee brusquely rejected the offer. For the first time Sarah was aware that something could be wrong.

'That's daft,' she said, 'when we've got the car.' Lee moved away and fiddled with the cutlery. The telephone rang in the living-room, bringing to a halt all conversation and laughter. Sarah looked at the mound of food. 'They don't need the three of us really,' she said, wishing she had not come.

A silence hung over the whole house. Outside, the rain could clearly be heard. A low murmur from the living-room, where Eileen was talking on the telephone, came to them. Sarah looked at one boy, then the other; she did not know what was wrong.

'Well,' she said, 'I'm going to take something in. Might as well work; it's not much fun sitting round here.' She moved to collect what she thought might be called for, selecting two dishes of chicken vol-au-vent.

Her back towards her guests, Eileen replaced the receiver with a face that would have wiped away any lingering remnants of hope for the evening's success. She was not pleased. She turned, forcing her face into a smile.

'That was the Franklyns,' she said. 'There's some ford they can't cross, seemingly.'

Only Harry, of those in the room, knew what that meant. He felt his spirits fall, and, seeing Eileen's set smile which he knew so well, his spirits sank.

'But there's no ford between here and Brecon,' he protested feebly.

'That is what they say.' His wife moved towards him. 'They send their apologies.'

The Austins and Tom Duncan were vaguely aware that something was wrong. Each put it down to the fact that a great deal of care and money had probably been spent and very few of them were going to be forced to enjoy it.

'Never mind, never mind!' cried Harry. 'Everybody's here that matters,' he lied. 'Why don't we have something to eat, Eileen?'

For one brief moment he thought Eileen was simply going to remove her energy and party spirit from the proceedings altogether, but then the door opened and Sarah, tentatively, appeared with food. The Austins and Duncan, skilled party-goers, did their best to cheer up.

'Somebody's a mind-reader!' cried Duncan.

'Yes,' said Gregory, 'Eileen's got them well-trained.' And everybody laughed. Eileen did not laugh very much. Sarah handed round the dishes as the Austins and Duncan took it upon themselves to keep the party going.

'Do you know Pant-bach?' asked Mary a little desperately.

'Yes,' said Tom Duncan with too much enthusiasm. 'Used to be a farm. Family called Rees used to have it.'

'That's the one!' said James.

'It was in their family for generations,' said Duncan, coming to sit at Mary's side.

She smiled, 'That does not astonish me.'

James sat in a fireside chair 'You ought to have seen the state it was in when we took it over. Took us two years to get it right. We come down whenever we can.'

'A holiday home,' added Mary. 'We live in London — Swiss Cottage.'

Seeing his guests doing their best encouraged Harry to act the host. 'James is one of those financial wizards who's something in the city,' he exclaimed. They talked a while of James' job, then talk turned to Duncan's work on the Estate. Gregory expressed his gratitude. 'We don't know what we'd do without Tom,' he said.

Mary nodded knowingly. 'Trying to get anything done round here is a nightmare,' she said.

'Don't tell us!' said Harry. 'Never leave anything to the locals.' He felt better now, food was passing round and he was beginning to be slightly anaesthetised by the Scotch; he felt expansive. 'Never leave anything to the locals. It's the same world over. Mañana, baksheesh. The language may vary but it's always the same.' They laughed a little at this.

Sarah, as the only local present, kept her mouth shut and her attention on the dishes, as she threaded her way between the guests.

'I must say,' said Mary taking a vol-au-vent, without thanking Sarah, 'we find the locals a bit soggy.'

'It's the climate!' Duncan said.

Again there was some laughter and, at last, Eileen, seeing Harry working hard to resuscitate the almost moribund celebrations, felt deep-down a sense of duty urging her to support his attempts.

'Excuses, excuses!' she cried expansively. 'How can it be the climate? Look at Harry and me — we positively radiate Rhodesian sunshine.' She beamed at them as they laughed and laughed and laughed, wondering how soon they could decently make their excuses and leave.

Alone with Lee in the kitchen, Matthew screwed up his courage. 'I want to talk to you,' he said. Lee made no reply. 'I've got to explain,' insisted Matthew.

For the first time Lee faced him. 'Explain what?' he said. 'You just froze. You'll be a riot in those bloody Paras of yours.'

Matthew dropped his eyes from Lee's cold gaze. 'It wasn't like that,' he murmured. 'Just let me talk, we mustn't let them get away with it.' Lee's eyes quested over Matthew's face, as he lamely continued, 'We could . . .' He shrugged. 'What I mean is, that I can . . .' His words petered out.

Lee shook his head. 'No point. Where I come from, if a guy

won't help his mate, he's not a mate.' Lee turned away and moved to take up a bowlful of salad. Matthew moved towards him, desperate to explain what he knew had no explanation, but Eileen's voice called him from the hallway and he had to move away to see what she wanted.

At nine o'clock the telephone rang again, for Tom Duncan. He took the call, the rest of the guests talking quietly and politely, making a point of not listening. Duncan also talked quietly.

'What kept you?' he said. 'I'm on my way. See you soon,' and he put down the telephone and turned with earnest apology towards Eileen and Harry. 'That was June,' he said. 'She's worried about water rising in the cellar or some such thing. I think duty calls.'

There was a murmur of concern and sympathy from the company.

'She's on her own and the house is a good way from anywhere. I'd better go,' he added.

Gregory tried to prolong his stay. 'One for the road?' he suggested.

Duncan politely declined. 'Thanks all the same, Harry,' he said. He turned to Eileen. 'Eileen, I'm sorry.'

Eileen smiled glacially at him. 'I hope it's nothing serious,' she said.

Duncan, knowing that she knew, shrugged. 'You know how people can fuss,' he smiled.

Mary, quickly catching her husband's eye, sensing an escape-route, added, 'What a shame.'

Sarah and Lee washed dirty plates in the kitchen. 'I thought you *wanted* me to work here with you,' she said quietly. 'Why do you think I'm doing it?'

Lee shrugged. A growing sense of something being wrong had been hardening throughout the evening. She looked at the impassive boy.

'Have you been hearing things about me?' she asked. He handed her a plate for drying. 'What have you been hearing?' she continued firmly. Lee made no reply. 'You don't want to believe everything you hear,' she said. Lee washed another plate and held it out; she took it. 'They're a vicious lot round here sometimes,' she added.

Lee moved to dry his hands on the towel. 'Vicious is right,' he murmured.

'Why do you say that, Lee?' She moved towards him. 'Has somebody done something to you?'

Duncan came through the door. 'Hello,' he said. 'Can one of you find my coat?' He was aware that he was breaking up something, but could not guess at its importance. Lee moved past him through the door and he followed. Sarah dried the final plate, now very anxious indeed.

'And who are you?' asked Tom Duncan, as Lee helped him into his coat in the hall.

'I'm nobody,' said Lee. 'Just working.'

Duncan smiled. 'You're not local, with an accent like that.'

'My uncle's got a farm here,' Lee said, stepping back.

The man turned, zipping up his coat. 'Which farm?' he asked. Lee told him it was Blainau. Duncan looked at him with interest. 'So, you're the great white hope of Blainau. I've heard great things of you.' Lee was puzzled. Duncan smiled again. 'Have you had much experience?'

Lee looked at the man as if he were mad. 'Sorry?' he said, confused.

'Much experience in husbandry?' Duncan explained. Lee wondered what the man was talking about. Duncan would not let the matter drop and continued, 'You've worked on farms before, presumably? You'd be too young for Agricultural College.'

Lee felt maybe the man had confused him with somebody else. Half-smiling, he said, 'I'm not going to Agricultural College.'

'What experience have you had then?' asked Duncan, also beginning to think that he was speaking to the wrong boy. They looked at each other in casual confusion.

'Who are you?' Lee asked, at last, politely.

'I manage the Estate your uncle rents his farm from.'

Lee made the connection in his mind and was worried. 'What's my uncle been telling you?' he asked.

Duncan saw his concern and grinned. 'Forget it,' he said. 'Listening to Morgan I've got the wrong end of the stick.' He turned to go.

'What's your name, please?' asked Lee.

Duncan was amused. 'Tom Duncan,' he said. 'What's yours?'

For some reason, Lee felt embarrassed about giving it, about involving himself. Duncan saw he was to get no reply, smiled, and moved on.

'Lee Turner,' said Lee.

Duncan turned to face Lee. 'I like Morgan,' he said, 'but he's not a realist. Do you know what I mean?'

Lee was wary. 'I don't know what he's been saying,' he said.

Tom nodded. 'Morgan's pinning a lot of hopes on you, but I imagine you know that.' He cast a professional eye over Lee's thin, wiry frame. 'I should think they have to anchor you down in a strong wind,' he smiled. 'Thanks for the coat.' He moved away. Lee watched him go, wondering what all that was about.

Sarah was waiting for Matthew as he came into the kitchen, carrying three dirty plates. 'What happened to Lee?' she demanded.

Matthew was evasive. 'When?' he asked.

'I don't know when,' said Sarah, tired of it all. 'Last week sometime.'

Matthew scraped the plates into a waste-bin and took them towards the sink. 'You know what happened,' he said in a low voice.

Sarah followed him. 'I don't know what's happening at all,' she said plaintively. 'That's the trouble. Tell me.'

Matthew looked up at her, realising she was being entirely truthful. With that strange sense of power that comes from knowing more than someone else, and feeling cruel because of his guilt in the matter, he said simply, 'Lee got beaten-up – you know who by. Does that make you feel good?'

Sarah suddenly understood the evening's tensions and felt wretched. Matthew's dark eyes held hers.

'Now you know,' he said, 'keep it to yourself. You've caused enough hassle between us, okay? Just don't tell him you know.' He made to move from the room.

Sarah asked quietly, 'When was this?'

'The Sunday before last,' said Matthew, and, with a final twist of cruelty, smiled at her. 'You must remember Sundays.' Then he was gone.

The Gregorys stood at the open door of the hall as Tom and the Austins, in full waterproof gear once more, took their leave. They were effusive with their thanks. It had been a lovely party, they said, and they were very sorry to have to go, but Tom could give them a lift to their very front door, which would prevent them being soaked all over again. A cacophony of goodnights, thank-yous, of intentions to meet again, took the Austins and Duncan out into the driving rain, then the door closed and Eileen moved back towards the living-room, slowly, even majestically, her face set. Harry knew this mood well and, had he been entirely sober, would have been very anxious indeed. In silence they walked to the living-room door, passing Matthew who also stepped back, sensing unknown danger.

Eileen came through the living-room door, suddenly cold, tugging down her cardigan sleeves. She slumped into a fireside chair. Gregory dared not speak; he poured two large glasses of spirit.

'Utter fiasco,' Eileen pronounced, as Gregory brought the drink, which she received in silence. She looked around the room. 'Complete and utter fiasco.'

Sarah opened the door and looked in nervously. 'Shall I clear up, Mrs Gregory?'

'You can do what the hell you like, little girl,' said Eileen, leaning back and disassociating herself from the whole terrible event.

Sarah felt dreadful. More than ever she wished she had not come. It had been a night of rejection, and she dimly remembered how she had been looking forward to helping out, seeing a little more of life than her father's farm and school, being with Lee.

Harry, through his drunkenness, saw her disappointment and nervousness, and warmed to her. 'Come in, come in,' he said. 'Go and get the boys. Bring a dish or two. There must be a pâté mountain out there. Go on, Mistress Sarah,' he smiled broadly at her as she left. He turned on his wife. 'Don't take it out on them,' he said. 'They've done their best. They all turned up.'

Eileen took no notice of the accusation. 'The phone call was blatant,' she said, 'and the Austins couldn't get their coats on fast enough.'

'Spilt milk, spilt milk,' said Gregory, coming towards the fire. The silence had suddenly turned dangerous.

Sarah and Lee entered, each bearing a plate with a few of the many leftovers.

'That's the way,' said Harry jovially. 'Put it down there on the table. Tuck in.' Lee and Sarah put the food down. Neither felt like eating. They stood about waiting to see what would happen.

'Give them a drink,' barked Eileen. Harry dithered, knowing so well this dangerous mood of his wife's. He looked across at the children and began to ask them what they would like, but Eileen interrupted. 'Just give them a drink, for God's sake! We don't need a public enquiry.'

Gregory, intimidated, waved a vague hand towards the table where Sarah moved to take the top from a small bottle of tonic.

Eileen considered them and it suddenly seemed to dawn upon her that her servants were one short.

'Where's Matthew?' she demanded.

Sarah was nervous; she had never met people like this. 'He's gone to bed,' she said quietly. The reaction was startling.

Eileen sat bolt upright. 'I beg your pardon?' she said. There was a pause as Sarah wondered what was so terrible.

Gregory sensed her unease. 'What's the matter?' he asked Eileen mildly.

'If I'm paying him, he stays until I decide otherwise,' she snapped.

Gregory turned to Lee. 'You know Matthew's room, old boy,' he said. 'Go and tell him to come down.' And as Lee made no move, suspicious of the situation turning in a direction he could not foresee, Harry added, 'Go on, yes, chop-chop.' Lee left.

Eileen was now very much the focal point of all attention and suddenly smiled. 'Fascinating,' she said. 'Tom Duncan comes and he's from Hereford — forty miles away. The Austins *walk* here and they're from London.'

'They didn't walk from London,' Gregory murmured.

'You know what I mean,' said Eileen sweetly. '*They* managed to force themselves through our front door, but our neighbours can't walk one mile to us and our bank manager invents some fatuous fable about being cut off by a water-wall of biblical dimension.' She smiled, enjoying herself.

Gregory knew her moods well and tried to defuse the situation. 'Why is it fascinating?' he asked. 'It sounds extremely boring to me.'

Eileen needed to make herself understood: 'The foreigners can make the effort,' she mused, 'but as far as the salt-of-the-earth locals are concerned, we can go to hell.' She really seemed to mean it, embarrassing Sarah.

Gregory smiled at her. 'Sarah's not like that, are you? Come and sit down, yes, come on.' The girl moved towards the fire and gingerly sat at the edge of the sofa, as far from Eileen as possible.

'She's being paid,' protested Eileen. 'If there had been money involved, they would have burst down the door.' She leaned back triumphantly, as Sarah felt herself stung to defend neighbours and friends.

'I don't care about the money, Mrs Gregory,' she said bravely. 'You just said you wanted some help.'

Eileen slowly swivelled her gaze upon the nervous girl, to Sarah's embarrassment, and scrutinised her minutely.

'Clever girl,' said Eileen thoughtfully. A smile came over her face which was not really a smile. 'Which one of the boys takes your fancy?' she asked brightly. 'The Lee boy, I suppose. I can't see any girl going rosy for the potential paratrooper.' Sarah looked at the floor and Gregory smiled, pleased to have the heat turned from him.

The door opened, and Matthew came in sheepishly, with Lee behind him. 'I thought you'd finished with us,' he said.

'I had not,' said Eileen imperiously. 'I had not finished with you.'

Gregory smiled. 'Help yourself, you two,' he said, waving towards the drinks, feeling suddenly very tired and very drunk. No one moved.

Eileen suddenly stood and walked to her husband's side. 'Come along,' she called brightly, 'amuse us.' There was silence again. Gregory laughed. Eileen pointed to Lee. 'Get everyone a drink.' She turned to Sarah. 'Amuse us.' She smiled encouragingly. 'Let-me-entertain-you,' she sang.

Gregory laughed delightedly. The mood seemed to be changing at last. He moved forward anxious to do his bit. 'I remember – ' he began.

'Not you.' Eileen cut him off dead. 'I've heard every damn thing you've ever done, twice over. We want to be amused, not bored to death.' She turned again to the youngsters. 'Come along. Songs. Recitations. Charades.'

Sarah looked up at her in mute appeal. 'I don't think I'm very good at that sort of thing,' she said.

Gregory laughed again. 'Ah, the post-telly generation,' he smiled happily.

Eileen was smiling too. She moved behind Sarah, making for Lee, standing at the drinks table. 'What *are* you good at, little girl?' she asked, holding out her empty glass to Lee. 'What *is* she good at, Lee?' she asked innocently, as Lee reached for the gin bottle and poured. Eileen smiled again. 'Of course I'm forgetting, you haven't been here long enough yet for the rolling-in-the-hay season, have you?' She moved along and Gregory laughed delightedly.

'You wicked old woman,' he called. 'Leave them alone,' and, following her example, he moved to Lee for more drink, placing an avuncular hand on Sarah's shoulder in passing.

'The moment that horny old hand slips south,' advised Eileen, 'scream.' The hand dropped from the shoulder and the silence intensified in embarrassment. Eileen turned to them blankly. 'So nobody's going to amuse the pensioners.'

'I think we've had enough amusement for one evening,' said Gregory mildly.

Eileen fixed incredulous eyes on him. 'You found tonight amusing?' Beneath her gaze Harry's bonhomie tottered. Lee asked if they could go, but Eileen said sharply, 'You can go when you've made us laugh.' Then, seeing his surly expression, she smiled more widely. 'Come along,' she encouraged him, 'An ee-by-gum lad like you should do a mean George Formby!'

Harry looked up eagerly at Lee's uncomprehending face and suddenly realised the boy had probably never heard of George Formby. 'I'm leaning on the lamp-post at the corner of the street, in case a certain little lady comes by,' he sang encouragingly.

It was embarrassing. The young people kept their eyes on the floor and Eileen held her husband in a gaze of cool contempt. Harry's drunken desperation increased.

'Oh me,' he sang, 'oh my, I hope a little lady comes by.' He wandered round the room plucking an imaginary banjo until he stood before Eileen. 'She's absolutely wonderful and marvellous, and fabulous' – the silence in the room suddenly struck him like a blow. He knew he was making a fool of himself; he knew the evening had been, as Eileen had said, a complete and utter fiasco. All the energy drained from the man, he looked from one face to the other, then dropped into a seat at the edge of the room and was silent.

'I'm going,' said Lee.

'You'll stay if I say so,' snapped back Eileen sharply. But Lee had had enough.

'You want to invest in a television set,' he said. 'You can be amused when you want without upsetting people.'

The words hung in the air and Eileen seemed to consider them very seriously. She nodded slightly, fixing Lee with the look a snake might bestow on a mouse, as she glided slowly towards the door. Among the children she stopped, a slight smile on her face as she looked from one to the other. None of them would meet her glance.

'Three sour little virgins,' she said quietly. 'What a crime – to have all that energy, all that freedom.' She waited for any answer; none came. 'You make me sick,' she said, deadly serious. 'You make me sick. All of you.' She turned and moved from the room.

A moment of deepest embarrassment hung in the air. Then

Lee suddenly turned and left the room, anxious only to go, to be at Blainau, or anywhere.

'More food!' shouted Gregory after him. 'More drink. Whatever you like.' His white head slumped forward. 'The bloody bank manager won't come now,' he murmured.

Lee cycled through the torrential rain towards Blainau and barely noticed the dreadful conditions. Gusts of wind buffeted him, but he determinedly kept his feet pumping the pedals until, eventually, the bicycle skidded and slithered on the mud and he could see, at the top of the road, a light in the upstairs window of Blainau. He drove himself on as if sheer effort could drive away the distaste and anxiety of the evening. It was not a time for thinking and his thoughts, in any case, would have been too complicated. He pedalled through the driving rain, concentrating on the effort.

Morgan was in his mother's room, gently dusting her photographs. He breathed softly at the glass of the photograph taken forty-eight years ago at his parents' wedding, then dabbed at it with his duster. He looked up as the front door opened, closed, and he heard Lee's footsteps on the stairs.

The boy was early. Morgan was not displeased; he had had more than enough of being alone and evenings were his bad time. Morgan carefully replaced the photograph in its precise position and moved out to meet the boy.

'You should have rung,' he said. 'I'd have come down and picked you up. You said you'd be back at eleven. It's early yet.' Lee said nothing. 'You want to get out of those wet clothes, boy,' Morgan added helpfully.

Lee, still silent, made no movement and Morgan began to appreciate that the boy had something on his mind; was not his usual self. He waited anxiously for Lee to tell him his trouble.

'It's all gone wrong for me here, Morgan.'

Morgan thought the words over. They made no sense and he considered that Lee might be drunk. 'Come downstairs,' he suggested tentatively. 'We'll get you drying.'

'No, listen,' Lee repeated. 'It's all gone wrong.' Morgan felt a coldness take him as Lee struggled to explain. 'This last week . . .' he began, but Morgan finished his sentence for him:

'This last week you've been quiet. Everybody gets quiet sometime.'

Lee noticed the duster in Morgan's hand. 'What have you

98

been doing tonight?' he asked. Morgan could not connect the line of the boy's thought. He explained that he had been seeing to the Old Lady's room.

'Why?' asked Lee.

'To keep it nice.'

'Why?'

'Because she'd want it.'

Lee nodded, moving past Morgan into his grandmother's room.

Morgan appeared in the doorway and the boy asked casually, 'What did you tell Tom Duncan about me when you went to see him?'

Morgan was pleased for the chance to impress the boy. 'I told him you were a strong lad; a good lad – quick to learn.'

'I saw him tonight,' said Lee. 'He said you were pinning hopes on me. Did you tell him that?'

Morgan saw danger sidling up and played for time. 'Damn and I can't recall every word I said. I was in a fret, boy.'

'So what you told me, in this room, wasn't something you'd suddenly thought,' asked Lee.

Morgan stopped trying to find the drift of the boy's mind. 'What you saying, son?' he asked quietly.

Lee turned to him. 'I'm going home tomorrow,' he said. 'When Pugh's daughter brings him in the morning, I'll go with her to Abergavenny station.'

Morgan could find nothing to say. He stared at the boy's unyielding face. 'Why for?' he asked softly.

'I told you,' said Lee. 'It's all gone wrong.' He turned and moved from the room.

Morgan stood near his mother's bed, struck down by the thought; bewildered by the reasoning that had led to it. He moved stiffly towards the photographs and began dusting them again. He began with the picture of Val on her wedding day, which was next in routine, once the glass on his parents' photograph was clean.

Lee, unlike Morgan, enjoyed an untroubled night. Now that his decision had been made, he allowed the events of the last month to fall conveniently into place. He was not one to look back over his shoulder. It seemed to him that his sentence had been served, and due penance done. If he felt nagging moments of guilt over leaving Blainau and his uncle, he did not allow them to do more than nibble at the edges of his own brand of common sense and, when he woke next morning, the long storm had passed, leaving a cold March morning whose sky was rinsed and clear.

He and Morgan made no reference to the events of the previous evening. Shortly before Jean, Pugh's daughter, delivered her father for his day's work, Morgan silently handed Lee the money his mother had left when she had brought the boy to him, and if either Pugh or Jean were surprised at the sudden turn of events, they did not show it. Lee bid a low-key farewell to Morgan and Pugh, shaking hands politely; no meeting of eyes. He petted Cap briefly and took his lift to Abergavenny where, waiting for the train, he bought cigarettes, two cans of Coke and a paperback thriller to wile away the journey.

The train slid north through Hereford, Ludlow, Shrewsbury and eventually to Crewe. Waiting for the Manchester train, he finished the paperback and threw it in a waste-bin.

He arrived at Manchester in mid-afternoon. Having phoned his mother, at work, he took a bus to collect the house keys from her and let himself into the empty house at last. He visited each room relaxing into the neat comfort. Making himself a coffee, he planned a riotous homecoming.

When Val hurried in from work, early, she was pleased by the ill-concealed relief and affection of her son. She was glad Alan was away, delivering south of Northampton, for it would give her time to assess Lee's mood and form an appropriate response. Neither she nor Lee talked about Morgan or Blainau; nor did they discuss Alan. Lee had already discovered that the spare room, which had been Alan's when he left, was now completely empty, and that there were two pillows on his mother's bed. Each was aware that there were important things to be said, but neither wanted to raise them, fearing the wrong moment or the wrong mood. Instead they chatted happily enough about the train journey, Val's day at work, and enjoyed her mock horror at the stream of dirty washing that seemed to pour, never-ending, from his rucksack. As she soaked them before washing, she was aware of how much she had missed her second role, as a mother.

At seven o'clock Lee left the house to meet Colin and his girlfriend, Ros, and, within an hour, the riotous homecoming was well under way.

They enjoyed a few drinks at their local pub before catching a bus into the centre of Manchester and were full of jokes about Wales. In a Chinese restaurant Colin demanded leeks and larded his conversation with 'Boyo' and 'Look-you', in spite of Lee's laughing protestations that he had never heard either spoken in Talgarth. The pub-crawl began about nine and ended when time was called at the final stop. They rushed to catch the last bus to their estate, on the outskirts of the city, rocked a few cars – running screaming away when one, whose untrusting owner had fitted an alarm beneath the bonnet, began shrieking at them.

Neither Colin nor Ross had talked much about Lee's exile, taking their cue from him, while, on his part, it was better joked about. They did discuss Lee's sex life, at which he grinned modestly, and all three expressed drunken sorrow at the sudden engagement of Carol, who had worked with Lee at the supermarket, to Lee's replacement there. It was not a moment of deep tragedy for Lee and they enjoyed some dirty jokes at her expense, too. They staggered from the bus and bade each other a tipsy farewell. Colin promised to return Lee's fish, minus the four that had died, the next evening. He could not spend the day with him since he was now working. His father had found him a job on a building-site. Lee expressed scandalised horror at the idea and Colin grinned, not saying how much more he enjoyed having something to fill the days, and money in his pocket to pay for evenings such as the one they had just enjoyed. Lee watched them go, their arms wrapped round each other. There had been a heavy shower of rain and Lee was very wet, enjoying the novelty of rain that fell, vertically and harmless. He weaved an unsteady path to the house where his mother and Alan lived.

Lee swayed into the kitchen in a silly mood, almost knocking to the floor the rack of shirts and underwear now washed and drying. He fought to pull the complicated arrangement back into place and, having done so, saluted it. The noise brought Val from the living-room.

'What's all this then?' she asked, smiling a little, her hands on her hips in the traditional stance of receiving drunk sons or husbands.

'All this then is me,' replied Lee happily, as he made a clumsy attempt to unzip his anorak. His mother came to help him, shaking her head, but amused, and they wrestled for a few moments, dragging the sodden anorak from his back.

Lee moved to the draining-board and picked up a tea-towel. Val took the work-stained anorak and laid it on top of a ruined pair of training shoes and torn jeans. She looked back at her son, happily rubbing his hair dry with the tea-cloth, and remonstrated. Smiling sheepishly, Lee slumped into a chair at the table and began folding the cloth − it suddenly seemed very important to fold it as neatly as possible − but, failing, he grinned up at her as she smiled back.

'Coffee?' she asked.'

'Definitely,' Lee nodded.

As she moved to reheat the kettle which she had been keeping ready for his return, Lee noticed the pile of anorak, jeans and shoes.

'What are you doing with them?' he asked, indignantly.

Val glanced over at the pile. 'Chucking them,' she said. 'They're ruined − like you are,' she added, pouring boiling water into a cup. Lee nodded blearily.

'Alan sends hello,' she said tentatively. 'He'll see you tomorrow. He's on an overnight.'

Lee, recognising the first test asked, 'He's okay, is he?' and Val smiled, pleased.

'Fine,' she said. 'He phoned about an hour ago.'

Lee nodded again. 'Great,' he intoned, making another attempt on the tea-towel. 'You're both okay then.' He gazed up at her, unable to resist lifting his eyes towards the bedroom above, and Val could not help but smile again, although mildly embarrassed.

'Fine,' she repeated.

She moved to the sideboard and found her purse, from which she took three ten-pound notes which she laid before Lee on the table. He looked up enquiringly.

'A new anorak,' she said. 'New jeans and a new pair of trainers too − if it will run to that.'

Lee looked seriously down at the money. 'I'll pay you back,' he murmured, but Val grinned and brought the coffee to him as he stood upright, with difficulty.

'Can you carry this up without spilling it?' she asked sceptically.

Lee saluted her with great panache and accepted the coffee which he immediately spilt. His sudden distress amused Val. She laughed and kissed him quickly on the cheek.

'Go to bed!' she ordered. Lee grinned and tried to return the kiss. Val waved him away and pointed to the door. 'Bed!' she insisted. Lee turned and, elaborately careful, weaved his way around the cluttered kitchen and through the door.

Lee negotiated stairs, landing and even bedroom door without spilling more coffee. He turned on his light and gently laid the cup on his bedside table and, clumsily kicking off his shoes, fell back, dizzy but contented. He looked round his room and sat up too suddenly. On his shelves stood a new television set – portable. He levered himself from the bed and sat before it. It was plugged in and ready for use. He jabbed at the switches, revealing a late-night film, a burst of static, anonymous music over a still photograph, and a chat show. Switching back to the film, he gazed at it avidly.

Behind him, the door opened quietly as Val entered. 'Welcome home from Alan,' she said. 'Sorry it's only black and white.'

He gave her a delighted look. 'No,' he protested. 'It's great.' 'It fell off the back of a lorry,' his mother said ironically, nodding her head towards his radio. 'Just like that and half the things in this house.'

Lee switched the set off and sat briefly in the silence. His mother guessed he was ready to talk.

'What happened at Blainau?' she asked softly. Lee smiled vaguely and shrugged. 'Too much for a town boy?' she said, helping him out.

Lee took grateful refuge in the generalisation. 'Something like that.'

'Morgan phoned while you were out on the town,' Val said. 'Just to see if you got back all right.'

Lee thought this over, feeling further explanation was called for, but not much. 'It was okay for a bit,' he murmured. 'He's got this room,' he said, 'his mother's room – *your* mother's room,' he added. 'It's really weird.' Val knew about her mother's room. Lee continued. 'And people there – it's not just that they're different. Here you know where you stand. Okay, it's maybe not working out, and, okay, you get a bad feeling about somebody, but you know the score.' He turned back and jabbed a finger at the set; blank screen and static briefly appeared before he pressed another button which took him back to the film. 'Back there, they change right in front of your eyes,' he said quietly. He turned the set off decisively.

Val judged that that was as far as they could talk about Blainau for the moment. She came to him. 'Forget it, love,' she said softly. 'Sleep well. Glad you like the telly.' She moved to

103

the door, hearing him add, 'This telly, it'll keep me in my room, will this.' She shot him a swift glance, trying to assess the direction of his words. 'Alan cares more for you than you think,' she said. Lee nodded as she closed the door. The boy got slowly to his feet and began undressing, grateful for the sounds of traffic and the dim sodium lighting of the street.

Alan returned and all three settled down to a determined attempt at happy families. The two men steered with great care away from any topic which might bring them into conflict.

The next morning, Sunday, Lee and Alan cleaned the cab of the lorry together. There was horse-play, a few jokes — Alan liked jokes — and a quick drink at the local while Val prepared Sunday lunch. In the pub they talked of neutral subjects — football, Alan's journey south of Northampton, Colin's new job, Lee's fish. Alan enquired after Carol, adding that what Lee needed was a good woman to steady him up, and was duly sympathetic at hearing of the termination of the relationship. 'Plenty more fish in the sea,' he said.

Back at the house, Alan made an elaborate show of appreciation for the meal that Val had cooked, taking her firmly in his arms, despite her protestations of vegetables boiling over and the joint ready to come out of the oven. She laughed, enjoying the game, and Alan winked at Lee over her shoulder. Lee made himself smile, and when the men had finished the washing-up, and Lee had gone upstairs to watch soccer highlights on his set, Val sat in the living-room and read a Sunday paper, while Alan repaired the flex of an iron by her side.

Val was surprised and content at the way the three of them seemed to be working out. She was aware of a change in her son, guessing that his weeks at Blainau had been more complicated and intense than either of them pretended. He was quieter, more appreciative of small comforts and seemingly more accepting of Alan. She supposed she should be more than grateful for that. Nevertheless, she was aware also of the careful avoidance of any topic that might suddenly raise trouble.

'You didn't give him that T.V. set to keep him up in his room, did you?' she asked suddenly.

Alan paused in his work. It was the first time since his return that she had said anything possibly critical of his behaviour towards the boy. 'You've got a devious mind,' he laughed, stripping wire, 'of course I didn't.' He leaned across to kiss her. 'Happy?' he asked.

She smiled. 'And you?'

Alan nodded. 'So far so good.'

Val turned her attention back to the paper. 'He must know we're sharing a room now,' she said quietly.

Alan laughed again. 'So what?' he said. 'He's been fine. He's grown up a bit. I said he would. On a farm it's all sex; pigs, cows.' Val began to laugh and he looked over. 'What did I say?' he asked, smiling.

At length she laid down the newspaper and her face slipped into seriousness, 'He's quiet,' she said. 'It's not like him; he's down. Can't you have a word with the boss?' she said, turning to Alan.

He leaned back in exasperation; they had covered the topic many times in the last twenty-four hours.

'Val, love,' he protested. 'We've got a few off sick, sure, but they'll all be back at work within a week.'

She could not let the idea go. 'Colin's father got Colin a job,' she said.

Alan smiled. 'That's a rotten blackmail.'

She leaned affectionately across and kissed him. 'Go on,' she said. 'Have a word with Bob.'

He grinned again. 'And that's another!' Alan was well aware of Val's need, both to do well for her son and to bring them closer together. Uneasily he said, 'What can I do?'

She had it all worked out. 'Take him on a trip with you,' she said. 'Just to break the pattern.' She leaned over to kiss him yet again. 'Do it for me?' she pleaded.

The day of the trip started badly and ended worse. Looking back on it, Lee was bewildered at the contrast between the way the day seemed simply to stretch — the early start; the waiting; the driving; the deliveries and a collection; snacks; meals — and the speed of the deterioration, in spite of dogged goodwill, of his carefully nurtured relationship with Alan. It was as though elastic were stretched, slowly, lengthening to a tautness which was realised too late; when the snap came it was sudden, a shock, but inevitable.

Val made them an early breakfast and there were a few jokes, about hitch-hiking teenage girls, and breathalysers and stopping off at strip-joints on the way home — all of which were lost on Lee, whose experience at early starts were limited to Morgan's quietness as the day fell into place at Blainau.

Alan and he checked in at the depot and linked the cab to the container section of the huge, articulated lorry. The boy settled himself in the cab while Alan collected the necessary paperwork from the office. It was a bleak morning, cold and damp.

The first stop was Preston. Alan pushed the immense truck along the M61 in good humour, overhauling slower lorries, cheekily edging past in the fast lane when he took a particular dislike to a car or its driver from behind, and occasionally glancing at Lee, grinning for approval at his skill with the vast machine. He was a good driver and liked it to be acknowledged – which, at first, Lee did, though soon running out of admiring terms which he didn't mean anyway. Such a skill seemed strangely irrelevant. He wasn't interested, his tractor exhibitionism conveniently forgotten. Eventually he fell into a doze: the cab was warm and comfortable. Alan glanced over and smiled. He pushed him awake. 'Too early for you?' They hammered on.

At the Preston yard, the boy worked hard. Alan went to the office, leaving Lee and a loader called Barry to move six crates to the delivery bay. Barry was old and more than content to watch the boy take the major part of the load. Barry was also a pain, believing himself to be a character.

'I'm what they call the Genuine Article,' he boasted.

The pressure of being a character was obvious: the man could not shut up, nor would he let Lee hit a rhythm in the heavy shifting of the crates. He sang, joked obscenely, talked football, family and snooker, farted, belched and, as a last resort, when silence seemed briefly imminent, laughed loudly for no good reason. Lee gritted his teeth, giving no encouragement. He thought that he would cut his own throat if he were Barry.

Alan appeared at the door of a Portakabin unit, checking lists.

'You see that man?' Barry said, farting. 'The Sir Galahad of the motorways; if a maiden's not in trouble when he finds her, she will be by the time he goes'. He leaned on a crate which Lee was trying to lift. 'See that paperwork?' He put a finger to his lips confidentially. Lee glanced at Alan.

'Paternity summonses,' the old man confided. 'This is the passion wagon. If that cab could speak.' He winked and belched. 'Showing you the ropes, is he?' Barry leered. 'Get him to tell you his sexual doings. He'll turn your ears inside out.'

Lee jerked the crate free, dislodging Barry, who smiled

106

indulgently as he toppled to lean on the crate behind.

'How is it, you mad beggar?' he shouted to Alan.

'How's yours?' Alan called back, tossing the paperwork into the cab as he came towards them.

'All limp and wrinkled,' Barry laughed.

Alan jumped up to the loading bay. 'You know what that is?' he said, nodding towards Barry. 'That's the Genuine Article.' Barry laughed hugely.

'Yeah,' muttered Lee, edging the crate from the truck. 'A real character.'

Alan took the crate from him easily, knowing the knack. 'You should be finished here,' he complained.

From Preston they drove north towards Carlisle, on the M6, in a cloud of spray. Barry had jangled Lee's nerves. Alan laughed.

'You don't want to take any notice of Barry. He's an old joker: famous for it. Gossip keeps him going. Little things please little minds.'

They sped on. Alan edged past a plum-coloured BMW, shut in behind a large van in the middle lane, completely obscuring the car with spray.

'He won't need a carwash,' Alan laughed. They moved on. Alan glanced over at Lee, bored and sullen. 'Look,' the man said, 'I don't say I lived like a monk before I met Val, but don't forget she had your father.' Lee said nothing. The plum-coloured car managed to pass them, the driver glaring up at Alan. 'I don't want to speak ill of Ken; never knew the man. But he never made your mother happy. Know what I mean?' Lee fidgeted. 'Never made her feel like a real woman. Know what I mean?' he repeated.

'Yes, yes, bloody yes,' the boy said. Alan laughed and pressed his foot down hard.

They pulled off the motorway for sandwiches and a drink near Kendal at a pub which Alan knew well. They played two games of darts, which Alan won easily, and he was scornful and amused when Lee wouldn't contest a third. Lee didn't see the point: he didn't like darts, seldom played darts; Alan was The Winner, fine. Alan misconstrued that Lee was a poor loser, and the more Lee tried to explain he didn't care who won, the more Alan believed it. Eventually, the boy gave up and listened to another obscenely sexual story that Alan had from Barry. Lee was becoming very bored with dirty jokes now: they were all the same, reminding him of the sniggers and anxious giggles that had greeted such jokes in the school lavatories when he was twelve or thirteen. He still had goodwill; he smiled dutifully.

The store of goodwill became sparser by the time they had driven over Shap and begun the descent towards Penrith, where they were to drop the last of the load. Val's mistake had been in believing that the enforced intimacy of the cab would force them together, whereas they were tiring of each other's company in the knowledge that the trip was less than half over – would not be half over until Alan picked up machinery at Carlisle for the home depot. The conversation steered dangerously towards taboo subjects, as they both ran out of small talk but saw the more insidious danger of long silences being misunderstood.

At one point Alan raced against another huge truck and Lee made the mistake of showing his alarm. Alan did not appreciate any doubting of his professional skills, and found greater speed, until they had to pull onto the hard shoulder and stop while Lee was sick. When Alan insisted on helping with the final unloading, shifting half as many crates again as Lee and the amiable loader of about his own age, Lee felt he was unsubtly being put in his place, left them to it and sat in the cab, waiting.

'Why the competition, Alan?' he complained. 'We were doing okay. Why the need to bloody show off?'

Alan slammed the truck into gear and moved to the gates. 'I'd have waited all day for you two fairies,' he muttered. They drove through the town, heading once more for the M6.

'What do you think you are proving?' the boy persisted. 'That you can drive a lorry better than me. That you're bigger and stronger than me. Wonderful. Fantastic.'

'Just stop whingeing, can you?' the man snapped. 'I didn't want to bring you.'

'I didn't want to come,' muttered Lee. They drove north in silence.

The mood lifted slightly as they took on board the load at Carlisle. Neither apologised, but an unspoken agreement crept in, now they were five hours from home and heading south again. Each tried harder, and when Alan retold yet another Barry joke, Lee forced himself to laugh and even tried to tell one back, forgetting the punchline – which Alan supplied: everybody knew that one. Alan laughed at the hopeless mistelling, so Lee supposed he had done his bit. Eventually silence grew between them and they let it surround them comfortably, with a degree of relief.

They pulled from the motorway, at about five, for a meal. Alan parked the lorry among several others and they moved gratefully to a transport cafe which Alan rated highly. They stretched, breathed the sharp evening air and strolled towards the low building, their minds only on food.

It was a popular eating-place for long-distance drivers; clean and friendly. As they sat in the warmth and ate their mixed grills, each felt better, each more relaxed. Alan grinned over the table at Lee and asked him how he was feeling.

Lee smiled back, glad of the gesture.

'Knackered,' he grinned.

Alan bisected the rich yolk of an egg so that it oozed onto his fried bread. 'Told you we'd put some muscle on you.' He grinned again, forking a mouthful between his lips. Alan ate like he lived, Lee thought: confidently and untidily. He wondered what his mother saw in the man; she was worth more than this.

Alan speared a sausage whole and bit off half, chewing briefly. 'Old Val was chuffed, this morning – seeing us both off on a job together.' Lee agreed, pushing his plate away, leaving a messy egg. Morgan could always get an egg right, he thought. Morgan should give this place lessons. He smiled to himself. Alan, seeing the smile, returned it and, chewing his bacon, he said, 'I'll tell you another of Barry's stories.' He chuckled, wiping bread around his plate. Lee's spirits sank. He took a sip of strong tea.

'Man goes into this chemist's, looks around for a male assistant; no luck – just a frosty old cow behind the counter. Anyhow, he goes over and orders one dozen packets of Durex: "Dozen packets of Durex, miss," he says. "I got a heavy night ahead."

'So this old cow goes all woman's lib or whatever and she says, "Don't you miss me".

' "Okay", he says. "Make it thirteen".' Alan scanned Lee's face for reaction, grinning. Lee nodded.

He had heard worse today; this was clinically wholesome in comparison to most. He suddenly saw a line connecting all the stories Alan had related with such enthusiasm; it had never struck him before. Without considering the ramifications, he said, in genuine interest and surprise, 'You don't like women much, do you, Alan?' The man was still scanning Lee's face. His chewing ceased; his grin demoted itself to a slight smile. Lee instantly regretted his thoughts and sipped his tea apprehensively.

Alan began chewing again, his eyes hard on Lee. 'What do you mean? Are you saying I'm queer?'

The reaction surprised Lee. 'Don't be thick,' he said, keeping his eyes on the table.

Alan's knife and fork lay motionless in his hands; he swallowed a mouthful, the smile still loose on his face. Lee grew more uneasy. He twisted in his seat to look round at the other eaters.

'I wouldn't call anybody thick if I were you. Not if I were in your shoes.' Alan's tone was light, like his smile. His wrists still rested gently on the table. He was like a boxer — balanced, deceptive, ready to attack. All this Lee wretchedly understood. He looked back at the table.

'I got my school exams. Bloody sight more than you got, Sunshine. I've got a good job. I've got money in the bank.'

Lee raised his eyes to Alan and shrugged. The man was prepared to accept the gesture as an apology. He dug his fork hard into a tomato and sliced it in half with his knife.

'I just wouldn't go calling other people thick. Not in your position. All right?' He swallowed the half tomato and dug up the other half. 'All right?' he repeated aggressively.

Lee pulled back in defence: 'All right, yes; all right,' he said. 'You love women. You're God's gift to women.'

It seemed to have been the wrong thing to say again, for Alan's wrists dropped lightly to the table and his eyes held Lee's. A burst of laughter rose from another table. This time Alan didn't smile.

'You don't give a toss what you say to upset others, do you? But if they get back at you, look out — you squeal like hell.' Lee felt easier for recognising the truth of the statement. He stayed silent. A moment passed. Alan began cutting his food again. 'You're a mess, Sunshine,' he said blandly.

It was Lee's turn to be stung. 'Stop calling me Sunshine!' he said loudly. At the next table, a diner turned a surprised head. Lee felt foolish. He sat in silence as Alan chewed and swallowed angrily.

'What time do we get back home?' Lee asked, fed-up with the long day and suddenly dispirited.

'When I get us there.' The response was sharp with irritation. Alan dropped his wrists again. 'You're pure one hundred per cent mother's boy, aren't you?' he sneered. Finding no response, he peremptorily wiped his plate clean and pushed it aside.

Lee felt the energy drain from him. Into the void came the question, 'Why does he hate me?'

'Why do you hate me?' he asked.

The question shocked Alan. He examined the boy's tight, tired face for sarcasm or irony. There was none. 'I don't hate you. The hate's all in you. You resent me because –' the man paused. Seeing the small hesitation, Lee looked up. 'You know as well as I do. Because your mother and me . . .' Again he paused.

Lee winced. 'You always drag it back to her,' he cried. Again the man at the next table glanced over, then back.

Alan shook his head. 'You can't take it, can you? I thought you'd grown up a bit, being sent away to your uncle.' Then, suddenly aggressive, picking up his knife and pointing it; 'I pay my way in that house.'

'I know,' said Lee, wretchedly.

'I look out for Val and for you.'

'Oh sure.'

'I do. Yes, I do. But you can't see past the bed, can you?' Alan threw his knife to the table. The raised voices had attracted attention. Behind the counter, a woman paused in handing over change to a driver. Both stared.

Lee was deeply embarrassed; deeply resentful at this public display of private troubles. 'Shut up, Alan' he said.

Alan was hot and angry now. 'You, your father, your uncle – you're all soft, Sunshine, soft. No guts; no balls.'

Lee was on his feet before he realised it. He picked up his anorak.

'Yeah,' jeered Alan. 'Walk away. That's something you can do!' and, as the boy moved fast to the door, 'piss off!'

Lee pushed the door open and walked, stiff with anger and confusion, almost in tears, out into the cooling darkness and away, fast, from the parked lorries. A raised section of the M6 was visible in the distance, high and lit. He walked faster towards it.

Back at the table, Alan looked round. The few glances he met fell away. Coldly furious, he felt for a local evening paper in the coat at his side and unfolded it. He didn't know if Lee would wait at the locked cab, and didn't care. He turned to the sports page and reached for his thick cup of tea.

It was about ten when Alan reached Val's house. He drew up opposite, and let the engine idle, as he concentrated on the

111

downstairs lights and pictured Val waiting for his return with her son. He briefly considered driving away, avoiding the scene he knew he was about to endure. He had called for a few drinks and could feel them catching up. He swore beneath his breath, switched off and jumped down from the cab.

He dropped his coat in the kitchen, hearing Val's cheery greeting, as he walked through to where she was already turning off the television programme to welcome the men home in the living-room.

She saw his face. 'Hello,' she said again, looking puzzled and, glancing towards the kitchen, she asked, 'where's Lee?' Alan sat down heavily. Val switched her attention back to him. She smiled uncertainly. 'Where's Lee?' she repeated, and, receiving no reply, 'has he had an accident? Is this a joke?' She was still smiling.

'He'll be home. Just as fast as he can pull himself along the umbilical.'

Val was puzzled. She moved warily to stand before him, watchful of his mood. 'Have you been drinking?' she asked.

Alan nodded emphatically, keeping his eyes down. 'I have been drinking,' he affirmed.

Val felt her heart sink. 'What happened?' she asked quietly.

'We parted company.' His eyes stayed carefully down. He added, 'I was in two minds about coming back myself'. He leaned back. 'I'm tired.'

Val didn't move. Her voice hardened. 'Are you telling me you dumped him?'

For the first time, he looked up at her. 'He's not a child. He can look after himself.'

Val asked, composed, 'Where is he?'

'Carlisle', he replied. 'Penrith, Preston. How do I know'. The moment took a sharp focus of imminent danger. Each knew it. Alan's eyes dropped down. Val moved into the kitchen.

She walked to the cooker and turned it off: there was to be no welcoming meal. Alan appeared uneasily in the doorway behind her.

'How about a cuppa then?' he asked gently, trying for normality.

She kept her back firmly to him, unwilling to show her distress. 'You know where everything is,' she said.

Alan moved to collect the cups, glancing towards her, now irritated.

'What did you mean,' she asked, 'in two minds about coming back?'

The man was suddenly fed-up with the whole miserable business. 'I'm just a simple guy, Val. I don't want hassles, or complications, or agonisings.' He banged the cups down and moved to the fridge for milk.

'You think I do?' Val's voice rose.

'I never drifted through life like he does,' he said, his voice rising to match hers. 'I had my share of problems, like anybody else, but I never made my life a misery. Or anybody else's.'

He did not dare move past her to the cooker, to boil the kettle. She turned to him. Very quietly she asked, 'What did you think of the place where I was born?' Her calmness unnerved him; he made no reply. She took a step towards him. Again that calmness. 'I know you told Lee how wonderful it was. What did you really think?'

Alan could see no direction to the conversation and looked at her, puzzled. She laughed quietly at his lack of understanding and came closer to him. Their eyes locked, above the table.

'I had a father,' she began, 'whose every word was Holy Writ and who was ignorant about anything, except how to bring animals up alive and keep them living until he wanted them dead. He cared more for them than he did for me — except that maybe I'd make good breeding stock when it came to it.' Alan could still find no direction. If the words had not been calm, he would have believed her to be hysterical. She went on, 'I had a mother who wanted no hassles or complications, no agonising, so she let it be; there had to be a master. So she cooked, she worked, she brought me and Morgan up. She taught herself to keep accounts and learned to keep her mouth shut and her eyes closed.'

Her voice had risen in intensity. He recognised the need she had to explain, but still could not understand what. She took a quick step nearer the table. Their eyes stayed threaded together.

'I said to myself,' Val continued, emotion hardening behind her words, 'I said to myself that there must be more to life than this. I said to myself: if ever I have children, they'll be free to do what they want.'

Alan suddenly saw the shape of her thought and opened his mouth to turn the argument, but she gave him no chance. 'When I was Lee's age, I left home for any job, anywhere. At my father's funeral my mother told me I'd broken his heart.' Her eyes filled with tears. 'So don't talk to me about lives made a misery. If my son doesn't live up to your high-and-mighty standards, at least he's living his own life the way he wants.

Don't blame him. Blame me. You just don't know the alternative.'

Val's passion intimidated Alan. He had never seen her so moved. She held him like a puppeteer. 'Do you want to go?' she asked bluntly.

Alan cleared his throat. He began to speak, but she cut through his evasions. 'Do you want to go?'

Quietly, he began, 'I've tried, Val. I've given.'

'Try harder. Give more. Don't just take.' Her intensity held. 'You're a selfish bastard, Alan', she said bitterly. 'I grew up expert on that. I cut my teeth on being expected only to give and be grateful.'

He could take no more. He picked up his coat and moved to the outside door, cold, insulted, angry.

'He hasn't got a key!' Val shouted despairingly at his back.

'Tough!' he said, slamming the door behind him.

Val stood at the table marooned by the ebbing of her intensity. After what seemed an age, she heard the truck engine turn, catch and fire. She heard its rumbling progress through the estate, into silence. She rubbed her eyes, guiltily, and sat at the table, feeling unhappy and confused, wondering what she had just done and where her son was.

Her son was in the passenger seat of a Cortina belonging to a rep returning late to Blackburn. Lee had also been in a Citroen 2CV and would travel in a Volvo, jammed among a well-spoken family who were into wholemeal bread and organic vegetables, before being dropped at Prestbury, where he would phone Colin who came in a taxi to collect him.

Downstairs, in Colin's home, they smoked a quiet cigarette together before making up a bed on the sofa. Lee related the whole day, exaggerating nothing, leaving nothing out. His mate listened until the very end.

'Two things about a man you should never criticise,' Colin said sagely. 'His driving and his masculinity'.

Too tired to disagree, Lee kicked his shoes from his aching feet and nodded in agreement. 'Now you tell me,' he muttered.

When Val listlessly opened her front door to take in the milk, Lee was on the doorstep, curled up for warmth. It was seven o'clock. She had spent a wretched night, hoping for his return, but despairing also at the idea of driving Alan away. Needing anything, rather than the empty house and the thoughts and fears moving endlessly round her tired head, she picked up the bottles and moved wordlessly inside, leaving open the door. After a while, Lee followed.

The boy stood in the hall, unwilling to progress further. Shutting the fridge door and seeing his stillness, Val reassured him.

'Come on,' she said dully. 'He's at work.' She straightened up. 'I suppose he's at work,' she added. Lee came into the room and sat silently at the table as his mother lit the gas and set the kettle above the flame. She remembered there was supper for three congealed in the cooker. 'I waited up till two. Why didn't you come home?' she said. 'Why didn't you phone?'

Lee recognised the stress in her. 'I stayed with Colin.' Val pulled composure round her, fearful to let the boy see her upset and identify it as the loss of Alan. 'What did he tell you?' Lee asked, in a monotone.

Val tried desperately to make light of her fears. 'Just that you'd had some sort of row.' She moved behind him, wanting and not wanting to put her around his stiff, unyielding shoulders; above all, not wanting to blame him for Alan's absence, which weighed in her heart like lead. 'Then we had some sort of row,' she added, 'and' – lamely – 'he sort of went.' Her eyes began to fill. Angrily she fought them. 'Sorry,' she said, 'I'm just tired,' rubbing her eyes quickly. She turned towards Lee. 'He didn't mean it, love.' She sat opposite him. 'He's not used to families. It's not his fault.' She was passionate in his defence.

Lee knew she needed Alan. The urgency of her words and her distress made it quite clear just how much. He nodded, suddenly so sorry for her. He knew the cost to her of the humiliation at having to show it, and looked at her exhausted, anxious face. Unable to bear his glance, aware she was letting him down in excusing the man, she twisted in the chair, trying hard for the light mood that would not come.

'So you stayed with Colin.' She attempted chattiness. 'Anyway, we'll all get over it. We'll manage, yes?' Her words fell into a void of silence. She felt humiliated and twisted back to face him. 'What happened?' she asked, half-accusingly.

Lee could not bear her distress. He forced a small kind smile. 'I fell off the back of a lorry.' His eyes said: I understand.

His kindness split her resolution totally. She stood, tears sliding over her cheeks and, her back to him, lied that she'd go and get dressed, told him to make himself a coffee, barely able to speak. His sympathetic stillness drove her finally from the room. When she was able to face him again, half an hour later, he was gone. He had turned off the flame beneath the cooker. That one small act released the floodgate. She wept uncontrollably, not knowing whom she had lost nor why, blaming herself for either or both.

Lee waited at the depot gates for almost an hour before the familiar truck rolled towards him. Seeing the boy step forward, Alan slowed, then braked. He wound down the window. They looked at each other in silence. It was Alan who eventually spoke.

'Things just came to a head.' He shifted the gear lever, his foot on the clutch: reverse, neutral, first, neutral. 'I shouldn't have . . .' The words tailed away. 'You know what I mean?'

Lee nodded. Alan stopped fidgeting. 'She's okay, is she?' he asked carefully, needing to know.

'Go home tonight, Alan.' Lee was very calm.

Alan fidgeted through the gears again. 'Maybe,' he said. 'It's not as easy as that.' Neutral, top, second, reverse.

'Alan,' the boy said, calm and strong. 'Just go home tonight.' He turned and walked away.

Alan called after him. 'We ought to talk. If it happens again . . .' Once more the words fell into space. Lee turned.

'It won't,' he said. Lee watched Alan carefully, then turned and walked from the depot.

Alan watched him go. A shout behind jolted him back to where he was blocking the path of a van. He wound up the window and found the low gear. Slowly and evenly the truck moved forward, passing Lee who kept his head down. It did not stop again but gathered a little speed and, at the junction ahead, indicated left and slid from Lee's sight.

Chapter Five

Lee moved back to Wales and it was no great drama. Val made token remonstrances but knew, in letting him see her need for Alan, that she had in some way rejected him and, in her complex of emotions, did not want to bear his reproaches, imagined or real. Alan returned to her house after two days to find Lee already gone. Neither told her of Lee's last visit to the depot, and Val's relationship with Alan took on a new aspect: she had revealed a secret part of herself to him which he came to explore and exploit.

The boy hitched to Abergavenny, which took him most of Tuesday. When Morgan returned to the Land Rover in the market car park, he found Lee seated in the back. There was no show of emotion and no call for explanation: Morgan was quietly delighted to have him back. A few days later Lee told him some of the events and conflicts which had happened, and he made little comment, which pleased them both. Lee settled back gratefully into the simple routine.

Lee was surprised to find Matthew spending much of his time with Morgan and Pugh, helping out where he could. Matthew was glad to have Lee back but his failure to support his friend in the confrontation, and the memory of the horrendous party at Plas Newydd was not easily accepted by Lee, in spite of all Matthew's efforts, and Lee was generally quieter, more self-contained. Occasionally he was likely to turn upon Matthew, Morgan and particularly Pugh, when he remembered the distress of his mother at losing her lover — which stayed bitter and hard in him. Pugh tried, mistakenly, to joke him from such moods, whereas Morgan and Matthew generally ignored them. Morgan saw the split between Lee and his friend and it saddened him; he made a point of putting them together when a job needed sharing. Lee, for his part, was aware of visiting his moods upon the others but could not, or would not, make much of an effort to change. Sometimes he felt a strange satisfaction in the role of not-quite-secret sufferer. The emotional stalemate was broken by the arrival of Matthew's sister, Louise.

When Lee had been back at Blainau for five days, and Matthew and he were stacking logs around the living-room fire, Matthew confronted him with the unfairness of his selfishness.

'I deserve it — if it helps. Morgan doesn't. Pugh doesn't.' Lee handed more logs to the boy, knelt to build up the stock.

'Bad times at home,' he replied aggressively. 'Okay?'

'So you had a tough time in Manchester. You're not in Manchester now. Look' — he stood before Lee — 'come down tonight and we'll go out for a drink or whatever you like. Just take it easy.'

Lee looked at Matthew's earnest face and suddenly wanted things to be as they once were. Matthew saw his hesitation. He smiled. 'You're not exactly perfect, yourself.'

Lee shrugged non-committally as Matthew pressed on. 'I'll pick you up here. Seven-thirty; eight.' Lee nodded. Sensing he should leave the subject, having at least not been rebuffed, Matthew asked, 'What do you want me to do now?'

Lee, too, was content to leave it there. 'I'll go and help Pugh,' he said.

Matthew nodded. 'Okay, I'll help Morgan.'

Neither moved. Then Lee turned towards the door. Matthew, relieved, was about to follow when the stack of logs collapsed and, muttering, he turned to rebuild them.

That evening Lee cycled down to Plas Newydd. He was pleased with his bike — he had seen it before he had returned home, advertised on a card in the Talgarth newsagent's shop and, feeling a need for a mild independence, had called on the vendor and bought it cheaply. He pedalled along the winding back road, sitting back occasionally on the saddle to blow on cold hands. It was the end of March and, though early spring was just apparent, the evenings were still chilly. The great ruin of the house appeared and he skidded the bike into the drive, leant it against the wall near Matthew's Honda and, shaking his fingers to restore their circulation, ambled — a little self-consciously — to the door. He had not been here since the party. He rang the bell and blew again on his hands.

The door was opened by the most beautiful girl he had ever

seen. Louise was slim, nineteen; a cascade of blonde hair fell beyond her shoulders. Lee gaped – hands still clenched at his lips. She raised an imperious eyebrow in enquiry.

'Matthew.' Lee heard his voice crack and cursed his rough working clothes, which were being swiftly and expertly scrutinised. Then Louise turned, without a word, and stepped back into the hall. Lee's eyes fell instinctively to her long legs in fashion jeans. She wore a waistcoat over an expensive-looking shirt.

'Matthew?' Louise called from the foot of the stairs and, without a second look at Lee, walked elegantly into the living-room.

Lee stood in the open doorway, deeply impressed, staring at the space that the vision had recently inhabited.

Eileen looked out from the kitchen. 'Close the door,' she said. 'This house is hard enough to heat. Come and talk to me.' Her head vanished from sight. Lee hastily moved into the hall, closing the door tight behind him.

Eileen was laying the table. 'Why haven't you been to see us since your return from civilisation?' she demanded, dropping the last cutlery into place.

'There's a lot to do on the farm,' he replied, uneasily. Eileen bent to check something in the oven.

'So Matthew tells us. I suppose he should know: he seems to spend most of his time there.' She straightened. Lee said nothing. Eileen's frightening behaviour of a fortnight ago was a sharp memory; he didn't intend to cross the woman again. Some similar thought must have slid into Eileen's mind. 'Did Bwana ever pay you for your work at our fiasco of a party?' Lee nodded and she saw his uneasiness. 'You don't want to take much notice of us; you're too young to be prudish.' Lee realised he was being apologised to, and was seeking a neutral response when the girl came into the kitchen and made for the fridge.

'Are you looking after Himself?' smiled Eileen.

Louise smiled back, taking ice from the freezer. 'Himself and I are getting on very well.'

'Plenty of ice,' Eileen suggested. 'It may cool him down.'

Louise smiled again and broke cubes into a dish.

'Keep him at arm's length, and don't let him drink himself stupid, and remind him we eat within the hour.' Eileen took the icetray to the tap.

Louise grinned. 'Don't worry,' she said and moved to the door, throwing a cool, cursory glance at Lee who gave what he hoped was a suave smile. She and Matthew crossed in the doorway.

119

Climbing the vast staircase, fast, and once out of earshot, Lee put out a hand to halt Matthew. 'Who the hell is that smart piece?' he asked urgently.

Matthew looked at him blankly. 'Louise,' he said, as if it were a fact universally known.

'She's a bit of all right,' Lee grinned foolishly, lasciviously.

'My sister,' said Matthew, continuing on his way.

Lee gulped. 'Sorry,' he said as he followed.

Lee helped Matthew move his clothes and bed-linen from his room to make way for Louise. Matthew was quite resigned to such treatment: unthinkable that a beautiful and sophisticated girl should sleep − as he would have to − in Harry's study − a small, crumbling room, barely waterproof, where he occasionally took refuge from Eileen − on a shaky camp-bed which the Captain had kept from his war-service.

'She gets the full treatment,' Matthew said, a shade proudly. 'It's always like that with Louise.' Among her other habits, Lee learned that she frequently turned up, at whim, unexpected and unannounced. The boy was amazed that Matthew had never mentioned her. 'I did,' he denied. 'I told you I had a sister.'

'You never said she was like that,' Lee complained. Matthew grinned as they took another load downstairs.

Lee was an only child. He tried to imagine what it would be like to have Louise as a sister, but her physical attraction was too much of an obstruction. Back in the room they made up her bed and brought up her luggage. Lee was delighted at the three cases which meant, presumably, that she intended to stay for some time, though Matthew did not know. In fact, Matthew seemed neither to know nor to care much about his sister altogether. He did know Louise liked riding and was to ride, the next day, with a local pony-trekking centre, managed by a man Lee had seen several times, on the common and the roads, called Boulton. They had once had an argument when Lee, exasperated at being trapped behind the plodding line of ponies, on the tractor, had eased his noisy way past, alarming the riders. Morgan and Pugh were scornful about the extensive trekking, which fouled the roads in summer and had turned narrow sheep-tracks in the hills to wide avenues of mud in spring and autumn. Nobody liked Boulton.

Louise had excited Lee: he had never met anybody like her before and he grew exasperated at Matthew's seeming disinterest. When the room was finally fit for such a grand presence and he was about to cycle back, he asked Matthew tentatively if he were intending to work the next day at Blainau and, if so, would he lend Lee the motorbike. Matthew agreed, pleased to see his friendship with Lee moving back towards how it had been. Lee was so profusely grateful that Matthew began to laugh.

'What's the matter? What's funny?'

'You're talking; you're smiling. It's a transformation.'

Lee smiled and agreed. They sprayed the room with one of Eileen's perfumed air-fresheners and left.

At precisely eleven o'clock the next morning, Lee sat astride the Honda Super Dream on the high point of the common, waiting for Boulton's string of ponies to appear along a broad, rutted avenue running down from the base of the hills. He wore his new anorak and best jeans; he had washed the mud and grime from his training shoes.

The line of ponies swayed slowly down, on time. Since it was midweek the trek only comprised six riders, led by Boulton, a small, dark Englishman who made the point frequently that it took the English to show the Welsh a good thing from the point of view of business. This did not endear him to the locals. As Boulton's mount picked its way along the avenue, Lee fired the bike and turned a slow circle to face the avenue. He recognised Louise at the back of the string.

Plodding its tedious way, the trek inched onto the common. Behind Boulton was a woman in middle age, then three children, then a man with a beard and, finally, Louise. Only she and Boulton were in full riding gear. The woman and the children bumped in the saddles like sacks. The beard swayed showily, but his jeans and sweater gave him away. Lee grinned and waited until they were well onto the common before gunning the bike noisily forward, hoping his own lack of experience would not be as apparent. He swooped down upon them from his vantage point.

Boulton twisted round in his saddle at the sound of the approaching bike, frowning as he saw its direction, and glanced behind him where his riders' attention was also being drawn to the machine. The ponies plodded lethargically on, all except Boulton's special mount, interested only in keeping the tails of their predecessors before their own noses. A child tugged nervously and unnecessarily at the reins. The beard glanced imperiously towards the advancing Honda.

Lee opened the throttle further. He was about two hundred yards away, heading for the centre of the line. Another child called nervously to her pony. Boulton gave some smooth advice.

'Hold them tight. Turn the heads away if they seem nervous. Don't worry.' He waved a stiff arm dramatically, as if warding off an attack. 'Get away. Go on: get away!' he shouted at Lee.

Lee throttled back and drove a wide circle round the blank-faced riders. A pony or two looked up from the tail ahead. Lee circled them again. The beard's pony danced a little, sideways, as the bike came past and the man made a great show of controlling it. Boulton raised a vertical arm and the string ground to a halt. Lee passed Louise who looked down on him coolly, with the trace of a grin, then he was moving round again towards Boulton, who shouted.

'Will you get away!'

Lee took the bike out of gear and considered Boulton's furious face. 'It's common land,' he called back.

'This is not a road. It's a footpath.'

'You're not on foot.'

Lee clicked the Honda into gear and began to circle. He looked up at Louise: she was definitely smiling. He grinned at her. The beard looked haughtily away and the woman coughed. A child giggled.

'Let's be sensible,' pleaded Boulton, trying not to grit his teeth. 'I've got people in the group not used to ponies.'

'Shouldn't be riding then.'

'Go away!' shouted Boulton. Lee peeped his horn. Boulton regained his composure. Two ponies bent their necks down to chew grass. The smallest child tugged its animal's head back to tail-height. The pony, irritated, danced a little and the child almost lost the stirrup. Gathering dignity, Boulton called out smoothly.

'Let's press on please.'

He tapped his heels smartly on his pony's flanks. Seeing tails flick and progress, the ponies plodded forward, past Lee. As Louise rode by, he called out, 'I bet he promised you a long gallop along the bottom of the hills. You won't get it. He always says this. It never happens.'

Boulton, who had recently promised his string a long exciting gallop on the last stretch home, turned in his saddle angrily. He met the enquiring eyes of the woman behind him who had been looking forward to it. Lee revved the bike.

'It's boring that way.'

He moved towards the distant Blainau road. Louise glanced towards him. Lee looked over his shoulder and smiled. He beeped his horn again.

'Take no notice of the fool!' called Boulton.

'Boring!' called Lee, revving the engine again. The string plodded across the common, Boulton sideways in the saddle, glaring back, his left hand on hip.

Louise thought: why not? She clicked her tongue and wheeled her pony from the line and expertly urged it into an easy canter towards Lee, waiting hopefully a hundred yards away. Boulton was amazed and furious, unused to having his authority flouted.

'Where do you think you're going? Come back here!'

Louise cantered past Lee. 'Which way?' she called. Lee revved his bike ahead, leading her. Boulton swung his pony's head round, determined to chase. Automatically the second pony followed, and the third. Nervous murmurs rose.

'Better dismount! Everybody dismount!'

With varying degrees of expertise, the riders kicked their feet from the stirrups and swung from the saddles. Lee and Louise were on the edge of the common, about to vanish in the trees lining the Blainau road. Boulton doubted he would even catch them and gave up.

'Everybody back in their saddles then.'

The last of the children had just made it to the ground and all five novices began the more difficult task of mounting. Boulton heard the beard mutter and the children giggle. The woman behind him sighed loudly. Boulton ground his teeth in exasperation, and by the time he had his plodding customers on the move again, Lee and Louise were laughing together as they made for Blainau, just coming in sight.

No one was at the farm. Lee propped the Honda on its stand and showed Louise where to tether the pony.

'You were right,' she laughed. 'He did promise a gallop.'

'Knew he would,' Lee replied suavely. 'He's a right wally, that Boulton.'

He related a few of the locals' comments on the man as they moved inside.

Louise looked round the living-room, which was shabby and dark. Lee was apologetic. 'It's a bit of a mess,' he said. 'Didn't really think I'd get you here. We only light a fire at nights,' he added, wondering if he should build one now.

'I'm not cold.' Louise wandered round the room, looking at the pictures, fingering the occasional knick-knack of which Morgan's mother seemed to have been so fond.

'Who lives here besides you?'

'Just my uncle.'

Louise moved into the kitchen. 'Where's my brother?' she asked idly.

'Working outside somewhere.' Lee kept very close to Louise, aware that he was building an image which he would have to maintain.

'Tea?' he asked. 'Coffee?' He thought of the image. 'Whisky?'

'Black coffee,' she replied. 'No sugar.'

Lee rushed to boil the kettle, suddenly aware of the greasy and stained cooker. 'Chair,' he said, flicking one out for her from the table as he passed. She sat, smiling, looking round.

'That was really good,' she said quietly, 'the way you pissed that man around. I liked it.'

Lee was deeply gratified. He moved from the cooker to stand the other side of the table. Her bright, clear eyes rose to meet his.

'Do you ride?' she asked.

'Sure,' lied Lee, hoping it wasn't too hard.

'Have you got ponies on the farm?'

'Got one.'

'We could go out tomorrow, if you're not working.'

Lee's excitement began to intensify. He pulled his image tighter around him.

'I please myself about work.'

'That's a bit of an accent.' She smiled.

Lee shrugged, thinking that her cut-glass Home Counties boarding school voice might also be a bit of an accent, but deciding not to push his luck. Instead, he reached for his cigarettes on the table.

'Yeah. Well, I move about.'

'I don't like smokers.'

Lee paused briefly. He pushed the cigarette back into the pack and tossed it nonchalantly on the table.

'You were looking for me specially then?'

Lee cast briefly about for an impressively cool reply, but failed. He fell back on the simple truth.

'Yeah,' he said, quietly.

Louise enjoyed that. Lee enjoyed her pleasure.

'Lee.' She drew his name experimentally on her tongue. 'I like your name.'

'I like yours,' he said quickly.

She grimaced. 'Puke-making cute.'

The porch-door opened and Morgan came in. Seeing Lee, he

entered the kitchen and stopped, noticing Louise at his table. Lee proudly hastened to make introductions.

'This is Matthew's sister, Morgan,' and to Louise: 'my uncle.'

Louise was polite and charming. 'Hello,' she said. 'I like your farm.'

To Lee's dismay Morgan was cold and offhand. He ignored her, merely asking the boy if the kettle was on the go. Knowing well that Morgan could see it was, Lee tried to crowd Morgan into civility.

'Louise ran off from Boulton's string on the common,' he grinned, aware of Morgan's feelings towards the man.

Morgan washed his hands. 'She'll get some stick when she takes the pony back,' he said.

Lee was annoyed. 'No she won't. Boulton never gets back to the Trek Centre before three.' Morgan moved to the roller towel.

'I'd better get the pony home before three then.' Louise stayed charming, indifferent to Morgan's behaviour.

Lee turned to her. 'How will you get back to Plas Newydd afterwards?' He was full of concern. 'Matthew can take you on the Honda. I've got the spare helmet.' He turned back to Morgan. 'That's okay, isn't it, Morgan? He can go early?'

Morgan turned from the roller towel. His eyes briefly met Louise's charm and swivelled away. 'I expect he can,' he said. 'Is Pugh down for his tea yet, or the lad?' Hardly waiting for Lee's reply, Morgan moved into the adjoining room.

Louise was amused at Lee's concern for Morgan's brusqueness. She rose from the table. 'I think I'd better go,' she said.

Lee moved swiftly close. 'Don't take any notice. He's not used to having people about.'

Louise thought it over a second. She was used to having people like her, if she chose — as she had chosen that Lee should. 'I'll make the drinks,' she said, pulling cups from the dresser hooks and taking them to the table. She turned her eyes wide upon his. 'And you're still on for riding tomorrow?'

Lost in the exciting depths of her eyes, Lee nodded violently. She laughed at the puppetlike motion. Smiling widely, Lee said 'It's two coffees, three teas then.' She found the tea caddy and pot.

Mimicking his accent she intoned, 'Two coffees, three teas, comin' oop.' Lee laughed.

*　　*　　*

In the kitchen of Plas Newydd Eileen and Harry Gregory sat, wrapped against the mid-Wales spring, waiting for Louise to come down. He gloomily cradled a tumbler of Scotch, while she checked the temperature of the Aga's oven. They had just taken a phone call from Boulton, from the Castle Inn, where the trek stopped for a packed lunch.

'Boulton is a repulsive little man.' Eileen moved to gather up her own glass. She had never met Boulton.

'Be that as it may,' Harry replied. 'One of us is going to have to say something to the girl.'

They heard her come along the passage and Eileen laughed shortly. 'If you feel the compulsion to speak, then speak.'

Harry rose and held the sherry bottle to the light. There were a few measures left. He collected a glass as Louise breezed in. 'Sherry?' he asked. Louise smiled.

'Please.' He poured a precise measure and handed it to her, sitting again to nurse his tumbler. Louise noticed a chill in the air, not wholly due to the climate.

'I'm sorry to be so early.'

'It's only a casserole,' Eileen said. 'It'll be ten minutes.'

Harry felt the need to speak. 'We had notice of your early return. An irate Mr Boulton rang.' Louise moved to stand beside Eileen, knowing where support would be.

'He has nothing to complain about. The pony's groomed and stabled. I paid for the whole day; he's lucky I'm not demanding a refund.'

Eileen smiled and sipped her gin and tonic. 'Repulsive little man,' she smiled conspiratorially at Louise.

'So you keep on saying,' murmured Harry.

'He'd phoned his wife, too,' Louise said happily. 'I was expected. She blathered on about the dangers of riding off alone and how much I'd upset her husband. Cheers.'

She sipped her sherry, thinking she had killed the topic, but Harry murmured that Mrs Boulton had a point. But Eileen was scathing. 'What possible harm could Louise come to in piddling little hills like these?' The girl nodded in agreement.

'In any case,' Louise continued, indignantly, 'we weren't even riding in the hills. I was lured from the common by that strange young man with the accent who was here last night.'

She felt that the revelation had not gone down too well. They disapprove, she thought; so much the better.

126

'Did you go to the farm and see Matthew?' Eileen was sharp in her question. They disapprove of Matthew's being there, too, thought Louise. She was non-committal: he'd been about somewhere. She saw a glance flash between the Gregorys. God, she thought, they're so dreary.

'Plenty for young Matthew to do here,' grumbled Harry.

'He spends far too much of his time on that farm,' agreed Eileen, for once. Louise decided to stir the evident resentment. She smiled charmingly.

'Can you sort me out a pony from somewhere else? I said I'd go out tomorrow with Lee. That's all right, I suppose, since he's a friend of Matthew's?'

They didn't like that. 'We can phone round,' Harry said unenthusiastically. Louise smiled and kissed Eileen.

'What did you say to Mrs Boulton?' the woman asked.

'I told her I hired the company of the pony, not that of her husband, and on balance I preferred the pony.'

It was the right thing to say. Eileen laughed loudly and clapped an appreciative hand on the table. Harry chuckled into his Scotch. Louise grinned and drained the sherry glass which Harry rose instantly to refill.

Louise was proving a sharper cause of conflict at Blainau. Lee and Morgan, alone, confronted each other across the living-room. It was the first time they had been angry with each other.

'You didn't have to be rude.'

'Damn, boy, and if I'd wanted to be rude, you'd have seen me bloody rude.'

'So what was wrong?'

'Nothing was wrong.'

'You keep on saying that,' protested Lee. 'Something was wrong.'

Morgan made no reply. Their eyes stayed locked together.

'I told her you were shy — not used to company. I felt a right berk having to apologise for you.'

'Nobody need do that.'

'I'm telling you I did.'

'And I'm telling you, you didn't need.'

Lee shook his head in frustration. Morgan glared at him.

'By God, there's a change here,' he continued, accusingly. 'Ever since you came back from home, it's been silence, and grunting, and letting everybody know you was none too pleased and now look at you! I'm the one who's bloody rude and you can't barely shut up two seconds!'

Lee saw the truth behind this.

'Wonderful thing: a pretty girl,' Morgan concluded. Lee dropped his eyes. He moved towards his anorak, hanging near the door.

'Why be so bloody embarrassed? That's all I'm saying,' he muttered, as he felt in a pocket.

Morgan saw that he had made his point. He withdrew his glance also. 'I'm shy lately,' he said quietly.

The anger had passed. Lee came towards his uncle, holding out two ten-pound notes. Morgan raised his eyes enquiringly.

'I cashed my first Giro from the D.H.S.S.,' Lee explained. 'Take it. Food and keep and things.' Morgan shook his head. 'Go on,' Lee persisted. 'It'll buy a few more nuts and bolts to keep this place in one piece.'

Morgan took the notes. 'It's me should be paying you,' he murmured, half-ashamed. He held one of the notes towards Lee, who took it back; an honourable compromise. 'It's appreciated,' Morgan affirmed quietly, folding the note carefully.

'Morgan? Matthew's working tomorrow. There's not much to do. Can I take the morning off?'

Morgan was puzzled. A recent innovation — Lee's idea — had been a list of jobs, a rota for the Blainau workers. He had hit upon the idea, seeing a large work-chart in Alan's depot office.

'I thought we was all for keeping to the list,' Morgan protested. 'Good idea, your list — getting the jobs organised.' He had been able to tell Tom Duncan that he had four working on the farm now and the work listed efficiently. Duncan had shown polite interest, recognising Morgan's pride in this tiny efficiency. The list hung on the workshop wall and even Pugh, who seemed to find it hilarious, was careful to cross out the jobs as they were done. Morgan looked steadily at Lee who shrugged, embarrassed. A slow smile spread over Morgan's face. He looked at the ten pounds in his hand.

'I've been bribed, is it?'

Lee slowly smiled back. 'Thanks,' he said.

After an indigestible, almost indefinable supper at Plas Newydd and the ritual of coffee — instant, but served in a Royal Doulton coffee-pot — Matthew and Louise retired to Louise's temporary room. He checked a sick Angel fish but found no improvement, as she sat at the dressing-table combing her long, luxurious hair.

'Was I being obscurely warned off?'

Matthew left his tank and sat on the bed. He didn't understand.

'Warned off your thin friend and his weird farm,' she explained, feeling the flow and pull against her scalp. 'The Gregorys don't like you spending your time there.'

Matthew nodded; he knew that.

'Comb my hair for me?' Louise slipped into a little girl voice. She looked over at her brother. 'Please?'

Matthew was uneasy. He knew Louise's tricks. He had loved to play with her hair, brushing, combing, when they had been younger. The game had been mutually abandoned when he had realised the sensuous nature of the act. 'That was when we were kids,' he said quietly. Louise's voice held its childlike innocence.

'Not that long ago.'

Matthew considered. He was glad to have Louise with him. Anybody who could help dilute and divert the bitterness of Harry and Eileen would have been welcome. At length he rose without a word and moved behind her, taking the comb, knowing how to please her: light, short strokes, moving soon to harder, longer ones; the hair behind, first. Louise closed her eyes.

'Why do you put up with this place?' she murmured after a while.

'It's not for long. Only until I go to Aldershot.' He combed on, moving to the side.

'Daddy says you're mad. He told me to try to dissuade you from the Paratroops, by the way,' and, feeling him pause briefly in his practised movements, she added quickly, 'don't worry. I don't care what the hell you do.' She inclined her head forward to increase the tension of his combing. 'That's lovely,' she murmured.

Matthew combed on for a while. 'How are they?' he asked.

Louise smiled. 'Same as ever; him rushing around being big and important and her taking care that everybody can see how modestly indispensable she is.'

Matthew nodded. It sounded true enough. He found a tangle near her ear and teased it loose. He combed on, and Louise found the pressure and rhythm hypnotic. Silently she reached both arms behind her, encircling his thighs. She pulled him closer.

He stopped immediately. The game had become knowing again; he had been right – they were too old for it. Louise opened her eyes, equally aware.

'Lee's a friend of mine,' he said. A warning.

She knew instantly what he meant and released her arms, standing to take the comb from him. 'I know he is,' she replied innocently. Running the comb through her own hair, she wandered to the tank with the Angel fish and rapped the glass with her knuckle.

'Fish are cold and useless.' She glared down at them. Turning to her brother, she said angrily, 'I hate sharing a room with cold, sickly fish.' But Matthew was smiling and then giggling at her words. For a second she stared slowly at him, then she, too, was giggling. The pleasure of being together and the recent sexual tenseness broke in a boisterous return to childhood. They began shrieking helplessly. Louise fell on the bed and Matthew collapsed at her side. The laughter rang on. At a moment when it seemed likely to falter, Louise whispered, 'Hospital Game?' and that set them off again. Helpless, Louise put a hand over Matthew's mouth.

'Quiet,' she tried to say, 'or you'll have the sniffling geriatrics up here!' But that only made it worse.

The next morning Lee and the farm's sturdy Welsh pony watched each other with mutual suspicion as Morgan tightened the saddle girths. Pugh came to Lee with a switch which he had just cut from a tree. The men gave each other a conspiratorial glance: they were enjoying themselves. Lee turned to smile at Louise, already mounted and waiting.

'Get up there, Harvey Smith!' Pugh shouted, grinning.

Lee took the worn reins and lifted his left leg to slot his foot through the stirrup. The pony's misgivings having been confirmed, it began to walk towards the gate of its field. Lee was forced to hop at its side, looking ungainly and undignified.

'More like Hopalong Cassidy!' called Morgan to Louise, who laughed, and, taking pity, stepped forward to hold his pony's head. The pony stopped circling and Lee hauled himself inelegantly across its back and into the saddle. Morgan pushed and slapped the animal in Louise's direction. She called a smiling farewell and Lee nodded to them while still trying to get his foot into the stirrup. The ponies walked along the road towards the common, their riders already chattering happily.

Pugh and Morgan watched them go. 'I thought you was

taking that pony of yours up the mountain for strays,' Pugh said accusingly. 'It's down on the list, boy.'

'Let them have their fun,' Morgan murmured, watching the youngsters more further down the road.

Pugh moved away: he had a stone wall to rebuild. 'I said the famous list wouldn't last ten minutes,' he called cheerily.

On the road the hooves broke into a more rapid rhythm. Lee could be heard shouting in mock alarm and Louise laughing.

'He'll break his bloody neck,' Pugh volunteered darkly, as he crossed to the field where he was working with Matthew. But Morgan watched the couple until they rounded the bend and could only be heard. He felt an unusual and unwanted sadness: a sense of regret for what he knew to be good and enjoyable, but had never himself experienced. Cap walked over to him, wanting work. Morgan knelt thoughtfully and made a great fuss of the dog.

Lee and Louise trotted across the common in the general direction of the church. Lee was being a great success — not for his skill but for the lack of it. He played up his alarm and rueful misery, pleased at its effect, as he jiggled unevenly in the saddle like a mad puppet. Louise, rising and falling in an effortless trot, gave such advice as her laughter allowed her. Her pony broke into a canter and Morgan's followed suit. Lee was delighted: he could do that with more dignity and comfort. Louise called over that she wanted to see the church: the Gregorys had said she'd like it.

The whole day was a huge success. Louise enjoyed Llanelieu Church, pointing out the unusual features to Lee, who enjoyed feigning an interest. He preached a brief sermon from the pulpit, which was less witty than he hoped, and they rang the bells before running guiltily out to the ponies. They took sandwiches and cider at Plas Newydd, because Harry and Eileen were shopping in Hereford. They rode to the base of the ancient hill fort, Castel Dinas, and climbed on foot to the ruined keep, holding hands. They surveyed the extensive views and talked tentatively about themselves.

Lee gave more than Louise but she was skilled in encouraging this and the boy didn't notice. He told her a little about Morgan and a lot about Alan and their conflicts. Still aware of his image, he made the complications of his mother's house sound like an adult hassle, self-imposed, which he had graciously returned to resolve, for their sake. Louise pretended to be fascinated. Lee told her of Carol, leaving the impression of tragic young love unconvincingly in the air.

'What about you?' Lee asked.

'I'm not into that sort of thing. I just like good times.' Louise rose from the stones where they had been sitting. Lee sensed she had been less impressed that he had intended.

'Sure,' he agreed. 'Me, too.'

She brushed the dust from her jodhpurs. 'I get bored. That's why I came here. When I'm bored here, I'll go. So don't let me down, okay?'

Lee was not entirely sure what she meant. She explained.

'If things work out, Lee, and we get something going, then we have a good time, and when it's over, it's over; no letters or phone calls.'

Lee could hardly believe his luck. He nodded eagerly in agreement. 'That'd be boring — phone calls and letters.' She smiled at him, and held out her hand. They wandered down to the ponies. Lee was in love.

Limping into Blainau kitchen, an hour later, Lee found Pugh ready to leave and Morgan washing a deep cut on his finger from renegade barbed wire. They were amused at the boy's discomfort — the inside of his thighs ached like iron from gripping the wide saddle — and pleased at his good humour. Pugh suggested a cold shower for the cause of his problem, rather than a hot bath for the symptoms, and assured Morgan that Blainau would soon be echoing with the scamper of tiny feet. 'And I don't mean mice neither,' he said. Everyone was happy. Morgan's earlier shy misgivings seemed to have been swept away: Louise had charmed him and he found interest and pleasure in Lee's obvious delight. When Pugh had left for Talgarth, and Lee was wrapping a plaster round Morgan's wound, the boy couldn't resist capitalising on his uncle's mood.

'Are you doing anything special tonight?' Morgan looked enquiringly at him as Lee pressed home the dressing. 'Only I told Louise you'd drive us into Brecon.'

'Squared it with Mr Gregory, have she?' he asked, flexing the finger.

'Nothing to do with them,' Lee replied, affronted. 'We're not kids.'

Morgan nodded as he took the First Aid tin back to the

sideboard. 'You'll have to take a brush and cloth to the old Land Rover.'

Lee smiled. 'Thanks, Morgan,' he said warmly. 'I'll do it after my bath.'

He walked wide-legged and wincing from the room, exaggerating a little to make Morgan laugh, which it did.

They drove to Plas Newydd at eight o'clock to collect Louise. The Gregorys were not of Lee's opinion that the visit to Brecon had nothing to do with them. Eileen, in particular, was annoyed at losing Louise: the evenings were tedious enough to her, without being denied the entertainment of a girl in whose sharpness and independence she saw much of herself when young, before she had settled for Harry and the orthodoxy of marriage. Also, she resented the way Blainau seemed to be capturing her young people, and had not forgotten, or forgiven, Lee's aggressive outburst to her at the party.

Nevertheless, it was Harry who had to meet Morgan and Lee at the door and deliver Louise into their company. Matthew came to see them off, primed by his sister to reject any suggestion that he might accompany them, if Harry asked. In any case Matthew intended to spend an hour cleaning his carburettor unit on the kitchen table. Harry led them all to the door and drew Morgan back for a quiet word.

'Look, drop them off wherever you're taking them, and call in here on your way back. We'll have a drink and a chat, yes?'

Morgan sensed that this was important, noting also a touch of embarrassment. Politely, he agreed. Harry thanked him once more for driving the youngsters into Brecon and saw him to the Land Rover.

'What did he want?' asked Lee as they drove along the rutted drive to the gates.

Morgan did not know. 'Wants a chat,' he said. Lee found Louise's hand in the darkness and forgot about the Gregorys.

Harry moved into the bleak kitchen to fuel the Aga. He wondered exactly what he was going to say to Morgan. Matthew was seated at the table, before sundry parts of his Honda on a newspaper. 'She'll kill you when she sees it,' Harry said gloomily, as he tipped the coke from the hod.

The wine bar in Brecon was busy and cheerful. Lee was impressed; it had, surprisingly, been Morgan's suggestion, feeling that Louise's sophistication called for more than a pub-crawl and a

Chinese takeaway, which had been Lee's intention.

They sat at a corner table. Louise gazed round, seeing only provincial presumption. 'This place is okay,' she pronounced.

Lee agreed happily. 'Not bad.'

She laughed, trying him out. 'Come on!' she said. 'It's pathetic!'

Lee looked round again; maybe it wasn't that good. He smiled and nodded, condescendingly. 'Terrible,' he said, grimacing. Tapes played gentle Vivaldi.

'Am I going to see you tomorrow?'

Louise looked at him, tossing her head, freeing her hair. 'Let's get tonight over first.'

A waitress brought them two glasses of wine, which Louise had ordered. They sipped and looked round them. Lee wished he'd felt able to ask for beer.

'So what is Lee Turner going to do with his life?'

It was not the type of question Lee Turner was often asked, and he took another sip of the sharp white wine, wondering what answer would most impress. In truth, he was finding the image he had chosen inconvenient and ill-fitting, but was stuck with it. He smiled a worldly smile.

'It's more a case of what's life going to do with him.'

Louise raised an elegant eyebrow. 'What?' she said. 'A man of action like you?'

Lee looked at her sharply, and decided he was not being mocked. Trapped in his mantle of easy independence, he began to speak, reiterating his home difficulties, but saw Louise glancing round, bored. He stopped as soon as he could.

'I like Morgan,' Louise said suddenly.

'He's okay,' Lee affirmed. 'Just shy.'

Louise disagreed. 'He wasn't shy tonight.'

Lee hastened to prove his point. 'No, he is. He told me.' He felt a distant guilt at belittling Morgan to demonstrate his own percipience.

Louise said, 'Daddy believes being shy is being afraid.'

Lee saw a way to exonerate Morgan and keep the lofty all-knowing line.

'Morgan's not afraid of anything. The Estate — that's the people Morgan rents the farm from —' Louise nodded, interested. 'They want to take the farm away from him; it's been years in the family. Morgan really stands up to them.' Enough of Morgan, he thought. 'I got him to make a list. I'll show it to you sometime.'

He waited for her to ask details of the list, but she was gazing

134

round the wine bar. He waited for her attention to be with him again.

'I know precisely what I want from so-called life.' Lee felt she was too interested in a man at a nearby table; an older man, easy with his company, smartly-dressed.

'How d'you mean? Husband and kids and all that?' She looked at him sharply. He smiled uneasily.

'I go up to university in the autumn,' she said brightly. 'York; modern languages. I can get a good degree there. That'll take me to the Sorbonne in Paris, then I'll train as an interpreter and work my way up to simultaneous interpretation at Brussels. United Nations in New York at thirty.'

She watched him, for the effect. He almost gaped. 'If you don't know what you want,' she added airily, 'you can't moan if you don't get it. Do you want another drink?'

Lee was deeply impressed. He knew nothing of foreign languages and had never heard of simultaneous interpretation, but, whatever it was, he recognised it as extraordinary. University itself meant intelligence and determination, but Paris, Brussels and New York? The next ten years programmed. He gaped briefly and Louise laughed, gratified.

'You're amazing,' he whispered.

He could not take his eyes from her now. She looked modestly down. Vivaldi played on. He cleared his throat.

'What you said today – if things work out – about having a good time . . .'

She met his eyes.

'Yes?' she said. Lee laughed delightedly.

'You're amazing!' he repeated.

'Then things are working out,' she whispered.

Lee tried to judge her mood. Hardly daring to ask, he began, 'Only – if you wanted – tomorrow, Sunday, Morgan goes to church, and sees people. And Matthew doesn't work Sundays. Or Pugh.' She steadily held his begging eyes. 'Only – if you like – I'll be there on my own most of the day. Please.'

Louise leant forward and kissed his lips.

'I like,' she said.

Lee could hardly believe it. He leaned back and shook his head.

'You're amazing,' he said yet again.

'And hungry.'

Lee obediently dragged his eyes from her and looked around for the waitress.

*   *   *

At a different table, in Plas Newydd's kitchen, drinks were not affecting such an easy mood. Harry poured himself a Scotch and glanced uneasily at the square back of Morgan, who was sipping uncertainly at a glass of beer.

'Do you never take spirits?' he asked equably, coming to sit nearby.

'Christmas. Or when the cold's bad.'

'Wise fellow.'

Gregory took a slug of whisky and wondered how to begin.

'It's just that Eileen's a little concerned,' he said, willing to allow himself the luxury of petty disloyalty.

'There's Matthew spending quite a lot of time at your farm.' He glanced up at Morgan, meeting his frank eyes. 'We're very fond of Matthew,' he faltered. 'Naturally we like to see as much of the lad as we can.' Is this true? he thought. 'His parents are good friends of ours' — not true he thought — 'They have become good friends,' he amended. 'Please don't misunderstand me: we're delighted he's of use to you.'

Morgan wondered, yet again, why he had been asked here. He was used to oblique approaches: he himself would not dream of coming directly to the point before circling round it for a while. He pondered what he had seen of this house; not wealth, certainly.

Morgan said, 'He won't take wages.'

Dear God, thought Gregory, he thinks I want money. 'No, of course,' he said quickly. 'Good of you to offer.'

'He likes the work, he says. Building himself up for the Army.'

Gregory switched the subject: Matthew was getting in the way.

'And now there's Louise. A law unto herself.'

He smiled at Morgan who smiled back. 'Pretty girl,' he affirmed.

'Very pretty. But again, Eileen feels' — he could not stay with this sneaky disloyalty — 'and I confess I see some sense in what she says, that we'd like to see as much of Louise as we can — the more so since she could rush away at any time.' He took a drink, steeling himself. 'And this friendship with young Lee . . .'

Again, he was intimidated by Morgan's frank gaze. He fell briefly silent.

'The boy knows how to treat a lady.' It was quietly said.

Gregory ploughed on. 'We know of course that she's nineteen and appears well able to take care of herself, but . . .' he faltered again.

136

Morgan once more quietly led, helping him. 'Would Mrs Gregory think the boy's common?'

Harry was briefly appalled. And yet, maybe it was simply this. He denied the probability vehemently.

'Please, no. I wouldn't want you to think us snobs. We like Lee; of course we do. We like him very much.'

Harry did not like Lee very much; he did not like anyone very much. At this moment, he did not like himself at all. 'I'm putting this very badly,' he said.

Morgan stood. He drained the last of his beer. Gregory glanced up at him wretchedly.

'Thank you, sir, for my drink.' Morgan placed the empty glass on the table. 'He's loyal to you, that boy of mine. The night he came back after your party, he was upset — damn, he was; next morning he was back off home to his mother, so something bad must have happened. But he never would say. I'm sorry he's good enough to work when you call, but not to take the young lady out for an hour or two.'

Gregory could find nothing to say. He waved his glass in a vague conciliatory gesture. Morgan moved to the door. Gregory stood and followed him.

'Look,' he said, wanting to make peace, 'why don't I pick them up and bring them home? To save you the journey?'

Morgan made no reply. He stalked through the hall towards the front door and Harry suddenly felt dispirited and tired. He called to Morgan, needing to explain, but knowing he could not; he did not entirely understand it himself. Morgan turned at the door and read the unease in the man.

'I know, sir,' he said, quietly. 'Not your words. Not in your nature.'

Gregory was grateful. 'Goodnight, Mr Thomas,' he said, stepping past to open the door. 'Thank you for calling in.'

Morgan moved into the still, frosty night. He put on his cap.

'The young lady'll be here at eleven, sir; safe and sound.'

'I know it.'

Morgan turned and walked angrily to his Land Rover. Harry closed the door.

'Well?' asked Eileen, from the top of the stairs.

He swung round to face her. She saw his set face and felt his cold temper slap at her like a fist.

'What is it about you that forbids anybody to have any sort of fun?'

She paused at the turn in the staircase. 'I beg your pardon?' she countered aggressively. He turned dismissively and walked away towards the kitchen.

'Louise is nineteen, not nine,' he said. 'The boy, Lee, is a perfectly nice, ordinary boy.'

She would not allow herself to be crossed in this way. She moved to follow him, calling, 'It's the perfectly nice, ordinary people who turn round and do nasty, extraordinary things.'

He turned back, annoyed at the humiliation she had caused him. 'Why do you make me do these things?' he snapped. 'I realised suddenly that I had no idea – no real idea – why I was there objecting to Matthew helping him out, or why Louise –' She cut across his objection.

'You are so stupid!'

'Eileen.' Gregory took a step towards her. 'Matthew spends much of his time at Blainau: not here, yes? And Louise prefers to be out with somebody – not us – somewhere: not here. Yes?' She fought to keep her blank, defusing gaze. It did not, this time, deter the Captain. There was a brief moment of silent confrontation. Upstairs Matthew's door opened and closed. 'Think about it,' Harry said. The boy's steps creaked along the landing. The bathroom door opened, closed.

'Do you think I don't,' hissed Eileen, dangerously, as she walked into the kitchen. Gregory turned and walked towards his study, forgetting it was temporarily Matthew's bedroom.

Morgan drove home, shaved, changed into his suit, polished his shoes and scrubbed the dirt from his nails. Nobody would say he did not know how to behave in polite society. He sat for three quarters of an hour reading the flimsy, local paper, cover to cover, before starting out for Brecon.

He parked the Land Rover as close to the wine bar as he could, and climbed the stairs towards the music and chatter. At the doorway he paused, seeing young people, casually dressed; he felt out of place and awkward. Screwing his cap in his hand he stepped in, looking round for Lee and Louise.

She saw him first and was glad of the diversion. Lee had begun to be boringly sentimental.

'I think I love you.'

That had been funny enough and had set her laughing. He searched her face, bewildered, trying to understand the joke.

It was then that she saw Morgan, red-faced and ill at ease. Her laughter faltered, then increased.

'My God,' she giggled. 'The Chauffeur!'

Lee followed her gaze and was moved, knowing that Morgan had taken trouble, was feeling out of place, shy.

'Don't laugh,' he said sharply. His urgency surprised the girl. 'No,' he insisted. 'Don't laugh.' She looked at him, amazed. He really means it, she thought.

Then Morgan had seen them and was threading his way towards them. Lee got up and asked what he would drink, making much of his still-aching thighs to draw any further amusement upon himself. Louise turned her charm upon Morgan. They stayed for another half hour and were at Plas Newydd by eleven, where Matthew had been detailed to wait up for her.

Sunday was a bright, clear day of solid, early spring. On the common Louise, riding up, saw Morgan's Land Rover on its way to church. She had spent the morning avoiding the Gregorys. Eileen had been vague and distant; Harry had been overfriendly. Louise could not decide which of them bored her more. Matthew had hovered uneasily, sensing an atmosphere, but he had always been easy to deal with: she had told him simply to keep out of her way. She had also forbidden him to turn up at Blainau while she was there. Wales was proving less diverting than she had hoped. She kicked the pony hard and its pace hardened into a gallop. She hit it with her crop, sharply, enjoying the increase in speed and the living power beneath her, desperate to please and totally in her command.

Lee, meanwhile, was making a great effort to coax Blainau into cosiness. The moment Morgan left, he lit the fire, plumped the cushions and wiped down the kitchen table. He had been able to tidy his room earlier and make his bed, which he usually did only before sleeping in it; he had turned on the small electric fire as soon as he had woken. His bedroom was warm when he checked it.

He heard the pony's hooves a moment or two before Cap began barking, and was glad he had shut the dog in the workshop. As Louise spoke reassuringly to her pony, tethering it in the yard, he took a quick look round, ran a hand through his hair and checked his breath in a cupped hand. He waited for her.

Physical attraction and sexual desire were nothing new to Lee but the intensity of his feelings towards Louise produced a tension that he felt as a hardening pain in the pit of his stomach. The freedom of the farm, which he considered his, in the way the Manchester house would always be his mother's, also played a part. He was adult here; there was none of the guilt he had felt when Carol had once come to his room at home. He felt in control and vibrant. He was ready at the porch door the moment she knocked.

Louise came into the room, noticing only that there was now a fire in the range. Lee could not keep away from her. Seeing it, she moved closer and kissed him deeply. Lee felt swept away, lost, totally enchanted, in love. As he pulled her closer and met her tongue with his, she deftly disengaged, smiling softly. She moved to warm herself by the fire.

'I saw Morgan driving down to church.'

'Did he see you?' The moment the words were out, involuntary and unwanted, Lee wished them unsaid. Louise raised a cool brow.

'I expect so? Why?'

He had no answer. He asked if she'd like a coffee. She declined.

'What time will Morgan be back?' she asked.

'Sometime after one,' he said. It gave them two hours. Louise surveyed the room. 'Don't you find all this a bit oppressive?'

'It's Morgan's stuff. And his parents'.'

'Where do they live?'

Lee was sure he had told her; maybe she hadn't listened.

'They're dead. The Old Lady and Old Gentleman — that's what he calls them.' Lee smiled, hoping the quaintness would amuse or impress her. She moved towards the stairs, putting her head into the kitchen. Lee guessed she was making sure nobody else was around.

'Nobody's here,' he confirmed. She grinned at him and climbed the stairs, making them creak, deliberately finding the squeakings, even stepping back to a particularly noisy step. They laughed.

On the tiny landing, Lee pointed out the doors. 'That's the bathroom. That's Morgan's room.' Louise looked casually into the latter. 'Nothing special,' Lee apologised. 'My room's here,' he said quietly.

Louise took a step towards the door and Lee put a hand on the door handle. He felt a surge of excitement as Louise took his other hand.

'What about that one?' She was nodding towards the Old Lady's room.

'That's his mother's room.'

'But you told me she's dead.'

Lee hesitated briefly — enough for Louise to see that he was uneasy. 'I know. That's what he still calls it anyway.' She led him by the hand to the Old Lady's door.

'He keeps it locked.' Lee's excitement was immense; he found it difficult to keep his voice level. He wanted to be in his room; this was frustrating.

'Maybe she's still in there.' Louise was smiling. He smiled back as well as he could.

'Why does he keep it locked?' Oh shit, thought Lee. She's interested.

He shrugged. 'He just likes to keep it the way it was.'

'When she died?' Louise was intrigued. Lee realised he would have to bear with the diversion. It never struck him she might wish to see the room. Unwittingly, he encouraged her interest by hoping to defuse it.

'Suppose so. Actually it's a bit creepy. You know? Her clothes and things.'

'Where's the key?'

The room suddenly became dangerous. The enormity of opening the shrine to an outsider weighed hard on the boy.

'Morgan keeps it downstairs. He doesn't like anybody in there. It's sort of private and special.'

'Have you been inside?'

Lee nodded unhappily. 'Let's go to my room,' he pleaded. But Louise was interested: a secret room, locked; Lee's uneasiness; forbidden pleasures. For the first time she began to feel excited.

'Go and get the key. I want to look.' It was a direct order. Lee still could not bring himself to allow it.

'There's nothing in there.' He spoke sharply.

'You said her clothes and things are inside.'

'Please, Louise. Morgan wouldn't like it.'

She withdrew her hand from his. She turned to him. She was cold and precise. Lee felt a panic at this sudden reversal.

'I thought we had a lot in common: the way you sorted out that Boulton man; the things you've been telling me. Now you're peeing your pants in case Morgan saw me coming here, and you won't let me see this room you've got me interested in. Get the key.'

Lee stood miserably before her scorn, feeling the grand image melt away to reveal a scared kid. She laid a hand on his neck and drew him gently towards her.

'You weren't going to let me down. We were going to have fun.' She kissed him, half-forgiving. Lee's body seemed a separate entity from his mind. He turned and ran downstairs, returning immediately with the key. Hearing his hurried steps on the creaking stairs, Louise smiled.

Lee put the key in the lock. His mind briefly reasserted control.

'Don't tell Morgan.'

Louise leant her body gently along the length of his back.

'Why the hell would I want to tell Morgan?' she murmured. Lee

141

turned the key and opened the door for Louise to pass inside.

'Good God.'

Louise stood, bemused and fascinated. She looked slowly around and drew in a deep breath.

'Windows don't get opened.' Lee was apologetic. He glanced involuntarily to the open door, as if half expecting Morgan to return.

'He's keeping her locked in here, isn't he?' Louise moved to the photographs. Her eyes widened.

'These are you.' She let her eyes rove to the largest frame. 'That's got to be her and the Old Gentleman. Who are they?' She pointed out the wedding picture of Val and Ken. Lee shrugged, claiming ignorance, not wanting to provide any further interest that might prolong her visit.

'My room's next door,' he suggested feebly. She took no notice, circling the room wide-eyed, coming to the wardrobe which she opened. She drew out a frock of small, bright, floral pattern and took it to the dressing table, holding it before her, watching herself in the mirror.

'Morgan might be early coming home,' Lee said, knowing that the words were whining. And then, bewilderingly, he felt that all the excitement, the anticipation and longing had drained away. He was simply Morgan's nephew who was permitting a dreadful wrong; he just wanted her out, easily, letting him keep the tatters of his image, for dignity.

She bunched the material and buried her face in it. 'It still smells of her.' To Lee's enormous relief she replaced it, moving back to the dressing table and examining the contents.

'He locks her in this room so she can't get away.' Louise was still fascinated.

'I don't like it,' said Lee abruptly. She turned wide eyes on him.

'She probably doesn't like it either.' She put down the brushes; she took up the heavily ornate comb. She held it up as she sat down.

'Comb my hair.'

'It's all wrong. Come to my room.'

'Comb my hair.' This time it was a command.

Lee did not know what to do. He knew Morgan wouldn't be back — shouldn't be back — early. He guessed that this new, rapt Louise was beyond his experience and could become difficult. He chose to humour her, hoping to get her out of the room immediately afterwards. He stepped unwillingly behind her, taking the comb. She watched him in the mirror.

He began awkwardly, not knowing the game, but she took his hand, guiding it, training him. She closed her eyes, breathing hard as the teeth of the comb caressed her. Her obvious excitement transferred itself to Lee. He felt the pain in his stomach. She dropped her hand, leaving him to choose where and how he should comb.

'Harder.'

He combed harder, lengthening into strokes that ran from her crown to the ends of her luxuriant hair. As suddenly as it had seeped away, his sexual tension returned and hardened. She sighed, reaching round and behind to draw him tight against her. The contact electrified Lee. His hands dropped. She took her hands from his thighs and turned in the chair, twisting up in one fluent movement to lay her lips hard against his. His arms held her to him as she rolled her warm, wet mouth over his. She clasped a hand behind his neck, pulling his head closer. Their tongues twisted and lapped.

She drew away. Taking his hand, she led him the few paces to the bed.

Morgan returned, as he had promised, at one. He had wiled away the hour after the service, talking sheep with a near neighbour in the Tower Inn at Talgarth, wanting the young people at Blainau to have their time of freedom. He had no real idea of how they might have spent it; much, he imagined, as they had spent the previous evening at the wine bar, chatting, laughing. He swung the yard gate open and called to Cap to shut up.

'Here comes the master,' said Louise.

They were sitting apart, as they had felt entirely apart for most of the hour that Morgan had spent in the Talgarth pub.

Lee stood and moved vaguely to meet Morgan; he felt terrible and wished he had found the courage to tell Louise to go.

'Don't worry,' she mocked.

'I'm not worried,' he muttered. The porch door opened.

'Fun?' Louise queried. Lee had no time to decipher the code before Morgan came in, and Louise turned her bright, dangerous eyes on him.

'How's Morgan?'

He smiled. 'Not too bad.'

'Would you like a cup of tea? Lee will put the kettle on.'

'Why not?' Morgan looked round the room: the boy must have cleaned it up after he'd left for church. He approved. Lee did not move. Her brittle brightness worried him; he did not know the game she was playing.

'Lee?' The voice was sharp enough for Morgan to notice. 'Coffee for me,' she added. He dared not disobey her: he had given her total power over him. He forced himself into an appearance of ease, moving swiftly into the kitchen, straining his ears to catch the conversation.

'Not long until spring,' she smiled.

'Not too long, no,' Morgan agreed, warming his hands. Louise laughed.

'Not too bad. Not too long.'

Morgan laughed with her. 'That's the farmer for you,' he said. 'He never takes nothing for granted. The businessman — he'd say "my glass is half full"; the farmer'd tell him "Damn, mine's half empty!" '

Louise squealed with laughter as Morgan sat in his chair, gratified. Lee hurried the kettle from the sink to the cooker and lit the gas. He heard Morgan ask what they'd been doing and Louise reply that they'd been talking. Both looked up as he rushed through the door and smiled foolishly.

'Sit by me.' It was another demand. Lee sat. She looked at the men either side of her. 'So,' she asked, 'how was church?'

'Same as ever.' Morgan was slightly surprised at the question; nobody had ever wanted to know.

'Pretty.'

Morgan nodded. 'It is,' he said.

Her bright eyes stayed on him. 'Is that where the Old Lady and Gentleman are buried?'

Lee felt the beginnings of panic.

'They're there, yes.' Morgan shifted his polite gaze briefly to the boy.

'I was telling Louise about the old days.' Lee explained hurriedly.

'Fascinating!' she said.

She kept her eyes on Morgan, drawing his full attention again.

'Lee showed me the list of all the work to be done.' It was a lie. Lee forced a smile. He shrugged to Morgan.

'She was interested,' he lied, too.

Louise was pleased. The conversation was between her and Morgan but the contest had become Lee against her. She had made him lie. She asked Morgan how he would manage when Matthew joined the Army and was delighted when Lee replied, 'It won't be for a while,' with an edge of aggression, but could not identify any reason. Morgan looked from one to the other.

'The Gregorys think he spends too much time here. They don't like him slumming — their words,' she added swiftly. 'They're snobs.'

Lee stood up, drawing attention. He looked down at Louise's too-innocent face. 'Come and help me in the kitchen, Louise.' It was Lee's turn to demand. She smiled gently.

'But I want to talk to Morgan.' She looked back to the man. He had not liked 'slumming'.

'We managed without him before.'

'Yes,' said Louise with apparent concern, but you'll need all the help you can get, if the Estate's not going to take the farm back.' She saw Morgan flash a look at Lee. She had got them both. Excitement began to build in her. 'That pony of yours needs schooling by the way, Morgan,' she heard herself say.

Lee shifted uneasily somewhere behind her, and she felt her heart begin to beat faster. Thrilled, she realised that she could barely control herself.

Morgan rose, trying to conceal his anger at the confidences Lee had tossed away. Angry at them both. 'I'm away,' he muttered. 'Away to get out of this suit. Work to do.'

Louise rose, too, moving towards the fire: the excitement was driving her like an engine out of gear — wild and dangerous.

'I think Matthew should work here full time. You'd be doing him a favour. You don't think this Paratroop nonsense is actually going to happen, do you? Why doesn't he live here?' She fought to control the tremor in her voice. 'He could use the spare room.' Forcing her face into bright charm, she turned to face them.

She opened her eyes wide in mock-surprise at Lee's dismay and Morgan's set, angry face. Morgan spoke to her, low and threatening.

'Make the boy a coffee. One for yourself.'

She could not stop herself now. Apprehensive and thrilled, she spun the words breathlessly.

'It's a decent-sized room, Morgan.' She saw the hurt crease his face, saw Lee's drop wretchedly. It was too late for drawing back, even if she could. 'It's a bit stuffy and smelly, but Lee says you never open a window. It's cluttered with junk, but there are shops who'd take that sort of stuff off your hands.'

She almost fainted with fear. Then she said, 'And it's got a good bed, hasn't it, Lee?' His head stayed hung in despair. 'Lee?' she insisted. 'Hasn't the Old Lady's room got a really good bed?'

She gnawed her lower lip anxiously, expecting that whatever would happen to them all would happen now, but she was wrong.

Morgan stared at her, distastefully.

'You go now, miss.' He was quiet and disappointed. Louise, too, was disappointed. She wanted the man's feelings turned upon Lee.

'I like the dresses, by the way.' Her voice rose, losing control. She dug into her pocket and brought out the ornate comb which she began to move through her hair. 'And I liked the things in the drawer and —'

Morgan roared like a wounded beast. '*Now*, miss.' His eyes glittered, and fear thrilled her into silence. Nobody moved. Alarm held her in a new fever. Then the excitement left her. Quickly, almost timidly, she hurried to the door. As she passed Lee, she held out the comb almost as a challenge, and he took it dumbly. They heard her quick steps in the yard and, in moments which stretched unbearably, the hooves of the pony at last; and still neither moved. The gate hummed on its hinges and clanged shut. Cap barked. The hooves doubled into a canter and rapped into the distance.

Lee raised his head slowly and looked at Morgan.

'It's just a room, Morgan,' he pleaded, 'only a room.'

The blow took Lee high on his cheek and swung him off balance, felling him instantly. He felt no pain. Shocked and dazed, he lay before the fire, the comb still tight in his fist. With dignity Morgan stepped up and took it from him. Lee's senses settled. He heard the sideboard open, and the muted clink of a key. He heard Morgan's heavy steps on the stairs. Pain poured into his cheek as he propped himself up on shaking arms. A door opened and closed upstairs. Then there was silence.

Time stretched further. Lee climbed slowly to his feet and walked delicately through the porch door and into the yard. Suddenly dizzy, he leaned against cool bricks until the fuzziness cleared. He rubbed his face and made his way uphill, anywhere away from the farm and the man he had wounded so deeply.

The enormity of what she had done escaped Louise. Entirely self-centred, she saw matters only in terms of her own reactions. Once in the saddle and riding fast — too fast for the narrow, blind roads — she had almost forgotten Morgan and Lee: memory, to Louise, was self-selective. Her sudden fear, at Morgan's cry of pain, did not outlast his presence. As she kicked and flicked her pony into a wild gallop across the common, she felt only the exultation of the moment, but, moving into busier roads, slowing to a walk, her mind turned more slowly and carefully too. By the time she returned the pony to Plas Newydd's neighbours and walked the

146

final mile to the crumbled gate posts, a complicated mixture of justifications, motivations and doubts had arisen. Lee had let her down; Morgan had asked for it; she had shown them. But Matthew was Lee's friend and would soon know something of what had happened. Morgan might come to Plas Newydd. She had no intention of being belittled or found at fault. Anyway, Wales was cold and depressing. She was a child who had been secretly naughty and feared the humiliation of discovery. She told herself she was bored.

Annoyingly Matthew was in the bedroom, collecting a clean sweater. She breathlessly told him she was bored and would leave tomorrow. Pulling down one of her cases from the top of the wardrobe, she began to fill it with clothes to hand, as if the simple act would somehow bring forward the coming hours that she would be forced to act out.

Matthew watched her silently, recognising the fear and excitement underlying her false packing. It was how their games had always ended. She would not look at him.

'What's happened?'

She took no notice, finding clothes, a magazine, toiletries to throw into the case. He repeated his question.

'Have I said something's happened?' she snapped back. She swung the lid closed.

'Where are you going? Have you got money?'

She smiled absently. 'I'll go to London and cable Mummy.' She pulled a comic face. 'She fixes everything.'

'What about the Gregorys? You've only just come here.'

She glared at her brother, suddenly angry again.

'Does it matter about the Gregorys?'

The bravado deserted her. Matthew watched her levelly, seeing the moods switch and display like a kaleidoscope. He knew she had done something.

'What's wrong?' he asked quietly.

Louise wandered towards his all-action montage and traced a picture of a soldier with her forefinger. 'Lee is like you,' she mused. 'Boring.' She looked at him quickly from the corner of her eye.

Matthew was instantly alert. 'What have you done to him?'

Seeing his concern for Lee, she grew petulant. 'You're not jealous? He's not your very special little friend, like the one at prep school you used to tell me about?'

Matthew said evenly, 'Take it easy.'

'Dirty little boys together? You might be; he wasn't very good at

147

the other.' She traced the soldier again. 'Daddy thought maybe that was one of the attractions of your macho Paratroop Regiment,' she said, idly. Matthew was annoyed.

'Shut up, Louise,' he said sharply.

Instantly she turned to him, a wide-eyed child. 'Comb my hair?' she pleaded.

'What have you done?' Matthew persisted, taut and unmoving.

Suddenly she simply dropped all pretence. 'I've done something bad, bro. To your friend in the hills.'

He moved to the door.

'They won't want you. Not now. Tomorrow.' She moved towards him. 'It's private now; between Morgan and Lee.'

He looked steadily at her, unable, as he always had been, to decide if she were lying. She knew it.

'Honestly. This is the truth. Honestly.' She began to smile. 'I'm telling you the truth.' With something like despair, she felt the smile broaden. She began to laugh. She shook with laughter, but her eyes stayed troubled. When the tears began, neither could tell if she were laughing or crying. Matthew watched her, fascinated and disgusted. She held out a hand.

'I can't help you,' he said.

Louise made an immense effort. Her breathing regularised harshly. She quickly wiped her eyes with the back of a hand.

'I don't need your help!'

She stepped quickly across the room and peeled off her jacket. 'I'm taking a bath now. Maybe I'll tell you what happened later. Maybe not.'

He still hovered, not knowing what he should do. She smiled experimentally. 'Go on. Get out. I want to change.'

Still uncertain, he walked slowly out. Louise took a deep breath and began to undress. She caught herself being ogled by a fish and ogled it back, giggling. Then she was thoughtful. Then she forgot about Lee and Morgan.

It was after dark when Lee came down from the hill. He was very cold and still frightened. The pain in his cheek had subsided to a dull throbbing. He came down knowing it was all he could do. He could not run again to Manchester. Most of all he owed it to Morgan that the man should say what he must, even do what he must. He guessed that he had given Morgan possibly the worst moment of his life, apart from the two deaths his uncle still bitterly mourned.

The fire had died and the room was in darkness. Switching on the light, he saw Morgan in his chair, still in his suit, straight-backed and unblinking, hands resting on his knees.

Lee took a step into the room. He had no notion of what he could do or say to lessen the hurt and guilt. He stood silently, not daring even to look at the man. The now familiar sense of time expanding occupied him wholly.

Morgan stood and moved before him. For a while, each stood heads bowed, humble before the events of the day, then his uncle slowly raised an arm and laid it gently on the boy's shoulder.

In the hours on the hill Lee had rehearsed many possibilities, run through the likely actions, but he had not foreseen this. It broke all barriers. Lee clung to the solid body of the man, weeping, trying to explain, regretting, begging forgiveness. Morgan made gentle sounds of reassurance, moved and aware of a responsibility he had never before been called on to assume. No human being had ever clung to him for comfort or honoured him with tears.

His arms went round the boy, firm and forgiving.

'Hush now, it's just a room.'

Lee's sobbing wracked them both. 'No,' he cried. 'Not just a room.' He gasped in his distress. '*Now*, it's just a room.'

Morgan felt Lee's misery as if it were his own.

'I always ruin things when they could be good,' Lee wept. Morgan stroked the boy's head. 'My fault, Morgan, my fault. I like it here. Help me.'

And only his poor sick sheep had ever asked that of him in their dumb beseeching. He felt the tears prick his own eyes

'Hush now,' he repeated softly. 'I'll help you, son. You help me.' He encircled the boy with what he recognised as love and the sobbing slowly ebbed. 'Hush now,' he breathed.

Chapter Six

The Friday before Easter weekend, a Morris 1000 van pulled into Talgarth square and parked among the vehicles outside the small supermarket. Talgarth was busy, the increase of tourist traffic combining with the usual mêlée of locals and farming vehicles. In the bus shelter beneath the Town Hall three young boys, no older than thirteen, sat together smoking and trying to look hard. The van was remarkable for its battered state and its colouring. The original bottle-green had faded; one wing was bright blue — a replacement from a scrapyard — and the overall green was mottled where filling had been used to cover dents but not painted over. Two bright yellow stars adorned the bonnet and each of the back doors bore a Snoopy transfer. The multi-coloured vehicles had always attracted amused attention in Manchester, but in Talgarth, more accustomed to unorthodox visitors, no one gave it a second glance.

Colin, Ros — his girlfriend — and Greener stood in the queue at the checkout desk with two wire baskets of food and drink. They enquired at the till if she knew where a farm called Blane-awe could be found, but, uninterested, the blonde girl shook her head and tapped away at the growing bill.

While loading the boxes of provisions into the back of the van, Greener asked a comfortable-looking lady, hurrying by with her shopping bag, the whereabouts of the farm, Blane-awe, but she took fright at the vehicle's appearance and hurried by. Colin took a scrap of paper from his pocket and showed it to some farmers, chatting near a tractor, by the newsagent's and Ros joined them, clutching an Ordnance Survey map. Together they worked out Lee's whereabouts. As they took the road to Llanelieu, Colin peeped his horn at the three young hards in the bus shelter, but they stared blankly at the van. Laughing, the three rattled from the square in the multi-coloured transport, in search of the elusive

Blainau, which they had just learned how to pronounce.

Blainau had more than its usual share of visitors that day. While Matthew enjoyed himself hindering Lee's attempts at baking a cake, Tom Duncan was walking a high field with Morgan, Cap trotting at their side. Morgan carried his shotgun with him, broken for safety, and balanced it easily over his arm. He pointed out work recently done.

'New fence in there. That stretch down by the road hedged since last year. Ditching done tidy.' They walked along the hedgerow. 'Making the effort,' said Morgan. 'Damn and you was right, Mr Duncan, I let it go. Shock see: the old lady passing on sudden.'

Duncan paused to admire a stretch of hedging, wanting to please Morgan.

'You couldn't say I wasn't doing my best,' said Morgan, anxious for approval.

Duncan looked up to the heavy clouds gathering above the ridge. 'I've never said that, Morgan. Let's get down to the road.'

They moved along the hedgerow. About a hundred yards from Blainau Duncan's stationwagon stood, and, far in the distance, a battered van could be seen threading its way towards the farm.

'It's all mad is this,' protested Lee. 'I was taught metric.' He peered down at the ancient cookery book. 'Eight ounces?' he complained. 'What's eight ounces?'

Matthew, at the table, grinned. 'Don't ask me,' he said.

While Lee juggled with a set of scales, Matthew moved to the sideboard and took down the work-list and, with the stub of a pencil specially for the job, he marked off his day's work.

'I shan't be here on Monday.'

Lee looked up from measuring flour. 'Why not?' he asked.

'Interview at Merthyr,' replied Matthew. 'Some major at the recruiting centre.' He replaced the pencil. 'There's nothing I can do, anyway,' he said. 'I don't know anything about lambs.' Lee nodded as he carefully shook flour into the scales.

Matthew picked up his helmet. 'I'll be away then.' At that moment there was a fusillade of tooting from a car horn. Annoyed at the interruption, Lee wiped his heavily-floured hands on the roller towel. He was fed-up with people who got lost and thought farmers had nothing better to do than to point out the way back to the main road.

Ros gazed at the farm. 'Is this it?' she asked disbelievingly.

Colin folded up the map and threw it in to the back of the van.

'That's what the map says,' he replied, tooting again on the horn. Ros climbed out of the vehicle and moved to the back to free Greener and looked around again. Greener stretched and saw Matthew's Honda parked in the farmyard.

'Is that Lee's, do you think?' he asked, leaning on the gate, as Ros joined him.

'There's posh, look you,' she said in grotesque mimicry. Leaving the engine running, Col joined them. All three hung over the gate, looking round the dirty, cluttered yard. Lee appeared at the porch door and his face split into a wide grin of delight.

'You want to do something about this road,' admonished Colin sternly.

'And this address,' Ros added, smiling.

Lee hurried towards them. 'Come on in!' he shouted. 'Bring the van in the yard!'

They climbed down from the gate and Colin fiddled with the latch. Seeing his difficulty, Lee laughed and came to help him. 'How are you, Greener?' he asked.'

Greener was scrutinising the high ridge behind the farm with something like awe. 'I'm great,' he said vacantly.

Lee grabbed Ros by the shoulder and gave her a quick kiss. 'How are you, Ros?'

She kissed him back, then she too, looked round. 'This place is amazing,' she squealed. Lee swung the gate open.

'Is that yours?' said Greener, pointing to the Super Dream. Matthew had arrived at the porch.

'No, it's his — Matthew's,' grinned Lee.

Climbing back into the driving seat, Colin called equably to Matthew. 'How are you?' he shouted. Matthew said he was okay. To much unnecessary advice and insult, Colin manoeuvred the van into the yard and Greener swung the gate shut behind him. Lee looked at Matthew, grinning with pleasure.

A hundred yards away, where the road turned towards Castel Dinas, Morgan and Duncan came to the Subaru. Duncan opened the door and sat down, easing off his green gumboots. He had given no great satisfaction to Morgan.

'What do you say then, sir?' Morgan asked at last.

'The Estate needs the land. It's not personal, Morgan. I've offered you a reasonable deal and we can do more with the land than you can.'

Morgan was not pleased at the answer. He looked up at the sky to where crows wheeled, crying in the sharp air. 'I've got time yet,' he said quietly.

Duncan tossed his boots into the rear of his car. 'To do what?' he asked easily. 'It's not just a case of running a clean farm. Yes, I've seen far worse than Blainau.'

'The land's only fit for sheep,' snapped Morgan.

'Of course,' said Duncan patiently, 'but high subsidies won't last forever and your sheep aren't sufficient to support the farm.' He swung his legs into the car and shut the door, winding down the window. 'You've done your best. Times change.' Morgan would not look at him. 'You're still going to appeal to the Land Tribunal?' Duncan asked.

'I got time,' said Morgan.

Duncan nodded. He had not expected any different, 'You'll need a solicitor,' he warned, finding his car keys. 'Does your accountant know the position vis-à-vis the tenancy?' Morgan made no reply. Duncan switched on the engine and grinned up at Morgan. 'Or are you hanging on, hoping you'll get a better deal from me?'

Morgan's eyes met him squarely. 'I don't want nothing but fairness and squareness from you, sir,' he said sharply.

Duncan reached out a hand to wind up the window. 'That's what I'm trying to give,' he said, a hint of exasperation creeping into his voice. 'Thank you, Morgan. I'll see you again.' He put the car into gear and it moved away. Morgan watched it out of sight, then turned and moved towards Blainau.

In the living-room Matthew, still nursing his crash helmet, stood near the door, while Lee and Colin relaxed among boxes of provisions, a small suitcase and three plastic bags, grinning and delighted to be in each other's company again.

Colin fished in his pockets for a packet of cigarettes, and offered them to Lee who shook his head.

'No, ta. I've just given up.'

Colin smiled knowingly and shook the pack. Lee grinned and took one: he'd lasted a week.

Greener and Ros came in, Greener carrying a battered rucksack and Ros yet another plastic bag. 'It's all right for some,' she accused.

'How are my fish doing?' asked Lee, suddenly remembering.

Greener dumped the rucksack. 'Swimmingly,' he said, and they all groaned. Colin and Lee lit their cigarettes; Ros took one and lit it from Colin's. They all relaxed.

Colin looked idly over at Matthew, noticing the camouflage trousers, military boots and khaki sweater. 'What do you do here?' he asked.

Matthew shrugged. 'I help Lee.'

Lee grinned. 'He's waiting to go into the army.'

Colin twisted his face into a mask of comic disbelief. 'You must be mad,' he said.

Greener was interested, 'What branch?'

'Parachute brigade,' replied Matthew.

Colin shrieked with laughter and rocked back, hugging his knees. 'He is mad!' he yelled, and Lee grinning, replied, 'Yeah, he's a bloody nutter!' The three of them laughed. Matthew smiled, feeling redundant and out of things.

Pugh and Morgan stood looking with suspicion at the van. 'What time did they come?' said Morgan.

'I see'd the van when I come off the hill,' Pugh answered, and they both looked towards the house.

'Ain't been in yet?'

'Not my friends, boy,' said Pugh, walking towards the safety of the workshop.

The youngsters chattered happily in the living-room, each now with a can of beer.

'We're on our way to Devon,' said Ros.

Lee was scornful. 'What do you want to go to Devon for?'

'Bit of a change,' said Colin.

'You can have a bit of a change here,' suggested Lee.

Morgan pushed open the door. In the silence Morgan noticed the litter of bags, rucksack and boxes of food. In their turn they were aware of his unsmiling face and the gun in the crook of his arm.

Lee jumped up to introduce them. 'Morgan?' he said happily. 'This is Ros.' Ros grinned and said hello. Morgan looked at her bright fluorescent hair.

'How do?' he said, bemused.

'My mate Colin,' Lee pointed. 'I've told you about him.'

'Colin jumped up and put out his hand which Morgan took. 'Don't believe a word!' he said. 'How are you, Morgan?'

Morgan nodded. 'Not too bad,' he said.

Lee pushed Greener's small frame forward. 'And Greener.' The boy nodded gravely and Morgan nodded gravely back. There was an awkward pause. 'They can stay for a couple of days, can they?' To his friends he explained, 'Morgan's my uncle. This is his farm.'

'It's a great place you've got!' enthused Ros. Morgan looked at her hair and made no reply.

Lee smiled anxiously at him. 'That's okay then, is it Morgan? They can stay?'

'We brought a tent with us,' said Colin quickly and Lee stepped in to support his mate.

'It can go up just outside.'

Lee watched his uncle, hoping there would be no awkwardness. 'I expect so,' he said at last with no enthusiasm. They murmured an exaggerated, 'Thanks'.

Lee hinted to Colin 'Do you want to put the tent up now?' The boy took the hint at once.

'I'll help you,' cried Ros.

'And me,' said Greener. They all left.

Lee came up to Morgan. 'They're my mates, Morgan. Old friends.' Morgan looked steadily at him. 'The tent's for the girl, I expect.' Morgan considered this; as far as he was concerned it made no difference.

'What about the other lad?' he asked warily.

'He'll be great kipping down here on the settee. It's okay, Morgan. You'll like them; they're great. It's really good to see them again.'

'How long for?' Morgan demanded.

Lee began to feel exasperated. 'I don't know! Tonight, over the weekend! Look, they've brought their own food.'

Morgan nodded unhappily once more, as Matthew moved towards the door calling, 'I'll see you both tomorrow, okay?'

Lee, more concerned with Morgan, called over his shoulder, 'Okay, cheers, Matthew,' and Matthew left, squeezing past Pugh in the doorway. The old man had watched the happy chaos as the tent was unrolled, outside.

'My God,' he said, 'It's all coming and going today. Too damn much of it. What do you say, Morgan?'

For a moment it seemed that Morgan might agree. To Lee's delight, he said. 'It's good to see old friends; the boy's mates from home.' So saying, he followed Matthew, promising Lee he'd show Colin where the tent would best stand.

Lee knew Pugh well enough to know that the old man was uneasy and out of sorts. Long-sufferingly, he said 'All right, Pugh, what's wrong with them?'

'Hippies, boy,' the man was entirely serious.

Lee stared at him amazed. 'Hippies?' he cried. 'Hippies died out in the sixties.'

'Have you seen that van?' said Pugh. 'And there's hippies every year under the hill over towards Hay — whole camp of 'em when the mushrooms comes up in autumn. Damn mess it is too,' he muttered.

Lee was patient. 'Col's old man runs a D.I.Y. shop,' he said. 'His mother's dead and he's been working his guts out on a building site all winter.'

'Ros' mother works with Val, my Mum, and Ros helps out at a day nursery; she's just out of school, okay?' Pugh shrugged, unimpressed, as Lee felt himself being carried away by his spirited defence. 'Greener's still at school — sixth form college, if you want to know. He's got eight O-levels and he's bloody brilliant. You're more of a hippy than any of them three!'

Seeing the slightest hint of a smile from Pugh, Lee forced himself from his righteous indignation, feeling foolish. He said quietly and simply, 'They're my friends.'

Pugh pursed his lips in thought. 'Dare say we'll survive, boy,' he said, half-amused.

Aware that grudging enthusiasm was about the best he could hope for, Lee said sarcastically, 'I'll make sure I lock the bantams up tonight.'

Pugh moved into the kitchen. 'We got enough to do, boy, without running Butlins,' he called over his shoulder.

Morgan watched Colin, Ros and Greener pegging out the tent in the place he had advised. Watching their simple and obvious enjoyment at the novelty of being on his farm, some of his misgivings melted. He began to smile shyly at their chatter and jokes, while Cap had also decided that the visitors were worthwhile and moved barking from one to the other, frisking away as they bent down to hold him. Morgan laughed.

On the road the Honda started up. In the excitement Morgan had forgotten Matthew. He realised, suddenly, that the boy had been quiet in the house, standing apart and saying nothing. Morgan knew about loneliness. He walked across the yard and leaned over the gate to where Matthew, astride his bike, was starting to put on his helmet.

'Feeling out of it?' suggested Morgan quietly.

Matthew smiled. 'They're old friends of his.'

'You're his friend from here,' said Morgan firmly.

Matthew considered this seriously and nodded. Suddenly turning to Morgan, he quickly said, 'I've got my interview on Monday, then selection, then Aldershot.' He looked back along the road.

Morgan watched him intently. 'You don't want to leave?' he asked.

156

Matthew smiled, 'If they didn't take me I'd still have to leave. There's nothing for me down here.' Morgan felt sympathy for the boy, he knew what it was like to be the outsider in a group; he knew too, about a life that seemed to be without alternatives.

'You do what you want, son,' he murmured. 'There's enough of us have took the least line of resistance. You're a good friend to us and it's appreciated.'

Matthew was grateful. He fastened his helmet and switched on the machine. Suddenly he smiled up at Morgan, sat hard down in the saddle, clicked his engine into gear and moved fast down the road.

Pugh came to ask Morgan what he wanted him to do before he went home.

I've got three strays for Tom Griffiths in the corner field,' he said. 'Give us a hand to get them in the Land Rover.'

Matthew was surprised to find Gregory in the kitchen of Plas Newydd working at a table covered with large sheets of paper and lists. He looked up as Matthew came through the door. 'Hello, young man,' he said. 'I didn't know you were around.'

Matthew wandered over to the table. 'What are you doing?'

'Playing around with an idea or two — nothing you need worry your head about.' Harry casually folded the largest sheet of paper so it obscured the rest. 'Are you all set for Monday?' he asked, changing the subject.

Matthew shrugged and moved to pour himself a glass of water. 'It's just another interview,' he said unenthusiastically.

Harry, who had enjoyed army life and considered himself a bit of an expert, frowned. 'Just a minute, Matthew,' he objected. 'If you go in there with the "just another interview attitude", it'll be noted. You've got to show them you're keen.'

Matthew poured water into a glass and drank. 'Where's Mrs G?' he asked, rinsing the glass beneath a tap.

'Having her hair sand-blasted into place somewhere in Hereford. Spring is in the air,' Harry said jauntily.

'Is there anything you want me to do,' smiled Matthew.

Gregory leaned back from the table, thoughtfully. 'A little digging at the front of the house would be appreciated,' he suggested. 'Eileen has plans for much colour when the blooms are out — if ever.' Matthew nodded and moved from the room. 'Cup of tea together at four?' asked Harry. 'Peaceful sort of day.'

Matthew turned at the door. 'She'll be back by night,' he warned.

Gregory appreciated the joke, chuckling. 'Will you be in for supper tonight?' he asked.

Matthew thought for a moment. 'No,' he said. 'Lee's got friends up at Blainau and I'll probably go back.' Gregory was already busy with his plans again. Matthew vaguely wondered what they were and why he preferred working on them while his sharp-tongued wife was absent.

The farm office in Tom Griffiths' house was a model of neat efficiency. A shelf of files contained stock records; there were clipboards on the wall for receipts and invoices; a row of labelled hooks held a spare set of keys for every farm vehicle; a rota of holidays covered much of one wall. There was a filing cabinet, an armchair near the door and a roll-top desk with a modern swivel-chair. Morgan was unable to avoid the contrast with Blainau.

Tom Griffiths sat at his desk and gestured for Morgan to take the easy chair. Griffiths swivelled to face him and waited for Morgan to tell him why he had come.

'Thinking about my Blainau' — Griffiths nodded encouragingly — 'only it don't pay. Sheep don't pay on a place like Blainau any more.' Griffiths nodded; Morgan hated this necessity for advice. 'Only it has got to pay,' he finished lamely.

There was silence for a long time, 'What are you asking me, Morgan?' inquired Griffiths.

Morgan steeled himself to what he hated most of all: anybody knowing. 'They want me from there,' he said abruptly. 'The Estate. You can give me a bit of advice like. I've got the place really tidy now. I got a bit of help, good lambing. Only, Duncan says it ain't enough. Times change, he says.' Morgan lapsed into silence.

Griffiths knew what it must have cost him to say that much. 'Have he made an offer of a deal?' he asked quietly.

'I expect so,' said Morgan.

'Take care of you, does it?'

Morgan was suddenly animated. 'It do take Blainau from me.' Then he relapsed into silence, staring at the floor.

Griffiths coughed and aimlessly swivelled his chair a little. He asked, 'What's the offer?' and, meeting only silence, continued, 'This is between me and you, Morgan. Damn, and I'd likely come to you if I wanted advice on sheep.'

This was fair, thought Morgan. He raised his eyes to his friend, 'Give the land and house over to the Estate, sell off stock and machinery — capital to live on, and he'd rent me a house, low rent.'

'Take it, Morgan,' said Griffiths without hesitation.

Morgan was surprised and disappointed. 'Damn and how can I?' he protested. 'Fifty years we've been there, man. The Old Gentleman brung it up from nothing. They'd never rest quiet.'

Griffiths' voice was soft. 'Think of yourself, Morgan. If you had kiddies it would be different, but who gets Blainau after you're dead and gone? No need to struggle on for no reason, man.'

'I got the boy to think of,' said Morgan tentatively. 'He's family; he could take care of the farm.' Griffiths regarded Morgan steadily. He had not heard this before and Morgan sensed his disbelief. 'Damn and he could!' he affirmed.

Griffiths fiddled with a pen on the table before him. 'Land Tribunal?' he asked quietly. Morgan nodded. 'When?'

'Twelve month from term date — next September, plenty of time.'

Griffiths thought it over; 'Plenty of time' — that was Morgan. 'You got the addresses for the Union?' he asked. 'They'd likely help with solicitors.'

'I don't need no solicitors,' snapped Morgan.

Griffiths had known Morgan all his life. He knew the man's simple strengths in the face of the Land Tribunal, and he knew Tom Duncan — could imagine the powerful case the Estate would put. He suspected that Morgan had come, not so much for advice, but for confirmation of the decision he had already made.

'It's all bloody nonsense anyways,' muttered Morgan at length. 'They won't get it from me.'

'You mean they're just trying it on?' said Griffiths hesitantly.

Morgan thumped the arm of the chair. 'You've got it. Giving me a scare before they likely puts the rent up. They've got the wrong man if they thinks . . .' but Morgan's anxiety tethered his tongue. He searched for words which would not come and suddenly stood, bringing the interview to an unexpected end.

'You don't mind me coming?'

Griffiths stood. 'Damn, no, we've known each other some years now,' he said, wishing Morgan would sit again so that they could methodically go over the whole business. He would like to help Morgan but guessed that the man's mind was made up. However, he thought, he could be some help, but not now. He moved past Morgan to open the door for him. 'You've told the boy he'd have Blainau?' he asked innocently.

Morgan's eyes flickered away from him. 'Not yet. Not told him yet,' he replied as they left the office.

Outside the farmhouse Morgan politely thanked his neighbour for his tea. Griffiths politely thanked him for his strays — now being led away by Price and Graham. Griffiths raised an arm in farewell and stepped back inside.

'You want to get that boy of yours to see to your Land Rover, Morgan,' Graham called, as Morgan moved to the vehicle. 'Antiques like that should be kept clean.'

They watched him go. 'It's only the dirt keeps it together, man,' Price grinned to his mate. They laughed and kicked the sheep on their way.

Sarah was surrounded by books, revising for mock O-Levels, when Tom Griffiths opened his living-room door.

'What did Morgan want?' she asked, keeping apprehension from her voice. Any connection with Blainau still worried her, and when the school bus drove her past, she kept her head in her books.

'Just a bit of a chat.' He lowered himself into his armchair. Reassured, Sarah concerned herself with revision. Griffiths knew he was a lucky and successful farmer and that Morgan was not; he would do what he could to help . . . if indeed, Morgan would accept help, which he doubted. Griffiths was fortunate in his family, too. That was another strength and comfort denied to Morgan. He gazed fondly at his daughter. 'Come here,' he said holding out an arm.

'I'm too old for that,' she smiled. 'But you can test me on history dates.'

She moved to sit at his feet, an arm over his knees, and handed him her notebook. Both were content with the compromise. He asked questions about the first Labour administration and she replied, allowing an arm round her shoulders.

Morgan, too, felt curiously content as he sat, relaxing, after a good supper, cooked by Greener. A boy cooking and cooking well, he thought. Times change. The house had seldom been so full and never with so many youngsters. He looked up from the fire to where Lee and Ros were happily talking. They suddenly laughed. Morgan smiled too, unseen.

In the kitchen Matthew and Greener were finishing the washing-up, while Colin sat at the table, watching and smoking. Matthew's boots, camouflage trousers and military-style sweater struck him as showy and peculiar. He didn't like the quietness of the boy and the slightly refined accent grated upon him. He couldn't understand what Lee saw in him.

Greener scraped a few fragments from the final plate into a plastic bag. 'Don't suppose you get dustmen here.'

He grinned. 'Yes, we do.' Matthew still felt uneasy in the boisterous company.

Greener dropped the plate into the sink. Matthew washed it carefully. 'When?' Greener asked, drying his hands on the roller towel.

'Week next Friday.' Matthew smiled slightly as Greener grinned at him and moved from the room.

Matthew shook the suds from the plate and dried it. He emptied the water from the sink and hung up the drying-cloth. He took the plate to the pile on the table, aware of Colin's silence. Colin took a cigarette from the pack and lit it. He offered the pack to Matthew.

'No, thanks.'

Matthew carried the plates to their place in the sideboard.

'Pure in body; pure in mind?'

Matthew smiled politely. 'Not that I've noticed.'

'Into uniforms? In the scouts, were you? Fancy yourself as a killer?'

Matthew had taken enough. He moved towards the door. 'I don't fancy myself as anything,' he muttered. Colin smiled as he rose.

'There's kids back home half your age could eat you for breakfast and spit out the bones,' he said, following him from the room.

They came into the living-room to find Morgan cleaning the shotgun, rested across his knees, and Greener engrossed in a magazine about pig-breeding. Colin moved to sit by Ros.

'What did you think to Greener's cooking, Morgan?' he asked.

'Very fair,' replied Morgan; a real compliment.

Ros smiled. 'He was the only boy in the domestic science class. Got an A grade at O-Level, didn't you, Greener?' Greener shrugged modestly. Matthew moved quietly to sit on the floor near Lee. Lee looked over to Ros.

'Do you ever see anything of my mother?'

She nodded. 'She was in the corner pub with Alan last Sunday. I don't know what you've got against Alan. He gives you real nice things.'

'Bastard,' Lee murmured.

'Yeah, well, you can be a pain when you want,' she said. Colin laughed and Ros giggled.

Greener dropped the magazine to the floor. 'You don't keep any pigs on the farm, Morgan. Why's that?'

Morgan carefully wiped oil from the double barrel of his gun. 'The Old Gentleman — my Dad — he was the pig killer here till he passed on,' he said quietly.

161

Lee looked up. 'I never knew that.'

'We all had pigs, them days. Farmers, cottagers, some of the pubs down Talgarth. He killed for a good five miles round. Cruel old business, but he done it till round about 1950. He could kill six a day when he was rushed. November to March — the worst of the weather — and it was all walking then. . .'

He had their attention. He squinted briefly through the barrels and laid the gun against the wall. He looked round, surprised to see the interest he had caused.

'Did you help him?' Ros asked.

'I'd be sharpening the knives on a stone in the yard by the light of a lamp at five in the morning. One knife for the killing, two for the cutting up.'

They gazed at him, seeing a way of life that had turned the corner for good. They wanted him to go on. Morgan warmed to the task, the memories crowding round.

'He had to start early to catch the men still at the farm, see. It took two strong men and the Old Gentleman to get the poor beast up and tied to a bench. Because that poor pig — he knew what was coming: three men with rope and a bucket instead of the kiddies with scraps. By damn, he'd know, and he'd fight, and he'd squeal.'

He remembered the terrible squealing and how the children would be sent away, some crying bitterly for the pet they had fed during the year. He remembered how some — the tough ones — would jockey for position to see every cruel detail. It was a clean death, but cruel. He remembered how the crying pig could be heard up to two miles distant on a calm, frosty morning. All this he told them. They were spellbound.

'How did they kill him?' Even Colin's voice was low, reverential.

'Slit the throat. You'd see the blood fly six feet. Some'd catch the blood in the bucket, for blood pudding.' Nothing of the pig would be wasted: he remembered his mother making faggots, chitlings — a clear picture of her washing intestines at the tap in the yard; another of his father delicately eating the brains with a fork.

'But he'd squeal. Boy, he'd squeal. Then he'd lose his strength as the blood come from him, and the squealing got quiet until it was nothing. Then he'd be gone.'

He told them how a thin fire of fern or straw would be laid on the carcass and the bristles burned; how some kept an old tin can to scrape the pig smooth; how the pig was washed cleaner, dead, than he'd ever been in his snorting, grubbing life.

'What next?' breathed Matthew.

'Day or day and a half later, the Old Gentleman would go back for the cutting up. Ribs out for fresh meat and then you'd salt him for three weeks; he'd soon go to stink if he didn't have the salt. When he was just flitches of bacon, he'd go up on the hooks.'

There was total stillness in the room. The memories were sharp: so many memories. They stalked through Morgan's mind, cocooning him in the past. He had been nearly half the age of his audience when his father stopped killing pigs.

'You had to be a hard man to kill the poor pig. He wanted me to follow him on, but I was too soft.' The memory of his father's scorn slashed him, like the knife. 'Too damn soft! That's what he said.' Morgan felt moistness in his eyes. He pulled himself back to the present. 'No money in pigs today.' He tried to smile. 'And damn, I couldn't look at one anyhows.'

He suddenly stood up, embarrassed at the emotion his memories had stirred. He took his gun and hung it high in the beams. He lowered his arms.

'But he never did forgive me for not following on. ''Too damn soft, boy.'' That's what he said.'

Morgan felt the pricking in his eyes. Too damn soft to follow on. And now he could lose the whole farm. He turned and walked fast to the door, taking his jacket as he left.

'What's wrong?' asked Colin. Lee got quickly to his feet and the spell slowly unwound. Ros leant against Colin. Their eyes rose silently to the beam where Morgan had hidden his gun; to the sharp, rounded hooks where the poor pigs had hung, reduced to cuts of meat.

Morgan was rubbing Cap's ears in the yard when Lee came up to him.

'Stupid old stories,' the man said.

Lee laid a hand on his shoulder. Their eyes met.

'Best take a walk round the sheep,' Morgan said briskly. Lee removed his hand.

'I'll come with you.'

But Morgan was already moving away, the dog dancing at his side.

'Damn and I shan't get lost,' Morgan called back.

Lee watched them go, through the small gate, uphill to the ewes waiting to give new life. He waited until they were lost from the thin spread of light around the house. Sensing the presence of man and dog, the sheep called anxiously to each other in the dark. Lee turned and went back into the house.

The next day, Saturday, passed happily for the visitors. They enjoyed being allowed to join in the farm life, knowing that it would never move beyond novelty. They privately agreed that they would find the muck, smells and physical work unbearable after a week or so. The remoteness and sense of huge space was also unsettling to city youngsters.

Greener attacked the house, ruthlessly cleaning, tidying and wanting to leave Blainau a brighter place altogether. Colin chopped wood and accompanied Lee wherever he went. Ros, refusing to join Greener in domesticity, attached herself to Morgan who was quietly proud. She adored Cap, which was mutual. Pugh and Matthew, less swept into the spirit of the weekend, found work well away from the farm.

In the afternoon Colin drove Greener to Talgarth with a shopping list, and Ros hung around the cowshed door, fascinated and frightened at the dark, moving bulk of cows; she made her excuses (to make tea) and left when the animals swayed free in the yard, while Lee cleaned out the muck-straw. Morgan laughingly offered her five pounds to ride on the back of a docile heifer; she offered to do it for a thousand.

Matthew ate at Plas Newydd that night and ran through a question and answer hour with Harry in preparation for his Monday interview. The Gregorys were pleased to have his company for an entire evening and made an effort to be pleasant.

At Blainau, Greener made a large pie of minced steak, and, afterwards, Colin played his guitar while Ros sang. Morgan did not offer more memories. Ros asked him once, but Greener stepped in to object — Morgan had put him off bacon for life. They talked and laughed; drank beer. They watched grainy football on television, before Colin bullied Ros into the tent for an early night, to much joking in which Morgan shyly joined. It had been a good day.

While Morgan donned his Sunday suit and his guests slept late, Eileen and Harry prepared to leave Plas Newydd for morning drinks with their bank manager. They dressed with care, indulging in their room in another question and answer session, this time with each other.

'One,' said Harry, tying his regimental tie, 'it is an historic building.'

'So is Stonehenge,' replied Eileen smoothly. 'I wouldn't pay to spend a night there either.' She scrutinised her image in the wardrobe mirror.

'Two: I have experience in man management.'

'I wouldn't press that particular button too hard.' She turned to find her handbag and Harry crossed to the vacant mirror, throwing her a glance of annoyance. She protested mildly. 'You asked me to play Devil's advocate.' At the door she paused waiting for him. He slipped a clean handkerchief in his pocket.

'Three: we have certain friends who would be interested in providing capital.'

'Pass,' she said, moving onto the landing. The damp behind the panelling seemed to be spreading. She put a hand to it, confirming her suspicion. Harry shut the bedroom door and they hurried down the stairs. She called to Matthew, busy fish-gazing, that they were leaving now; he called back an acknowledgement.

'And grants would be forthcoming because we would be bringing in tourists.'

'Where they swarm in anyway.'

'And we would employ local staff.'

'In an area of low employment, where there are plenty of hotels already.'

In the hall Gregory held out Eileen's coat sullenly. She shrugged it on.

'But not in historic buildings,' he insisted. 'Not offering what we could offer.'

They moved to the door. Eileen smiled at her husband, infuriatingly patient. 'You don't convince me. But then,' she said, waiting for Harry to open it, 'I know you better than all the land agents, tourists boards and bank managers in the world. Thank you,' she added, stepping into the cool morning. He closed the door. They walked to the car.

'You joke about it,' Harry said quietly, 'but – ' She kissed him on the cheek, suddenly softening to his dogged optimism.

'I know,' she said, pointing at the passenger door, which he opened for her.

Morgan laid a small bunch of wild spring flowers on his parents' grave and stood to rub bird-droppings from the headstone with the cloth he kept specially in the Land Rover. It had been an average service; none had truly impressed him since the heady, false revelations two months ago. He stepped quietly back for his weekly atonement with his parents. When he turned to join the path, he found Tom Griffiths and his wife waiting for him. Griffiths had something for him at home. Would he come to the farm for a cup of tea or a drink?

Greener and Lee had been exiled. The lovers had found passion in a tent cold and strangely public, so the two boys ambled through the fields to Plas Newydd, where Lee enjoyed Greener's surprise – ruin or not, the sheer age and bulk of the place was impressive. They came to the door and Lee knocked loudly. He had already warned Greener to take no notice of the Gregorys, who were peculiar.

'Just three living here?' asked Greener, stepping back to survey the crumbling and buttressed façade.

'Yeah,' Lee grinned.

Matthew opened the door. He was still in pyjamas, a worn dressing gown pulled over them. He let them in and Lee explained they'd been ejected from Blainau, as they followed him upstairs. Greener looked at the dingy grandeur of the hall and staircase.

'How old is this place?'

'Four hundred years: some of it.'

Matthew led them to his room.

'You know that old plough in the field by Blainau?' Lee asked. 'Greener's decided to do it up!'

Matthew glanced over his shoulder. 'It's falling to pieces,' he protested.

Lee winked at him; he knew Matthew would be as amused as he had been, when Greener had dragged him enthusiastically to the implement, rusted and half-buried in the earth.

'He's going to paint it up and write "Blainau" on it.'

Greener had seen the wink and was unabashed. 'No, it's interesting,' he said grinning. They entered Matthew's room. Greener wandered around. He had no interest in the fish, but found the military display extraordinary.

'Where are the Gregs?' Lee asked.

'Brecon. Drinks with somebody.'

Lee was disappointed. He enjoyed impressing Greener and two more odd exhibits would have been a bonus. Matthew straddled a chair. Lee lay on the bed. Greener was examining a plaster of Paris model of Falkland Sound.

'Thought you might have come up last night.'

'I was sick,' Matthew said.

Lee laughed. 'That's Greener's cooking.'

'Or Morgan's stories,' Greener called.

'Yeah.' Lee gazed at the ceiling. He sat up. 'What about your interview tomorrow?'

'I'll be okay.'

Greener walked to the fish tanks and flicked one idly, watching the fish spin away. 'What's the interview?' he asked.

'Over at Merthyr. Some major at the recruiting centre.'

Greener gazed at the fish in the breeding tank. 'Colin thinks you're crazy,' he said mildly.

Matthew slapped the back of his chair with the dressing gown cord. 'He's got it all wrong,' he murmured.

Greener sat cross-legged on the floor, smiling. 'It's been known,' he agreed. Lee knew little about the antagonism, other than it existed. He saw Matthew's tight face.

'You don't want to worry,' he said. 'Colin's just got a thing about uniforms.'

Greener stretched out on the floor, close to the paraffin heater. 'Cubs, Guides and Brownies,' he murmured, smiling.

Lee took up the idea. 'Chief constables, lollipop ladies!'

Greener's face split widely; he pushed the fantasy on – 'Sea Scouts!' he laughed, 'Firemen! Gnomes on toadstools! Action Man!' Lee and Greener spluttered with laughter. Matthew slapped the chair with the cord.

'What's the interview about?' Greener asked, sitting up, looking at Matthew. Lee was still giggling, Matthew glanced at Greener suspiciously.

'I'm just interested.'

Matthew took a breath. He had met with too much derision. He needed to be taken seriously.

'Look,' he said, 'Right or wrong, we've got armed forces.'

Lee had flopped back giggling on the bed. 'Bang bang.'

Matthew slapped the chair hard. 'Okay,' he murmured, 'forget it.'

'No, go on.' Matthew looked hard at Greener but the boy showed nothing but genuine curiosity. Matthew tried again. The words tumbled out.

'It's a career. You learn a trade. Parachute Regiment's the best; the hardest to get into – one in ten make it in the end. That's worth something. You get to travel – see something of the world.'

'Northern Ireland?' asked Greener seriously.

'Yes. Right. Probably.' Matthew swivelled to face him, passionate now. 'But that's a hell of an involvement. It's a real responsibility and I want that; I want to take responsibility for myself. The Paras teach you to push yourself to the limit.'

Matthew was suddenly embarrassed at his own fervour, but Lee lay flat on the bed, eyes closed, and Greener was levering himself to his feet, his attention caught by a photograph on the wall. Marooned, Matthew shut up. He slapped the cord against the chair. 'The photo's of the farm at Mvurwi,' he said quietly.

Lee raised his head. 'Where?'

'The place the Gregorys had.' Lee let his head fall back on Matthew's pillow.

Greener studied the picture of the long, low building. 'Were they there for the war?' he asked.

'What war?' Lee was vaguely interested. Greener turned to face him.

'I did it for part of a project at school. It was interesting. You know – the attacks, landmines, ambushes. They had this system called Agri-alert. When the guerillas broke through the wire round your farm, there was this red button you pushed and an alarm went off at the Army Headquarters and they tried to get to you in time. It went off in neighbours' farms too; then you got your guns and got over soonest. Panic button.'

Lee briefly pondered this new vision of the Gregorys. He laughed.

'They're still prats!'

Matthew paused in slapping the cord against the chair, feeling that his vague, passionate advocacy had been subtly called into doubt by Greener's second-hand, vivid detail.

Sarah was tending the earthy flowers in the border round the farmhouse when her father's car pulled up, followed by Morgan's Land Rover. She paused and watched them walk together along the path towards her. Morgan stopped and shook his head.

'Damn and I forget flowers. The Old Lady liked her bit of garden.'

He looked with pleasure at the small, bright blooms, while Mrs Griffiths went ahead to make them tea. Morgan seemed lost in memories again. Griffiths put a hand on his shoulder, moving him gently towards the door.

'Sarah will cut you a few to take home.'

Morgan nodded. He smiled at the girl, who smiled politely back. She returned to her work as the men walked, talking, through the doorway.

Griffiths had done what he could for Morgan. A tidy pile of pamphlets and papers waited on his office desk, crowned by a page of typed addresses. Griffiths waved an arm to it and ran through the information he'd been able to gather. He explained the addresses: a good farmers' solicitor, local and not too expensive; two contacts from the Farmers Union − one local, one national − who specialised in hill farming problems; two farming friends who had successfully appealed to the Land Tribunal and one who had not.

'And I rung up our advisory service − A.D.A.S. − for you, Morgan. They're good to us boy. Now this man here,' − he jabbed a finger at the final name on the page − 'he's a useful man. He can come out to see you next week. I told him end of the week: Thursday morning.'

He tapped the pile for luck.

'Anyway, there it is. It's a start. You don't want to leave it too late.'

Morgan stared down at the intimidating pile which demanded action and initiative. Griffiths pushed it towards him, but he made no sign of acceptance or gratitude. Griffiths said quietly, 'I can't tell you what to do, Morgan.'

Morgan shifted his weight and screwed his cap tightly in his hands, his eyes warily on the dangerous pile before him.

'Only I might be from the farm, Thursday.' He was evasive.

Griffiths tried one last time. 'He'd come out after Easter then. Give him a ring.'

Morgan was wretched. 'College boy, no doubt.'

'He knows his job.'

Morgan turned to Griffiths. 'Only last time I come here to you, I was in a sweat. That Duncan − he give me a scare, trying it on.'

Griffiths held his gaze steadily. Morgan's eyes beseeched him to let him go free of this obligation.

'He was just trying it on. He was. No doubt,' he repeated.

Griffiths nodded, disappointed but not surprised. Morgan turned his back on the desk and glanced towards the open door.

'You know your business best, Morgan,' Griffiths said quietly. 'Let's get that tea now.'

Greener and Lee, still forbidden the house on their return from

Plas Newydd, were sanding down the old plough in the workshop, watched by an incredulous Cap who sneezed now and then as the rust filled the air. It had taken half an hour to dig it out and carry it into the outhouse.

'This is going to look really stupid,' muttered Lee. They worked on, occasionally slapping the sandpaper free of the clogging rust.

'Is Matthew's father in the army?'

'He's a doctor or something.' Lee stepped back. There was little to show for their effort.

'What's he going to do with his fish?'

Lee was fed up. 'I don't know,' he said, glad to hear the familiar Land Rover and to see Cap's ears prick up as he darted into the yard, barking. Lee hoped Colin and Ros would hear the warning too.

'That bedroom of his is weird.' Greener flapped dust from the wedge of sandpaper and bent to begin a new section.

'What's this sudden interest in Matthew? What's weird? His books and wall and things?'

'It's interesting. Like he's got to keep persuading himself. Like he doesn't really want to do it so he surrounds himself with all the hope-and-glory bit.'

Lee was affronted for Matthew. 'Of course he wants to do it. He's doing it. There's this interview. He told you his reasons.'

'He talks like a recruiting advert. That's excuses, not reasons.'

Lee considered this seriously, knowing Greener was no fool. He wondered how best to defend Matthew but gave up.

'Does it make you popular: knowing everything?'

Greener grinned as Morgan came in, clutching a small bunch of flowers. 'Not a lot,' he said. Lee turned to his uncle.

'Is this all right? Painting this up?' He half wished the man would forbid it.

'I expect so.' Morgan peered at the implement. Cap sneezed and trotted into the yard. 'What's it for?' Morgan asked.

Lee shrugged. 'Don't ask me. Ask him.'

Morgan stepped past them and looked into a wooden box. He handed Lee a wire brush. 'Better than sand paper.'

Greener straightened up and stretched his back. 'Hungry?' he asked, moving to the door. 'I'll call you when it's ready. Bet the table's not been laid,' he called over his shoulder.

'Bet Ros has,' shouted back Lee. They heard Greener laugh and knock elaborately at the porch door. Lee and Morgan gazed silently at the plough. Morgan smiled. They moved into the yard.

'Morgan?'

The man stopped and turned.

'Thanks.'

Morgan was puzzled. 'Why for?'

'For letting them stay, and being okay and everything.'

Morgan blushed behind his red, weather-beaten complexion. 'Damn and we said as we'd help one another, son.'

They walked together to the porch where Lee repeated the elaborate knocking and Morgan coughed long and loud. Ros opened the door to them, sheepishly coy.

It began to go wrong that afternoon. Ros and Colin took a walk through the fields and found the scattered circle of torn wool which meant a fox had attacked a sheep nearby. They did not know this until they almost stumbled across the carcass, eyeless from crows, stomach gaping, and torn where the fox had savaged it.

They ran, screaming down the road, scared but enjoying it, claiming sightings of a wolf close behind, frightening each other until they crashed through a weak stretch of hedge, onto the road where they clasped each other, laughing and panting and childishly disgusted at the gaping, eyeless creature in the field above. They continued their walk happily, intending to tell Morgan of the horror.

Within the hour sixty pregnant ewes had followed them through the breach, determined to get at the fresher, juicier, longer grass, at the verges of the roadside. Morgan had driven to see a sick acquaintance in the hospital at Bronllys, so Lee and Greener had the humiliation of being called out by Graham and Price who, driving past, had almost collided with the milling sheep blocking the road. It had been chaos. Lee could not work Cap to round them up; he did not know in which field to put them, once the four of them had managed to gather the anxious flock in.

It had taken almost an hour. Colin and Ros returned to the farm unknowing, ready with their comic saga of the sheep and the wolf and their headlong flight to the road, expecting amusement, but finding Lee sullen. Morgan returned, made light of the matter; but Lee was not to be mollified. It was not Morgan, Colin or Ros who had been made to feel inadequate or endure the scorn of Price and Graham. When it became clear that Colin and Ros had caused the hassle, the atmosphere turned cold. They had let Lee, and Blainau, down.

That evening Greener buried his head in a book, *Mysterious Britain*, and was half lost in the world of ley-lines and UFOs. Morgan relaxed by the fire, watching a wildlife film on rabbits. Colin and Ros, refusing to be chastened, sat on the sofa nudging each other into guilty giggles, and Lee carved a piece of wood, apart.

Ros glanced at Morgan. 'We saw some rabbits today, didn't we, Col?' she said, trying to initiate normality. Colin agreed.

Without looking up from his book, Greener intoned, 'Oryctolagus cuniculus. The Normans brought them from France in the twelfth century.'

The screen showed a cross-section of a burrow. Colin glanced over at Lee and grinned, wanting peace, but Lee would not give way. He hacked at the wood. Colin sighed loudly. He turned to face his friend.

'Look, we just didn't think.' Colin was becoming edgy: all this fuss for a few stray sheep.

'It's obvious, mate. Break a hedge down and what do you expect?'

Colin was exasperated. 'We didn't break it down.' Ros agreed: they didn't, not deliberately.

'Okay.' Lee's voice was cold, clipped. 'So the sheep never got out.'

Morgan stepped in, to smooth the moment. His eyes firmly on the television, he said quietly, 'Sheep'll get out any place this time of the year.'

Lee said nothing. He threw a piece of wood across the room into the fire. Colin and Ros exchanged apprehensive looks. Colin clapped his hands.

'Come on,' he called. 'We're all going out; we can get five in the van. We'll buy everybody a drink and forget it.'

'Right,' Ros said. 'Come on. We go.'

She stood up, hoping for action. Nobody else moved. Colin called to Greener. He said 'thanks' but shook his head, engrossed now in the Glastonbury myths. Ros moved towards Lee.

'Come on, Lee,' she begged.

'We could go,' Morgan said. He had enjoyed the easy atmosphere of the last two nights; he did not want it spoiled.

But Lee shook his head, and, in sympathy with the boy,

172

Morgan murmured that the pubs would be crowded, come to think of it, with tourists.

Ros asked once more, with no success. She looked at Colin, exasperated. He too had had enough. Taking her hand he moved to the door. 'See you then,' he said curtly. Greener lifted an arm in farewell and Morgan nodded. They left. After a moment or two, the van started up and the yard gate clanged. Lee stood.

'Where are you going, son?' asked Morgan softly.

'Listen to my tapes.' He moved towards the stairs. Morgan turned off the television set.

'Actually,' said Greener, without looking up, 'I don't think Colin and Ros have much to learn from rabbits.'

Lee turned and was forced to a smile as he moved upstairs, and Morgan saw the joke, laughing out loud. Greener looked at Morgan over the top of the book.

'You're a loner, are you, Morgan?' he said conversationally. 'You must be, living here.'

Morgan looked sharply at the boy, but met simple, friendly curiosity.

'Not from choice, no,' he replied quietly.

'Loners never get the choice.' Greener's eyes fell to the Glastonbury chapter once more.

'What do you know about it?' Morgan's voice was quiet.

'I'm a loner too. It's good!' He laid the book on his knees. 'Loners of the world unite!' he grinned.

That was clever, thought Morgan, grinning back. He rose from his chair and crossed to the sideboard.

'You as sharp at the old draughts?' he said, finding an ancient board and its battered box of checkers on the lower shelf. 'I got him ready, if anybody wants to play,' he explained.

Greener rose and made for the sofa where Morgan was setting the board. 'Fast mover are you?' he asked. Morgan sat opposite, rolling up his sleeves.

'Blink, boy, and you'll miss me,' he chuckled, glancing briefly up as Lee's music seeped through the ceiling.

Monday, it rained — a miserable, dogged rain, with low clouds shrouding the hills. Lee worked determinedly, making good the hedgerow that his friends and sixty sheep had broken down; it was not a job on the list, that would have to wait until later. He wondered how Matthew would be feeling as he drove to Merthyr. It was the first real step towards his permanent departure. The rain spattered against the foliage around him, but, thankfully, there was no sly wind behind it. He paused before collecting the new stretch of wire he had brought from the tractor box. Bloody Col; bloody Ros. He had heard them talking in their tent when he left the farm that morning and Greener had still been curled in his sleeping bag on the sofa. Bloody rain. At least they would be harmless around the farm; they would not venture out in weather like this. He walked to the tractor for the wire, vaguely aware of his dark mood. He forced himself to hum. It sounded ridiculous and he shut up.

Morgan checked the spinner that would be throwing fertiliser across the drying fields on to the springing grass in a week or two. Even through the closed doors of the machinery shed, the loud music intruded boisterously. He wondered when his guests would be moving on.

Greener lay flat on the living-room floor, clicking his fingers to Colin's Buddy Holly tape. In Morgan's chair Colin hammered the singing, half-mime, half-mimic; he spun his guitar following the chords comically. Ros, on the sofa, squealed with delight. The fire was piled high with logs − almost half the day's supply. Their late breakfast lay uncleared on the kitchen table.

Lee noticed the music as soon as he switched off the tractor engine, and smiled to himself. There was no sign of Morgan, but when he entered the workshop to return the tools, he found Pugh seated on a bale of straw, reading a week-old paper. Pugh did not look up.
    'Coming for dinner then?'
    Pugh read on.
    'What's the matter?'
    Pugh would not look up at him. 'I been told off enough about nagging, boy.' Lee felt a surge of annoyance. He bought time, looking at a couple of weak lambs in the pen. He threw a glance at the old man but the newspaper was up; a defiant shield. A burst of laughter and applause came from the house. Lee turned and left.
    Lee noticed the chaos of the kitchen table the moment he came into the house. The high spirits which had made him smile in the yard seemed out of place, and, suddenly, infuriating. Greener and Ros were dancing a parody of rock and roll. Colin was hitting indiscriminate strings, shouting with Buddy

Holly. Ros saw him and called out a welcome. She squealed as Greener twirled her off balance.

'What did you say to Pugh?'

They could not hear him over the tape. Lee flicked his radio into silence. Colin's grotesque song and accompaniment jangled, wobbling, in the sudden silence, then stopped. They looked at him.

'Pugh,' he said firmly.

They stared. Colin said, puzzled, 'Pugh?'

'What happened?'

They could not mistake his annoyance and looked at each other, genuinely unaware of any fault. Colin smiled, amicably. 'What are you talking about?'

'He put his head in and went,' added Greener. 'What's wrong?'

Lee felt a strange conflict of loyalties. He tried to explain. 'Look, Pugh likes a quiet dinnertime. He's not used to . . .' He waved, embarrassed, to his radio. 'To tapes and . . .' Their gaze of total bewilderment daunted him. He shrugged unhappily.

Colin lay down the guitar in silence. Greener began to collect coffee cups. Ros moved to Colin and sat at his feet. Lee felt marooned: a killjoy. 'I know it's raining,' he said miserably.

Colin gazed at him, hardening into irritation. 'What's got into you?' Greener passed him, taking cups to the kitchen. Ros looked at him and shook her head in disbelief. Water could be heard filling the sink as Greener began washing up their breakfast plates.

'It's different here,' murmured Lee.

Ros nodded slowly. 'Sure is,' she said.

Morgan and Pugh stood talking quietly in the workshop as Lee came in, cold and angry at the position he seemed forced into.

'It's okay now,' he said. Morgan and Pugh made no reply. 'They're just bored. In the town, you just – I don't know.' He tried hard to diffuse this small offence, unworthy of the effect it seemed to have produced. 'Just stay in and hang about with friends, if it's raining. That's all.'

Pugh looked up. 'This ain't the town, boy,' he snapped.

Morgan added awkwardly, 'Any farm's a place of work. You know that.'

Exasperated that they would not let the event die, Lee took a step towards them. 'Why do you want to make a big thing out of it? Nobody said anything to upset you, did they, Pugh?' The old man shook his head. Lee turned directly to him. 'Why didn't you just say something? Ask them to be quiet? Why does it have to be me?'

In the silence Colin came to the door. 'Greener wants to see the bookshops in Hay-on-Wye,' he said quietly. 'See you.' Before he could leave, Lee had put a hand on his arm.

'You don't have to go.' It was a plea for the return of easy normality.

Colin smiled briefly at Pugh. 'Are you okay, Pugh? Sorry and that. You only had to say.' And, turning finally to Morgan, 'Nothing you want from the shops?'

Morgan also felt the complications of changing moods and Lee's difficult position; he also sympathised with Pugh. Unable to unravel the strands he snapped, 'Don't ask me, boy! I don't know what I got and what I ain't got, these days!'

Lee saw Colin stiffen at the attack. 'No thanks, Col,' he said quietly. Colin nodded and left. They heard him call breezily to Cap as he made for the van.

'I thought you liked them here!' It was Lee's turn to harden his resentment into aggression; Colin had got it right – the event had been nothing and he was treating it as such. The van doors slammed. 'You two are amazing!' Lee swung round and left to open the yard gates for his friends. He had hit out at everybody now. But Colin had it right. Lee hoped to smile and joke his way back into their favour in the seconds before they left.

Pugh turned belligerently to Morgan. 'How long you got to get Blainau in order?' he demanded directly. 'Twelve months, I hear.'

Morgan was still unsettled. 'Who's been saying that?' he murmured.

Pugh came close to him, sorry for his friend, but determined to make him face the realities of the situation. 'Get the professional help. What use a few days' labour from a bunch of kiddies?'

Morgan looked patiently at his old friend. 'Pugh,' he said mildly, as if to an infant, 'if they wanted it so bad, why didn't they try for it when the Old Gentleman passed on?'

Pugh was not to be pacified. 'You don't listen.' He moved to the corner of the workshop where old sacks covered the plough that Greener was painting. He pulled them off, revealing the garish colours and the nameplate: BLAINAU. He glared up at Morgan, annoyed to see him smiling at the offending object.

'Impress the Estate, that will,' Pugh mocked. 'Farm name painted on a bit of old wreck.' He threw the sack over the plough. Morgan laughed and shook his head.

'Give the little lad his fun.'

Pugh moved to the door, affronted. 'Fun is it?' he called over to Morgan. 'And a bit of company?' Morgan nodded. The old man turned at the door. 'Sand to put your head in, boy. Like an ostrich. You heard of that?' He was gone before Morgan could reply.

At Plas Newydd Harry poured a Scotch for Tom Duncan. Eileen had left them together while she prepared lunch. Tom took a quick look at his watch. 'Going away for Easter?' he asked.

Who would invite us? Harry thought. He replied that they were not: too much to do around the house. He handed Tom his glass. 'I want to float an idea,' he began. Tom's spirits fell; he kept his face neutral and nodded in minimum encouragement. Gregory stood before him, his face furrowed in important concentration. Tom hoped silently it would not take too long.

Harry had prepared his speech well — after two hearings even Eileen could not fault its presentation. His preamble was that the Estate was progressive, looking always for new ways to increase assets in an area of outstanding natural beauty and safeguard a traditional way of life. In such an area there were two industries: farming and tourism; the former in decline — hill farming anyway — and the latter on the up and up. Tom Duncan nodded; that much was obvious.

'Eileen and I sat down the other day and put the point of a compass on Plas Newydd. Extraordinary range of facilities within a radius of ten miles.'

Harry named them all: the expected — climbing, canoeing, riding, camping — and the more rare — Llangorse Lane with its water-skiing, pot-holing near Gilwern, hang gliding from Hay Bluff, the airstrip at Pengenffordd.

'God almighty!' he laughed. 'I hear there's even a dry ski slope at Llanigon!'

Tom Duncan waited for Gregory to make his point: he'd done some homework, but so what?

'Come and look at this.' He led the way to a table where his amateur plans lay folded and ready. He took a small swig of Scotch, nervous now that he had arrived at his purpose. He unfolded a large sheet of paper and smiled more confidently than he felt. Duncan peered at the plan, dutifully. It was Plas Newydd, drawn roughly to scale.

'Historic building,' Harry intoned. 'Most of it Tudor.'

Tom scrutinised the drawing. He saw the drift of Gregory's mind immediately. 'It would cost a fortune,' he protested mildly.

'And it could make a fortune.'

Harry explained his scheme to turn the out-buildings into a completely separate and self-contained centre for pony-trekking. The stabling existed already. Here would be the dormitories, the dining hall, which would double as a recreation room, and there the kitchen and bathrooms. He jabbed a finger at the house itself.

'Plusher accommodation for plusher guests. Kitchens. Rebuild the wall here and there's the original dining-hall. No jolly medieval junketings: just peace and quiet and excellent cuisine.'

Duncan pointed to a circle in the field behind. 'What's this?'

Harry beamed. He believed it a masterstroke.

'Helicopter pad. Jaded executives; bring them in from Bristol, Cardiff, Birmingham, London.'

He stepped proudly back. 'Do I make sense?'

Tom thought carefully, unwilling to commit himself. He had seen crazier schemes. What part exactly, he wondered, did the Gregorys see themselves playing? Harry almost read his mind.

'We'd want an option on the lease. No taking it over once it's under way. We've been squeezed out once before.'

Tom knew every detail of the Rhodesian debacle. 'That was a revolution,' he said.

Harry took Tom's glass for a refill. 'So is this, dear boy,' he smiled.

Tom stayed neutral. He knew the Gregorys must have taken time and trouble over this. He moved from the table towards the fire.

'Our architect's with us after the Bank Holiday. Why don't I send him along?'

He hoped his answer was neither encouragement nor a put-down. It seemed to meet with approval. As if pre-arranged, Eileen joined them for a final drink before lunch.

Lee had spent most of the afternoon walking the hills, exasperated with Morgan and Pugh, and obscurely guilty for the part he had played in — as he saw it — driving his old friends from the farm. The rain had petered out into April showers and then died away altogether, leaving a cool freshness in the air. Part of his difficulties had been in identifying where his loyalties should lie. He had not lunched with the men, needing to show his dissatisfaction, and having no stomach either for bread and cheese or their grumbling disapproval of his friends. Instead he had cleared out a ditch — his job for the afternoon — and finished work early.

A balance slowly came to him as he trod the wet paths. Colin was not one to harbour a grudge; it would all have blown over with luck, so long as Morgan did nothing to create a new storm, and he thought that unlikely — his uncle clearly enjoyed the company, and Ros, in particular, would be soothing and sympathetic towards him. Once Pugh had gone home the atmosphere would improve.

Dusk found him in the neighbouring valley and Lee was pleased to recall how, only a matter of weeks ago, nothing would have persuaded him to be two miles from Blainau as the day died and shadows merged into the general night. It was nothing to him now. About seven o'clock he came down to the path below Castel Dinas and walked the final quarter of an hour to the road; he would see Blainau's lights soon after.

Cap came up, barking, as Lee climbed the gate into the yard, noticing Greener's plough sitting incongruously on the roadside. He crouched to fondle the dog, who jumped up to greet a now familiar friend with much tail-wagging. A burst of laughter turned Lee's head towards the house. He straightened up, tired and hungry, and walked across the yard, pleased to hear more laughter and shouts, and curious at its intensity. Cap danced round him, eager for attention, jumping up, yelping, joining in the jollity.

They had made Morgan drunk.

Lee found his uncle staggering across the living room, clutching what seemed to be a half-pint mug of cider, while Ros and Colin lay helpless with laughter on the sofa. Morgan was laughing too, sweat streaming from his face, hardly able to stand as he reached vaguely towards his chair. All three were drunk. Morgan was very drunk indeed. There was no sign of Greener.

'And honest to God now,' — the words pressed unclearly through his drunken delight — 'if any bugger had told me then

179

as we should have electric along this old road, I'd a laughed in their face, I would.'

Morgan swung to face Colin and Ros, his laughter uncontrollable, seeing their faces.

'And phones and cars and vans by damn!' He fell into his chair. 'It was all bikes and ponies then!' He brought the mug to his mouth; the cider spilled between and below his lips. He screamed with laughter, coughing and spluttering. Colin waved furiously, conducting the man's gaping chaos.

'More!' he shouted. 'More!'

Lee stared at his uncle and friends, bewildered and uncertain. Ros at last noticed him; she waved him in, tipsily, crying out his name. Colin saw him too.

'Get a drink. We're having a drink.' He waved a glass.

'Morgan's having a bloody good drink!' shrieked Ros.

They collapsed into laughter again, watching Morgan clown his way through wiping away the cider and the sweat.

'It's hot in here, boys,' he said, suddenly serious. The sudden change of mood provoked further delight and, seeing it, Morgan clowned more, hooting with helpless laughter. Colin and Ros looked at each other; Ros slipped to the floor, intensifying the mad roaring.

Colin glanced with alcoholic affection at Lee. 'Help yourself mate!' he called. He waved vaguely behind him at a box standing on the sideboard which held a variety of cans of beer and cider. Greener came silently from the kitchen. Lee threw him a puzzled look; Lee did not know what had happened. They had been drinking heavily; only that much was obvious, and Morgan was being encouraged to play the clown, which Lee hated. Greener nodded, unseen by the others, towards a bottle, half-hidden on its side behind the box. It was a bottle of vodka, three-quarters empty. They had spiked Morgan's cider. Greener moved quietly to a chair near the fire and picked up his book.

The laughter seemed likely to lapse. Morgan seemed ill and bemused. He almost retched as he fumbled to undo his shirt buttons. Colin continued to orchestrate his confusion.

'It was hot last summer, Morgan.'

Morgan gazed blearily in his direction. He nodded violently.

'Damn and you be right, son! And Seventy-six when the old hill catched fire.'

Colin mimicked his Welshness. 'Old hill catched fire?' he asked, heavily incredulous.

'You can see the black still!' Morgan was animated again.

Ros leant against Colin, crying with laughter. It set Morgan off once more. 'I'm sweating like a pig!' he shouted gleefully. Ros shouted back.

'So long as you don't start squealing like one!'

Morgan was delighted. He threw back his head and squealed, long and grotesquely. Colin slipped to the floor and clung to Ros. All three screamed uncontrollably. Morgan's shirt was soaked. His head fell forward, distressed. He choked back vomit.

Lee had seen enough. Repelled and angry, he moved to take Morgan by the arm.

'Come on, Morgan. I'll help you get up to your room.'

Morgan threw off his grasp. 'I'm marvellous here!' he insisted. Lee took hold of him again, roughly pulling him from his chair. The humiliation of Morgan disgusted him. The man choked again.

'Hey, take it easy, Lee!' shouted Ros, suddenly caring.

'Greener?' Lee called the boy to help. Between them they hauled Morgan, swaying, to his feet. Colin and Ros complained bitterly at this hard handling of their drunk companion.

'You ain't going to tie me to the bench, say?' Morgan was becoming comatose. Colin and Ros called happy approval, but Greener and Lee slowly manoeuvred Morgan's bulk towards the stairs.

Suddenly, Morgan seemed to realise he was making a fool of himself.

'Let me be,' he insisted quietly. They continued to pull him on. He shook them away, violently. His voice rose to a surly shout. 'Leave me be!'

Colin winked, grinning at Ros: this was a new twist in the entertainment. They watched, giggling.

With surprising control and dignity, Morgan stood, swaying like a tree about to fall. He gaped uneasily in the direction in which he must move, and set one foot before the other with extreme care. He walked slowly from the room. His measured, uneven progress could be heard, as he climbed the stairs. The landing creaked massively and a door slammed.

Lee moved angrily to Colin and looked down at the grinning boy. 'What have you been giving him?'

Colin smiled up equably. 'He thought it was straight cider.' He suddenly giggled.

'Wrong!' squealed Ros, climbing with difficulty back onto the sofa.

181

'He's not used to strong drink.' Lee's cold belligerence began to break through their haze of good humour.

'He bloody *bought* half of it.' Colin threw out a hand towards the box. 'He wanted a party. He drove down to Talgarth to get that.' His grin slipped from his face. 'What's wrong with you?'

'That's true Lee.' Ros, seeing the mood turning dangerously, was anxious to explain.

'He can't afford it.'

'He just bought beer and cider. It was Col drove to the pub for the vodka.'

Colin nodded agreement. 'He wanted to make it up after this morning. Morgan was enjoying himself.' He was no longer amused or entertained. His eyes on Lee's cold face, he murmured, 'It's you that's got the problem, not Morgan.'

Lee said nothing. Colin smiled.

'Come on old son,' he said, offering a truce, 'I've seen you worse.' He climbed to his feet, throwing an arm around Lee's shoulders. Lee shrugged it off. Ros giggled.

'He told us about your little Louise.'

Remembering the drunk, sentimental story, Colin chuckled. 'And the sad story of the Old Lady and Gentleman.' He composed his features, suitably solemn, but Ros spluttered amusement. 'No,' Colin rebuked. 'Very sad was that.' But he could not hold his laughter. Colin and Ros set each other giggling.

Sudden anger rushed blood to Lee's face. He turned and moved fast towards the kitchen.

'Where are you going?' called Colin. His temper was beginning to shorten; he had had enough of Lee's unmerited disapproval.

'To get him coffee.'

'He's a big boy. You're not his bloody keeper.' Colin watched Lee's tight shoulders. 'Look,' he called, 'what have we done? We had a row, this morning; now we're friends again. What's wrong with that?' He found himself talking to space — Lee had moved into the kitchen. He swung angrily to Ros, seeking support for his justification.

'Our friend is not being friendly.' Ros shook her head, tipsily sad.

Colin threw a look to Greener, who was reading his book, and ran after Lee.

Lee was lighting the gas below the kettle. He heard Colin

move angrily into the kitchen and took no notice. Colin stood at the table, glaring at his back.

'I've had enough of this.'

'Get stuffed, Colin!'

'No, I have. We come specially to see you —'

Lee turned to him. 'All right,' he said wearily.

'All right, yes. You remember, do you? Back at home? Griping on about this place? Yes?'

'All right, Colin. I remember.' Lee was tired and dispirited. He wanted peace.

'So we come down specially —'

'You were going to Devon.'

'But we detour, yes? And we help out on the farm?'

This was too much for Lee. He felt himself colour. He snapped back. 'And you upset Pugh and you let sheep out —'

Colin slapped the table in frustration. 'Jesus Christ!'

'You get Morgan on at me, then you lace him up and get him pissed. Big laugh, right?'

Colin gazed at Lee's cold, unfriendly face. 'Since you mention it, yes.'

For the first time in their lives, they were dangerously close to coming to blows. Lee turned and moved to the cupboard for coffee, backing down.

'Just go,' he said quietly.

'Just what?' Colin was quiet too. The danger suddenly swelled again.

'Go, okay?'

'Go where?'

'Next door, anywhere.'

Lee had half-opened the cupboard when Colin stepped in front of him, knocking the cupboard door shut. Their faces were close, confronting.

'You're going soft. Like Morgan. Like your new mate, Soldier Blue.' The resentment poured out. 'Like the old man — too scared to tell us we were bugging him.' Colin dropped his arm from the door. He laughed, humourlessly dismissive. 'You've found your place here. You've really changed, haven't you?'

He was right. It was the cause of everything that had happened over the weekend. 'If you like,' Lee said unhappily.

'I don't like.'

Lee pulled the cupboard door open, against Colin's weight. 'Then you know what you can do,' he said, controlling his shaking hand as it reached for the jar. He turned and pushed past Colin to find a cup. 'You made a fool of Morgan.'

Colin searched his eyes. He suddenly shrugged and smiled bleakly. 'Well, you can't improve on nature, Sunbeam,' he said jauntily, turning towards the door.

'Get packed!' Ros and Greener looked blankly at Colin. 'We're going to Devon. We were on our way to bloody Devon!' Colin moved to collect his guitar, leaning against the sideboard. Greener objected, mildly aware of Colin's brittle moods. 'Devon's a couple of hundred miles yet.'

'I know where Devon is.'

Ros, too, was wary of his moods. 'It's dark,' she complained. Colin swept up Greener's sleeping bag and flung it at her. 'Then put a bloody light on!' he shouted.

Greener and Ros exchanged a brief glance of misgiving, seen by Colin as he ranged around the room, gathering their random belongings. 'We'll find somewhere for tonight,' he muttered.

Ros picked up her sweater and a magazine, not daring to cross Colin's mood. The effects of her drinking had quickly diminished; she felt tired and slightly sick. 'What's happened?' she asked, hardly able to see at what point the earlier fun had slid into disagreement, and now this rush to depart. Colin made no reply. He moved towards the porch door.

Greener as yet had packed nothing. 'You're drunk, Colin,' he said. 'Wait for morning.'

Colin shouted over his shoulder at the door. 'You can come with us or stay. Please yourself.' Greener crouched to gather up the books he had bought in Hay.

Ros, more and more hungover as the exodus gathered pace, called to Colin's back, 'What about the tent? Are you taking it down?'

He fumbled with his armful at the door, unable to turn the handle. 'No, I'm leaving it here!' he mocked. The handle turned and he stumbled out into the yard. 'Put this outside light on!' he shouted. Cap barked uneasily at his dark, laden shape. Ros followed him, turning on the switch.

Lee paused at the foot of the stairs as Greener stuffed books and clothes into his rucksack. Lee had heard Colin's decision and the rounding up. Miserable, but resolute, he shook his head. He carried a cup of coffee. Greener smiled.

'I'll make them stop in Abergavenny.'

'Plenty of camp sites there.'

Greener began to roll up his sleeping bag. 'Look after

Morgan and say goodbye for me. Did you see the plough at the gate?'

Lee nodded but could not smile. He regretted Greener's departure and almost considered asking him to stay on. The idea blew out. It was best to get back to the old ways as soon as possible. 'I'll see you before you go,' he said. Greener nodded. Something should be said, but Lee could not find it. 'It's all wrong, is this?' he murmured, a foot on the first step.

Greener paused and looked across the room to him. His brow furrowed in puzzled disagreement. 'No,' he objected mildly. 'It's interesting.'

Lee carried the coffee upstairs, hearing low voices as Colin and Ros lowered the tent. Greener had thought it all interesting; he recognised it as a compliment but was too miserably tired to analyse it.

Morgan pushed bales into the rack below the workshop ceiling, feeling slow and sick.

'I made a fool of myself,' he said for the third time to Pugh, who was oiling the chainsaw at the bench. The sound of hard hammering intruded from the yard, where Lee was securing a loose sheet of corrugated iron on the roof of the bantam shed.

'You're not the first,' the old man muttered. Morgan looked at the lambs that had been gathering strength in the makeshift sheepfold, during the wet days. His head thumped. He was glad the outside hammering had stopped.

'I'm sorry for the boy: no fun chucking out old friends.'

Pugh grunted in agreement as he lifted the chainsaw to its shelf. Lee came in. He moved to replace the hammer and the tin of nails. Pugh smiled at him, wanting to show a definite end to hostilities.

'Here he is,' he called. 'What we got on the famous list for today?'

Lee was grateful for the warmth in Pugh; he wished it could make some difference.

'I've done the roof. Could you check round where the hedges came down again?'

It was a kind, comfortable job. The weather was better today: warmer with some sun. Pugh sorted out a few tools which might be necessary. 'Slave driver is it?' he asked, winking. 'You're getting like us boy. Strangers is a nuisance: they puts you on edge.' He lifted a hand to both and moved into the yard.

Morgan began to urge the animals towards the open door. He

and Lee had avoided any reference to the sudden absence of old friends. The boy looked at the square, stocky strength of the man, gentle with his lambs.

'Sorry, Morgan,' he said. He stood aside, not wanting to alarm the sheep.

'I can look after myself,' his uncle said gruffly.

'I know,' said Lee swiftly.

The lambs at last got the message and barged through the door into the yard. Morgan called Cap to them. He turned to the boy.

'Sorry, son.'

Lee made himself smile briefly.

'Forget it.'

They moved outside.

Pugh held the yard gate open and Morgan called Cap to take the sheep through, as Lee shut the workshop door. The buzz of the Honda hung in the sunlight. Soon Matthew's helmeted and leathered figure could distantly be seen.

'Here's the man from Mars!' Pugh grinned, leaving the gate open for Matthew and following Morgan behind his sheep across the road and into the field opposite. Lee waited for the boy. Matthew slowed the bike, braking and swinging the rear wheel dramatically. He sat, smiling, idling the engine. He nodded down to the garish plough and nameplate.

'God, that's terrible,' he laughed.

Lee was glad to have Matthew back. He had only recently realised how redundant and out-of-place he had allowed him to be in the excitement of seeing old friends. Matthew noticed the absence of the tent; the yellowed oblong of grass where it had been.

'Where are the others?'

'Devon,' said Lee simply. 'They were only here for the weekend.'

If Matthew guessed anything of the complications behind the bald statement, he said nothing, unclasping his chin strap and glad to have his hair free in the sun. He drove his bike into the yard.

'How did the interview go?'

Matthew hesitated a second, before his toe clicked the bike into first gear and he began to move it to his usual parking place.

'Couldn't make it,' he called back. 'I was sick all day.

Tummy bug, according to the Captain. Bloody nuisance.'

Lee stared. 'But you'll get another interview?' His voice took on an edge of anxiety.

Matthew switched off the Honda's engine. 'When they can fix it up.' Their eyes met. Lee knew he had flunked the interview; Matthew's face silently asked him not to pursue it.

'When?' Lee's voice was sharp, insistent.

Matthew climbed from the machine. 'When?' Lee repeated. Matthew made himself answer easily.

'Sometime,' he said, making for the house. 'Soon.'

Lee looked down, all-knowing, at Greener's plough, then moved off towards the waiting tractor at the roadside. It was Matthew's concern. He tried not to be disappointed.

Chapter Seven

Some time after Easter winter finally loosened its six-month grip on the hills, and a brief period that was identifiably spring softened the land. Grass began to push strongly through the heavy clay and Lee found himself needing his heavier clothing less. The sheep seemed happier and the year's lambs lay in warmer content or rushed about in gangs, to no noticeable purpose other than high spirits.

With the better weather came the tourists. Boulton's Trekking Centre doubled its plodding strings, which could even occasionally be seen cantering across the common. Gliders were in the sky above the ridge from the airstrip at Pengenffordd, and almost every day cars dotted the roadside verges as the occupants walked the hills.

Pugh said it wouldn't be long before the cows were sent out from the sour-smelling gloom of their shed to the strengthening pastures. A lorry-load of blue plastic sacks was delivered and stacked against the yard wall: fertiliser to thicken the all important grass. When the cows were released summer would be in sight. Work would be harder, more varied, but infinitely more pleasant. The turning of the year gave Lee a sense of well-being that he had never previously felt.

But Morgan became more morose and taciturn as pressures, unseen by Lee, built slowly round him. Duncan's warnings of economic troubles ahead for Blainau began to be justified as the scope and pace of work increased: the delivery of fertiliser had cut into his account at the bank. While withdrawing money, one day, Morgan found the manager at his side, polite and casual, enquiring about the prospects for the year. His accountant in Abergavenny had never found it easy to persuade Morgan to deliver the statements, invoices and receipts necessary for him to provide Morgan with the service the farm needed. Now it began to be more difficult still. Some of the Blainau bills became even more outstanding. He had to buy more winter feed, which diminished his account further, and the lamb sales which would ease the situation were months ahead. Morgan explained none of this to Lee. The man felt at siege.

Tom Duncan brought an architect to Blainau, explaining that if, at some future date, the farm reverted to the Estate he would need plans and specifications ready for any prospective buyer. Morgan sat, angry and dispirited, in the living-room with the Estate Manager while Lee, puzzled, accompanied the architect, Rivers, around the house. Morgan forbade entry to his mother's room and insisted he be called Mr Thomas, rather than by his Christian name, which Duncan had long used. Duncan caught his mood of elaborate anger and the two men became overpolite and distant. Lee saw this and was worried; Pugh, silent at tea in the kitchen, knew also that it was a pointless and dangerous mistake on Morgan's part.

Rivers took a few Polaroid snaps of Blainau's exterior, used, like Duncan, to awkwardness from independent farmers who felt threatened by the least hint of interference or criticism. He joked and chatted to Lee, whose attention was more on Morgan and Duncan as they walked, in pointed silence, to Duncan's car, and waited for Rivers to join them.

'Nobody'd turn a sitting tenant off a tidy farm.'

Duncan nodded vaguely. 'In which case, Mr Thomas, you'll have to be prepared for other changes.' He glanced at Morgan, seeing the farmer's eyes narrow in suspicion. 'If the Land Tribunal decides in your favour, the Estate will have to put money into this farm. A lot of money.' Duncan looked towards the gate, pleased to see Rivers hurrying towards him. 'I shall need to recoup some of that money. There may well have to be a rent increase.' Morgan smiled, as if expecting something like this. 'Probably a severe increase.' Duncan added. Today he had found Morgan more irritating than ever.

Morgan continued to smile knowingly. 'I knowed it'd come down to that,' he sneered. Rivers and Lee joined them in silence. Duncan sat in the estate car and reached over to click the passenger door open for Rivers to climb in. Lee noted Morgan's knowing smile. His uncle turned to him.

'Now we got it straight,' he said to Lee. 'It's all to put the rent up.' He laughed.

Duncan was not amused. He could see that Morgan was prepared to believe that all his advice and offers of a deal were merely a smokescreen to increase rent. The man was too simple.

189

'Do you pay this boy the correct agricultural rate?' Duncan was annoyed with himself for feeling the need to strike out at Morgan, but the words were out, too late to withdraw. He looked squarely up at the farmer. 'I noticed an envelope on your sideboard.' Morgan said nothing and Duncan turned to Lee. 'Do you draw benefit?' The boy did not know how to answer. Glancing to his uncle for guidance but finding none, he shrugged, alarmed. Duncan switched on the ignition. The engine caught, revved, idled.

'If you can't afford to pay him the full rate, fair enough, but you'd have to explain why. You can't expect Social Services to pay his wage for you. The Land Tribunal might find it interesting that you can't afford a boy's labour.'

At Duncan's side, Rivers was surprised to hear Tom needling the farmer. He doubted if it was the sort of evidence the Tribunal would show interest in, and it was unlike the manager to lose even the slightest cool. He looked over and saw Lee looking anxious and Morgan angry.

'Sharp practice, sir!' Morgan shouted. 'Threats now, is it? Damn and you must be unsure of yourself — that's good news to me. Rent increase and the police, is it?'

Duncan sighed. 'Nothing to do with the police,' he said, 'and I'm just warning you: the D.H.S.S. make random checks.'

He backed off a little, feeling increasingly guilty at trying to scare the man who had more than enough problems anyway. He smiled up at Morgan apologetically and began to say goodbye, but Morgan had turned and was already moving back towards the yard gate, leaving Lee standing uncertainly by the car. Tom nodded to him and, slipping his car into gear, he moved away. Duncan smiled at Rivers, and shook his head in exasperation. Rivers grinned back and settled down into his seat, snapping on the safety belt.

Lee hurried to catch up with Morgan. 'Is that right?' he asked, 'about the D.H.S.S.?' Morgan was too angry to reply. What right, thought the man, what bloody right to talk like that? Fifty years in the family. Bloody college boy! What right? They strode in silence into the yard, where Pugh was manoeuvring a sack of fertiliser to the spinner. The outdoor phone bell shrilled and Lee was glad to leave and answer it.

'When did your rent go up last,' Pugh asked.

Morgan thumped the gate in annoyance. 'He's trying it on, man. It have stayed the same a year — year and a half. He can't fright me.'

Pugh tugged at the awkward sack. 'He have let you off cheap

190

then. Every other damn thing have gone up since.'

Morgan turned upon the man. 'Whose side are you on? Bloody old fool, you are!' The hurt showed in Pugh instantly. Red-faced, he hauled the load near the spinner Morgan regretted the outburst at once.'He gets me on edge. Plans and pictures with the camera,' he said. Pugh heaved the sack into place and rested. His eyes stayed down.

'Morgan?' Lee called from the door. 'Phone.'

Morgan opened his mouth to frame an apology, then, knowing he was too wound up to make it generous, he walked fast into the house. He would keep it for later; the old boy knew him better than to believe the insult was personal.

Pugh slit open the sack with his knife as Lee came up to him, and together they lifted the sack and tipped its contents into the funnel of the spinner. The events of the last hour had shaken them both. Morgan's lack of his usual massive stability and control was unsettling. Pugh, knowing the man well, was less surprised than Lee; he had seen Morgan's confidence dwindle, in barely noticeable ways, over the last few weeks.

'Will he lose this place, Pugh?' Lee spoke softly, asking the question neither had dared raise until now. The visit of Rivers and Duncan, and their purpose, had suddenly made the issue real for the boy. Pugh was still upset and affronted.

'Nothing to do with me,' he murmured. They shook the sack empty.

'It's Morgan's accountant on the phone.' Lee needed reassurance, but Pugh moved stiffly to collect a second sack. Lee turned and walked resolutely into the house.

Lee had intended, first, to ask what Morgan had said to upset Pugh, but, seeing him at siege on the phone, denying there were papers to be sent to the office, complaining that he had a farm to run and was no office boy, agreeing that there were other accountants if he were dissatisfied, the boy's determination was defused. He was fascinated and distressed by Morgan's eyes, which reminded him strongly of animals in distress: that sideways flick towards an unseen danger — that wide open panic.

Morgan saw Lee and put the phone hard down in mid-sentence.

'What did he want?'

'I sent him papers,' Morgan protested. 'Sent him plenty: all I got. Done it when the Old Lady passed on.' He turned defiantly to face Lee. 'I ain't no office boy.'

'She died seven months ago, Morgan.'

Lee watched Morgan twist and turn in his frustration.

'It's all threats, this morning, boy.' Morgan forced a smile which was grotesque, begging for Lee's acquiescence. 'He can choose for himself if he wants my custom,' he said, unconvincingly righteous.

Lee was not to be diverted. The unexplained moods he had seen Morgan suffer clarified a little. Seeing the frightened eyes had given him the clue.

'What papers, Morgan?'

The eyes flicked sideways again. 'I got all the papers safe,' he murmured evasively. Lee knew where the papers were. As long as he had been at Blainau, he had seen letters, mostly in brown envelopes, torn roughly out and read, before being pressed into the sideboard drawer.

'The Old Lady was a wonder with the paperwork.' Morgan's half-hearted boast had no weight behind it. Lee moved towards the sideboard.

'Clear the table in the kitchen.'

Morgan's eyes pleaded with Lee not to face him with this proof of his inadequacy.

'We got work to do,' he protested lamely.

'This is work.' Lee pulled the drawer free. It was so packed with paperwork that the upper edge of the dresser scraped the top level of random receipts and bills from the drawer and they fell to the floor. Lee stood calmly. Morgan slowly bent to gather the fallen papers. He dropped them on top of the rest. Lee moved to the kitchen.

'You're your own worst bloody enemy,' he said. 'Look at all this.'

Morgan followed him wretchedly. 'Leave me be,' he begged.

Lee dumped the contents of the drawer on the kitchen table. He noticed one envelope that had not been opened. Then another. A third.

'Get it all sorted now, Morgan. Take it in tomorrow.' Morgan made a vague, dismissive gesture but Lee was insistent. 'You usually go into Abergavenny for the market. Take it tomorrow.' Morgan made no movement. Lee grew exasperated.

'You've got to get real help. This Land Tribunal – what's it going to be like? Somebody's got to know. Have you got a solicitor?'

'Ten pounds to stand on a solicitor's carpet.' Morgan still made no move. Lee turned and walked into the living-room. When he returned, Morgan was standing at the table, opening a sealed envelope unenthusiastically. It was a start. Lee held out his Giro cheque from the D.H.S.S.

'I'll be cashing this tomorrow. Will it pay for a solicitor?'

Morgan looked at the boy's steadiness and was ashamed. He was proud, too, that the boy cared so much. He sat at the table and began to work, smoothing crumpled scraps of paper, removing letters from envelopes.

'Keep your money, son,' he said quietly.

Duncan and Rivers were pleased to find a more enthusiastic, not to say effusive, welcome at Plas Newydd. After a swift sherry Rivers produced a set of architect's plans, thirty years old, and they all moved outside. Tom and Eileen watched Harry as he scampered around Rivers, who was trying to collate the deterioration since 1950, pointing out a feature, explaining an idea, wanting to be a help.

'Harry's a real optimist,' chuckled Duncan.

She smiled. 'An optimist is merely someone who hasn't heard the bad news yet.'

Tom laughed, 'Eileen, Eileen!' he admonished. 'You're going native. That's local doom-and-gloom if ever I heard it.'

They watched Harry directing Rivers' attention to a particularly ornate carving above a boarded window. She smiled thinly.

'My husband is a born starter-up of hares. Unfortunately, it's always others who seem to enjoy the jugged benefits.'

Duncan grimaced briefly; he liked Harry Gregory, so long as the doses were small.

'His ideas are in line with Estate thinking.'

Eileen felt the mild rebuke. She turned her cold amusement full upon him. She beamed.

'Then let us hope we're all around to share the happy outcome. Would you stay to lunch?'

Duncan was forced to smile inwardly; she could be a pain, God knows, but she had style. Although the invitation had been more than polite, he knew better than to accept. He made a show of consulting his watch and, professing a heavy day ahead, said no, they had better move on, thanks all the same: Ted Rivers wasn't often in Wales and they had other properties to see.

They moved to join Rivers and his persistent satellite.

It had been, in short, a difficult day for everyone, and everyone, in various ways, was glad to see it over.

While Morgan sat alone, slowly filling a cardboard box with material for his accountant, Pugh sought out Lee to check that the famous list would soon include picking stones from the higher fields, the maintenance of which earned an easy subsidy. Lee made a note to ask Matthew up the next day; they could pick stones together. The old man and the boy sat around in the workshop, in silent solidarity, unwilling to intrude on Morgan's unenthusiastic concentration. Pugh was relieved to hear his daughter's car arrive to collect him.

Eileen and Harry were silent, too, wondering what the official response would be from Tom Duncan. Eileen had not enjoyed seeing her husband scamper like an ageing puppy around the architect. Undignified. The Captain, in his turn, entertained misgivings that Duncan and Rivers may have misread his show of enthusiasm for mere amateur meddling; eccentricity. He listened to the radio news at six o'clock, sipping Scotch in his study. She read *Horse and Hound* and drank gin and tonic in the kitchen.

Tom Duncan and Ted Rivers drank coffee in Tom's ornate estate office in the big house, reviewing their day. They quietly made decisions which could alter the lives of their tenants. Blainau was no problem: Ted's office would supply plans and drawings within the week, sufficient to show off the scope of the place to any possible buyer or new tenant. Rivers suggested a small-scale scheme for Plas Newydd, which would keep the occupiers off Duncan's back. Rebuilding of barns at Tredustan would pose no problem. The derelict cottage under Castel Dinas was more tricky: to make it an attractive proposition as a holiday home, it would have to be rebuilt from scratch. All this Tom approved.

Morgan prepared to leave for Abergavenny market the next morning. The cardboard box sat in the passenger seat of the Land Rover. Pugh helped him pack three sheep into the back.

'Who'll buy three sheep?' Pugh still held some of the surly mood of the previous day. Morgan, virtuous after his paperwork, seemed to have forgotten how he had suddenly turned on the man. He secured the canvas carefully.

'They're tidy enough. I'll get a price.'

'To pay the accountant, say?'

'I'll get a fair price.'

Morgan nodded to Pugh and climbed into the cab. The Land Rover moved from the yard and turned towards Abergavenny. As the vehicle progressed along the road, Matthew approached from the other direction. Pugh closed the gate behind him.

Matthew switched off his engine and climbed from the Honda, pulling off his gauntlets.

'Where's Morgan gone?'

'Aber.'

Matthew removed his helmet, watching Pugh walk towards the workshop.

'Lee around?'

'Off on his pushbike. We got to pick stones from the top field, till he come back and relieve me.'

Matthew noted Pugh's unusually solemn mood, but could see no good reason for it.

'You okay, Pugh?'

Pugh turned and looked at him, seeing genuine concern. He grinned.

'Champion.'

Reassured, Matthew was about to move to the house, when a sudden burst of whooping broke through the morning. Clip-clopping past the farm came a string of trekkers who waved and shouted, wildly enjoying themselves. There were about a dozen riders, all dressed in parody of cowboys. They had taken some trouble and looked splendidly absurd. Gratified at Matthew's incredulity and Pugh's scorn, they waved cap-pistols and cheered. One, with a huge cardboard Sheriff's star pinned on a fancy waistcoat, called 'Howdy' in a grotesquely hammed-up Welsh-American accent, and the rest almost fell from their plodding ponies with laughter as they passed.

Matthew and Pugh moved to the gate to watch their comic progress. The boy turned grinning to Pugh who, amused in spite of his mood, smiled back, shaking his head.

'Who are they?'

'Up from the mining valleys. Come every year. One big joke to them, we are.'

They watched the string pass out of sight.

'I passed a couple of tents on the common.'

Pugh spat eloquently. 'I seen them, too. Hippies, boy.'

Matthew grinned.

'It'll be like Custer's last stand when they meet up.'

Pugh fervently hoped it would be.

Lee knocked at the office door and pushed it timidly open as Griffiths called from inside, looking up from the desk where he was working.

'Mrs Griffiths told me to come here.'

Griffiths waved to the chair. 'Come in then. You can sit down.'

Lee sat and waited for Griffiths to finish his morning correspondence. He looked round the office: so this was the way things should be done on a farm.

'Morgan want summat?' Griffiths picked up another letter and scanned it.

'He doesn't know I'm here.'

Tom Griffiths considered this and, laying the letter aside, he swivelled his chair to face the uneasy boy. 'Morgan's a good friend to me,' he said carefully, wanting to establish at once where his priorities lay. He waited patiently for Lee to get to the point. Lee was finding his visit more difficult than he had expected. Riding to the farm, he had rehearsed what he must say: it was not so easy.

'Only, Morgan needs some help. Advice and that.' Griffiths nodded slowly. 'It's the Estate. They want ='

Griffiths helped him out. 'I know about the Estate. Morgan have told me.'

Lee was surprised. He thought Morgan hugged the threat to himself; he thought only he and Duncan knew the full details. He raised an arm, indicating the neat efficiency all round him.

'Only, you've got it together here.' He saw Griffiths' puzzlement. 'You know how to make things work,' he explained. Tom Griffiths saw the boy's anxiety.

'Maybe it's you wants the advice, not Morgan?' he suggested quietly.

Lee leaned forward, needing to make the man understand his position.

'I don't know how I can help him,' he stated simply. Then, feeling suddenly guilty: 'It's bad is this. I don't like talking about him behind his back.'

Griffiths felt a surge of sympathy and wondered if Sarah would ever do as much for him; he liked to think she would.

'How long you been at Blainau?' he asked conversationally. 'Best part of four months?' Lee nodded. 'Then you know your uncle damn near as well as I do.' He searched for the right words and the best way to say them. 'Morgan don't face things square.' Lee nodded unhappily. Griffiths picked some forms from his desk and moved to file them in the cabinet, wanting time, wanting to say it well.

'Go along with how he sees things: that's likely the best way you can help. Keep by him. See him through. He has got more than a year. Can you stay?'

He moved to perch on a table at Lee's side.

'Between us, boy, you couldn't have no better neighbour than Morgan. Nice chap. But he's simple — not dull in the head, I don't mean that. But he sees things simple. His Mam and Dad was the same. Blainau should have changed in their lifetime.'

196

Lee listened with a sinking heart. He's saying it's too late now, he thought. Can I stay a year and then watch Morgan lose Blainau? Griffiths saw Lee's shoulders droop slightly.

'I was lucky,' the man said, as if he should be feeling guilty at his success. 'My Mam and Dad passed on early. I was left to myself. I was lucky in my wife: farmer's daughter − and a good farmer. She taught me new ways. Lucky.'

He smiled at his luck. Genuinely happy for the man, Lee smiled too, nodding.

'Now,' Griffiths said, suddenly brisk and businesslike, 'Morgan never had luck like that.' He moved back to his desk. 'Just him and his parents, getting older, fixed in their ways. Close − too damn close. I wouldn't want Morgan to know I'm saying this,' he warned. Lee reassured him; the boy knew he could never face Morgan with this alien view of family, too damn close in Blainau, letting time move on outside.

'I have made Morgan the offer of help, but he won't have it.'

Lee looked up, surprised again.

'Morgan's scared, son. He was scared of his Mam and Dad all his life − fearsome man, old Mr Thomas − and he's scared of them now, scared of letting them down.'

Lee knew this. He nodded helplessly.

'You ever do boxing at school? No? Well, boy, if you never steps up in that ring, then you never loses the contest.' Tom Griffiths spread his arms wide. 'That's Morgan for you.'

Silence grew in the room. Griffiths folded his arms and watched his visitor.

'I should just stay then? Go along with him?'

'Leave him his dignity. You'll have done your best.'

Silence fell again. Lee nodded, thanked the man and stood. Griffiths stood, too, he laid a friendly arm across the boy's shoulders, impressed at Lee's understanding and acceptance.

'You take time off from Blainau when you can. You're a bright boy. My Sarah's bright, too, and she spends too much damn time with those old school books. You come here when you needs help or company, and welcome.'

Lee was moved and grateful for the offer. He could not tell Griffiths how impossible it was to accept. He thanked him and they moved to the door.

'Not a word to Morgan, mind.'

Lee nodded silently one last time and they walked together to the front door.

Mixed feelings were also in order at Plas Newydd as Harry spoke jovially to Tom Duncan on the phone, aware of Eileen's presence at his side. He bid an affable farewell and replaced the receiver. He relayed Tom's greetings.

'How kind.' She waited for the news, knowing her husband well enough to sense that it fell short of his expectations, as everything always seemed to. He smiled too widely.

'Right,' he reported. 'Architect chap suggests we knock Matthew's room and the boxroom next door into one and put in a bathroom. Same across the corridor. Uncover the open fireplace in that barn of a room next to the kitchen and fit it out as a dining-room.'

She waited. That was all.

'Not a bad idea,' he said, trying for total enthusiasm and almost succeeding. She smiled.

'Bed and Breakfast.' She made it sound like a prison sentence.

'No,' Harry objected vigorously. 'Limited experiment. If we can get it done to catch some of the summer' — he almost said 'trade' — 'visitors, we review the situation in late autumn and take decisions about further extensions for next year.'

Eileen reached for her magazine. 'This year, next year, sometime, never,' she opined equably.

Harry was annoyed. 'I'm probing for a little enthusiasm.' Harry walked to warm himself by the fire.

'A little is all I can dredge up.'

'Tom says he has builders able to begin as soon as we like. They're bogged down in some project the other side of Crickhowell, which is lucky for us.' He looked down at his seemingly indifferent wife. 'I have to ring him back when we've talked it over.'

'Well, now we have.'

'Don't be silly, Eileen,' he said sharply. She raised blank eyes to him.

'You seem to have decided for us.' She smiled her infuriating smile. 'I'll believe it when I see it.' She turned back to her magazine, leaving him irritated and annoyed with himself: he had expected more from Duncan and knew he should have told the man.

Stone picking is a back-breaking, slow business, seemingly never-ending, and Lee and Matthew were duly tired when they drove back to Blainau, a full box of stones swaying behind the tractor.

Pugh had told them to get rid of the load in a stream about half a mile from the farm; they thought they deserved a break first.

There was no sign of Pugh, and Morgan had not returned from Abergavenny as they came into the kitchen. Matthew's complex involvement with the Paras had become, by mutual tacit agreement, a taboo subject. Lee supposed Matthew would talk of it when he was ready.

As Lee gingerly stretched to reach down the coffee, Matthew dug his fingers into his aching back muscles, provoking a flurry of aggressive horseplay which soon subsided: they were too tired to prolong it. They eventually sipped their coffee and examined tender, grazed hands in quiet content. They talked about Talgarth and Plas Newydd. When Matthew asked where Lee had been earlier on his cycle, he simply said 'Nowhere,' and they left it at that. Lee was entertained by the account of the Wild West procession; he would have liked to have seen Pugh's face when the Sheriff greeted him.

'Where is Pugh?' Matthew asked. It was unusual not to see him around the farm at teatime. Lee did not know. He offered his friend the latest fruit of his growing interest in baking, which was more enthusiastic than skilful. Matthew took a rock-cake, and dramatically toppled beneath its supposed weight, which provoked more horseplay. They washed the mugs and left to unload the stones in the swift stream near Cwm Farm.

Pugh watched them leave − Lee driving the tractor and Matthew perched behind on the rattling stones. He was sitting on a fallen tree, near the highest of Blainau's hedges, with the ridge at his back. He feared for Morgan; feared for this farm. He had spent most of the day thinking what he should do for the best and was coming slowly, with no pleasure, to a possible conclusion. The afternoon sun was briefly warm on his face, as it slanted down towards the distant hills of Radnorshire. He hauled himself to his feet and began his descent. Blainau's roof gleamed and dazzled in the setting sun. He noticed the school bus making its second journey of the day. His grandson would be out of school finding the back-door key in the secret place in the garden. He made careful steps across a wet patch in the field, noticing the quiet content of the pregnant ewes grazing richer pasture.

Graham and Price were enjoying the late sun as they drove across the fields in the pick-up truck to Griffiths' farm.

'All I say is you want to watch out,' protested Graham

mildly. Price grinned sideways at him.

'You're jealous, boy. It sticks out a mile.' Graham affably poked Price between the legs. Price yelled and swerved.

'That's what's sticking out a mile.' They laughed as they bumped through a rutted gateway onto the farm road.

'Sarah's not under age. She knows her own mind.' Graham laughed again. 'When she was under age, I didn't notice you much bothered.'

The truck turned into the yard and stopped. Price switched off the engine. He was thoughtful.

'Too many knowing, you reckon?'

'They was talking up Castle Inn.'

'Who?' Price was suddenly sharp. 'Not Morgan's boy or his brave mate?'

Graham got out and slammed his door. 'They know better,' he smiled. 'It was just general conversation, man.'

Price climbed from the vehicle and stretched. 'I'll have a word.'

They moved to set up the evening session in the long, low, milking parlour.

Morgan and Lee met on the road. They halted their vehicles alongside each other.

'How did it go with the man?' Lee called above the combined rolling of the motors.

'Not too bad.'

'Get a fair price for the sheep?'

'Nothing fancy.' Morgan nodded to Matthew on his perch. 'You picked some stones then?'

'Bloody awful job!' called Matthew, holding up his ravaged hands, grinning.

Morgan smiled back. 'It is,' he agreed. He engaged his gears and moved away. Lee was relieved; the meeting with Griffiths had left him apprehensive of next seeing Morgan, anxious of an appropriate response. That hurdle was over. He slammed the tractor in gear and toppled Matthew onto the stones. Lee looked behind, smiling, impervious to the threats and insults hurled at him by his friend.

Sarah was the last passenger in Mrs Lewis' minibus: the boys from Cwm had taken another day off to help their father in the fields. The girl had endured a long, tiring day at school, faced with the spectre of imminent O-Levels. She waved to Mrs Lewis as she reversed the bus in the farmyard and drove home to Talgarth.

Price stepped from a barn near the house and beckoned. She looked round quickly and shook her head. A meeting at this time was dangerous. Price, too, glanced round, checking, before beckoning her over again, more urgently. He stepped back into the barn. Sarah followed him swiftly, unwillingly, but accepting that whatever he wanted to say must be important.

The hay barn was large and modern, still a quarter full of bales — the modern silo nearby provided most of the winter feed. Sarah came in anxiously, screwing up her eyes as she moved from the bright sunlight. Price held out a hand which she took and they found a corner among the sweet-scented bales, invisible from the door. She asked what he wanted; it was dangerous to meet now — her parents could have seen the school bus and be wondering where she had vanished to. He grinned at her worried face.

'School uniform turns a man on,' he said.

She smiled back. 'It's supposed to turn men off.'

He pulled her towards him and they kissed, but she was still uneasy. 'What do you want?' she repeated, moving apart.

'You heard anybody saying anything?'

She was instantly alarmed, but Price was reassuring. 'No need to worry. Just wondered — only Graham's been hearing things up Castle Inn, he says.'

Her fear sharpened. 'Dad drinks there,' she said, dismayed.

Price put out a hand and stroked her hair. 'They wouldn't have dared talk with him listening. Just that we better be careful a bit. Okay?'

She nodded. Price saw that he had frightened her. 'Come here,' he murmured, drawing her close again, pressing her to him. She pressed back, closing her eyes.

They kissed for a long time. She began to murmur about leaving, but Price opened his mouth on hers. She felt his tongue move around hers and groaned, holding him hard. Her eyes opened and she saw her father at the corner of the stack of bales. She froze in panic.

Price barely had time to realise something was wrong before Griffiths' fist hit the side of his face, knocking him off balance, away from his daughter. The farmer was shouting, almost incoherent with rage.

'You bugger! You bloody bugger!'

He pushed the staggering Price wildly back, half-sitting in the hay. Sarah stood where Price had been holding her. She tried to speak.

'Bloody get off me!' shouted Price, struggling to his feet. The man swung at him, missing, and Price raised his own fists.

'Dad –'

Griffiths twisted to face Sarah. Shocked, she tried again to force the words. He shouted at her.

'Get to the house!'

She could not move. Then Griffiths took a step in her direction and she found herself clumsily pushing through the hay, frantic for escape. The low sun slanted into her eyes as she broke through the door and ran, crying, towards the house.

Griffiths' temper cooled slightly. He turned back to Price, who, expecting a new attack, was hot and at the ready. The two men confronted each other.

'And you,' snarled Griffiths, 'you get from here now!' Price saw the anger leaving his boss. He dropped his arms.

'Be reasonable, Mr Griffiths.'

Griffiths flared up briefly. 'By damn,' he shouted. 'I should kick you back to bloody Cardiff!' They stared each other out.

'All right,' murmured Price. Each imperceptibly relaxed, knowing the time for violence had passed. Price felt his face and flicked hay from his overalls. Griffiths controlled his rasping breath.

He looked at his labourer with distaste. 'Just get right from here. I'll send you your cards tonight.' Price began to walk stiffly towards the door. 'Cardiff boy,' sneered Griffiths. 'Wild boy. Give us a chance, you said, come begging for a job.'

Price turned. 'I'm not taking all the blame,' he said. 'It takes two and you know it.'

Griffiths moved belligerently towards him. 'You just keep your mouth shut, boy!' Price shook his head in disbelief as the farmer came close.

'I can take you any time, old man,' he said quietly.

Griffiths pushed him hard. 'Bloody try it!' His voice was quiet and dangerous, too.

Graham appeared, looking scared, in the doorway. The shouting and Sarah's flight to the house had drawn him. He said nothing and did not move. Neither Price nor Griffiths, their eyes locked together, seemed to have noticed him. But the presence of a third must somehow have registered. Again the possibility of violence dulled and receded.

'Get from my farm.'

Graham's appearance drew a response from his mate. Price smiled at him and gathered up his canvas bag, his thermos and coat, near the door. He winked at Graham who nodded uneasily back.

'Who told you?' he casually asked Griffiths as he packed his thermos.

'Nobody. No need. I seen you.'

'Saw the old bus and wondered what your wonderful daughter was doing, meeting a scruff like me!' Price grinned at Graham. 'Not been telling tales on me, have you, friend?' he asked. Graham saw the coldness behind the grin. He shook his head. Price nodded, believing him. He stepped into the yard. 'Plenty of overtime for you now, Graham.' He turned to look at Griffiths. 'I'm glad to be shot of this place.' He spat and moved towards the vehicle shed. 'Bring my money down the house tonight and we'll celebrate, eh?' he called over his shoulder.

Griffiths came to the door to watch him leave. 'You knew about this, did you?' he murmured to Graham.

'Tried to warn him, Mr. Griffiths. Swear to you, sir. Been trying to warn him, ages.' Graham shifted nervously beneath the cold, angry gaze of his employer.

'How long's it been on?' asked the man softly. Graham licked his lips anxiously, saying nothing. 'Last year?' He sharpened his eyes sternly. Graham nodded. 'Longer?' Graham nodded wretchedly again. Griffiths walked into the fading light towards his house. Graham leaned back against the barn door, exhaling, relieved.

In the living-room, Griffiths found Sarah, still sobbing, with his wife trying to comfort her; the girl could not break through the shocked tears to explain. Her mother looked up as he walked through the door.

Before Sarah could say anything, he slapped her violently across the face. Mrs Griffiths stepped forward, protesting, but caught a quick glance of cold anger from her husband and stood very still.

'You stay here, my girl, while I check that man of yours is from this farm and then you'll answer some questions. Damn and your life's going to be different now.' He looked at his wife. 'Bloody teasing,' he explained, 'and leading men on.' He strode to the door, shouting, as he turned to shut it, 'I should take a belt to you!' The door slammed, Mrs Griffiths moved to take in her arms the daughter whom she must now no longer think of as a girl. She had gathered some small gist of the events, but none was so poignant as the need for that sudden adjustment.

The hospital section of Blainau's workshop had only one patient — on his slow descent from the high fields, Pugh had discovered a newborn lamb, more dead than alive, and carried it gently inside his coat, giving it the warmth of his older, sturdier body.

When he looked in, ready to leave for the town, Morgan was gently lowering it into a wooden crate containing a battered, one-bar electric fire. He had tried to encourage milk from a teat on a bottle between the feeble lips, but the lamb was too far gone; all he could do was keep it warm now. With great gentleness he set it in a corner of the crate and slotted a mesh of wire between the helpless creature and the fire.

'Got him in intensive care?'

Pugh came to join Morgan who murmured, 'Poor little bugger.' He laid a roof of tin across the crate and slowly stood.

'Will he last?' asked Pugh, deferring to Morgan's expertise.

'I expect so.'

Morgan turned to Pugh and smiled.

'We'll have him out on the hill soon, and the rest. Then the cows'll be out in the fields and summer's here.' Pugh kept his eyes down on the crate among the bales of straw and asked the question he had been considering all day.

'Morgan? Keep hold on the farm, will you?'

It had been a long day: market, the accountant, farm work. Morgan felt it had been a good day overall. The warm sun had helped. He had done his best.

'You and the boy,' he said bluffly. 'You do worry a damn sight more than me. Who knows what's ahead, man? A whole damn year to get Blainau to rights.' He smiled again.

Pugh had asked the right question. The answer was wrong. He tried again. 'But Duncan, from the Estate —'

'Could he save a lamb?' Morgan's complacent serenity provided Pugh with his answer, however unintentionally. The old man kept his eyes down.

'Likely not,' he murmured.

Morgan moved to the door where Cap waited. The dog wagged his tail briefly and stretched. Pugh's eyes lifted to the sturdy frame of his friend, as he shoved the door open and stood framed in the last of the sun. Pugh's eyes were full of sympathy.

A car approached. Morgan turned. 'There she is,' he called. Pugh was watching him, intent with sadness and Morgan was puzzled. The car drew up and a horn tooted. Morgan kept his surprised eyes on the man all the way to the gate, wondering at the unaccustomed seriousness and lack of the usual wave as Pugh climbed carefully into his daughter's car.

                    *   *   *

Lee cooked a simple meal, after which he and Morgan washed up. Each was slightly wary of the other: it showed in the silences, smiles and politeness, which each assumed to be his own reaction to the day's events. Lee had accepted Tom Griffiths' advice to acquiesce in his uncle's decisions, and was anxious that Morgan should not notice the tricky seam between his pushy self of the previous evening, when he had forced Morgan to do the paperwork, and the supportive role he was now to play. Morgan had something to say which he hoped would not diminish the boy's determination to stay and battle on with him, for Blainau. They were both skirting the topic gingerly, waiting for the opportunity to react to the new situation.

'You worked damn long hours today.'

'Yeah. Those stones were bastards.'

Lee rinsed the final pan. Morgan carefully dried a plate.

'Give you a game of draughts, Morgan?'

'I'd like a good, long game. Bit of a change.'

'Or we can go to the pub?'

'I'm content with the old draughts, boy.'

Morgan picked up the milk jug and shook water from it. Lee crossed to light the gas and set the kettle over it.

'Sure?' he asked. 'If it's money's any problem, Matthew took me to the post office to cash my Giro.'

Morgan paused briefly as he screwed the tea towel deep inside the jug, seeing his opportunity. He kept his voice quietly casual. 'It'll take more than that.'

Lee didn't understand. He asked, 'Sorry? What will?'

Morgan placed the dried jug on the table and reached for the frying pan. Lee replaced the jug on the sideboard, waiting for the reply.

'Only we got to cut back a bit, see. Not to be extravagant. Not long till shearing – not long really – and then the lamb sales: good money in fleeces and lambs. We'll be wonderful then.' He laid the pan on the table and looked at Lee, smiling and embarrassed. 'But just now we got to be careful.' Morgan kept his eyes keenly on Lee's face, wanting to show optimism; wanting Lee to understand.

'Can't you get money from the bank?'

Morgan hung up the towel. 'Got to have money *in* the bank to take it from there.'

'I mean a loan or overdraft or something. I don't know about banks.'

Morgan moved closer to Lee. 'No sense to get in deeper,' he said. 'Come the sales, we'll be champion.' He saw Lee's concern. 'Look,' the man said simply, 'that chappie in Aber — the accountant man — he took a fair bit from me today for V.A.T. and to be set aside for the old tax man.' Lee opened his mouth to speak, but Morgan continued earnestly. 'I'm just telling you so you don't think I'm holding it back from you. Trusting you. I'm doing it, son; I'm trying to get the damn money side straight. Trying — like you wanted.'

After a while Lee nodded and smiled a little. Morgan left to set out the draughts board while Lee made the tea and coffee.

Lee slept heavily that night. It was not only physical fatigue; a mental and emotional tiredness drained his energy and he had gone to bed early, after three games — they often played seven. He had expected that life would somehow muddle on to the point when he left: he had no idea when this would be. He had not foreseen any great changes in the pattern but it concerned him obscurely that, just when he had followed Griffiths' advice and been willing to make the adjustment to this pattern — Morgan's pattern — Morgan himself had decided to change it. The problems of money registered little: as he had told his uncle, he knew nothing of banks. But it was a huge step for Morgan — or rather for Lee's vision of Morgan — to move into the bigger, colder area of V.A.T. and tax, where the Old Gentleman and Lady held no place, nor did Cap, nor Pugh, nor the famous list. Had he known it, he was taking on characteristics of the border people, going native, apprehensive of what *they* could do to you if you moved outside your patch onto unfamiliar ground, where rules were different and people held other views. Lee had found a comfort and partial peace in moving towards Morgan's small, protective world, only to discover that, partly to please him, his uncle had put one foot outside, and might, now he was committed, have to step further.

Morgan knocked on his door at seven-thirty, and again at eight. He called from the yard before taking the tractor to plough the high stone-free field. All this Lee heard, but he was unable to break through the dull net of fatigue that drew him back to sleep. It was almost nine when a calling voice finally penetrated his heaviness; a female voice, inside the house. At first he thought he was dreaming. He glanced at his watch as he called back, struggling into jeans and T-shirt to run barefoot downstairs and find Pugh's daughter, Jean, smiling as she waited just inside the porch door.

Lee knew Jean well enough. He liked her Welsh sing-song voice and her cheerfulness. She was middle-aged, a comfortable lady, who looked after the office of an Abergavenny garage, whose husband was an engineer for British Telecom. Lee had never before seen her outside her car and she was shorter than he'd imagined.

'Someone's sleeping late,' she grinned, showing a sudden and startling similarity to her father. 'I didn't think there was anybody in, maybe.'

Lee was apologetic. 'No. I'm sorry. Must have overslept,' He waited for the purpose of the visit, not knowing if Pugh was about or not. He glanced to the pegs inside the door: Pugh's working-coat was still hanging there from yesterday.

'I saw Morgan up in the fields on his tractor but he didn't notice.' She smiled cheerfully again. Lee shrugged and smiled back. His feet were cold on the flagstones.

'Only, Dad won't be coming up,' Jean smiled.

Lee was concerned. 'What's wrong with him?' he asked.

'Nothing wrong.' The cheerfulness persisted. 'Only, we had a good, long talk last night – the three of us: me and Dad and my husband – and he won't be coming up.'

'No?' asked Lee, puzzled.

Jean moved closer to the door. She grasped the door-knob which was a comfort to her: she would have preferred not to have come into the house in the first place, but nobody had responded to her knocking. She would have much preferred not to come at all, but it was only fair. She opened the door, her message delivered. Seeing Lee's bemused face, she added, 'We had a good, long talk. He's getting on and we think it's best. All right?' The hand turned the door-knob.

'When's he coming back?'

'You know Dad,' Jean smiled and moved around, anchored by her hand on the door. 'He wants to do what's right – not to let anybody down – but he's getting on. All right?'

Lee forgot the chill under his feet. 'I don't know what you mean?' he lied, hoping he did not.

'Only, it's no good for him. He's done his best; fair play. He said for me to call and tell you. You'll see Morgan, will you?' She moved to stand at last in the doorway itself.

'Not coming back ever?' The enormity twisted his stomach. He felt sick.

'All right?' asked Jean brightly. 'You'll tell Morgan then? It was getting him down. Not fair really.'

She turned the door-knob once and then stepped out into the

welcome daylight. 'There's some traffic on the roads,' she confided. 'Better be away or they'll be giving me the sack. Goodbye then.' Jean walked briskly towards the waiting car, glad to make her escape. Lee was running, in his boots, to the field behind Blainau by the time the engine of the car was a distant, disappearing drone in the air.

Lee ran hard uphill, his breathing harsh and laboured. He clambered uncaring over the barbed wire into the second field and pounded on, his legs beginning to ache. His heart thumped as he raced diagonally across the rough ground, still slippery from the dew, to where he knew Morgan was working. He hung, briefly, across a gate, for respite, before hauling himself over and on, along the hedgerow and into the final field, staggering now and gasping. He saw the tractor and tried to shout but his breathless cry had no force. He forced himself towards Morgan, stumbling across the furrows. Cap saw him and came bounding and barking towards him. Morgan saw him as the tractor turned, lifting the plough like a dainty skirt, at the edge of the field.

It was some time before Lee could gasp the complete, devastating message and crouch down on the deep-scented earth, his back leant gratefully against a massive tractor wheel and his mouth wide open, drawing in the cool, restoring air.

Morgan stood at his side, saying nothing. He had been alarmed to see the exhausted boy staggering over the ploughed ground, his arms flapping for balance like some grotesque parody of a bird. He had rushed to meet him, prepared for bad news, and yet, when he had grasped the gist of the boy's speech, his feelings had retreated within him, bit by bit. Now they were entirely hidden.

Lee turned his face to Morgan, wide-eyed in anxiety. His breathing was nearly normal.

'Did he say anything to you yesterday?' Morgan turned his attention to the ridge where a group of walkers were silhouetted, making for the high plateau. 'You'd better get down and see him.' Cap had found a rabbit burrow: he barked and dug with fast front paws. Morgan clicked his tongue in encouragement. 'You didn't say anything to upset him?' Cap gave up the search and trotted to Morgan who knelt to whisper amused endearments.

'What are we going to do, Morgan?' The question came out directly and harshly, from frustration at the man's refusal to listen, to appreciate. Morgan straightened and glanced towards the walkers. He moved stolidly towards the tractor.

'I got work to do,' he said.

Lee forced himself to his feet, as Morgan climbed into the seat and pressed down the starter.

'Morgan!' shouted Lee, but the roar of the engine drowned out any possibility of conversation. The machine swung in line for the new furrows and the plough dropped. Its blades sliced into the heavy clay, carving it sweetly. Lee walked fast downhill, distraught and aching.

When the phone rang in Plas Newydd, Matthew and the Gregorys were working upstairs. Eileen contrived still to look cool and elegant in the faded, baggy trousers she had worn on the farm at Mvurwi, topped by a slowly unravelling sweater of Harry's and a headscarf. She lugged in a plastic sack of rubbish from a disused room and dragged it to the top of the stairs. Harry and Matthew, looking simply scruffy, bore the bulky wardrobe from the boy's room onto the landing, where most of his furniture and clothes were already stacked. They had all been working for more than an hour when, to their annoyance, they heard the ringing downstairs in the living-room. Matthew moved to answer it, acknowledging demands not to carry dirt and dust downstairs. There was enough floating around the first landing as it was.

Harry moved into Matthew's room to dismantle his bed. Eileen surveyed the chaos of the landing. 'I hope this is a good idea, ' she said acidly.

Harry, who was enjoying himself, called, 'Don't let's start that again,' and wrenched the bed frame free. 'Half an hour at the car,' he shouted. Eileen was carrying a load of decaying curtains downstairs. 'Do you hear?' her husband yelled.

'Yes,' she yelled briefly back. They were driving to buy new wallpaper and curtains from Cwmbran.

The living-room door was open. Eileen could clearly hear Matthew's conversation. She'd guessed it would be for him: nobody, apart from Tom Duncan, ever bothered with her or Harry.

'What does Morgan think . . . ? No, Pugh didn't say anything to me. Do you want me to come up then?'

Oh no, thought Eileen. We talked this over last night. We need your help. Your place is here. She stood in the passsage, listening.

'I don't know what you expect me to do . . . All right. Take it easy. I'm on my way.'

With a slight look of irritation, Matthew walked into the passage.

'On your way where?' asked Eileen sweetly.

Matthew started. He had not known she was there. 'Blainau,' he said. 'Why?'

Eileen explained as if to a child — 'The Captain and I have to see builders in Crickhowell, as you know, after which we are shopping in Cwmbran. Meanwhile, there is your room to clear, not to mention two others.'

I can do some when I come back.'

'You are needed here.' The voice was calm, firm and totally authoritative. Matthew knew he would stay, though he tried again.

'It's the old guy that works on the farm. What I mean is, he's not working there any more. Or something. Lee was in a bit of a state, so I said I'd go up.'

Eileen was adamant. 'You are needed here. How many times do I have to say it? You know nothing of farming. What help can you be?' On that point, Matthew agreed, albeit silently. 'I have never understood the fatal fascination of this remote farmstead, but it has never much mattered before. Now it does. You agreed last night to help us. The builders are available for only a short time. They begin tomorrow, should you have forgotten.'

There was no crossing her will. In any case, most of what she said made sense to Matthew, who simply felt he might be letting Lee down, and once, he had promised himself, would be the only time.

'I just told Lee I'd go up.'

'Then phone your flat-vowelled friend and tell him you have other obligations.' Seeing him still uneasy, she strode into the room. 'What's the number?' she demanded.

'I'll do it,' protested Matthew. She smiled and moved towards the door and dustbins. The phone rang unanswered in Blainau, and Matthew was still hanging on when she returned and sweetly ordered him back upstairs.

One evening Pugh had left behind at Blainau a dozen eggs necessary to his daughter's baking; Lee had delivered them on the motorbike, following Morgan's carefully-drawn map, so Lee knew where the old man lived. It was a surprisingly large and venerable Victorian house, set slightly back on the road to Llangorse. Pugh had been well pleased: Wells Fargo, he had called him, laughing.

Pugh was not laughing now. He and Lee sat in a pleasant front room, beneath whose window Lee's cycle leaned. He had ridden very fast and was still flushed from the ride. Everything was reversed. Pugh was usually the one with the red face, yet, in neat grey trousers, a clean sweater and shirt, he already seemed a different man, not the Blainau workman. While Lee sat, glowing, in muddied jeans and working anorak, awkward and fidgeting, Pugh was calm and dignified.

'Won't they let you come back?' Lee still could not conceive of a Pugh, even this different Pugh, who would leave Blainau of his own volition. Pugh looked at him, upright and assured.

'This winter's done with, and the lambing. I seen him through that.' Lee could not hold up beneath the cool gaze. He shook his head in disbelief.

'Being cruel to be kind, boy.' Lee's eyes came up again, wanting to understand. 'Know my old farm? The Garn out past Trevecca?' Lee shook his head. 'The Garn near did for me, it's all a man got, is his health.'

Lee remembered Griffiths' advice. 'What about his dignity?' he asked pointedly. Both knew they referred, obliquely, to Morgan.

'If a man's lost his health, he's lost his dignity.' Pugh leaned forward urgently. 'Morgan have got to face up to it. With me there, he can pretend he've got a good farm running. I took more weight at Blainau than you knows, boy.' He paused. 'Cruel to be kind,' he repeated softly, leaning back in the chair. 'And he can pay you now, 'stead of me — no trouble with the police. It's all for the best.'

Silence re-established itself in the room. There seemed nothing more to say. Lee could not find it in his heart to accuse the man of disloyalty, ingratitude and the other spiteful insults he had half-considered on the twenty-minute ride to comfort him.

'The kiddies'll be from school soon for dinner. You'll like my grandson; he's only ten but sharp as a knife. He'll make us a drink and a sandwich. Stay on a bit, why not?'

Another view of Pugh. Grandfather with a grandson sharp as a knife. Lee shook his head and stood.

'Better get back,' he said dully.

Pugh stood and moved towards him, his fierce eyes full on Lee's. 'You done him proud, boy. I never thought you'd stay.'

Time stretched. Lee wondered if he were going to cry and was shocked. He examined dispassionately the complication of feelings from which emerged one new thought: he would miss Pugh terribly, whatever the extra problems his absence would bring Blainau. Christ, he thought. I *am* going to cry. He turned away, towards the door.

'For all the good my staying's done,' he said. 'Waste of time.'

Pugh spoke gently, seeing the boy's eyes moist, 'Nothing's wasted, son.'

Lee needed to be hurtful, realising it was a reaction of some former self. 'Tell that to Morgan.'

The half-cruel jibe was instantly regretted. 'Sorry, Pugh,' he murmured.

The old man seemed to have accepted the spite as his due. 'I'm too old, boy,' he said. 'I been through it once with my own farm. Too damn old now to see it happen to a friend.'

The uphill journey to Blainau took Lee almost three-quarters of an hour. Tired and dispirited at first, the rhythmic pressure on the pedals soothed all his feelings to a dull apathy. In this mood he was not particularly surprised to find Harry Gregory in his car outside Blainau's gate. The Captain, on the other hand, was shifty and embarrassed, as he felt the need to explain that they were on their way to Crickhowell, so Eileen thought she'd call for a word with Mr Thomas. Lee parked his bike and walked to the porch. He could clearly gather the gist of the conversation and moved closer to listen.

'Matthew is a charming boy, Mr Thomas, and very willing to help you when he can. You will, however, understand that it's not fair to divide his loyalties. We're quite content, of course, that Matthew should pay you the occasional visit when he has nothing better to do at home. We know he and your nephew are friends. Lee is always welcome at Plas Newydd.'

Morgan nodded, awkward in his work-clothes. As Eileen glanced, smiling, round the room, he was aware that it was cheerless and untidy. 'I know it,' he muttered, 'and thank you.'

Eileen let her eyes dawdle on the sofa, piled with dirty clothes, making a point. 'Anyway,' she concluded, 'we were driving past and Matthew asked me to call and explain.' She drifted towards the door. 'He's a boy made easily anxious, and I do ask you not to suggest he spends his time here when we need him at Plas Newydd.'

As Morgan saw her to the door, he did not know Lee had overheard much of the one-sided conversation and would have been embarrassed to know it. He was not often made to feel so shabby. He watched her delicately pick her way through his filthy yard.

Harry and Eileen were already driving along the main road towards Crickhowell before she learned of Lee's presence during their visit.

'Why on earth didn't the boy come in?' she mused.

'Pedalled off like a wild thing,' added Harry.

Lee had listened no further than Eileen's bland declaration that Matthew had asked her to call, and he did not know it was a lie. Not that she would have called it that, exactly.

He now faced Matthew angrily; Matthew was not sure where his exact fault lay, except he knew he had promised Lee he would drive to Blainau at once, but had not. His protestation that he had telephoned without reply made no difference. Lee stood in the middle of Matthew's room, now almost empty: a pile of his military books was stacked ready for removal and he had been about to turn his attention to the fish tanks.

'She said you're not coming up. She said you're working here now and you told her to tell Morgan.'

Matthew gave Lee a smile that was half-apology, half-embarrassment. 'That's just like her,' he said. 'You know what she's like.'

Lee was not to be diverted to Eileen's shortcomings. 'That's right, is it?' he demanded. 'You're packing it in, too?'

Matthew found Lee's anger disproportionate. He frowned, irritated. 'I'm clearing rooms. There's some builder coming in tomorrow. It's a pretty big thing for the Gregs.'

'It's a pretty big thing for me and Morgan when Pugh walks out on us. You said you'd come up straight away. Now suddenly you're working here.'

Lee had found Matthew's weakest point but Matthew still couldn't invest it with such significance. 'Take it easy, Lee,' he muttered.

'You pick your moments, don't you? We're supposed to be mates. You let me down rotten, time after bloody time.'

Matthew refused to reply. He knelt to pick up his books. The bitter failure to support Lee in his fight with Price still lay sharp and shameful in his memory. He looked up angrily.

'What can I do at Blainau? Tell me.'

'Just bloody be there.'

Matthew flipped open a book to cover his annoyance. He shut it and laid it on top of the pile. 'You're over-reacting,' he said, controlling his voice. 'Blainau's going to go on ticking over like it's always ticked over. What's the panic? Pugh was old, and Morgan's got you. You're here; I'm here. I do my share for Morgan – that's great: I like it. Now this is important to the Gregs and I'm helping them for a while. I'll come up tomorrow when I've finished. Okay?' He picked up the book again, unused to revealing his feelings. He dropped it back on top of the pile. For a few seconds neither spoke.

Lee said quietly. 'I went to see Pugh. He says he's doing this to

213

make Morgan face facts. Not to let him go on fooling himself. What do you say?'

Matthew was quiet, too. 'Nothing to do with me.'

Lee casually kicked over the stack of books. 'So tell me about this shit,' he demanded.

Matthew sighed heavily. 'What was the point of that?' he asked patiently, as he collected the books and rebuilt the pile.

'Greener got your number. You don't want to join your wonderful, bloody Paras.' Lee's voice was deadly with scorn. 'You puked up as soon as it looked anywhere near real.'

Matthew paused, rebuilding the books. His whole body visibly tensed. 'I was sick,' he said, so softly that Lee barely heard him.

'When's the next interview?'

'How the hell do I know? They let you know.'

'Then you'll puke up again, or bust an ankle. Plenty of time, is there?' Lee jeered. 'That's what Morgan says about Blainau.'

Matthew knelt, tense and dangerous. 'Don't take Blainau out on me,' he said quietly.

'You let yourself get pushed around by anybody.' Lee's voice rose. 'Is this what all this Para crap is about? The excuse to push someone else around? You could have started, up in that car park,' he added bitterly.

Matthew spoke calmly, still tensed like a spring wound one notch tighter by the memory. 'I explained that: my medical was the next week.'

'You were shit-scared,' mocked Lee, kicking down the pile of books again.

Matthew suddenly shouted at him. 'Don't keep doing that!'

Matthew's outburst proved satisfying.

'Stop me,' Lee said conversationally. 'Let's see the fighting man.'

Matthew slowly got to his feet, ignoring the scattered books. 'Let's leave it there,' he whispered.

Lee threw out a hand and pushed Matthew off balance; it was experimental, not aggressive.

'Don't do that, Lee,' Matthew said sharply, angry but feeling a dull fright creeping over him. He had last felt that exact paralysis in the car park.

Lee shoved him again, harder. 'Why not?' he mocked.

Matthew fell back a step. 'Stop it!' he shouted.

Lee scrutinised his taut face and smiled. 'You're even scared of being scared.' He knocked Matthew back another step.

Recoiling, Matthew shouted, upset, 'Why are you doing this

to me?' He felt a wall at his back.

Lee suddenly had had enough. His earlier, dull fatigue overcame him and he shook his head, feeling almost sad. 'Big talk and army toys,' he murmured, turning towards the door. 'Face facts, Soldier Blue. You're a joke.' He walked from the room.

Matthew never moved until Lee's steps had gone fast along the landing and creaked downstairs where, soon, a door slammed and there was silence. Then, slowly, he slipped down to a position, half-sitting, half-crouching, backed into a corner.

Lee made one final call. It was late afternoon as he forced the pedals towards Tom Griffiths' farm, where he had been offered respite, a welcome and advice, and now needed all three. The school bus was in the yard. He saw Sarah climb down and move towards the house. He rang his bell, needing neutral friendship. She glanced across but hurried to the door where her father stood and walked past him, head lowered.

Griffiths walked to the garden gate as Lee drew up. Mrs Lewis smiled and waved to them as she steered the bus towards Talgarth.

'Can I have another word, Mr Griffiths, please?' Lee asked quietly.

The man was stern, unsmiling. 'Off you go, boy,' he said.

Lee was puzzled. 'Sorry?' he enquired, fearing he had misheard.

'Wasps to the jampot, you young lads.' The voice was low and surly. 'I won't be the laughing-stock. I've had enough.'

Lee dawdled, confused, not knowing if there was a joke somewhere. Still on the saddle, he uneasily rolled the bike forward and back. He smiled tentatively. 'I don't know what you're talking about.' Griffiths examined his face grimly; Lee's smile evaporated under the scrutiny.

'You knew what was going on with my girl and that Cardiff bugger. You been working your way in here. Worried for Morgan, is it? Wasps to jam. Well now I'm in on the arrangement, too.' Lee's face showed such total bewilderment that Griffiths' certainty faltered. 'It ain't the right time, boy,' he said gruffly. 'Maybe you know what I'm talking about and maybe you don't. I ain't giving you the benefit of doubt. You get from here.' He turned and walked stiffly towards his house.

'You said you'd help,' Lee called, but the door was already shut to him. He wheeled his bike round and moved away, hurt and confused.

Morgan had beer waiting, as Lee came home through the dusk.

They had not seen each other since the panic of the morning and Morgan was anxious for him; the beer was a small gesture towards admitting his concern. The boy slumped onto the sofa, too tired even to warm his freezing hands at the well-built fire. It had been the most complex and emotionally wearing day of his life and he had pedalled twenty miles as part of it. Morgan saw his exhaustion and despair; he put a can of beer into the boy's cold hands and built the fire brighter, before sitting down in his chair, his eyes searching for clues in the pale, tired face.

'Where have you been? I was worried for you.'

Much of Lee's day and energy had been spent worrying for Morgan. If he had been less leaden with fatigue, he would have smiled.

'How will you manage, Morgan?'

Morgan raised his can of beer to his lips and drank. Wiping his mouth, he replied evenly, 'We'll get by.'

'How, Morgan?'

'I have always managed.' The man guessed that Lee had seen Pugh.

'What do you want, Morgan?'

The solemn string of questions forced serious thought upon Morgan. He had never seen his nephew like this and did not know how best to reply.

'Can we manage? Without Pugh?'

The shift to 'We' seeped through Morgan like a proud, warm draft. 'Just you and me,' Morgan said simply. 'Family.' Their eyes met. Knowing that it was hopeless, but right, Lee nodded slowly.

'We'll keep Blainau running, then,' he affirmed. 'We can cut right down on what we buy. Until we get through to when things are easier.'

'That's the way,' breathed Morgan, dismayed at the boy's new and complete acceptance of events. 'We got to ginger up – the Old Lady said that.' He tried to keep the despair from his voice as he studied Lee's exhaustion and knew, from the depths of his own experience, that Blainau and family had taken the life from this tired, young boy, had laden him with the burden he would not, himself, wish on anyone. He saw the mirror-image of himself when young. Lee nodded again, slowly and seriously. He carefully laid his beer can against the arm of the sofa and reached for the crumpled pack of cigarettes in his jeans' pocket. It was empty. He tossed the packet into the flames.

'It's bad for you anyway, is smoking,' he said. They sat in

silence for a long time, Lee staring into the fire and Morgan watching him, seeing himself.

At about this same time, the Gregorys returned to Plas Newydd with rolls of discreetly patterned wallpaper, tins of paint, a toolbox and metres of curtain material. They bore the tools and paint towards Matthew's room, gathering righteous indignation at the still cluttered landing. It was dark in the room. The one naked bulb dimly lit the scattered books, the fish tanks, the montage on the wall and Matthew, crouched silently in the corner. Harry and Eileen were, at first, simply irritated.

'Matthew! What's this? You promised you'd have this room empty.'

'The landing's still overflowing.'

The boy didn't move. Harry dropped the heavy tools on the floor. Eileen laid down the tins of paint. They stared at him, then at each other. The boy neither spoke nor moved.

'What is this nonsense?' demanded Eileen.

Harry was less aggressive. 'Come along, old boy.'

Matthew seemed not to register their presence.

'Matthew!' Eileen said sharply.

They glanced uneasily at each other. Harry tried to tease the boy from his impassive enchantment.

'He's hypnotised by the fish. I always said they were peculiar, damn things.'

The boy still didn't speak or move. Eileen threw her husband a dangerous look, whose meaning was a clear command not to be so ridiculous.

'I have a builder arriving early tomorrow,' she said to the boy. 'He intends to begin work on this room. Are you sick? Do you need a doctor?'

Harry, too, began to feel a growing annoyance and frustration: neither was used to being ignored. 'You'll have to learn to rise above personal feelings in a fighting unit,' he snapped. 'What's wrong with you?'

Eileen looked coldly down at him. 'You wouldn't find your sister crouching in some corner like some frightened child.'

'Exactly,' Harry added. 'And what would your father say?'

It was hopeless. The boy refused to respond. Eileen felt the beginnings of temper flare inside her. She threw an angry, imperious glance around the room and back to their sullen, silent charge. 'I shall make tea,' she said, controlling her anger, 'and you shall clear this room. Is that understood? I shall return

217

in half an hour. Have it done by then!'

The temper was building; she knew she must leave the room. 'One half-hour,' she called back, as she strode through the door.

Harry, usually milder, was, on this occasion, inclined to agree. 'What will you do?' he said. 'How on earth will you cope? It's aggression the Army demands. Not this.' He followed his wife onto the landing.

But Matthew had heard them, had registered each further detail in the catalogue of his failures. When Lee had walked from the room after his clumsy but effective demonstration of Matthew's passive helplessness, his mind had been a void. But, in the emptiness, other remembered voices had spun other criticisms — teachers, parents, sister, friends, enemies; everybody who had ever found this quiet and remote boy lacking in affection, in determination, application, intelligence, in courage, in gratitude, all those who had ever controlled Matthew in any way, had come singly and at random at first, but, one echo awakening another, a pattern had emerged, charting his history of schools, holidays, minders. Matthew, like a drowning man, had relived his lifetime during the two hours between Lee's mockery and the Gregory's onslaught.

As a soothing counterpoint to the mockery and anger of the jangling memories, like smoke rising from a noisy party in a small and airless room, the idea of the Paras swayed and swirled. His positive motivations — serving a cause, comradeship in adversity, physical fitness, completeness, identity — gathered, moved and hung together like the montage on his wall. Then, as if somebody had, in disapproval, somewhere opened a window, his certainties had been drawn swiftly out into the cold, leaving only the derision of his uninvited guests, whose voices had ceased one by one, creating a new void. At that point the Gregorys had returned.

Harry and Eileen were three steps down the staircase when they heard the crack and smash of glass and a swift rushing like sudden wind. Hurrying to his room, they found Matthew sweeping the new hammer into the side of his second fish tank, the floor already awash with water and struggling, glittering fish, squirming for life. Appalled and shouting, they stood helpless in the doorway, as the hammer smashed through the glass. His eyes dull with despair, Matthew glared momentarily at them, gasping, and, before they could move, he was tearing at his wall. Harry hurried towards him, slipping on the soaked carpet, shouting for the boy to stop, while Eileen shut her eyes firmly and leaned against the door, swaying and nauseated.

It was over before Harry reached him. Energy simply deserted him. A valve switched off his adrenalin. In the sudden silence, Matthew's rasping breath and a curious whimpering from Eileen were the only small intrusions. Matthew dropped the hammer, to turn calm eyes upon Harry's wild, questioning face, then he became poor, quiet, remote Matthew once again. In little more than a whisper he told them he would like to phone his parents, please.

As Matthew smashed his life into fragments and waited for his parents to gather them up, and repair them, Lee lay in his bed longing for sleep's comforting ambush. He knew his leaden helplessness had worried Morgan, but explanation would have been impossible. Unable to bear Morgan's silent concern, he had gone early to bed. His uncle was next door now, in his grandmother's room. Morgan had knocked quietly on his door but had found no response, only the lock turned against him. Supposing that the man needed the advice and support of his dead mother's presence, Lee turned in his bed, away from the soft movings on the other side of the wall, and waited for sleep.

Lee slept more heavily even than the night before and did not wake until Morgan knocked long and loud. Lee dragged himself from sleep and bed to unlock the door, half-prepared for a beginning as bad as the previous day. Instead, he found Morgan bearing a mug of coffee in his large, careful hands. As he took it gratefully, he heard the lowing of cows in the yard. Morgan drew back the curtains and sunlight slanted in. Lee was amazed to learn it was eleven o'clock.

'I don't know what's happening to me,' he muttered, sipping from the mug. He still felt leaden: yesterday, he supposed. He sat blearily on the bed. 'You've got the cows out,' he said, for conversation, since Morgan was still hovering at the window.

'Taking them to the fields.'

Lee vaguely remembered that the time for the cows to move back to pasture was sometime late in May, early June. 'Thought that was for next month,' he yawned. He felt a stiffness in his neck; a nagging ache at the back of his head.

Morgan thought the boy looked tired and sick. No wonder, he thought, I have made the right decision. 'There's food on the table for you,' he said. 'You stay in bed a bit.'

Lee pressed a hand to the ache in his head; it seemed to be growing. He felt very tired. 'Thanks,' he said. 'I feel . . .' He didn't know how he felt. He noticed Morgan was in his suit.

'Going somewhere?' He lay back on his bed. His head ached less.

Morgan moved to the door. 'You rest,' he murmured. He half-shut the door behind him, then turned and opened it again. Lee looked at him, curiously.

'I have seen Tom Duncan,' Morgan said softly. 'I have taken his deal.'

Before Lee could react, Morgan had closed the door. Lee heard his steps, heavy on the landing and stairs. He shut his eyes. Tears began to slide beneath the lids, over his cheeks. The porch door shut. Lee began to sob.

As Morgan, ceremonial in his suit, swung the yard gate open and began, with Cap, to escort the six cows to the fields to early freedom, Lee wept bitterly for Morgan, for Matthew, for himself.

Chapter Eight

The dual sense of time, which seemed to be so much a part of Lee's months at Blainau, was never so apparent as in the weeks following Morgan's decision. On the one hand, the daily routine of the famous list stretched ahead and the gathering pace of the year made the days long with extra work; on the other, the finality of the date in late May when Morgan had agreed to vacate his farm imposed a different, more urgent rhythm – by such a date, Morgan would sell his small reserve of feed; by such a date, the stock would go to market; by such a date, the various machinery would be gone; by such a date, the contents of the house not needed in Morgan's new residence must be seen by the auctioneer's clerk and, on the final day, collected to be taken to the fortnightly furniture sale in Abergavenny. For three weeks little seemed to happen and then, suddenly, the tempo increased as Blainau ran down. All this Morgan bore with a resolute balance, of which Lee would never had believed him capable.

Tom Griffiths was a good friend to Morgan, paying moderately well for the farm's feed, for the more modern machinery – of which there was little – and, at Talgath market, for the best of the Blainau flock. He lent Morgan transport, which he insisted on driving personally to take, one week, the remaining sheep to Abergavenny market and, the next, the six cows to Hereford. He stood at Morgan's side during the auction, quietly at hand to ensure that his neighbour was paid a fair price.

What was left of the machinery and tools was bought by other local farmers, turning up at Blainau, 'as they were passing', and giving Morgan little profit. There was spirited haggling in the yard, slapping of hands in agreement and the occasional return of a pound or two as luck money, according to the custom. Lee was surprised to find Morgan equal to almost the best of them in his bargaining. It was an irony that this seeming efficiency and balance came in the ending of Blainau, and that, in one sense, nothing became Morgan so well as the disintegration of all that he had stood for. If Morgan shared any of Lee's surprise and dismay, he did not show it.

The strange weeks came to an end. For the last few days there was little to do and neither the boy nor his uncle had much to say to each other. Lee missed Matthew, who had suffered transportation to his parents in Zimbabwe, leaving Plas Newydd the day after his outburst with only the barest details revealed to Lee in a single, cool phone call. Lee regretted his part in driving his friend towards the debacle, but managed to rationalise the confrontation as an attempt to show Matthew that he, like Morgan, had been living a dream. Lee also missed Pugh. The dangers of living in a Never-Never-Land, where fantasy could easily predominate, shielded by remote hills and valleys, sharpened in a personal way. Lee began to think of his own future. Blainau had always been Time-Out and he realised that, very soon, he would have to take a part in the wider game of the Real World. Meanwhile, he and Morgan concluded, job by job, the adjusted rota of the famous list and each did well, determined to avoid the minefield of sentiment and guilt. Even Cap, though bewildered to find less work to do, seemed not unduly upset.

Val came for the final days of Blainau, anxious to see a smooth transition, and pleased to mastermind the removal to the new house, which was exactly that.

Five minutes' walk from Talgarth square the Estate had bought a block of six small houses on a site not yet fully built. They were brand-new, less than one month old, and, as she made a point of reiterating to Morgan, he was lucky to get one. The houses were on the very edge of the town — fields rose gently behind them. They were compact, tidy and comfortable; the exteriors uniformly white, with dark roofs. Lee, seeing Morgan's house for the first time, was dismayed. The house was not even on an end of the row, but boxed into the centre by other similar little white boxes. When Tom Duncan showed Morgan and Lee round, Morgan had been polite and impressed. Relieved, the Estate manager had produced a bottle of champagne and paper cups to celebrate a successful conclusion to a potentially difficult problem. One of the row was still empty, three were inhabited by Estate workers, and the one at the far end was not yet complete.

In the last week of May, with summer established, the lorry arrived to remove the last of Blainau's furniture and other random lots that might make money in the Abergavenny sale. The vehicle was small and open-backed; most of the Blainau furniture was already installed at the new house, where it sat, unhappily aged and massive, in tiny rooms of cold and dazzling white. Wyn Williams, the auctioneer's driver, carried a large cardboard box from the house, which clunked with a collection of excess crockery and ornaments; the Old Lady had been a great snapper-up of ill-considered trifles. He slotted the box into a corner of the lorry and, whistling, glanced towards the open door of the workshop where Lee knelt, watched by a curious Cap, binding together random old tools into lots that somebody might possibly buy. Williams wandered up to him and, seeing Lee's cycle half inside the shed, drew it out, bounced it experimentally a few times.

'This?' he asked.

Lee nodded, cutting his roll of binder-twine into a length for securing various hedging hooks into a lot. 'Yeah.' Williams bounced the bike once more and wheeled it to the lorry. He thought it might fetch ten pounds.

Val carried a final load downstairs from the bathroom, to where Morgan stood redundant, looking round at his home which was not his home. The walls, suddenly grimy and dark, were clearly etched with lighter blocks where his furniture had stood. He was determined not to surrender to the poignancy of the moment. He had made the biggest decision of his life and was determined to see it through, hurting nobody else with excess, or even due sentimentality. He did not, on the other hand, wish to deny Val the full, essential role she was taking.

He said quietly, 'I'll be glad to get done here, Val.'

She put down her load near the door and came quickly to him, enfolding him in her arms. 'You've done well,' she confirmed. They looked together at the final cardboard box and its contents.

'No sense to hold onto things for the sake of it.'

'No,' she agreed softly.

Val moved to pack the bathroom linen into a plastic sack. 'What are we doing about Mam's room, Morgan?' she asked, deliberately casual. Receiving no answer, she continued, 'Only, there's some good furniture in there, as I remember.'

'That's for me to see to. Later.'

She nodded and pressed down a thin, torn towel. 'Only it seems daft — with the lorry outside and waiting.'

Morgan turned and walked into the bare kitchen. 'It's clear in here,' he called, needlessly. Val laid the sack against the wall, having her answer in his moving away. She followed him as Williams whistled his way through the open door.

'Nothing more?' he asked. 'What about this?' He pointed to the sack.

'You leave that,' Val said sharply. Williams grinned and walked through the living-room towards Morgan's square bulk in the kitchen doorway. He was used to being snapped at; nobody loved a man who came to break up the happy home.

'That the lot then?'

'There's a box by the front door.' Val moved to join them. The kitchen looked small. Only the sink remained.

'You want to get that range in your other room taken out. Fetch a few bob.' Morgan murmured agreement. 'I know somebody who'd see to it,' Williams pressed on cheerfully. 'Cost you a bit, but it's a job for an expert, shifting an old range.'

'Leave it be,' Morgan replied softly.

Williams whistled a few bars of nothing particular and turned to collect the last box. 'Finished upstairs?' he checked. Val confirmed that they had. Williams stopped and turned.

'What are you holding behind the locked door up there?' he asked, grinning. 'Family fortune?'

Brother and sister were shoulder to shoulder.

'Private,' said Morgan curtly.

Val snapped, 'Not for the sale.'

Williams guessed he had pressed a sensitive nerve, but was not over-concerned. 'Right you are,' he said. 'You've got what you want and I've got the rest.' He moved into the living-room and headed for the yard. 'You want to think about that range,' he called, as he gathered the box. 'Get it cleaned up, stick it in a holiday cottage and it could fetch a few bob.' He walked out, whistling.

Val and Morgan walked slowly from the kitchen. They stood gazing at the range. Val smiled and turned warmly to Morgan.

'You remember when Mam — ' she began, but Morgan spoke sharply.

'No, Val,' he said. She understood. Collecting the sack of linen, she moved out into the bright day.

Lee was dropping the last bundles of battered tools into the back of the lorry when Williams carried the box to be stowed safely. The man walked to the open cab door to collect a clipboard. Lee turned to his mother and uncle as they left the house — grateful to see they seemed to be making light of the difficult moments. Val smiled and held out her sack; Lee hurried over to stack it in the full back of Morgan's Land Rover.

Morgan carefully checked the inventory on Williams' clipboard. Williams winked at Val. 'Careful lot, these farmers,' he joked, raising no laugh. Morgan signed and handed the list and board back.

'Right you are.' Williams moved towards his cab. 'Probably go in the sale Thursday week. The boss'll be in touch.'

Val thanked him and he wished her good luck. Whistling, he climbed on board and slammed his door shut. The engine fired. Lee turned from his task to watch brother and sister silently link arms, as much of their past was slowly driven through the gate. Williams pressed the horn in salute and the lorry turned laboriously left into the narrow road, jolting and rumbling its way from Blainau. Val and Morgan stood silently in the yard. The lorry was out of sight now, but could be heard climbing towards the Castel Dinas road, where it changed gear and laboured to the main road. Eventually, the low rumbling merged with birdsong and the high-distant drone of a plane.

Lee walked to them, anxious to defuse a difficult moment. 'When we eating?' he whined. 'It makes you hungry — all this carrying.'

Val turned, grateful for the diversion. She unlinked her arm. 'Come on then.' She glanced at Morgan, his head upraised, as if still striving to catch the drone of the lorry. 'Locking up, Morgan?' Morgan moved to the house instantly.

'See to the yard doors, boy,' he murmured.

Lee walked his mother towards the Land Rover, which was packed and waiting. 'You okay?' he asked. She smiled and squeezed his arm.

'Let's just get away, eh?'

'What about Morgan?'

'He's fine.'

Alone, he could briefly drop pretences. He looked round at the bare interior of Blainau, his face set as cold stone. The barn doors grated and clanged shut, one by one, a sound that had been such a part of his life that, until now, he had not noticed the detailed scraping on the yard stones and the brief rattling reverberation as they closed. He took the key from the lock,

225

where it had always been, and crossed the threshold. As he locked the door, Val watched him carefully. How can he bear it so well, she thought? Lee, at the yard gate, watched him too, admiringly. He approached the Land Rover without a sideways glance, calling Cap to jump into the back. He climbed in and shut his door.

As he briefly settled in the seat, he saw Val's anxious sympathy and almost gave way. Their eyes held together for a while, then he turned to switch on the ignition.

On the road the Land Rover waited while Lee swung the gate shut. The low organ note of the hinges played to Val's memory. She took a quick look across, but Morgan's eyes were determined and, unlike hers, dry; he stared fixedly down the road.

'What should I say?' she whispered.

There was no reply. She blinked a few times and swiftly pressed her eyes with the back of a hand. The door at her side swung open.

'Budge over.'

Val moved across, as Lee pushed in beside her and slammed the door shut. Morgan drove from Blainau. Lee and Val could not resist peering behind them, past Cap — slithering for footing amongst the boxes and parcels — to the farm, which would be empty that night for the first time since a burly, young farmer brought his bright-eyed wife through a wooden gate and into their new home a lifetime ago.

'Stay!' Morgan insisted. Cap, at the open door of the new house, was uneasy, anxious for reassurance. He wanted to be inside with Lee, wanted to follow Morgan, now carrying in the last of the load from the Land Rover at the kerb. Near at hand, a town dog yelped and Cap swung to the direction, noisy in reply. Morgan reappeared.

'Quiet dog.'

The man anxiously glanced at the window of the neighbouring house where a net curtain fell into place. 'Good boy,' he murmured as he moved back inside. Cap sat and waited for what was to happen, uneasy and confused.

Lee met him in the squashed, empty hallway; none of the Blainau furniture had been small enough to furnish it. Morgan smiled.

'Tidy little place.'

Lee was not convinced.

'You could take Cap around the back to his shed.' Glad to be active, Lee agreed; he did not think the dog would like it.

The living-room was cramped with Blainau's sideboard, chairs and sofa. Val had made a great effort — the room shone with polished wood and floors — but it contrived to look cluttered and bleak at the same time. She came from the kitchen, beaming, determined that Morgan should be pleased with his new home.

'It's convenient; I'll say that for it. Small, but you'll save on heating. No more wasting half a day cutting wood. It's good, is gas for central heating; I've got it at home. You'll be cosy enough here.'

She saw Morgan looking tired and dispirited, for the first time, and dropped the bright pretence. She sat him down and moved back into the cramped kitchen to make him tea. He was glad for the rest and the chance to be himself; he would not have relaxed his guard without Val's taking the lead. He spoke wearily through the open kitchen door.

'What'd they say to see me here, Val?'

She knew at once whom he meant.

'Look,' she said. 'Mam was practical whatever else she might have been. She'd see the sense in it.' She sat a kettle over the flame of the incongruous, stained old cooker — she had done her best with the wire wool, but had failed — and hurried back to him.

'You've not let them down. It's the other way round: they let *you* down. They let us both down,' she added bitterly. 'So don't feel bad.' She patted him on the arm. 'Ginger up,' she demanded, smiling.

Morgan smiled dutifully back.

'While the kettle's boiling, I'll see to Cap.'

He levered himself up and moved to the kitchen through the back door.

Cap would hate it, Lee was positive. The outhouse was windowless and cold, built in breezeblocks. Like the new house itself, it managed to be simultaneously cluttered and bleak. Morgan had brought tools that might be useful, which were stacked against one wall; he had also brought the old sacks on which the dog had slept in Blainau's workshop. It was not the same. The scent of straw, old leather, sheep, that had made the workshop unique and familiar, was absent here; the smell of wet concrete prevailed. Cap sat on the sacks obediently, wondering when they would go home — Lee was sure the dog felt that. As Morgan looked in, through the open door, Lee looked up at him, indignantly.

'Why can't Cap live in the house? He's retired, too, now'.

'Down boy; we're not retired. Always work for a good man and a working dog.' Morgan was indignant too.

'We'll get settled here and then we'll see about it. Anyway a working dog's not comfortable in a house'.

Lee nodded, petting the dog.

'He won't like it,' he murmured.

'He'll have to get accustomed. He wouldn't work for no one else.' Lee realised the truth of that. Morgan tried to cheer the boy up.

'I'll be putting a window in, for light, soon as I can. He got to make the best.'

Lee climbed to his feet.

'That's what you told me when I first came down here. Up to Blainau, I mean.'

Morgan told the dog sternly to stay. He half-closed the door and they looked round the tiny square of grass.

'Good piece of ground this,' said Morgan. 'Small, but it'll make me a tidy garden.'

'Room for a thin bunch of flowers,' muttered Lee, wishing he could find enthusiasm or at least match this admirable resolute enthusiasm of Morgan's. Morgan laughed.

'What would I do with flowers?'

Lee smiled a little. 'You might go courting one day. You never know'.

Morgan hooted. 'A few spuds, carrots and tomatoes'd be a damn sight more use to me, boy!' He took a step to the door.

'Morgan?' asked Lee, quiet and concerned, 'this is all right for you, is it? Being here?'

The man put an arm round Lee's shoulders and moved him to the door and tea. 'It's where I am and that's all there is to it,' he said bluntly.

In their absence Val had worked fast to create a table fit for a celebration. The best of Morgan's plates — which at Blainau had stood in the sideboard, strictly for show — lay washed and gleaming on a white tablecloth whose edges the Old Lady had embroidered with flowers. Cutlery shone in symmetry. There were red paper napkins and a small bunch of spring flowers. She stood back, beaming at their enthusiasm. She suggested that maybe some celebration booze might crown the event and Morgan picked up his cap willingly.

'I'll get some now. Shop's still open.'

Val laughed. 'Looking like that?' Morgan looked down at himself, puzzled. She smiled at him. 'You don't want to go about looking like that!' He was still in his farming outfit. 'It was all right for up in the hills, but you're a man about town now. What'll people think?'

Morgan nodded slowly and left to put on his suit, which Val declared was only fitting for a celebration anyway. Lee could not shake off his sense of unease. He told his mother he'd walk with Morgan to the supermarket. Val replied with quiet urgency.

'You stay with me. He's got to get used to being on his own in the town. He won't have us after tomorrow.'

Lee shifted uncomfortably. 'Yeah, well, I'm not sure about that.' She looked hard at him; he avoided her glance.

'Come and talk while I'm seeing to this meal,' she said quietly, moving into the kitchen. She hoped he wasn't going to complicate matters at this late stage.

A chicken was roasting in the oven, ringed by potatoes. It was doing well. She tested it expertly with a fork. Lee came into the doorway.

'It's not right. That's all,' he stated flatly. She was obscurely irritated.

'What's not right?' She closed the oven door and lifted the lid of a saucepan.

'He doesn't say anything.' She waited for him to come to the point, opening a packet of powder which would come near to a bread sauce. 'About being here. In this place.'

She turned to him sharply. 'There's nothing wrong with it. He's lucky to have it for the rent.'

Lee grimaced, leaning against the doorpost. 'He's just not right here'.

'Has he said that?' Lee admitted that Morgan had not. 'He's putting on an act.'

Val moved to her son and drew him into the tiny kitchen, shutting the door behind them. She did not want Morgan to overhear.

'Of course he's putting on an act.' Lee stared at her. 'He'll take time to settle, Lee. A long time. You can't just step from one way of life into another. He wants us to know he'll be all right.' She held his glance firmly, 'And he will be all right,' she added, turning to find milk in the fridge. 'It won't help Morgan if either of us makes a song and dance about it.'

She mixed powder and milk. Lee sat on the one wooden chair in the room.

'So when will you come home?'

'Quite like to go and see my father.'

Val spooned the paste into a saucepan. It was a long time since Lee had mentioned Ken. 'What's brought this on?' she asked quietly.

Lee shrugged. 'Don't know. Just thought I'd like to see him; talk to him.' He knew she would hate the idea.

'He won't put the flags out and kill the fatted calf.' There was an edge of bitterness in her voice. 'Not Ken.' She added milk to the paste and laid the saucepan aside. She guessed that Morgan's company and influence had somehow triggered Lee's imagination. 'You can't just turn up there,' she protested. 'Have you even got his address?' Lee stood and moved to look through the window onto the small square of grass and the outhouse which was Cap's new home.

'You don't want me to hear *his* side of things. About you and him.' It's true, she thought. 'Why did Alan go?' he suddenly asked, his back carefully towards her.

Val felt further threatened. 'You're too young to understand,' she countered. 'It's nothing to do with you'.

Lee turned, puzzled and annoyed. 'It's got a lot to do with me,' he protested. 'It were for him I got sent here. What are you talking about — nothing to do with me! I've got a right to know.'

'My life, my problem.' Val was firm. Beneath his steady gaze, her resolution faltered. 'He was a bully,' she murmured.

'I could have told you that. I did.'

'My hang-up, Lee. Okay? Men who look to have a bit of power.'

'Your dad was like that.' Her son's instinct was direct and unanswerable. For a second or two, it took her breath away.

'Look,' she felt obliged to explain, 'Alan and I, we just had enough of each other. We had expectations. When it came to it, his expectations weren't the same as mine.' It was as much as she could say about the ending of the relationship. It embraced but did not specify the growing disappointment, the rows and occasional violence. 'Now can we leave it, please?' Lee's eyes held her steadily. She moved to fidget with saucepans. 'Ken won't be like Morgan,' she added beneath her breath.

Lee nodded. It was his turn to be impressed with truth, striking in from a tangent. She turned wearily to him; it had been a long, tiring day.

'I'll give you Ken's address before I go,' she said flatly. Lee wandered back to the chair and sat down.

'I just know Morgan feels bad — really bad — for letting his old man down, and his mum.'

Val sensed an opportunity she had long sought for. 'Morgan's a believer,' she said. 'He thinks they're up there together, or somewhere, looking down and judging him.' He was silent. She looked quickly towards the shut door and moved towards him, her voice quiet but urgent.

'Listen. About your grandfather — he wasn't the way Morgan pretends. Neither was the Old Lady.'

Lee protested. 'Morgan knew them better than you.'

'Salt of the earth? With hearts of gold? If you've got the idea Blainau was some sort of paradise, forget it. They were narrow-minded, ignorant and cruel with it.'

She saw he was ill at ease with this new view of mythology. She moved closer. Her voice dropped further.

'Why do you think I got out of it as soon as I could? And once I'd gone, there was no escape for poor Morgan. Who'd do the work? Who'd look after them in old age? That's what they cared about.'

He protested again, more uneasily. 'This is just you remembering what you want,' he said.

'When I came down for my father's funeral — you came with me. Remember? — I walked in on Morgan in the bathroom. He had still got marks from the belt buckle. That's how much of an old gentleman your grandfather was.'

She saw him squirm at the idea. 'This is Morgan's chance, Lee,' she hammered urgently on. 'Maybe his last. To make a real life for himself!' He saw the sense of that. Miserably, he nodded agreement. Relieved, she stood back a little. 'I know you think anyone knocking on fifty's halfway to the knacker's yard,' she said, with the trace of an ironic smile, 'but Morgan could have half a lifetime ahead — now he's not chained to that place up in the hills.'

Morgan opened the door, smiling sheepishly in the formality of his suit. She scrutinised him approvingly. 'That's better,' she affirmed.

'Beer is it?' Morgan asked.

She came up to him and gave him a quick kiss on the cheek. 'For a celebration?' she mocked kindly. 'You can do better than that'.

He nodded. 'I'll be away then. Catch the shops.'

Lee suddenly stood. 'I'll come with you,' he said, refusing to meet Val's sudden glance.

Morgan was pleased. 'That's right,' he smiled. 'Stretch your legs.'

Val was dry and laconic in this small defeat. 'Stretch them any more,' she said, 'and they'll be up under his armpits. Go on then,' she added, 'and don't be long.'

Morgan shook his head in mock awe. 'Get an apron on a woman, boy, and she'll boss you something terrible.'

Lee thought of his new idea of the Old Lady. He forced a smile. 'Yeah,' he said. They left. Val turned back to her preparations, hoping she had not opened Pandora's Box. The boy had to know, she consoled herself, testing the golden chicken, turning the potatoes.

Lee and Morgan strolled towards the square.

'It's all right, is this,' proclaimed Lee happily, lying for his uncle's sake.

'Bit of a change, like,' agreed Morgan equably, to help the boy in his lie.

'I decided to stay on another day.' Morgan looked sharply at Lee. They passed a young woman pushing a pram who smiled shyly.

'A bit of independence, say? From the apron?' The man suggested.

Lee smiled. 'Yeah,' he agreed. 'Just a bit.'

They turned right between more new houses. Lee began to think his mother had been right. Morgan would settle in time.

The celebration meal was a success. The novelty of a new house, a good meal, a bottle of wine, and the close family relationship of the three diners — all determined to avoid any difficult topic whatsoever — made for a happy end to an enigmatic day. Cap was allowed to lick plates at the kitchen door. It was a positive contrast to the only other time that Val, Morgan and Lee had eaten alone together, five months ago on the boy's first night at Blainau.

When Lee had retired to bed with all the washing-up done and goodwill maintained, Morgan moved his favourite chair experimentally round the living-room, finding it a home — without the focal point of a fire, it was unsettling. Val came down from settling Lee and they joked about Morgan's manoeuvres. He found a place for the chair and sat. Val brought her unfinished wine to the sofa and stretched gratefully back. They were pleased with the way the evening had happily unrolled.

Tired, brother and sister chatted essentials. Had Morgan

money enough to live on? He claimed he had; he would find work easily enough – Griffiths had asked him to call and discuss terms. When Val advised him not to rush into anything before he felt settled, Morgan smiled and pointed out that rushing into matters was an accusation nobody had ever thrown at him. It was all easy. They talked about Lee: how Morgan would miss him; how he was determined to see his father, which was Morgan's unconscious doing; how he would surely want to visit the new house regularly in the future; how pleased they both were that he had discovered a new base, had stuck to his task. All easy.

Morgan rose during a calm silence and laid a small box in Val's hands. It was her mother's jewellery. He sat and watched Val gently sort through the pieces.

'You never got your rights from the Old Lady,' he murmured. 'No worth in any of it, I dare say, but something to remember her by. She was fretted about you in her lifetime, but she'd want you to have it now.'

Val picked out a brooch: silver and enamel. Pretty. She remembered it clearly against the dark dress her mother wore for best. It was even a shock: she had forgotten the brooch and dress for twenty years. She quietly put the jewellery box aside, moved.

'She never forgave me and never forgot. Nor did he.'

Morgan watched her. Her eyes rose to meet his. 'And what about you Mor? Have you ever forgiven me?' He dropped his glance abruptly. Val was careful with her words. 'We always got on well, you and me. If we'd still been together when we grew up a bit . . . maybe we could have stood up for ourselves?' There was a complete stillness and silence in the room. 'I thought I'd left it all behind me,' Val said very quietly. 'Then you phoned.' She looked at her brother, trying to gauge his unmoving silence. Briefly, all defences were down. Each knew that Blainau was in the blood for ever; they would never entirely escape it.

'Morgan? The boy knows it's a hard time for you. Let him go easily.'

The importance of the request was appreciated by both.

'He'll go free,' Morgan replied softly.

The next morning was all hurried preparation for Val's departure. Eventually, shortly before ten o'clock, she briefly hugged Lee, knowing better, now, than to hedge him round with advice and instruction. He knew where she was if she was needed. She gave him Ken's address and five pounds before taking her seat in the Land Rover. As Morgan started the motor she felt overwhelmed with a sudden need to see Blainau once more, but fought it down as a self-indulgence. She knew Morgan would have to enter it soon, to clear the Old Lady's room. That would be hard enough. She could not face him with the sight of the empty farm simply for a whim of her own, no matter how strong.

'Ready?' Morgan was looking at her; she had the impression he had read her thoughts. She nodded and smiled. The Land Rover moved away. She waved back until her son was out of sight.

There had been changes since Lee last saw Plas Newydd. Scaffolding towered around one of the windows and careful flowerbeds were bright with colour, as Lee ambled towards the door which was open to the soft warmth of early summer. He peered in and called.

The hall had changed too. A smaller tower of scaffolding rose to the top of the wall, where somebody had been cutting away crumbling plasterwork and rotten panelling. He called again.

'Did you want something?'

He turned to see Eileen behind him. She must have been working outside, a pair of secateurs in her hand.

'I'm away tomorrow,' he explained. 'Saying my goodbyes.'

There had been no connection between them since Matthew's departure. Eileen decided to be pleasant.

'Say them in the kitchen,' she commanded, shutting the door into the garden. The kitchen also showed changes.

'You'll have to make do with me,' Eileen said. 'The Captain is in Brecon, moving in the world of high finance.'

Lee pointed at a new set of wall units. 'Different since I was here last.'

Eileen nodded graciously, permitting him a thin smile.

'Have you heard from Matthew?'

The smile thinned even more. 'Should we have done?' she asked. 'I imagine he's safely with his parents. He was merely a paying guest.' She waved vaguely at a chair. 'Sit down.' Lee sat. 'We always thought he was unstable,' she added airily.

Lee frowned. 'Not all his fault,' he objected. 'Things just came to a head.'

Eileen was not persuaded. She lit herself a cigarette. 'So,' she said brightly. 'You're leaving us.'

'Expect I'll be back sometime.'

'And what about your uncle and his peculiar little farm?' Lee told her Morgan had moved. Her eyes widened in amusement.

'Moved? One never thinks of farmers moving. One imagines them yoked eternally to their native soil. Where has your uncle moved to?' Lee told her. She laughed. 'Such an adventure,' she mocked. 'All the way to Talgarth!'

With entire and disinterested sincerity, Lee asked, 'Why do you always put people down?'

Eileen did not take the criticism kindly.

'I beg your pardon?' she said, affronted.

Lee smiled. 'I'm expected to curl up and get struck dumb by that, am I?'

'I beg your pardon?' she emphasised.

Lee shook his head, casually amused. 'Only, everybody else is rubbish to you.' He slid an ashtray towards her. 'No wonder you don't make friends.'

She stubbed out her half-smoked cigarette in ill temper. 'Did you come to say goodbye?' she enquired. He nodded.

'Goodbye,' she said firmly.

Lee got to his feet. 'Matthew was all right,' he said. 'You never treated him like your own son.'

'He was not.'

'I thought the point was you were supposed to.' Lee felt he had gone too far and was sorry. 'Sorry, Mrs Gregory,' he apologised. 'I didn't mean to get into all that.'

He moved through the door into the hall and turned.

'Goodbye then,' he said. She was still annoyed and distant. Lee had not intended this. He moved towards the outside door.

'Listen, child.'

Again Lee turned. Eileen was in the kitchen doorway.

'We lived in a hut of corrugated iron for the first two years of our married life, and we worked damn hard, trying to carve six thousand acres from the bush – against rains in the wrong season and, then, against tribal raids. We were looted twice – servants wore my jewellery and clothes in the local village. Then the war turned dirty, with terrorists, mercenaries, landmines; the police had to train me to fire and service guns. When it became too difficult and dangerous for a woman to live anywhere remote, we had to leave our men and move to the nearest town, not knowing if we'd ever see them again. Our nearest neighbour was shot and his body dismembered. Harry sat alone three nights waiting for his turn. After all that – after thirty hard years — we lost our land and most of our money.'

She paused, seeing him held by the sudden sense of having to readjust a network of casually built prejudices. She smiled, sympathising.

'So don't rush your judgements,' she said. 'Think on. Isn't that what you folk say, up North?'

Lee saw her pride and felt the injustice with her. He coughed to clear his throat. 'You'll get this place to being a hotel, then, will you?' he asked, feeling for the first time that they might.

'It won't be the end of the world if we don't.'

Lee understood that, too. He nodded. 'Good luck,' he called, meaning it. 'Say goodbye to the captain for me.' He moved into the warm air and walked towards the gate. It will make a nice place to stay, he thought.

Pugh was tending flowers when Lee called on his way back to the new house. They had not seen each other since the day the man had sent his daughter to Blainau to give his decision; both had regretted that meeting and were anxious to make this one a success. 'You come just the right time,' grinned Pugh, slowly straightening. 'Flowers is fussy.'

They sat in the neat anonymity of the living-room, talking over old times. Pugh forced biscuits upon the boy. 'You were always a great one for the biscuits,' he pronounced, satisfied at Lee's hungry munching. They had seen changes. Pugh asked if Lee thought he could now settle back into his home at Manchester, and Lee ruefully doubted it. The old man smiled.

'You've had a bit of breathing space to think about it, boy.'

Lee nodded and smiled back. He liked this Pugh almost as much as his Blainau counterpart. They were relaxed: old friends. Lee suddenly realised that he had never felt close to anyone of Pugh's age before; in the town such friendship would be considered bizarre by his mates.

Pugh watched him finish the last biscuit. 'I got to congratulate you,' he said quietly. Lee looked up questioningly, wiping crumbs from his lips. 'Fair play,' Pugh went on. 'You stuck with Morgan and made a deal of difference to him; give him some family; drawed him out of himself. He'll make friends better now.' He suddenly winked. 'You done all that,' he grinned.

Lee was not used to compliments from Pugh, especially of this intimate kind. He dropped his head and picked up a few crumbs from the carpet.

'Will he be all right, Pugh?'

Pugh considered the question seriously for several seconds; long enough to draw Lee's eyes up to his. The old man saw genuine concern there and was careful in considering his answer.

'I expect. It'll take time, mind.'

Lee nodded; he would almost have preferred an optimistic lie. 'I just can't see him fitting in anywhere else but Blainau.' He leaned forward. 'You'll call round on him regular?'

'Bound to, boy. And I'll see him round the town.'

Lee lay back on the sofa and gazed through the window. The trees in the garden were green with new growth. 'It all happened so quickly,' he murmured.

'We're all like that round here, boy.' Pugh was his joking self again. 'Slow on the boil — then watch that lid come off the kettle!'

They laughed quietly and easily. 'I'll keep an eye on him for you,' the man promised. Lee murmured thanks and they fell to silence.

'You'll be back, will you? And you'll come and see me?' Lee promised he would do both and Pugh was pleased.

'You won't forget Blainau.' It was more a statement than a question. Lee knew he never would. They sat and chatted quietly for a last ten minutes.

At the gate, Lee shook Pugh's hand. He took a scrap of paper from his pocket. 'Pugh,' he said cautiously, not wanting to be taken lightly nor to turn the mood too serious. 'If I give you my address and telephone number, if Morgan's not — you know — happy or anything, or gets sick . . .' He paused, holding the paper out, not knowing exactly how to continue.

'Give it here, boy.' Pugh found the exact balance between amusement and concern. Lee was grateful.

Lee walked through the mid-afternoon warmth and paused on the town bridge to lean over and see his reflected self fragmented in the water. A sadness and excitement ran through him; it was time to leave but it would not be without regret. He straightened and leaned upon the stones of the parapet, scrutinising the square of the town he had become a small part of. The slanting sun warmed the cold stone. He looked at the old, unlikely shop below the tower guarding the bridge; at the bank with its incongruous, modern extension; at the wool shop, the supermarket and the newsagent's. Time to go. He walked towards the estate of new, white box-houses, hidden behind the

Tower Inn. Pugh had promised to visit Morgan the next night. When Lee would be gone.

Morgan and the boy sat down to fish and chips in the living-room. Morgan protested that he had done nothing but eat and drink for the last two days.

'When you come to see me next, I'll be too big to get through that door, boy!' He seemed delighted with the novelty of fast food. Town life was a damn sight more simple. No doubt about it. They were both hungry, despite Morgan's misgivings, and ate in silence. The evening was warm and birdsong rippled in through an open window. A blackbird. There had always been a blackbird at Blainau, too.

'I'll miss you, boy,' Morgan said, suddenly gruff with emotion. Lee was determined to keep the evening as easy as possible and camouflaged his response with a familiar line in banter.

'You'll miss me all right. Nobody to fetch and carry, or bring your tea in the morning, or to do the washing.'

He kept his face down, as if totally involved with sliding chips through a pool of sauce. Morgan smiled.

'When was that then? I must 'a been looking somewhere else at the time!' Content to see the boy's lips twist into a grin, he, too, concentrated on the meal.

'I'll miss you, too.' Lee could simply not, at last, keep the words back. Neither raised their eyes, recognising dangerous territory. It was as Val had said: they were alike in their shyness of admitting they might be merely human. There were more words Lee needed to say and could not, for all his intentions, deny.

'You could get to like it then? Living here?' He tried to keep the question casual. Morgan looked at him as if the boy were half-witted.

'Why not?'

Lee looked carefully at his uncle's face. He saw bewilderment and was relieved. He laughed and shook his head. 'You can always surprise me!' he said. They turned again to the food.

'Your mam gave me a lecture.' Morgan threw a sly grin across the table. Lee grinned back.

'Things starting? Not ending?'

Morgan laughed. 'You got it too,' he said. He speared a chip. 'Well, damn and she's right,' he continued quietly. 'I done my duty to the Old Lady and Gentleman. I done my best for

Blainau. Nothing to feel bad about.'

Lee watched Morgan eating in his slow, deliberate way. The blackbird still sang. The boy found this new, positive attitude almost alarming, almost a betrayal. His feelings were very mixed.

'You'll miss Blainau, though.' He needed reassurance; he could not see the balance in Morgan yet. Morgan looked sharply up.

'Of course,' he affirmed urgently, needing to explain. 'Of course I will. I'll miss the quiet. But a man can get too quiet. When you came, you brung people — Matthew and his sister, your mates from the city; and Val came with her man. Good for me, yes. I don't say I liked it all, not all, but a bit of new life!'

It made sense. Lee thought of Pugh's words: that he had drawn Morgan from himself to a point where friends could be made more easily. He could understand. It would, as his mother said, as Pugh said, take time, but Lee felt he was seeing something new and optimistic. He was enormously relieved.

'And you can always take Cap up into the hills when you want a bit of peace and quiet,' he suggested. Morgan's need to prove his new self held strong.

'Of course I can. And that's where I'll be working. I called in on Tom Griffiths coming back from the station. I'm seeing him Monday morning, first thing.'

It was news to Lee, but what he had told Morgan was true: the man could always surprise him. The relief showed in his face and he found himself smiling at the prospect of Morgan at work with Cap in the hills, returning to the ease of this house and the novel convenience of town life.

'You're not just saying all this?'

Morgan paused and, again, considered him, as if the question had come from a simpleton.

'Why would I do that?'

'I don't know. To please me.'

Morgan swallowed the last chip and pushed the plate aside. 'You're pleased then?' he asked casually.

Lee nodded, grinning widely. 'Of course I bloody am!'

Morgan relaxed in content. 'That's two of us, boy,' he said softly. He pushed his chair back and reached for his glass of beer.

There was one more question Lee knew he would find himself asking, and he waited meticulously for the right moment.

'Morgan? Your dad — the Old Gentleman — did he ever take a belt to you?'

Silence filled the room. The birdsong had come to an end; a lick of breeze rattled the open window. 'Only Mum said . . .'

Lee needed to have a clear picture of the old life at Blainau; Val's image of scars from a buckle had disturbed it. He wanted to know whom to believe. He shrugged, embarrassed at his own need.

'I deserved it, I dare say.' Morgan's voice was matter-of-fact. 'Your dad never raise a hand to you?' The man looked casually at Lee, who knew Val's version of that incident at least was true; knew he had no right to pursue the matter further. They sipped beer, before deciding to go out for a drink at The Tower once the washing-up was done.

As each had foreseen, the next morning was the most difficult. It bore a strange similarity to the earliest of Lee's days at Blainau, when there had been much to say and discover, but unwillingness and unfamiliarity had shackled tongues, in a fear of any commitment which might immediately be regretted. Totally familiar now, the two men went about Lee's departure in a quiet, for the most part, silent way, avoiding each other when possible, keeping to neutral subjects when they spoke. The fear of commitment was now for the other. For Morgan, it was important to let the boy go free of too much regret at leaving him in a house that was not Blainau; Lee's purpose was not to make 'too much of a song and dance', for Morgan's sake, as his mother had said. They made a practical job of it and were waiting for the National coach at its stop on Pengenffordd hill by five to eleven.

There were three other passengers, two of them were walkers, in shorts and boots. The Land Rover was parked a short distance from them. Cap sat in the front seat between Lee and Morgan. The boy's luggage was in the back; he had arrived with a rucksack and was leaving with the addition of his radio and a full, battered suitcase that had once belonged to the Old Lady, for her annual one-week holiday to work on her own father's farm, near Rhayader.

Neither knew what to say. Lee squeezed Cap's neck below the ears. The dog turned its head and laid a paw on the boy's leg, wriggling closer to him. He brushed it away; the small gesture tightened the emotion of the moment, and Lee could not afford the luxury of letting himself flow with it. He had twice felt himself near tears already. What's wrong with me? he thought. It's only a bloody dog.

Morgan saw the movement. 'Here's another that's going to

240

miss you,' he said. Lee nodded, his face set ahead, staring through the windscreen at the waiting passengers. Morgan took an envelope from his pocket and held it out to Lee, his eyes firmly on the tourists who were laughing. One looked at his watch. Lee threw Morgan a glance. The man thrust the envelope nearer. 'Just take it.'

Lee took it. Inside were five ten-pound notes. The boy was appalled. 'I can't take this.'

Morgan would not look at him. 'You earned it. Your part of the sales at market.'

Lee looked again at Morgan's set profile. 'Morgan — I can't.'

Morgan swung his face sternly round. 'Just put it in your damn pocket and shut up!' he said sharply. Lee gazed at the fifty pounds uneasily. 'I got a good price for the stock and Tom Duncan let me off from the delapidations.' Lee sat in silence, not wanting to offend. Morgan's gaze moved back to the tourists. 'Do as I tell you just one damn time,' he said softly.

Lee slid the envelope into his jeans' pocket. The dog; now this. He felt the emotion tighten another notch. Morgan consulted his watch. 'Best get out to the road.'

Lee reached into the back of the Land Rover and brusquely laid his radio in Morgan's lap. 'Company for you,' he said, with difficulty. The man was moved, nobody had ever given him anything so valuable or valued. He knew how much Lee would miss it. Another notch seemed about to tighten. Lee forestalled it, opening the door and forcing a grin.

'I'd leave you my tapes too but I know what you think of them.'

He moved to the back of the vehicle to collect his rucksack and case. Morgan laid the radio carefully at his side and opened his door. Cap looked at the radio, sniffed it, cocked his head to one side.

Lee brought rucksack and suitcase to the front of the vehicle. He looked round to Morgan. 'Don't I get properly waved off?' he called.

Morgan came to him suddenly and took him close in his arms. Lee held him tight. No words were possible as the coach glided round the bend and slowed. As, many times before, time stretched and was suddenly in a rush. The passengers at the roadside gathered their luggage. The coach doors hissed open. Morgan dropped his arms but Lee clung on.

'Look after yourself,' he murmured. 'See you.'

'God bless you.'

'Yeah.' Lee's arms came slowly down. He gazed into the man's moist eyes. 'And thanks.'

The final tourist climbed into the coach. Morgan took a short step back. 'Get on the bus,' he said, roughly. Lee smiled and gathered up his luggage. He turned and hurried to the open doors. The driver was revving the engine, anxious to be away.

Lee threw the suitcase before him and manoeuvred the rucksack up the steps. Doors hissed closed behind him. He turned to look at Morgan, as the coach jerked into first gear and began to move, throwing him off balance. He saw a vacant seat, close at hand, and drew his luggage towards it.

'Been on holiday?'

Lee turned to see a woman smiling at him from a seat at his side. 'What?' He twisted again to seek Morgan.

'Holidays. Have you been on holiday?'

The coach was twenty yards from the car park now. Lee turned again to the friendly passenger.

'No. I've been working. I live here.'

He dumped his rucksack on the seat and looked for Morgan as the coach gathered pace and changed to a higher gear. Through the rear windows, Lee saw the Land Rover draw into the road and head in the opposite direction. No point in waving. Five seconds later the two vehicles lost each other between the bends. Lee smiled. Typical. When Morgan makes up his mind, it happens fast. Lee squeezed the case into the space at his feet and settled himself. He turned to the passenger who had shown an interest in him.

'Been working here. Up in the hills. Most of the year. That was my uncle in the Land Rover.'

The woman smiled politely and picked up a magazine. Lee relaxed in the part excitement, part regret of imminent change. He leaned back and closed his eyes. He felt in his anorak pocket to check that he had his father's address. He felt hopeful.

Pugh found Morgan in the outhouse, sitting quietly with Cap. The cheerful optimism of the previous day had collapsed. He had let the boy go free and it had cost Morgan dearly. Pugh was secretly surprised at the change in the man: he had aged, his eyes were blank and apathetic. He was glad he had come; the boy had been right to worry.

'No answer round the front.' Pugh smiled. Morgan's dead eyes moved to the old man's face. 'I come on a visit. I promised the boy.'

Morgan nodded and climbed heavily to his feet. He pushed past Pugh in the doorway and walked across the patch of grass towards the house. Pugh followed, sympathising, remembering how long it had taken himself to adjust from living as king in his farm to being just someone who lived in a town. Sharp. Bitter. He hurried along in Morgan's measured tread.

Pugh looked approvingly round the tiny living-room, exaggerating — as Val had done — the benefits of cosy convenience. He was anxious to keep the moment as cheerful as possible.

'I come prepared,' he grinned, producing a quarter bottle of Scotch. 'A gift to the house.'

Again, Morgan nodded silently. He walked to the sideboard and found two glasses. He'll need new furniture, Pugh thought. A mistake to bring memories to a new start. His sympathy held: he had some idea of how little cash Blainau had provided.

'This still your chair?' Morgan nodded once more, laying the glasses on the table. Pugh sat on the shabby Blainau sofa and leaned forward to pour the drink that was a gift to the house. He noticed the radio.

'Boy forget his wireless?'

'He gave it me. For company.'

Words at last. Pugh was relieved. He took up the idea eagerly. 'Very good. And you'll have more company now, in the town.' He picked up a glass. 'Here's drinking to the future, Morgan.'

Morgan laid down his glass and moved again to the sideboard. He dropped a sheaf of papers on the table before Pugh. A photocopy of a drawing lay on top. The old man peered at it for several seconds. The drawing showed a neat house, with suburban extensions either side of an area resembling a patio. Behind the sanitised clinical sketch, a ridge rose.

'Blainau?' Pugh asked quietly.

Morgan ranged around the box of a room.

'Tom Duncan brung me papers to sign. Brung me that, too.' He suddenly came to the table. 'For school kiddies down from London,' he said. His voice held an accusation that Pugh could not understand. Morgan jabbed a finger at features of the drawing.

'Kitchens. Drying rooms. Space to sleep twelve.' He took the sheaf of papers swiftly from the table, as if he could not bear acknowledging their prominence. He threw them down on the sideboard.

'Outdoor-pursuits-centre.' He bitterly tasted the words on his tongue. 'Duncan sells them the house. They pay for rebuilding. "Outdoor-pursuits-centre",' he repeated. 'A bit of walking, ponies, studying bloody plants, Duncan says.' Morgan walked the room again: an animal in a cage.

'That's the future of Blainau,' he said quietly.

Pugh tried to raise his spirits. 'Blainau'll be giving a lot of pleasure to a lot of people, Morgan.' He raised his glass, hoping to encourage his friend to take a drink, sit and relax. Morgan would not meet his eyes, but stopped to gaze through the window; a low hill rose behind the house, wooded near the top, preventing a clear view of the hills beyond. Just as well, thought Pugh; it'll all take time.

There was a question Pugh needed to ask. He was not shy of raising the matter; they had always discussed such things at Blainau.

'I'm worried for you about your sales. Griffiths was fair to you, but you could have got more. You damn near gave some of the tools and machinery away. I saw what you got for the beasts. See you through a year or two if you're careful. Likely you expected more.'

Morgan swung towards Pugh, his face intense with despair. 'Why did you do it?' he shouted, shaking his head as if to clear some sudden great pain. 'Why did you walk out on me? Said you wouldn't let me down. We could've hung on. Why, say?'

Pugh gazed at him, shocked and frightened. Morgan clenched and unclenched his huge hands, his eyes hard on the alarmed eyes of Pugh.

'I done it for the best.' Pugh's voice was a whisper.

Morgan bellowed like a beast in distress. 'Best for bloody who?'

Pugh played nervously with the glass. He moved his gaze from the accusing wild eyes. 'Blame me, is it?' he murmured.

'We was dead and done the morning you sent your girl up! Didn't have the courage to come yourself! Why, man?'

Pugh stayed silent, hurt and offended in the face of Morgan's despair. Morgan moved across the room and gazed down upon the architect's drawing of Blainau.

'You bloody old fool,' he said, quiet and bitter. 'I been good to you.'

The old man could bear no more. He drained his glass and stood up. Morgan would not turn to him.

Very quietly he asked, 'Why did you give it up, Morgan?'

The question wounded Morgan into silence for long seconds. He wondered if Pugh would understand.

'For the boy,' he whispered. 'I done it for the boy.'

Pugh understood. Some of the shock and hurt of Morgan's attack lessened under the knowledge of the sacrifice that had been made. He did not know the details, but could accept the love that had made Morgan leave all he stood for, so that a strange boy — family — should not suffer the numbing obligations and guilt that had chained Morgan to a life of inescapable commitment.

'I'll visit another time,' Pugh said. 'When you're settled.'

Morgan laughed shortly, he echoed the word 'settled'. He made it sound a total impossibility. He still would not turn. Pugh approached the door. Morgan stopped him with a question Pugh had hoped never to answer.

'You know'd them. You know'd my Mam and Dad. What you think to them, say?'

Pugh searched for a reply that was honest and would not hurt. 'Hard-working?' he ventured quietly.

Morgan nodded and almost smiled. Forty-seven years of daily obligation; duty and love; guilt and frustration — and for what? A couple who were 'hard-working'. It was a cruelly honest epitaph, in spite of Pugh's careful search. 'They done for me,' Morgan said.

Pugh stared at his squarely set shoulders. 'When you come to thinking that, Morgan?'

'I know'd it all the time.'

The full tragedy of Morgan's life confronted Pugh for the first time. In deepest pity for his friend, beyond words, he turned to go. As if sensing the pity and unable to bear it, Morgan moved swiftly to snatch up the bottle Pugh had brought and thrust it into his hands.

'Take this gift to the house.'

Pugh slid the bottle into his jacket pocket. 'I'll keep it for a better time,' he said quietly.

Morgan heard the front door shut and suddenly twisted, this way and that, as though suffering a seizure. He moved across the room, shaking his head to ward off unseen assailants. His hands clenched, unclenched. Then he began to sob. The tears he had fought wildly finally engulfed him. Morgan wailed. For Blainau. For Lee. For the Old Lady and Gentleman. For a lost life. Blindly he groped for the radio on the table, aware, here, of neighbours. He fumbled for the switch and Lee's favourite station drowned the gulping, retching, guilty sobs with a counterpoint of jangling banality. As Morgan wept ever louder for his wasted life, he increased the volume until he could barely hear his shameful distress and the two chaoses mingled and fought for supremacy. Locked in his concrete kennel, Cap, alarmed for his master, yelped and wailed and leaped at the door.

Man and dog stood, the next morning, in Talgarth square, unnoticed among tourists and shoppers. Morgan was shaved, neat in suit and tie; secure but uneasy, at the end of a leash of binder-twine, Cap flinched among the marching feet and petrol fumes. It was a warm, sunny morning. Morgan flicked the binder-twine, and man and dog threaded their way through the traffic to the Llanelieu road.

Each was glad to make the long journey to the common. Morgan watched Cap delight in familiar smells and territory and felt something of the dog's relief.

They met Harry Gregory, himself a refugee, tired of builders and decorators, wanting simply a brief time of sun and silence. The two men walked in contentment to where their way divided. Harry was surprised to learn that Morgan had left Blainau – Eileen had not thought it worth mentioning when she had indignantly relayed her last meeting with Lee. He suggested that, soon, Morgan should call at Plas Newydd; if he were any good with flowers there might be some work available. They parted amiably – Harry to wander to his car near the cattlegrid and Morgan to continue his journey to the Church.

When the vicar hurried from his car to pin upon the church notice-board a rota of good ladies responsible for the month's flowers, he was surprised to see a farm dog sunning himself near the porch. He did not recognise Cap; they all looked the same to him – he was simply grateful that the animal seemed friendly enough and did not bark or bare its teeth. He pinned up his rota and opened the door in case the dog's owner was inside – for what reason he could not think.

He recognised Morgan as a member of his congregation, but they had never been officially introduced and he did not know his name. Morgan sat stiffly in a back pew and did not turn at the heavy clicking of the handle. It was cold inside the church after the warm, May sunshine. Occasionally a tourist or two were to be found, looking round the church, but it was the first time he had found a worshipper – if that was what the man in the suit was.

'Good afternoon.'

Morgan nodded, sitting stiffly in the pew. He still did not turn. The vicar was uneasy. He glanced at his watch: it was almost lunchtime. His wife appreciated punctuality. He tried to make out what the man was doing, immobile and silent. He closed the heavy door behind him and moved to stand at Morgan's side, in the aisle. Morgan stared straight ahead, his face blank.

'Are you all right?'

'No. Not all right.'

The man's reply worried the vicar. Four miles down the road, towards Talgarth, was a sizeable psychiatric hospital; he hoped he was not a patient, but was prepared to be considerate if he were. He moved into the pew and sat at Morgan's side.

'Are you ill?'

Quietly, Morgan asked, 'My Mam and Dad — will I meet them?' If the words had not been so quietly and seriously spoken, the vicar would have been further persuaded that the man was a patient at the hospital, but, as far as he knew, no patients regularly attended his Sunday morning services.

'They're in the ground. Will I meet them?'

Again the vicar was impressed by the quiet seriousness. He wanted to help.

'Are we talking about the after-life?'

Morgan nodded. The vicar played for time, trying to gauge the problem. 'Well, I think it depends on what you mean by "meet".'

Morgan was quite clear. 'The Bible says I will.'

The idea seemed to worry the man. The vicar suggested cautiously that a more modern interpretation of life-after-death might not so much be a flesh-and-blood meeting — like the meeting between the two of them, here, now, in church — but that maybe the dead have their immortality by living on in their children. There was a long silence. The vicar secretly looked again at his watch. Morgan said softly, 'They live in me?'

'In memory and influence.'

The vicar studied Morgan's face, firmly set towards the altar, but could still find no clue to the problem.

'Honour thy Father and thy Mother,' said Morgan suddenly. The vicar murmured agreement. 'Love them?'

The vicar cleared his throat. 'Isn't that assumed?' He shifted in the pew, less and less at ease. Morgan's seeming composure contradicted the apparent lack of direction in his questioning.

'It's wrong then — a sin — to hate them?' That was sharply said.

'Parents are only human. We all find ourselves resenting —'

Morgan cut across him; the words were again sharp. 'Not resentment, no.'

'Hate?' Morgan nodded briefly. The vicar studied his averted face. 'Hate is always wrong,' he said quietly.

'Is it a sin?'

The questions came faster now. The vicar wanted desperately to help, he was concerned for the man at his side. 'We need to be very careful of using that word "sin".'

There were a few seconds of silence before Morgan suddenly stood, ending the catechism. The vicar stood, too. Morgan turned to him, 'Thank you, sir,' he said briskly. The vicar could not feel the thanks were well-deserved. His instinct sensed pain behind the man's composure. He asked if Morgan was feeling well.

'If I got hate in me, they passed it down, like you said.' Morgan moved a little towards the aisle. The vicar squeezed from the pew to let him pass.

'Are you saying you believe your parents hated you?'

Morgan drew his rolled cap from a jacket pocket. He turned to the door. 'Loved and hated me, like I loved and hated them.' It was a matter-of-fact reply: no guilt, no doubts.

'I'm sure you must be wrong,' the vicar murmured. At the door Morgan turned, his voice echoing across the still, cold space. He pronounced the kindest, most precise verdict on the Old Lady and Gentleman that he could find.

'They were God-fearing people, sir, in harder times.'

Without waiting or expecting a reply, Morgan pulled the door open and walked into the warm sun. Cap ran to his side and they moved to the churchyard gate. The vicar stood in the porch and watched them, aware that this strange meeting had been of importance, but not knowing why. He saw them pass the more recent gravestones without a glance.

Cap was content to be at Blainau again. He quickly lifted his leg at the usual places, marking his territory, and sniffed where strangers had been. Morgan enjoyed the dog's content as he pulled from his jacket the spare key to the front door he had not surrendered to Duncan. There were sheep in the field above — he could not identify the markings at that distance but guessed they were Griffiths'. He had to smile: Tom Griffiths was a smart one — no grass growing beneath his feet. He'd always wanted the field.

The house was quiet and Morgan felt a great peace within him as he climbed to the Old Lady's room and fumbled for the key in his pocket. Cap barked distantly.

Morgan drew back the curtains and hauled the window open with difficulty; it had been firmly clamped shut since his mother's death. He took off his jacket and tie, hanging them carefully behind the door, on the hook where the warm, faded dressing-gown still hung. Rolling up his sleeves, his attention was briefly caught by the stern, accusing glance of his father, yellowing slightly in the frame with the Old Lady. Morgan moved to the wardrobe and opened it. He drew out the clothes hanging there and laid them on the bed. On top of them he emptied the contents of the drawers and, when he had a suitable load, he drew together the corners of the counterpane and began hauling the load downstairs.

Cap was drilling Griffiths' sheep when he saw Morgan manoeuvre the unwieldy sack through the door and into the middle of the yard. He bounded happily from the fields to sniff through the interesting variety of objects dumped on the ground.

From the workshed Morgan brought a five-gallon drum of diesel oil and an armful of empty plastic sacks, which had held the fertiliser he had scattered on his fields only a month ago. He laid down the drum and walked back into the house, calling to the snuffling dog to leave the pile in the yard. Cap obeyed but with regret, remembering familiar scents.

The photographs went into a sack which was topped up with the smaller pictures. Curtains and bed linen filled another. Unhurried, at peace but decisive, Morgan stripped the room bare and carried its contents to the growing heap in the yard.

When the room contained only empty furniture and the crucifix over the bare bed, Morgan took his jacket and tie from the hook behind the door. He had forgotten the dressing-gown and took that, too. Leaving the door wide open, he walked downstairs and into the yard, where he tossed the dressing-gown onto the pile and turned to the full drum of fuel.

Diesel fuel, when ignited, will burn almost everything. The flames were low and cautious at first, but joining and redoubling, they grew higher. A pall of grey-black smoke hung above the burning pile. Cap nervously kept his distance, and, seeing his unease, Morgan walked round the pyre to reassure him.

The fire had settled to smoke, half an hour later, as Morgan sat on a fallen tree, high above Blainau, where the mountainside gave way to cultivation. He watched the thin, grey plume rise and mingle with the sky, Cap obediently at his side, enjoying the rare luxury of fondled ears and Morgan's heavy hand sliding up and down his back. They sat for maybe a quarter of an hour more before Morgan rose, and then they walked slowly down to the farm, towards the sun, now settling on the hills above Glasbury.

The smouldering circle of debris was beginning to scatter in the evening breeze. As Cap stalked gingerly round it, the stones warm beneath his paws, Morgan reached up to the beams of the living-room in the silent house and brought down the shotgun from its hiding place.

He came into the yard. A blackbird was singing from a tree near the road. Morgan stood in the last of the sun, enjoying the song. Seeing the gun on Morgan's arm, Cap assumed they were going to hunt rabbits and trotted to the man's side expectantly.

Morgan turned a slow circle from the familiar viewpoint, seeing the features he had known all his life; the cow and machinery sheds behind which a small plantation of trees was springing up; the road beyond the low stone wall with its gate whose hinges hummed musically; the hills to the south, low and tinged with blue at this time of the evening; the high solid block, Y Das, and the ridge that ran behind Blainau to join it. The blackbird was still singing. Morgan looked up at the sky; the weather would hold. It would be a fine day tomorrow. He found the two cartridges in his pocket and moved towards the open door of the workshed, calling Cap to follow which, puzzled, he did. The door closed behind them.

At which point, precisely, Morgan had decided to kill himself, he would not, himself, have been able to say. Sacrificing the farm to free the boy from the obligations he had himself suffered, had been the most dreadful decision of his life, knowing he would be called to account by the Old Lady and Gentleman and be, yet again, found wanting. 'Too damn soft' his father had always considered him, envying other farmers' sons. Tom Griffiths had always been the example to follow, and he had failed. The vicar had tried to convince him that he would not have to face the frightening man, who had beaten him to scars he bore to this day, and the righteous woman, who had allowed it; but the new and terrible idea that Morgan's life contained them both had been a white-hot revelation. The crippling obligations must come to an end. When Lee, defeated and depressed, had said he would stay, offering his youth and energy for as long as it would take, seeing no other way out, Morgan had seen the ghosts of his own past and now they had to be put to peace.

Morgan shot Cap first. The dog had been bred to serve Blainau and would work for nobody other than Morgan. He would be a misery to himself and everybody else in any other context. The roaring echo of the blast drove away the blackbird in panic. For much the same reasons, he placed the acrid, warm barrels in his mouth and pushed down the trigger with a stick, hoping that, however severely the taking of his own life might be judged, it would be set against the refusal to stunt a young, much-loved life. In the split second between pressing down the stick and oblivion, he blessed Lee, who had briefly been Morgan's boy and now would be only himself. The blast doubled and redoubled in the locked, stone shed. Outside, the lack of birdsong continued.

A selection of bestsellers from SPHERE

FICTION

THE SEA CAVE	Alan Scholefield	£2.25 ☐
THE JUDAS CODE	Derek Lambert	£2.25 ☐
MONIMBO	Arnaud de Borchgrave and Robert Moss	£2.25 ☐
KING OF DIAMONDS	Carolyn Terry	£2.50 ☐
AUTUMN TIGER	Bob Langley	£1.95 ☐

FILM & TV TIE-INS

WEMBLEY FRAGGLE GETS THE STORY	Deborah Perlberg	£1.50 ☐
MAROONED IN FRAGGLE ROCK	David Young	£1.50 ☐
THE DOOZER DISASTER	Michaela Muntean	£1.75 ☐
ONCE UPON A TIME IN AMERICA	Lee Hays	£1.75 ☐
THE DUNE STORYBOOK	Joan Vinge	£2.50 ☐

NON-FICTION

THE COMPLETE HANDBOOK OF PREGNANCY	Wendy Rose-Neil	£5.95 ☐
THE STORY OF THE SHADOWS	Mike Read	£2.95 ☐
WHO'S REALLY WHO	Compton Miller	£2.95 ☐
WORST MOVIE POSTERS OF ALL TIME	Greg Edwards	£4.95 ☐
THE STOP SMOKING DIET	Jane Ogle	£1.50 ☐

All Sphere books are available at your local bookshop or newsagent, or can be ordered direct from the publisher. Just tick the titles you want and fill in the form below.

Name_____

Address_____

_____

Write to Sphere Books, Cash Sales Department, P.O. Box 11, Falmouth, Cornwall TR10 9EN

Please enclose cheque or postal order to the value of the cover price plus:

UK: 55p for the first book, 22p for the second and 14p per copy for each additional book ordered to a maximum charge of £1.75.

OVERSEAS: £1.00 for the first book and 25p for each additional book.

BFPO & EIRE: 55p for the first book, 22p for the second book plus 14p per copy for the next 7 books, thereafter 8p per book.

Sphere Books reserve the right to show new retail prices on covers which may differ from those previously advertised in the text or elsewhere, and to increase postal rates in accordance with the PO.